Dare Come For the KING

HOPE PAGE

Published in the United States of America

ISBN 978-1-962730-22-8 (SC)
ISBN 978-1-962730-24-2 (HC)
ISBN 978-1-962730-23-5 (Ebook)

Hope Page Books
222 West 6th Street
Suite 400, San Pedro, CA, 90731
hopepagepublishing@gmail.com

Ordering Information and Rights Permission:

Quantity sales. Special discounts might be available on quantity purchases by corporations, associations, and others. For details, contact the publisher at the address above.

For Book Rights Adaptation and other Rights Permission. Call us at toll-free 1-888-945-8513 or send us an email at worksofhopepage.com

Contents

CHAPTER ONE

It's the first day of spring after a long, cold winter. The vibrant sunshine kisses KD Daniels, making her skin glisten as she briskly jogs alongside the Detroit River. The breeze flowing from the direction of the water invigorates her as she listens to music on her iPhone. She is focused on making it home, but John is focused on her.

KD unknowingly attracts the attention of John King, Detroit's most-sought bachelor, sitting in the backseat of a passing black Range Rover, going in the opposite direction. When John sees KD, his attention is immediately and completely captivated. His jaw drops as he moves closer to the window to get a better look. John sees everything he wants in her pink yoga pants.

John instructs his driver, Rock Henson, to turn around and stop ahead of her. John gets out the car to stand directly in KD's path. John smiles as he watches her jog toward him. KD never looks at him, and that makes John even more interested.

As she jogs pass him, John says, "Excuse me!" KD doesn't hear him through the music blasting from her ear buds. He quickly turns and grabs her arm. She is startled by his touch, but she stops. She turns to face him. She sees John's lips moving, so she removes her earbuds.

John says, "I didn't mean to scare you. I was asking for your help."

John smiles, staring directly in her eyes. KD is trying to read him to see if he is flirting or if he is selling something.

KD thinks, damn he is fine. She tries to conceal her interest in his physical form by focusing on what he is saying. Through her labored breathing, she asks, "How may I help you?"

John says as he looks in her pockets, "I saw you take something that belongs to me, and I was hoping you would give it back."

She steps back; she says, "Excuse me!" KD thinks, damn, he is crazy. She is disappointed.

John says, "I have to get to work, so I need you to return my stuff."

KD is confused, but John is smiling. John has made up his mind to command her full attention. KD turns to continue her jog, but John grabs her hand.

John says, "Don't leave before I get my stuff."

KD says, "Sir, I didn't take anything. I have no idea what you are talking about, and I really need to go."

She tries to pull her hand out of his, but he won't let go. John watches tiny beads of sweat slowly drip down her face. He sneaks a peek of her glowing cleavage illuminated by the sunlight sparking off her necklaces and reflecting onto her slightly sweaty chest.

John says, "I specifically saw you take it," as he memorizes her face and every curve of her body. He loves her lips, her cheekbones, and the curve of her hips.

KD asks, "What are you looking for?" At this point, KD wants John out of her face. She is convinced he's crazy.

John, smiling, says with a soft, low tone, "My heart, my attention, and my train of thought, you took them as I rode passed you. You either need to give them back or come have dinner with me tonight. I prefer you to keep it all and come hang with me."

KD smiles and says, "You can't be serious."

KD is so relieved that he is flirting. She quickly glances at his shoulders, arms, and chest before her eyes make their way back to his.

John says, "I'm so serious! Have dinner with me tonight!"

KD says, "You're crazy, you know that."

John says, "I'm determined. I'm interested, but I wouldn't say crazy. Sound mind and body, I want to spend some time with you. Have dinner with me tonight!"

She says, "I can't have dinner with you tonight because I have to work, and I don't go out with strangers." She tells herself she might as well play along.

John says, "I'm John. I've lived in Detroit my whole life. I work over there, and I live down there. What's your name and what time do you get off work?"

As John talks, KD notices his soft, pink lips, his bright, golden skin absorbing the sun, and the sparkle of his white, straight teeth.

KD's interest is piqued, so she decides to flirt back; she says, "I get off at ten, which is way past dinner time."

She smiles at him. She is feeling his approach even though it teetered on the lame side. She can't stop looking at his cute lips and picturing them kissing her.

John, still holding onto to KD's wrist, notices KD looking at his lips. He licks his lips before he says with a low tone commanding her attention, "Meet me at midnight. I'm not letting you leave until you say yes."

KD says, "I thought you really needed to get to work."

John sees KD is favorably responding to him; he seductively says, "The whole world can wait for you."

KD smiles at the comment. John is already in love with her smile. He asks [pointing to the apartments just ahead], "Do you live over there?"

KD says, "Yes."

John says, "Henson, my driver who I've known for twenty years, will pick you up at midnight. Henson is a dedicated married man. We both are fathers of daughters. You will be safe the entire time, I promise! There's a nice place that will be packed wall to wall. The food is great. The live music always has the crowd vibing. Henson will bring you home by two, and you never told me your name."

KD looks unconvinced. John says, "You are too beautiful for me to accept no. I will come back here every day, and embarrass you in front of your neighbors until you say yes. You might as well say yes, now. Save yourself the embarrassment."

KD plays coy; she says, "What if I have a man at home?"

John answers, "Leave his ass at home and give him a two-week notice because I'm taking you. I'm not playing games."

KD says, "You're giving orders!"

John winks at her. He says, "I'm just stating the necessary and obvious."

He smiles as he takes her phone out of her pocket to call himself. There's something about his smile that melted the walls KD built around her heart and mind to keep men away.

KD says, "I see!"

John says, "I'm serious. You will be mine and nothing or no one will stop that."

KD says, "You are very confident!"

John replies, "It's the weather. The sun makes me intuitive."

KD says, "It is a pretty day."

John says, "It doesn't compare to you. Your eyes are so lovely."

KD says, "Thank you," as she smiles.

John shows her the screen and points to the number. He says, "That's my number. Henson will be in front of your building at midnight in that [John points to the SUV.] black Range Rover. Will I see you tonight?"

KD says, "I guess so."

John says, "I got your number and I know where you live, so don't renege on me." John hands KD her phone. She looks at the time on her smart watch.

She says, "Excuse me, John, I have to go take my son to school." KD's eyes hint that she is interested, so he believes she'll show up for dinner.

John kisses her hand before letting go of her hand; he says, "It was a pleasure to meet you. Have a good rest of your day."

She replies, "You, too," as she puts her earbuds back in her ears. She turns to finish her jog home. John smiles as he watches her jog away. He gets back in the SUV with a new energy.

John asks Henson, "Did you see her? She is fine."

Henson burst into laughter. He asks, "What about your fiancée?"

John confusedly says, "My what?"

Henson says, "Your fiancée?"

John says, "Who?"

Henson continues to laugh; he says, "Raina! What about Raina?"

John says, "Huh?"

Henson pulls off while they laugh; he says, "The girl you've been dating for a year."

John asks, "I need you to pick that young lady up from those apartments at midnight. Bring her to the club and take her back home by two. Can you do that for me?"

Henson answers, "You have plans with Raina tonight. I'm supposed to pick her up tonight."

John says, "Focus! I need you at those apartments promptly at midnight. Forget all about Raina. That's a done deal!"

Henson says, "I got it covered!"

John says, "My man! You can drop me off at home. I'll drive myself to work. You take the day off. Get plenty of rest. I need you tonight."

Henson says, "You're the boss!"

While Henson drives John home, John texts Raina to end their friendship. The message reads: I've enjoyed the time we've spent together, but it's best to end our friendship. I appreciate the time you invested into our friendship. I wish you well. Take care of yourself.

Henson drops John off at home. As soon as John gets in the house, he goes through the house gathering all the remnants of Raina. He deletes any sign of her from his phones and social media pages. He unfollows her on every social media platform. John packs her stuff in a box. He removes the old to make room for the new. He doesn't even know if he has a real chance with KD, but he is willing to take a chance. He doesn't want Raina lingering around and blocking his chance with KD. After cleansing his life of Raina, John makes his way to the office.

After Raina finishes the morning broadcast, she sits in her dressing room, checking her messages. She is distraught when she reads the message from John. She repeatedly calls him, but John ignores her. After several missed calls, he blocks her.

Raina was never a real factor in his equation. He enjoyed her companionship, but he never saw himself having a committed relationship with her. John felt Raina saw him as the final piece to her desired perfect life puzzle. John and Raina had fun, but they didn't have the connection he desired. From his point of view, she was more interested in finances and status than being with him and loving him.

Raina is upset even though she saw the end coming. John has been distant and unavailable lately. Raina saw an opportunity to get at the other females John's spends time with. She knew John wasn't going to be happy, but she figured her love for him would overrule his disappointment in her. John saw her move as a betrayal. He immediately lost trust in her. That was really the end. It just hadn't been communicated.

John only saw her a few days ago because he was lonely and needed female companionship. After their rendezvous, she asked him to accompany her to a work event. He said yes to show appreciation for the sex, but he had no intention of going.

When John doesn't answer her calls, she goes to his social media pages. She notices all her pictures have been removed, and he no longer follows her on any platform. She knows this means he is done. Raina cries her eyes out, sitting in her dressing room, looking at her ring. She's been showing off her ring for weeks, and she is already embarrassed that everyone will know the relationship is over. She can't believe her perfect love affair is over.

John sits in his office thinking about KD after his morning meetings. John is smitten by KD already. He pulls out his phone to send her a text message. KD is making her rounds at the hospital when she receives the message. She smiles as she reads the message.

John: How's your day going?

KD: Good and yours?

John: It's cool. You never told me your name.

KD: Aren't you supposed to be working?

John: I'm focused on what's important: you. What's your name?

KD: I couldn't possibly be more important than your priorities. You don't even know my name.

John: Getting to know you is my priority.

KD: If I enjoy myself tonight, I'll tell you, my name.

John: I look forward to seeing you, and getting to know you.

KD: Have a good rest of your work day, John. I'll see you tonight.

John: Can't wait!

When John finishes his workday, he goes home to find Raina standing at his door. Her shiny, brand-new black Benz is in his driveway. John is irritated, but composed and calm as he prepares himself for the confrontation. He does not want to talk to her, but he knows they must have this conversation. He drives into the garage. He comes out the garage holding the box with her things. He hands her the box. He says, "Here's your things!"

Raina is heartbroken. She asks, "John, what's wrong? What happened?"

John says, "Raina, you know what's wrong. We don't want the same thing. The way you went about getting what you wanted wasn't cool." John walks toward his door.

Raina follows him to the door; she says, "John, baby, I'm sorry. I don't want to lose you."

John stops. He turns to face her; he says, "I don't want what you want. I can't give you what you want. Asking me to give in to what you want is not fair to me, and it wouldn't be fair to you to ask you to give up what you want. Letting go is best for both of us."

Raina grabs his arm; she says, "John, why now? Why today? I get I was wrong, but I thought everything was cool the other day." Tears begin to roll down her face.

John says, "Why not today? Why waste another day on something going nowhere?"

His words, his demeanor, his coldness hurt her feelings. Although intentional, his coldness wasn't indicative of his feelings. John didn't hate Raina. He only wanted to end the friendship. He thought a firm approach would better communicate his desire to end the friendship. He wanted her to get angry, so she would also want the relationship to end.

Raina turns to walk away, but she stops to ask, "Is there someone else? Who is she?"

John says, "There's nothing for someone else to intrude on."

Raina says, "I can't believe you are being so cold! John, you're the best man I've ever known. I can't lose you. I won't let you go. I love you too much."

John says, "You don't love me!"

Raina says, "How can you say that? What makes you think I don't love you?"

John says, "I don't feel it. You may love being around me, but you don't love me."

Raina says, "That's not true, John, I do love you! I tried to show you that you were loved every time we were together. I tried to make you feel loved just like you made me feel loved. I know you know in your heart that I love you. You're just distracted by someone else. She has taken your attention momentarily. She will never love you like I do. She could never take my place because she doesn't deserve you," as she turns to walk to her car.

John says, "Be good, Raina," before he turns to walk to the door.

She replies, "Not until I get you back! I'm going to find out who she is. When I do, I'm going to let her know you belong to me. I love you, John. I love everything about you, and this woman won't love you like I do. You'll be back once you see she's not me, and she can't do the things I can. Together, John, we are a power couple. We can have whatever we want. What you want is here with me, but I'll let you see for yourself."

John walks in the house unbothered by Raina's statement. He doesn't even know KD and is more willing to gamble on a new relationship with KD than he is to continue in the situation with Raina. John feels a sense of relief when Raina pulls off. For him, that is the end of the relationship.

At ten-thirty, John texts KD to see if she is still planning to meet him at midnight. KD texts back indicating she will be there. John is excited about the possibility of getting to know KD. Since the moment they met, thoughts of her smile, her eyes, the soft touch of her hand, the curves of her body, and her voice crowds his mind. He cannot shake the thought of her, and he doesn't mind. John likes being attracted to her despite not knowing her.

John showers, brushes his teeth, then goes through his closet trying to pick the right outfit. He wants to look good, but come across as charming and down to earth. It's imperative that he smells and feels incredible. He goes to his lotion and cologne collections to pick the right fragrance. Once John is dressed, he makes his way to the club.

At midnight, Henson picks up KD. As Henson helps her into the back seat of the Range Rover, KD questions herself. She would not normally make moves like this, but something about John's bright smile and intense personality made her say yes. She thinks to herself: KD, are you crazy? You're getting in a car with a stranger. As Henson starts the car, he calls John to let him know they are in route to the club.

Henson and KD talk as he drives through the streets of Downtown Detroit. Henson learns through their conversation that KD is nice and down to earth. They talk about their jobs and families. They make each other laugh. The conversation with Henson makes KD feel more comfortable. Henson is sure to mention how great John is as an employer and a friend. He explains how John's family treats him and his family like relatives.

KD says, "It's good you and he get along so well. It is important that your employer respects you as a person."

Henson says, "Many years ago, I had fallen on hard times. Things were rough for my wife and me, and it was all my doing. John never questioned or doubted me. John hired me as his personal assistant and he helped my wife get a better job. We bought a house. We've put our daughters through college. They both are very successful and married with children. My sons and nephews make a good living working in the factory. John is the brother I never had. I'm very fortunate that he took a chance on me."

KD says, "That's a powerful testimony. A fair chance is all we need. It's a blessing that you paid your blessings forward to your children."

Henson says, "John's that kind of guy. He is blessed because he blesses others."

KD says, "He sounds like a good man!"

Henson says, "He is!"

When they arrive, John is waiting outside the club to greet KD. He opens the door to help her out of the Range Rover. When John sees KD, he is stunned into stillness and quiet. After a pause to comprehend her beauty, John says, "Hello, Beautiful!"

KD says, "Hello, Handsome!"

He sticks out his arm. She puts her arm in his. They walk into the club. The club is packed just as John said it would be. The live band is jamming and the dance floor is packed. KD looks at the cheerful partygoers as they walk pass the dance floor. Several women in the club notice John with a new female. They look KD up and down with a smug expression on each of their faces.

John escorts her to a private dining room on the upper level of the club. John has a sexy vibe set in the room. Lit candles surround the room, the lights are dim, expensive dinner ware elegantly adorn the table, an Italian linen tablecloth covers the table, and essential oils give the room a pleasant aroma. KD is impressed. She compliments the effort John put into preparing the room.

John says, "You deserve five-star treatment!" KD smiles at him. He winks at her.

KD scopes the foods sitting on warmers on the table against the wall. John leads her to the table in the center of the room. He pulls out the chair to help her sit. John dips KD's hands in a silver bowl with warm mix of sanitizer and water. He stares in her eyes as he dries her hands. One of John's phones is vibrating in his pocket. He ignores it.

KD says, "Thank you!"

John dips his own hands into the bowl as he tells her, "You're welcome." KD grabs the other towel to dry his hands. John is impressed by the reciprocal gesture. It tells John she has a caring spirit. She looks into his eyes as she dries his hands. He smiles and says, "Thank you."

She says, "You're welcome!" He walks over to the table with the food.

He says, "I knew we wouldn't have a lot of time, so I took a guess at what you might like."

KD says, "You were right. You are intuitive. Your guesses were spot-on."

John says, "I'll make your plate. What do you want?"

KD says, "The steak looks good, the vegetables look good, the potatoes look good."

John asks, "Do you drink wine?"

KD answers, "Not if I have to work the next day."

John says, "I have juice, lemonade, and water."

KD says, "I'll take a glass of lemonade."

John asks about her day. She watches him pour the glass of lemonade. He puts strawberries and pineapples in her glass. KD sees the care he puts into making her drink. She concludes he is thoughtful and pays close attention to detail.

She answers, "My day went well." John brings her the glass of lemonade.

He says, "I'm glad to hear that!" John's phone continues to vibrate nonstop in his pocket.

KD says, "Someone really wants to talk to you."

John says, "You are who I want to talk to. You have my undivided attention."

John powers off the phone and slides it back into his back pocket. John knows it's Raina calling, but he has no interest in what she has to say.

KD says, "You must be an important man." She is trying to figure out if he is single.

John says, "That depends on who you ask."

KD says, "I'm asking you."

John says, "Hopefully, one day, I'll be important to you, but today, I'm just a man trying to get to know the most beautiful woman in the world."

KD smiles. She pushes her hair behind her ear. She says, "Well, I'm just a woman who would like to make the acquaintance of the most handsome man I've ever seen."

John says in a low, mesmerizing tone, "Let's make tonight count!"

They stare at each other. The attraction they feel for the other is a force, making them desire closeness. John resists temptation to kiss her. He smiles looking directly into her eyes.

She asks about his day; he says, "It didn't go by fast enough. I was rushing the day to get to you, but it was cool otherwise." John goes back to the table and begins to make their plates.

KD says, "I'm glad your day went well!" KD asks, "Mr. John, what do you do for a living?"

John says, "Manufacturing and shipping. What about you?"

KD says, "I am a RN," as she scopes John's attractive body from head to toe.

John brings the food to the table. He sits across from KD. KD lowers her head to pray over the food. John follows suit. After they pray, John says, "Nurse, honorable, hard work."

KD says, "Thank you!" KD begins to eat.

John says, "I respect what you do. My mother was a nurse. Nurses have caring hearts. They give a lot to their work. My mother was dedicated to her job. She loved helping people. My father worked until his dying moment at the same place I work."

KD says, "My mother was a nurse. My father worked in the same factory for forty years."

John says, "So, we both come from good, hardworking families. Keep talking, so we can see what else we have in common. I don't want to be a stranger after tonight. I can't have you hesitating on a second date."

KD says, "You can't be sure you want a second date already."

John was thinking the way your body looks in that dress, you damn right I want a second date, but he says, "I'm sure, already. I need you to be sure."

KD says, "Before I can agree to a second date, let's clarify that you are completely single because the way your phone was blowing up seems like some woman needs your attention."

John says, "She does, but she's not my woman, so she's not entitled to my attention. No woman is because I'm one hundred per cent single. What about you?"

KD says, "I wouldn't be here if I weren't."

John asks, "Were you ever married? I heard you say you have a son this morning."

KD says, "I divorced five years ago after twenty-two years of marriage. I have a daughter, Kelly, who is graduating from Michigan in May. My son, Daniel, is ten. He is in the fifth grade. What about you?"

John says, "Divorced twice many years ago. I've been single since the second divorce. I have six kids, three from each marriage. I have three daughters who work with me; two are married with children. I have three boys. They're married, and two have children. One is a corporate attorney, one is a pharmaceutical rep, and one owns several reception halls and this club."

KD says, "It's so awesome that your daughters work with you. What made them follow in your footsteps?"

John answers, "When my children were in high school, they wanted expensive shit, so they had to work. Each one of them came to work with me the day after their fourteenth birthday. The boys found other interests. The girls stayed, and worked their way up just like I did."

KD says, "That's awesome! I know you are so proud of your children."

John asks, "I am! Thank you! My marriages failed because we were not ready to be married. Why did you get a divorce?"

KD says, "Nothing I did made him happy. He had to go, so I could be happy."

John says, "I know the feeling. I don't want to say I regret the marriages because I love my kids and I'm thankful for them, but, man, I could've done without those marriages."

KD says, "Were you in love on your wedding day?"

John says, "I was scared because she was pregnant, and I had a girlfriend back home. She didn't know I was already involved with someone, and I couldn't tell her about my girlfriend after she told me she was pregnant. I thought getting married was the right thing to do.

"My side chick became my wife, and the one who thought she was going to be my wife had to settle into being my side chick, which made her bitter, very bitter. I wasn't even twenty when the pregnancy happened. I was young and not ready to be someone's husband. I wasn't a great husband, but I was intent on being a great father."

KD says, "Despite the difficult circumstances, it seems like you made the best of the situation for your kids and that's really all that matters."

John says, "Amen to that! My kids and grandkids are all I have."

KD asks, "Are you close with your exes?"

John says, "Absolutely not! My first wife, well, we were so young. I was barely present between work and a mistress. She divorced me and took the kids back to California. She didn't want the kids. She just wanted a way to control and manipulate me. I fought for two years, and I won full custody of my kids.

"When the first wife divorced me, I married my pregnant side chick. She wasn't prepared for the responsibility of raising a big family. It was fun when we were sneaking and creeping, but when three additional kids came to live with us, things got real.

"We weren't happy. Six kids running around and a distant, preoccupied husband had her stressed out. She left me and moved back in with her mother. When she left, she never looked back. She got the kids on the weekends and the holidays, but she was done with me."

The club's manager, Kayla, knocks on the door; she says, "Mr. King, you're needed downstairs."

When KD hears the name King, she thinks about everything he has said about himself: he's in shipping and manufacturing, the name of the club, Kingdom Come, and she finally puts the pieces together. She says, "You're John Michael King!"

John says, "I am!"

KD says, "I'm so sorry, I didn't recognize you."

John says, "Don't be. Excuse me, I'll be right back!"

John gets up to walk out the door. When John closes the door, Kayla whispers, "Raina is on the phone." John hangs up the phone. He tells Kayla to tell the entire staff not accept calls from Raina. John thanks Kayla and goes back into the private dining room.

When John returns, he apologizes for the interruption and gets right back into the conversation. He asks, "Are you cordial with your ex?"

KD says, "We have no reason to speak since my kids are in the position to communicate with him on their own. He picks my son up from school every Thursday. The weekends are his days, even holidays. If going to each other's home is necessary, we don't get out the car."

John asks, "Was the break-up terrible?"

KD says, "Terrible doesn't even describe it."

John asks, "Were you heartbroken when your marriage ended?"

KD says, "I was more embarrassed than heartbroken. Everything he did was so unexpected. He gave me hell the last six years of the marriage. I was embarrassed because everyone I knew was still comfortably, happily married while my marriage was falling apart. No one in my family ever got a divorce. I questioned myself as if something was wrong with me.

"I asked myself, why me and what did I do to deserve this. I had to remind myself that he is a grown man and his actions were about him. I couldn't harbor the responsibility for his actions. When it was finally over, I had to focus on me and my son. I didn't have time to be brokenhearted."

John says, "I'm sorry to hear that. I hope things have been good for you since the divorce."

KD says, "My life has been peaceful, so I'm happy."

John asks, "What is making you so happy these days?"

KD answers, "The peace, calm, and quiet after the storm."

John asks, "What do you do for fun?"

KD says, "Fun! I don't even know what that word means. I work overtime four to six times every week. I work most weekends and holidays. Fun is not an option for me right now."

John says, "Not to pry, but why are you working so much?"

KD says, "To pay private school tuition, to pay for basketball camp, to buy equipment and shoes for basketball, football, and soccer, and to buy video games every week. My daughter's scholarships covered her classes, books, and fees. I pay her car note, insurance, and her rent."

John asks, "Your ex-husband doesn't help you?"

KD says, "He manipulated every angle he could to get out of paying child support for Daniel. I wanted it to be over. I was tired of fighting. I told the judge to let him keep his money, his last name, and his presence away from me."

John says, "That's not right. He should contribute to his son's well-being."

KD says, "He said the boy can go to public school for free and the girl is grown, so he was no longer obligated to support her. My daughter loves her daddy, and they are very close. I don't ask her about him, but she has always gotten whatever she wanted from him."

John asks, "Is Daniel close with his dad?"

KD says, "No, they've never had a father and son connection. Daniel tolerates him because the court order obligates him to do so."

John says, "What man doesn't pay for his son's education? You shouldn't be out here hustling by yourself when your son has two parents."

KD says, "I would rather work my fingers to the bone than to deal with him. I work a lot, but I have peace in my home. It's worth it. My son has everything he needs, so I can't complain."

John says, "I'm not trying to be in your business or judge, but a man takes care of his kids. That's not right!"

KD says, "I get that, but my freedom was more important than getting a few dollars."

John says, "You know what's best, and you're making it work for you. That is the important thing. I believe a woman shouldn't have to parent alone after the relationship ends."

KD says, "That's honorable."

John asks, "What kind of men do you date?"

KD says, "I don't!"

John asks, "So, you haven't been in a relationship since your divorce?"

KD says, "I've been on a few first dates, but I've not been interested enough to go on a second date."

John says, "Oh! This is going to be a challenge. Can I interest this beautiful, unattainable woman enough to capture her attention?"

KD says, "I don't know! Seems like a mighty big feat, Mr. John Michael King."

John says, "I'm up for the challenge."

KD asks, "So what do you do when you're not out at midnight with strangers?"

John answers, "I play sports, travel, work out, and spend time with my grandkids."

KD asks, "What type of women do you date?"

John says, "I am interested in beautiful, Black women who are smart, driven, kind, fun, trustworthy, sweet, sexy, hardworking, caring, along with a few other things. I hadn't found one woman that embodies all the qualities I seek until I saw you jogging this morning."

KD says, "I can only imagine what the few other things are."

John says, "Nothing out of the ordinary." He gives her a look to confirm they're sexual.

KD says, "You can't say that I embody all those qualities. You don't even know me."

John says, "I never lose a bet. I'm betting you have all the qualities I am seeking in a woman." John sips his drink as he stares in her eyes with a serious face. She shyly smiles at him.

KD says, "If you're wrong, what will I win?" KD flirts with John with her facial expressions.

John says, "What do you want?"

KD shrugs her shoulders; she says, "I don't know. I don't gamble. What's a good wager?"

John asks, "What's one thing you've wanted your whole life, but never came close to obtaining?" John adds, "I'm serious about this bet."

KD says, "A red 1968 Mustang!"

John asks, "You love that car?"

KD says, "I love that car. My dad had one when I was a little girl. He would take us to Belle Isle every Saturday. On Sundays, after church we would ride around the city. I miss those days. I was so sad when he sold it to help my brother pay for college."

John says, "I'm betting that you are everything I'm looking for in a woman. If I'm wrong, you get a Mustang."

KD says, "What do you want if you win?"

John says, "A kiss!"

KD says, "A car against a kiss. That doesn't seem like an equal wager."

John says, "I guarantee I will love the kiss more than you love the car."

KD licks her lips after taking a bite of food; she says, "I'm not sure about that, but I'll take your word for it."

John says, "You know my full name. Are you comfortable with telling me your name now?"

KD says, "KD, just the two capital letters K and D together no space, hyphen or periods."

John says, "KD, that's cute. Does it stand for anything?"

KD says, "My father's name was Keith Daniels, and everyone called him K. D."

John says, "I like that! Your mother was very clever."

KD says, "Thank you!"

John asks, "Are your parents still with us?"

KD says, "My father died five years ago. My mother is still living. She's my backbone. She's super supportive with my son, especially since the divorce."

John says, "It's good you have a strong support system." He doesn't hesitate to ask, "How old are you?"

KD doesn't hesitate to answer. She says, "I will turn fifty this year. That's probably too old for you, right? You know what they say about you?"

John says, "One, I'm older than you. I'm fifty-two. Two, I don't know what they say, please, tell me."

KD says, "Playboy King has a different, young [she emphasizes young] girl every night."

John says, "Who says that?"

KD says, "I don't know specifically."

John says, "Well, luckily, I'm just John, and those people don't know John. Playboy King sounds like an asshole."

KD says, "I'm pretty sure Playboy King and John King are interchangeable."

John says, "I'm just a man named John. Being a playboy is not me or my intention. I have been searching for the one [he holds up one finger] woman God has for me, so you can say my experiences with women were purposeful research. I've enjoyed the company of many women over the years, but a different woman every night is an extreme exaggeration.

"Fifty-two take away thirteen is thirty-nine. Thirty-nine times three-hundred sixty-five is fourteen thousand two hundred thirty-five. Shit, I got a little game, but not that much. Not that I count, Ms. KD, but my number is way, way below that."

KD, side-eyeing John, says, "You count, don't you?"

John says, "Hell yeah!" They both laugh. He asks, "You want to know my number?"

KD says, "No! It's okay to have some secrets! And before you ask, you can count on one hand, and you will have fingers left."

John says, "You never strayed during your marriage?"

KD says, "No! I can't comprehend thirteen! How old was she?"

John says, "It was my birthday. She was twenty-one."

KD shockingly asks, "What! Are you serious?"

John says, "My brothers got her to do that."

KD says, "That's interesting!"

John says, "It was interesting. I was a good boy focused on school and sports. That night interrupted my whole trajectory."

KD says, "So they made you a hoe?"

John bursts into laughter; he says, "A former hoe." John likes that KD can make him laugh.

KD says, "So you're a reformed hoe!"

John says, "I've turned my life around." They laugh.

They stare at each other in silence, both enamored by the other's looks.

John says, "Ms. KD, you look amazing, and by the way, you're not too old for anything."

KD says, "Mr. King, you've done an incredible job of staying handsome."

John says, "There's something about you that I like."

KD says, "Like what?"

John says, "It could be your energy, your spirit, or your joy, I don't know how to describe it."

KD says, "When you can, please, enlighten me."

John says, "Only if you promise to give me a fair chance and get to know me. Don't listen to the rumors because they do not represent me."

KD reaches out her hand, and they shake hands. KD says, "Deal!"

John asks, "Did you grow up in Detroit?"

KD says, "Born and raised!"

John asks, "Do you have other siblings?"

KD answers, "No, just the one brother, Keith Jr. He is the oldest."

John says, "I had older twin brothers. They were both star athletes and super smart. They were seniors when they died in a car accident coming home from a party celebrating a win. They were speeding. They both died before the car finished flipping over.

"My parents were devastated after their deaths. My mother told my father not to buy teenagers such a powerful car, but he wanted to give his sons everything. That decision haunted my dad for the rest of his life, and my mother was never the same. I don't know how she pushed through, but she did.

"Their deaths left me feeling this extreme pressure to be the golden child. I couldn't do anything wrong and risk hurting my mother. My parents really kept a close eye on me. After the accident, I was either working for my dad or playing sports.

"I started at the bottom at fourteen. I had to hustle hard to earn respect. I couldn't have people saying I made it because I'm John King's son. I wanted people to see me as my own man. I studied the business and industry. I lived and breathed the company. My dad never gave me a position. I earned every promotion. I was thirty-two, single with six kids. My father really started to respect me as a leader when he saw I could perform at work while caring for my family. He made me his number two, and I took advantage of the opportunity.

"When my father died unexpectedly, and my mother put me in charge. She told me, 'Don't fuck up my husband's legacy! Son, I'm counting on you to be the man I raised. Make me proud.' Even though she's gone, I still try to make her proud."

KD says, "I feel your love for your family in that story."

John says, "Tragedy taught me the value of hard work!"

KD says, "So, that's how you became King of Detroit, The Hometown Hero!"

John says, "I'm just John. I don't call myself that."

KD says, "I like it! It sounds a little gangster. Just enough to make me feel protected, but not too much that I feel threatened."

John says, "You're always safe with me."

KD asks, "You promise?"

John says, "I promise!"

KD reaches out her pinky finger; she says, "Come on, you have to pinky promise." John smiles as they lock pinky fingers. KD says, "My son makes me pinky promise to everything."

John says, "I can't believe we've never crossed paths. How long have you lived in that building?"

KD says, "Four years."

John asks, "Where did you go to school?"

KD says, "Michigan."

John says, "I went to USC. Did you meet your ex in college?"

KD says, "Yes, but he went to State. We met hanging out."

John asks, "How was the relationship early on?"

KD answers, "At first, things were like a dream. I was totally blindsided when my life turned into a nightmare."

John asks, "Are you ready to dream again?"

KD asks, "So dating you would be like a dream?"

John says, "Not to brag, but I'm a great guy. I'll be good to you, spoil you. You will enjoy being with me because I'll be everything you ever wanted in a man that you never had."

KD says, "How do you know, Mr. King?"

John says, "We have a special connection, Ms. KD."

KD says, "Just to confirm, you're totally free to pursue only [she emphasizes only] me. If sharing is a requirement, I don't want any part of it."

John says, "There is and will be no one in the way of me getting you."

KD says, "I'm going to do something crazy."

John asks, "What's that?"

KD says, "Trust you!"

John says, "I appreciate that, Ms. KD!"

KD says, "Don't make me regret trusting you."

John says, "With me, you'll have no regrets."

KD asks, "Are you sure about that?"

John says, "I'm sure."

KD asks, "How can you be so sure?"

John says, "Why do you think people call me King of Detroit?"

KD says, "Why?"

John says, "I don't let people down."

KD asks, "Is that so?"

John answers, "Just ask around. I mean, if everyone knows about my sex life, they must know my character."

KD says, "I will take your word as truth. No one knows you better than you."

John replies, "I appreciate that!"

When KD is done eating, John says, "Let's go enjoy the music." When they get to the main floor, he says, "Can you play pool?"

KD shakes her head no. He reaches out his hand, KD takes his hand. He leads her to the pool table. As John walks with KD, a few of his friends spot him and notices he's with a woman that's not Raina. His friends point to KD as a way of asking John to identify her. John smiles, but doesn't respond.

As John explains the rules of the game, his friends watch. John puts the stick in her hands. He stands behind her to help her take the first shot. KD enjoys being so close to him. The smell of his cologne, the feel of his soft hands on her back, and the warmth of his body against hers comfort her. John is behaving as a gentleman, but being so close to KD is intoxicating to his maleness. The sight of her, the smell of her, and the silhouette of her body in the low light are all working in KD's favor.

John whispers in KD's ear, "I love your hair. Your bob is fire. The argan oil smells good."

KD says, "Thank you. I'm surprised you know those words."

John says, "I have three daughters."

KD says, "Right! Makes sense, you would know a lot about hair."

John says, "You wouldn't believe the hair drama I've been through over the years."

KD says, "I can believe it." After John takes a few shots, they stare at each other until KD shyly looks away.

John puts his thumb and forefinger under her chin to make her look up and into his eyes. He says, "I like you! I would like to see you again."

KD looks in his eyes; she says, "I would love to see you again."

He asks, "If Henson takes you home now, would you find time to let me see you tomorrow?"

KD says, "I go in tomorrow afternoon and I don't get off until Saturday morning."

John says, "I only need a few minutes to put my eyes on you so I'll know I'm not dreaming."

KD says, "You think I'm a figment of your imagination?"

John says, "When you meet the woman of your dreams, you have to make sure your mind is not playing tricks on you."

KD says, "Don't play with me!"

John says, "I'll do a lot of things with you, but play games is not one." She looks at him as if to say you're full of shit, but you're cute, so I'll listen.

John asks, "Do you think you could give me five minutes?"

KD says, "I can give you five minutes."

While KD sits at the bar, John gets her jacket and purse from the private dining room. He walks with her arm wrapped in his arm out of the club where Henson is awaiting her arrival to take her home. Before she gets in the car, John thanks her for hanging with him and tells her he can't wait to see her tomorrow.

She says, "I had a nice time. Thank you for inviting me out." As they stare at each other without speaking a word, the black Benz that rode alongside KD and Henson to the club lurks shielded in the darkness across the street from the club.

John breaks the silence; he says, "Hug my neck like you're going to miss me." KD wraps her arms around his neck. John embraces her; he whispers, "You're perfection in motion."

Raina sits in her car watching John and KD talk. Raina had a nagging feeling that there was someone new in John's life. None of John's female friends ever made Raina feel insecure. Since the day they met, Raina felt like she was John's number one girl. Something about the way John looks at KD tells Raina that KD is a threat to Raina's position.

KD, smiling, says, "Right back at you!" John smiles back.

John says, "I love the perfume you're wearing."

KD says, "Your cologne makes an impression." Neither wants to let the other go, but they manage to pry themselves apart.

John says, "A good one, I hope."

KD says, "I'm impressed."

John says, "Text to let me know you made it home safely." John pulls his phone out of his pocket. He powers on his phone as he says, "I'll be waiting for your text!" John wants to kiss her, but doesn't.

KD says, "OK! Goodnight, John!"

John says, "Goodnight, KD!"

John helps her get into the Range Rover and closes the door. John goes back into the club, but his mind is with KD as she rides home, thinking about him. His smile is the most beautiful thing she has ever seen on a man. As she rides home in the back of the Range Rover, thoughts of his smile light up her mind.

Raina follows the Range Rover, so she can learn more about KD. Raina watches Henson help KD exit the Range Rover and walk with her to the door. Henson and KD shake hands. She thanks him for the ride as he holds the door for her. Henson tips his hat and tells KD it was a pleasure making her acquaintance. KD thanks him as she waves goodbye.

Henson and John love KD's delightful personality already, but Raina hates her. KD's pleasant smile as she says goodbye to Henson irritates Raina to her core. Raina has had enough of KD. She pulls off to go home. At home, Raina is full of jealousy as she checks John's social media pages for any sign of KD. She finds nothing, but that only lights a fire in Raina to find out more about KD.

As John cleans up the room, he smiles, thinking about the conversation he had with KD. He liked talking to her. She engaged and interested him unlike any of the other women he encountered over the years. His phone vibrates. A message from KD is on his screen: I'm safely in my apartment. I really enjoyed hanging out with you."

John replies: I'm glad to hear that. I'm about to head home myself.

KD: Be safe

John: I always am. I can't wait to see you tomorrow.

KD: I'm looking forward to seeing you, too.

John: Goodnight, KD! Sweet dreams!

KD: Goodnight, John! Rest well!

One of the servers, Bella, comes to help John clean up. John is lost in thought with a gleam of happiness on his face. Bella asks John if he's okay. John smirks and says yes.

Bella asks, "You like her, huh?" John shrugs his shoulders.

She asks, "When did you meet her?"

John says, "It's crazy! I just met her this morning."

Bella says, "Boss Man, you got it bad. It hasn't even been twenty-four hours."

John says, "Is it that obvious?"

Bella says, "I saw the way you looked at her. It wasn't the way you looked at any other woman."

John asks, "Do you think she saw that?"

Bella says, "She only knows you with her. She can't compare. I've seen you with a ton of women, so the difference is very noticeable to me." John listens and agrees that Bella has a point.

She asks, "Where does this leave Raina?"

John says, "I ended that this morning after I met her."

Bella says, "So, it's true?"

John asks, "What's true?"

Bella says, "My grandpa told me that one look is all it takes for a man to know he wants a woman. He said a woman must first give a man something to look at, then show him something he wants to keep seeing."

John says, "We are visual creatures. He has a point."

Bella says, "She may be the one, Boss Man. Think about it. You had one encounter with her, and in that one encounter you saw or heard something that made you call and dump your girl of a whole year. It's something there. Everyone thought you were going to marry Raina."

John says, "That's the problem. Everyone except me thought that."

Bella says, "A man knows when a woman isn't right for him. You did the right thing, not letting the pressure keep you in the relationship with Raina. Good for you! You should go after what you want. If you like this woman like I think you do, get your girl." John smirks.

Bella says, "I wish you well, Boss Man!"

John says, "Thank you, Bella! You're a sweet, insightful, wise, young woman."

Bella says, "Boss Man, go home. I can clean up."

John says, "I can't leave my mess for you."

Bella says, "You have a lot to think about. Go home! I'm serious!"

John says, "Thank you, Bella!"

Bella says, "You're welcome! Boss Man!"

The mysterious black Benz is still outside the club when John gets in his car. The mysterious black Benz inconspicuously follows him all the way to his house.

The next day, KD and John text each other throughout the day. John plans to bring her food on her dinner break. After completing his work day, John meets his friends at the park to play basketball. As soon as John steps on the court, he hears Troy and Rocco describing John's new girl to Samuel, Stanley, Warren, and Matthews. Castle was also at the club last night, but he quietly stands with a disinterested smug look on his face.

Troy asks, "Who was that girl with you last night?"

John says, "Nope, Troy, not going there."

Matthews says, "You don't ask a grown man about his personal business."

Rocco says, "I guess Raina is sidelined."

Warren says, "Her ass is seated on the bench, looking sad because the coach took her out of the game."

Castle says, "Like the many, many women before her."

Warren, "How bad was the girl last night?"

Troy says, "Bad, bad to be forty plus."

Samuel asks, "She was full body bad? Face, body, like that?"

Rocco says, "Whole body bad!"

Warren says, "Damn! King, do the dollars and the dimes just fall in your lap?"

Samuel says, "That's what you call blessings from heaven."

Troy says, "Those kinds of blessings need to rain down on me. Lord, I am ready!"

Stanley says, "I didn't even know King messed with women over forty."

Rocco says, "Poor, poor Raina! I thought for sure she would last a little longer."

Castle says, "None of them lasts more than a year."

Rocco says, "That girl last night is definitely worth a year."

Stanley says, "King's greedy ass gets all the fine women and stacks."

Samuel says, "It's not his fault. It's the law of attraction. He has a success mindset."

Warren says, "Pour some of that shit in my cup. I need my cup to overflow with expensive shit and bad bitches." John doesn't like this conversation.

John says, "Maybe if you didn't call women bitches, beautiful women would come to you. She's not a bitch, so don't reference her in that way."

Warren says, "My bad, King. I wasn't saying it like that."

Stanley says, "King, you must really be feeling her." John doesn't respond.

Troy says, "King, what's up? Who was that last night? Where is Raina?"

John doesn't answer. He listens to his friends talk about him with an uninterested face of disapproval.

Castle says, "Raina is beautiful, young, rich, sexy, no kids, smart. And did I mention beautiful? You could've made things work with Raina." John doesn't respond.

Rocco says, "King, tell us about your new girl."

Samuel says, "Leave King alone! It's complicated being rich and handsome."

Castle says, "Don't forget old! Your old ass needs to settle down and quit playing."

Matthews says, "Cas, don't be so hard on King. We all have our crosses to bear. His cross happens to be fine ass women."

John gets tired of his friends talking about his love life, he says, "Can we play ball?"

Rocco says, "Whoever she is, she's fine. If you ghost her, pass her ass this way."

John says, "Don't speak on her like that. Don't look at her like that. It's not like that."

Castle says, "That's some bullshit, King. You found your next victim?"

John says, "She's different. She's special. I'm not on any bullshit with her."

Rocco says, "So you think you are ready to settle down?"

Troy says, "King will never settle down."

John says, "She's a good person, a hard worker, and a good mother. I really like her." All the men pause.

Samuel breaks the silence; he says, "Get the fuck out of here!"

Matthews says, "It was only a matter of time before he got caught in some woman's web just like the rest of us."

Samuel says, "King, every man needs a good person to hold him down. If you think this woman is that person for you, I am happy for you and I wish you well with your relationship."

John says, "Thank you!"

Stanley says, "I don't believe this."

John says, "Can we play ball?"

Stanley says, "It's so sad when the great ones retire. I guess we need to hang his player jersey from the rafters."

Troy says, "Look at you, King, looking like you're all in love."

Rocco says, "King, don't tell us you out the game, Player. I thought you would die on top."

Warren says, "Twenty-one-gun salute for the fallen soldier."

Matthews says, "King, you deserve a good woman. I hope this works for you. Now get your ass on the court. Let's play ball!"

John thanks Matthews, and tells Matthews and Samuels they are real friends. Troy, Rocco, and Stanley feel slighted.

Troy says, "We are your friends."

Rocco says, "Come on, King, don't be so sensitive."

Stanley says, "Why are you mad at me? They were the ones checking out your girl."

John says, "Forget y'all! Stop checking out my girl. It's disrespectful!" John, Matthews, and Stanley head to the court.

Troy says, "All right, King, man, I see you're in your feelings."

Rocco says, "King, we're sorry, man, don't be mad." Troy and Rocco keep laughing.

As soon as KD's break starts, John texts to tell her to meet him in the back stairwell. When she walks through the door, John is standing there with the food she wanted.

She looks at him and smiles; she says, "Hey!"

John says, "Hello, Beautiful! It's so good to see you."

KD says, "It's nice to see you!"

John says, "I know, I'm sweaty, but hug my neck!" KD wraps her arms around his neck. She thinks even his sweat smells good. She doesn't want to let him go, but she manages to pry her arms from around his neck.

John says, "Let me come over to care for you tomorrow evening. I'll massage your feet, rub your back, feed you, relax with you."

KD says, "I'd like that."

John says, "Does six work for you?"

KD says, "It works!"

John says, "Kiss me!"

KD pauses and says, "There are cameras in here."

John says, "They're not working for five minutes, and we've already wasted four, so come on, kiss me like you missed me."

KD put her hands on his shoulders, and slowly moves her lips to his. She looks at him to see his eyes are closed as he awaits the kiss. KD is unsure if she should, but John is so cute standing there. She stands on the tips of her toes. She lightly presses her lips against his bottom lip. KD slowly moves back. John smiles and opens his eyes. He did not want her to stop.

John says, "That made my heart flutter." KD smiles. John says, "Here's your food!"

She says, "Thank you," as she takes the bag.

John says, "If you find the time tonight, call me," just as KD's friend, Nanette, comes up the stairs. John speaks to Nanette (she smiles and says hello). John says bye to KD, and turns to go down the stairs.

Nanette asks, "You know John King?"

KD says, "Not really!"

Nanette says, "The way he smiled at you, he knows you."

KD says, "I only met him yesterday."

Nanette says, "He likes you."

KD says, "He doesn't know me."

Nanette says, "That's when men like women the most."

KD says, "I don't know if I should even think about going there."

Nanette says, "The most handsome man in the city who happens to be the richest man in the city smiles at you like that, and you're questioning it. Hell no, KD, I am not letting you say no to this one. You better strap on your seatbelt and enjoy the ride. I heard him tell you to call him tonight. You're going to call him tonight. I will come to cover for you for an hour after my shift. And don't worry, I will keep your secret."

KD is lost in her thoughts of John as she eats. She takes a deep breath as she washes her hands and she embraces the possibility of a relationship with John before she gets back to making her rounds. Her first stop is to check on Mrs. Arlene Gable, a lady from her childhood neighborhood whom KD has known her whole life. KD knocks to let Mrs. Gable know she's coming into the room.

As KD enters the door, she says, "Hello! How are you feeling, Mrs. Arlene?"

Mrs. Gable says, "I'm okay, KD!" As KD checks Mrs. Arlene's vitals, Mrs. Arlene says, "You've been hugging a man. He smells good. He's fine, too!" KD is at a loss for words.

Mrs. Gable says, "You like him. I can see it in your dancing, smiling eyes." KD shrugs her shoulders.

Mrs. Gable says, "I know you don't think so, but you're still young. You have a lot of life ahead of you. You don't want to spend the next thirty years alone, and don't worry about DJ; he wants you to have someone to take care of you.

"Trust me! I have been alone since my husband died over twenty years ago. I thought the respectful thing to do was to put that side of myself away to honor his memory. I regret that choice. I deserved to be a woman, regardless of being a widow and mother. Don't do that to yourself. You're too beautiful of a person to be packed away like an old shirt in luggage. You hear me?" KD nods yes.

Mrs. Gable adds, "Next time he comes to kiss you at work, bring him in here, so I can meet him."

KD says, "Yes, ma'am!"

Mrs. Gable says, "It'll be fine! You're grown enough to handle yourself, and besides, good things come to those who wait. You have patiently waited on the Lord. He wouldn't leave you after you've been so faithful. Trust me, this is a good thing."

KD says, "Mrs. Arlene, thank you!"

At midnight, KD goes to the break room to call John. John is asleep, but immediately awakes when he hears the phone. He grabs the phone. When he sees her name on his phone, he hurries to answer with a smile on his face. When he answers, she thanks him for the food; she says, "The food was so good."

John says, "I'm glad you liked it. Chef McClure is the best chef in town. He can make anything."

KD says, "You have to thank him for me."

John says, "I will!"

KD asks, "How was your day?"

John says, "It was cool!"

KD asks, "What did you do?"

John says, "I went to the gym, got some work done, played ball with my friends, mostly thought about you."

KD says, "Is that so?"

John says, "It's facts!" KD smiles.

KD asks, "Did you have fun with your friends?"

John says, "Yeah! A few of them were at the club last night and saw us together. They were all up in our business."

KD says, "My friends would be the same way if they saw us together, so I understand."

John says, "Who are your good, true friends that will come get you out of trouble or get into trouble with you?"

KD says, "Tricia, we call her Tri because she hates Tricia, and Mena; we went to every school together. They are like my sisters."

John says, "I bet you three have some stories to tell."

KD says, "Stories we can't tell and stories we can't stop telling."

John says, "I bet you do. Quiet girls are usually sneaky and adventurous. Is that you, KD?"

KD says, "I'm not telling. I guess you're going to have to stick around to find out."

John says, "I look forward to finding out!"

KD asks, "What did your friends say?"

John says, "They asked a bunch of questions. They made some judgmental comments, but they agreed one on thing: you're beautiful. They think I really like you, and they wish it works for us."

KD says, "Do you think you really like me?"

John says, "Absolutely!"

KD says, "Do you want to know a secret?"

John says, "I do!"

KD says, "I like that you like me."

John asks, "Do you think you like me?"

KD says, "If I didn't like you, I wouldn't be on this phone. My friend is covering my patients for an hour, so I can be on this phone with you."

John says, "I've got fifty minutes. I better make the best of it."

KD says, "Don't make me regret this, Mr. King!"

John asks, "Regret what, Ms. KD?"

KD says, "Liking you and admitting that I like you."

John says, "You'll never regret your feelings for me, I promise."

KD says, "You don't break promises? A man's measure is his ability to keep his word."

John says, "If I say something will happen, you can take it as if it has already happened."

KD says, "I don't break promises, so you can trust my word."

John says, "That's good to know."

KD asks, "How many times have you been in love?"

John says, "Outside of my ex-wives, I've been infatuated a couple of times."

KD says, "Maybe that's what this is with me?"

John says, "No, KD, my feelings for you are totally different."

KD says, "How do you know?"

John says, "KD, I won't lie, so don't ask a question if you don't want the answer. Do you want me to answer your question?"

KD says, "Yes!"

John says, "I genuinely enjoy talking to you and spending time with you. I want to know you and be near you."

KD asks, "What is it like when you are infatuated with a woman?"

John says, "KD, don't get offended because you wanted the truth. To say it plainly, I am interested in you, your mind, your heart, and your soul. When I'm infatuated with a woman, I'm interested in what's between her thighs. I'm not even on that with you, so don't think that."

KD says, "So when we are alone in my apartment tomorrow, I won't have to worry about you trying anything?"

John says, "I'm coming over to massage your neck, back, and feet. I'm going to feed you. I'm going to sit and talk with you. We will plan our next date before I leave to go home."

KD says, "That's it?"

John says, "That's the agenda."

KD says, "Uh huh!"

John says, "I'm so serious, but I wouldn't mind if you wanted to kiss me."

KD asks, "You don't want to kiss me?"

John says, "It's not that. I don't want you to feel uncomfortable or think I am after something. Do you want to kiss me again?"

KD asks, "I do."

John says, "When our lips touched, I felt fireworks in my heart and butterflies in my stomach."

KD says, "Even though it was a tiny peck, there was definitely sparks."

John says, "If we both felt something from a peck, imagine how we are going to feel when we hold each other and kiss deeply."

KD says, "You have a point."

John says, "It'll be amazing."

KD asks, "I bet it will. What's your sign? When is your birthday?"

John says, "I'm a Leo. My birthday is July twenty-ninth."

KD says, "The confident king of the jungle. That fits you perfectly."

John asks, "When is your birthday?"

KD says, "November first."

John says, "The secretive, sexy Scorpio. Is that you?"

KD says, "You're going to have to find out for yourself."

John says, "Okay, I'm up for the task."

KD asks, "Who is your favorite superhero?"

John answers, "I'll go with Batman. He has more swag than Superman."

KD says, "I have to agree!"

John says, "What's your favorite movie?"

KD says, " I have a few: *Beverly Hills Cop 2*, *Color Purple*, *I'm Gonna Get You Sucka*, and *Boomerang*."

John says, "Those are all classics. Of course, I like *Scarface* and *The Godfather*."

KD says the famous lines from the *Scarface* film: "I'm Tony Montana!"

John says another line, "In this country, you gotta make the money first." They laugh.

KD says a line from *The Godfather*. She says, "I'm gonna make him an offer he can't refuse."

John says another line. He says, "Revenge is a dish best served cold."

KD says, "What about this one." She quotes Inspector Todd from *Beverly Hills Cop 2*, "Don't think, Axel! It makes my dick itch." John cracks up laughing. KD says, "You know how irritating someone has to be to make someone's dick itch just by thinking."

John laughs. He says, "That's pretty bad! John says [mocking the actor from *Boomerang*], "You wanna come over for a cup of coffee?"

KD [mocking the actor's voice from the *Boomerang* film] says, "Not even if Jesus was pouring it."

John says [imitating the actor in the *Boomerang* movie], "Don't be pussy-whipped, whip that pussy."

KD says a line from the *Boomerang* film. She says, "My parents are in there hitting it."

They enjoy the lighthearted conversation, making each other laugh more. John laughs. He says, "I love talking to you."

KD looks at her smartwatch; she says, "I enjoy talking to you, too, but I have to get back to work."

John says, "I hate to get off this phone, but I won't be selfish."

KD says, "Go back to sleep and dream about me."

John says, "That's what I was doing before you called."

KD says, "Talk to you later."

John says, "Go save someone's life, Superwoman!"

John knocks on KD's door at exactly six o'clock Saturday evening. KD opens the door; she asks, "How did you know which apartment I lived in?"

John says, "I know people!"

KD says, "Come in!" John has Chef McClure and his assistant, Mario, with him. John introduces everyone. Mario and Chef McClure are carrying bags of food and supplies. KD compliments Chef McClure and Mario, as she leads them to the kitchen. She says, "Let me know if you need anything." They thank her before she returns to the front room.

John looks at the trophies and pictures on the walls and shelves. When John notices KD has returned from the kitchen, he reaches out his arms for a hug.

When KD embraces him, he says, "You smell good."

KD says, "So do you!" KD tells John, "Make yourself comfortable." John sits down.

John says, "I know those two are yours because they the spitting image of you."

KD says, "Yes, that is Kelly and that guy is Daniel. The other kids are my nieces and nephews." KD sits on the couch with John.

John says, "Your nieces favor you a lot. Gorgeous family!"

KD says, "Thank you! I tell my brother all the time that his karma for bullying me when we were little is God gave him three copies of me."

KD turns on the TV. KD says, "You know a lot of people. Who do you know at the hospital?"

John says, "A while back, the board invited me to a few presentations to convince me to donate money. As I went in and out, I would talk to the a few of the guys who work security."

KD says, "I bet you make friends everywhere you go because you're so charming. What friends do you have in this building?"

John says, "Full disclosure, I own the property management company that owns the building, but my daughter handles everything. I'm cool with the head of maintenance. The day we met, I called him to ask your name. When I described you, he knew exactly who I was talking about. He didn't know your name, but he knew your apartment number."

KD asks, "How did you describe me?"

John says, "I asked if he knows a beautiful nurse who lives in the apartment building with her son. She jogs, has pretty eyes, a cute haircut, in great shape, and a smile that will make you fall in love. He said, 'You're talking about the sweetheart in apartment 3B.'"

KD says, "Gerald is always very polite and kind to me."

John says, "You know him?"

KD says, "We are cordial, but I don't know him personally. I know his name from his nametag on his shirt." KD and John look at each other.

John says, "You pay attention to people."

KD says, "It's the polite thing to do."

She hands him the remote; she says, "Maybe you can find something worth watching."

John asks, "What do you like to watch?" John flicks through the movies.

KD says, "I'm usually asleep when the TV is on."

John says, "All I watch is sports."

John comes across a movie, he says, "I heard this is worth watching." John presses play before he sits the remote on the table. John puts KD's feet in his lap. He asks, "How was work?" as he takes off her shoes to massage her feet.

She says, "It was chaotic as usual."

John says, "I thought about you all night and all day."

KD says, "You crossed my mind in the chaos."

John says, "I can't shake you, and I don't want to. It doesn't feel like we just met. It feels like we're old friends. Are you comfortable with me?"

KD says, "I am very comfortable with you, which is strange because I usually don't let men in my space. With you, I feel no apprehension," as she watches him massage her feet.

John says, "That's good because I feel the same way!"

KD says, "You give a pretty good foot massage."

John says, "Only because you have soft, pretty feet. Your pedicure is immaculate. Soft, smooth skin, ankle bracelets, and toe rings, you're so sexy!"

KD says, "You are!"

John says, "This is new for me, this feeling."

KD says, "What do you feel?"

John shyly smiles and changes the subject. He asks, "What kind of music do you like?"

KD says, "I like jazz, R & B, neo-soul, gospel, some hip-hop, and a lot of old-school."

John says, "We have to catch some concerts."

KD says, "I'd love that!"

John points to the pictures on the shelves; he says, "You like to travel?"

KD says, "I cut the ex out of the pictures. We took a family vacation every summer. I haven't been anywhere since the year before filing for divorce."

John says, "You look happy!"

KD says, "My kids make me happy."

John says, "The fact that your marriage lasted so long is admirable. Both my marriages were over by our fourth anniversary."

KD says, "At first, I stayed for myself because I loved being married to him. When things got rocky, I stayed for my daughter's sake. I had to end it for my son's sake. I didn't want him to think a man leads his household the way his father was leading our family."

John asks, "What made him the one you wanted to marry?"

KD says, "He was very intelligent, sweet, kindhearted, tall, handsome with a beautiful smile. He was the first guy that captured my attention. He swept me off my feet. He made me feel loved while we dated. We would read and study together. We went to church every Sunday. We had similar beliefs. He came from a good family. He was working to build a lucrative career. I thought he would be a good father. In the beginning, we really loved each other."

John asks, "What changed things?"

KD says, "He never told me, but it was obvious that he was with someone else. I was completely blindsided. I loved him. I did everything for him. I cooked every day. I kept our home clean. I was a good wife to him and a good mother to our daughter. I raised our daughter to be respectful and have manners. I worked hard and earned my own money. We always had fun together. We had an incredible sex life. I did everything to please him, so I didn't understand why he needed another woman."

John says, "I'm sure his decisions were about him, so don't take that personally. Do you want to marry again?"

KD says, "I haven't even thought about it. At this age, falling in love, merging my life with someone else's, is it even possible?"

John says, "Anything is possible!"

KD asks, "Do you want to try again?"

John says, "I would love a chance to do it right and for the right reasons. All my interactions with women have been superficial. I haven't had a woman to love me, care for me, be my companion and friend, or felt that feeling when you know it's real. Taking a chance to get the things I've always wanted but never had would be worth the risk."

KD says, "That's wise. You're right, that would be worth the risk."

John asks, "What would you want in the next relationship that you didn't have in your previous relationship?"

KD says, "Protection, peace, fidelity, trust, stability, lasting love, and to be treated like a wife. All of that is secondary to having a good man as an example and model for my son. I do my best, but I can't teach him to be a man."

John says, "I know what you mean. As much as I love my daughters, I am not their mother. I always hated not having a woman in my life that they could bond with, talk to, and learn from. My girls are smart, tough, happy. We are super close, but there are times they need a mother even as grown women. I wish my daughters had someone that they could call to get motherly advice. Especially Kimma, my oldest. Her mother is so far away. Regardless of age or success level, anyone can benefit from parental support and love."

KD says, "I wouldn't have made it through without my mother, so I get what you're saying."

John says, "My mother definitely was my backbone."

Chef McClure comes in the room to let them know dinner is served. John and KD go into the kitchen. They praise Chef McClure and Mario on the presentation and smell of the food. Chef McClure and Mario pack up to leave. John walks them to the door, thanks and tips them.

KD opens the wine bottle. She pours John a glass of wine. When John gets back in the kitchen, he pulls out KD's chair. After pushing in her chair, he sits down. KD prays over the food. They eat dinner by candlelight as they continue to talk.

John asks, "Hypothetically, if you were to pursue a relationship with me, what would you want, expect, and absolutely not tolerate?"

KD answers, "I would expect mutual respect, honesty, and trust. I would want caring, kindness, and fun. I would not tolerate disrespect, cheating, or physical abuse. What about you?"

John says, "I would not tolerate unfaithfulness or dishonesty. I highly doubt either of those would ever be a problem. Once I get you, you won't ever need another man. You never have to lie to me. I can handle your truth.

"In a relationship with someone as beautiful and kind as you, I would expect and want real, pure love, endless romance, trust, honesty, respect, fun, support, constant communication just so we know where we always are, and the most incredible sex either of us has ever experienced. I can handle all your expectations and desires. Do you think you could handle mine?"

KD answers, "I was with you and everything sounded reasonable until that last one. That's a tall order Playboy King. I don't want to write a check that I cannot afford to cash. I don't know if I have the skills to pay that bill."

John says, "Something tells me Ms. KD Daniels has the skills, so I'm not worried about that."

KD asks, "How can, you be sure?"

John says, "Your vibe, your personality, your charm, your innocence, your quietness, your shyness, your smile, your appeal, your body, and your eyes. Those eyes are so beautiful."

KD says, "Well, I guess we'll see." That response makes John smile. KD smiles too.

John says, "So let's add to our bet. I bet you embody all the characteristics I need in a woman, and you will be the best and bring out the best in me. You win, you get the car. I win, I get lifelong access to your kisses."

KD says, "I accept your bet."

John reaches out his hand. KD accepts his hand and they shake on it. John says, "This is going to be interesting."

KD says, "It already is!"

After they eat, they clean up the kitchen before going back to sit on the couch. John massages her neck as they talk. KD relaxes, leaning her back against John's chest. John slowly kisses her neck. She gently places her hand on his head.

He says, "I better stop before you try to take advantage of me, and I don't give it up so easily or quickly."

KD laughs and says, "I have to wait and work for it, huh?"

John says, "Women have to court me before I even think about giving it up."

KD says, "It's good you're stingy with it."

John says, "You know how women are! After they get it, and they start acting funny."

KD says, "They just want you for your body, poor baby." They laugh.

John asks, "May I kiss you?"

KD turns to face him. They look into each other's eyes. KD slowly moves toward John and softly touches her lips to his. John closes his eyes. John wraps his arms around her. His lips and tongue roll, twist, and tangle with hers. His hands slide down her back. The kiss and his hands awaken places in KD that she forgot existed. KD is flooded with desire.

John follows the kiss with a peck and says, "I could kiss you all night."

KD says, "I was thinking the same thing."

John asks, "Was it everything you thought it would be, our first real kiss?"

KD answers, "And more!"

John says, "I think we can do better. Let's try again!"

They kiss again. This kiss is longer and more passionate. KD rubs his arms, shoulders, and chest as they kiss. John gently holds her face in his hands. They kiss like familiar lovers in need of each other's comfort. When they stop kissing, they sit forehead to forehead looking into each other's eyes. John gently presses his lips to hers; he says, "I knew it! You know what that says to me?"

KD asks, "What?"

John answers, "When we focus our energy together, there is nothing we can't accomplish."

KD replies, "You're that confident in us?"

John says, "I am! Come here, let me massage your back."

KD relaxes as John massages her back while they watch the movie. KD relaxes so much she falls asleep lying on John's chest. John covers her with a blanket, wraps his arms around her, and and soon falls asleep himself. Just after sunrise, John wakes her up; he says, "KD, I have to go."

KD says, "I'm so sorry! I can't believe I fell asleep and slept all night."

John says, "I enjoyed holding you! Go back to sleep. I will let myself out. I'll call you." John hates to leave, but he promised his grandsons he would come to their game. John kisses her forehead.

KD says, "Okay." After John leaves, she balls up under the cover and falls back to sleep until it's time to get ready to go to church with her mother.

John calls her later that day. He says, "We never did plan our next date. When can I see you again?"

KD says, "I can hang out Saturday night."

John says, "I don't know if I can wait that long to see you."

KD says, "We can go on a date Saturday night, but we can find time here and there to see each other before the weekend."

John says, "I'll definitely make time for you."

KD says, "I'm working tonight, but not Monday or Tuesday night."

John says, "Good to know! I know it's time for you to get ready for work, so I'll let you go."

KD says, "Enjoy your evening and sleep well tonight." John says, "I will if you think about me!"

KD says, "I promise, I will!"

John says, "Have a good night!"

KD says, "OK! Bye!"

John says, "Don't say bye. Say I'll talk to you later!"

KD says, "Okay, John, I will talk to you later!"

John says, "I look forward to that, KD!"

John sends a dozen long-stem red roses in a beautiful vase to the hospital early Monday morning. KD's co-workers rush to get the card that reads: The odds are in my favor. The cryptic message has her co-workers puzzled. They ask about the roses and card. KD reads the card, she smiles, and smells the roses, but she refuses to tell them anything. This starts the tradition of John sending a beautiful bouquet of flowers to the hospital every Monday morning with an unsigned card.

When she calls to thank him, he thanks her for being so beautiful inside out. They text each other throughout the day. KD beams from ear to ear whenever she thinks of him.

After nightfall, John calls KD. When KD picks up the phone, he says, "Come ride with me."

KD says, "Are you outside right now?"

John says, "Yes! Put on some jeans and gym shoes and come outside." KD slips on some jeans, socks, and gym shoes. She throws on a jacket over her t-shirt. KD peeks at Daniel who is asleep in his bed. She grabs her key and quietly sneaks out the door. She is expecting a car, but she sees John sitting on his motorcycle. She walks over to him.

KD says, "I don't know, I've never been on a motorcycle."

John says, "I told you, you are always safe with me. Let's ride through the city and enjoy this beautiful night. I promise I will bring you home in one piece. Your son won't ever know you were gone." John puts a helmet on her head. He helps her on the back of the motorcycle. They take off down the avenue.

KD holds on to John as they speed through the streets of Downtown Detroit. She surprisingly enjoys the ride. When they return to her building, John parks by the river. They walk over to the river's edge. John says, "How was your day?"

KD says, "It was okay. How was yours?"

John says, "My day was good!"

KD asks, "I'm glad to hear that! What are you doing out here this late?"

John says, "I couldn't sleep. I kept dreaming about you, so I came to see you."

KD says, "What happened in your dream?"

John says, "Dreams! I had more than one. I don't want to talk about any of them."

KD asks, "Were they bad dreams?"

John says, smiling, "Let's say I couldn't handle them, but enough about me. How is Daniel?"

KD answers, "He's well! His team won their basketball game today, so he was all smiles."

John says, "Congratulations! Good for him. Sports are a great way to help develop character. You're doing the right thing, KD. You're a great mother."

KD says, "Thank you! You're a great father."

John says, "Thank you; that means a lot coming from you!" John throws a rock into the river; he asks, "So, what does little man want to do when he grows up?"

KD says, "Both of my kids love computers and technology like their father."

John says, "It's the future. It's the now. Thank God you have smart kids."

KD says, "Amen to that! How is your family?"

John says, "I saw my lovebugs today. They're good. Everyone else is well."

KD says, "That's good!"

John says, "If you weren't a nurse, what would you be?"

KD says, "A seamstress or hair stylist like my grandmother. When I was a little girl, I would watch my grandmother work in awe of how she made things so beautiful. I was her free labor and only assistant. As I got older, I started practicing on my own, and I got pretty good. I braided a lot of the girls' hair at school and in my neighborhood back in the day. When I would make my own clothes, girls would buy my stuff off my back. I made so much money in high school that I was able to buy a car senior year."

John says, "Do you think hair, nursing, or fashion is your true passion?"

KD answers, "I don't know! I enjoy them all!"

John asks, "When was the last time you made something or braided hair?"

KD says, "The last thing I made was my daughter's and her best friend's prom dresses. Last time I braided hair was around Christmas. I braided my friend's and my daughter's hair."

John says, "I would love to see something you made. I bet it's beautiful."

KD says, "I'll look around for something or a picture of something. What about you? If you hadn't gone into the family business, what would you have done with your life?"

John says, "Roamed the Earth looking for you."

KD says, "Besides women! Professionally?"

John says, "The only other love I have is sports."

KD asks, "Did you ever think to pursue them professionally?"

John says, "No! I was focused on my father's business."

KD says, "Then, things are as they should be."

John says, "I hope you're right about that." John and KD look at each other. John says, "Thanks for coming out and riding with me. I really enjoyed your company."

KD says, "The pleasure was mine."

John says, "May I have a kiss before I leave?" KD looks at him. They get closer to each other as they stare directly in each other's eyes. John takes KD in his arms. She hugs his neck. Their lips touch, and John holds her tighter as if he's asking her to never stop kissing him.

Raina sits in her car hidden by the darkness of night watching them kiss. When they stop kissing, John takes her hand. John says, "I'll walk you to the door." Raina can't stand to watch him with another woman. She quietly pulls off, never seen by John or KD.

Standing at the door, KD says, "Call when you get home, so I'll know you made it safely."

John says, "Definitely!"

KD kisses John's cheek before she says, "Goodnight, Mr. King!"

John says, "Good night, Ladybug!" He watches KD walk into the elevator. They look at each other through the glass doors as she waits for the elevator's doors to close. When the elevator doors close, John smiles and shakes his head. He gets on his bike and drives off.

As John turns the corner, the mysterious black Benz pulls up behind him. The car speeds up, aiming to hit his back tire, but John speeds up before the car can reach him. John rides down the avenue never knowing how close the car got to him. The car follows John home, being careful to stay in John's blind spot. John makes it home, never noticing the black Benz.

John pulls into his garage and goes into the house. He sits on his couch to call KD. When KD answers the phone, John says, "It was nice to see you tonight. You looked so good. You're beautiful even with no makeup and your hair back."

KD says, "Thank you! You're extremely handsome in all situations."

John says, "That kiss! KD! Your kisses could get you in trouble."

KD shyly giggles. She says, "Your kisses make me want all the smoke."

John asks, "You're sure about that?"

KD says, "No doubt!"

John says, "You sound confident."

KD says, "Your kisses make me confident."

John says, "How old were you when you had your first real kiss?"

KD says, "Ninth grade, I was fourteen."

John says, "Thank that young man because he taught you well."

KD says, "I taught him. My skills are naturally inclined."

John replies, "So you were born a good kisser?"

KD says, "Absolutely! You are a great kisser."

John says, "My first real kiss was that night when I was thirteen. She taught me what to do. I was clueless about everything."

KD says, "She taught you well."

John says, "I'm going to let you go to sleep. Think about me. Dream about me. Call me tomorrow after you drop your son off at school. I'll stop by to say hello before my meeting."

KD says, "All right, Mr. King!"

John says, "Sweet dreams, Ladybug!"

KD says, "Sweet dreams, Mr. King!"

When KD returns from taking Daniel to school, she calls John who comes right over. When John comes through the door, he kisses KD, spinning her around and picking her up. KD holds on to him as if he is the love of her life. John backs up until he sits on the couch. KD sits across his lap. They never speak. They continually kiss as their bodies merge.

The kisses are so intense that they both forget that they just met. Neither can resist or stop. John is so close that KD can feel every bulging muscle in his body pressing against her. KD is enjoying the romantic moment when John whispers in her ear, "I hate to leave, but I have to go!"

He kisses her one last time before he carries her to the door with her legs wrapped around his waist and her arms around his neck. She hates to let him go. She kisses his neck as he walks to the door. When they reach the door, they kiss.

John says, "I'll think about you all day."

KD says, "I miss you already."

John says, "Have a good day at work, Ladybug!"

KD says, "Thank you, you too!"

John says, "I'll call you tonight!"

KD says, "I look forward to your call." She kisses him before he puts her down. They look at each other as John walks out the door. KD waves before John walks away. She closes the door. She leans against the door and rubs her fingers through her hair. She can't believe the feelings she has for him already.

John asks if she can skate as he drives into the parking lot. KD says, "It's been a long time."

John says, "I come out for old school night every now and then."

KD says, "So, you're nice on skates?"

John says, "I can roll a bit!"

KD says, "You're a jack of all trades!"

John says, "I like to try different things."

John gets out of the car, and he goes around to the passenger's side to open the door for KD. John helps her get out of the car. John puts his arm around KD. As they walk toward the door, John sees Raina with her friends standing next to her car in the parking lot. John's heart almost jumps out of his chest. John fakes a smile and manages to keep his composure. Raina stares at him with eyes that could kill, but John focuses on KD. He doesn't want Raina to ruin their good vibe.

They walk into the rink holding hands. John and KD walk to the counter to rent skates. John keeps an eye out for Raina while they put on their skates. KD and John skate around the rink like teenagers until two o'clock in the morning.

After they leave the rink, John asks KD what she was in the mood to eat. KD answers she's in the mood for a big, juicy cheeseburger with fries. John asks her about her favorite place to get a burger. KD answers the twenty-four-hour Coney Island on the avenue.

After getting food, they drive to the park. John parks his car near the river. They sit on the trunk to eat and talk. John says, "I've missed you. You haven't called me the last few nights."

KD says, "I've been getting in so late. I didn't want to wake you, but I missed you, too."

John says, "Call or text me every night before you go to bed, no matter what time it is." He sticks out his pinky.

They lock fingers; she says, "I promise."

John says, "Don't let the sun rise twice without calling me. You hear me?" John stares at her.

John adds, "I worry about you leaving out so late. You need to call and let me know you're safe, or I will come to the hospital every night to follow your home." John stares in her eyes with a straight face, waiting for her response.

KD smiles at him. She says, "I will call you! I promise!"

John says, "To show you I'm fair, I will check in with you daily. Texts are cool, but I want to hear your voice. Deal?"

KD says, "Deal!"

John says, "Kiss me!"

KD says, "No, I'm eating chili fries."

John says, "I don't care. I'm eating the same thing." John smiles at her; he seductively says, "Come here, Ladybug!" KD looks at him. He seduces her with his male energy and smile to get her to kiss him. KD leans toward him. They kiss. John says, "Even your chili fries kisses do something to me." They sit with their eyes closed forehead to forehead.

John says, "KD, I like you!"

KD says, "I like you, John!"

John asks, "You mean that?"

KD says, "Yes!"

John says, "I mean it, too!"

Raina sits in her car just outside the perimeter of the park, hidden behind parked cars. She watches with eyes full of jealousy and envy. John's smiles and happiness disappoint her. She wanted to be the one that made him feel that way. She can't stand to see him so happy with another woman, so she quietly pulls away. Raina cries as she drives home. She tries to convince herself to accept that the relationship is over, but a part of her can't accept losing him.

At the end of their date, they kiss so passionately at her door that John stops. He tells her goodnight before he goes home to call her. While on the phone, he admits he had to leave because he couldn't handle her kisses. KD admits she didn't want him to leave because she was enjoying his kisses. John tells her he's happy she enjoys his kisses before he tells her goodnight.

KD has been working overtime since their last date, but she's been keeping her promise to check in with him every night. Two o'clock in the morning, KD sends a text message that wakes John. He reaches for his phone to call her. When she answers, his deep, low voice says, "Ladybug, I miss you!"

KD says, "I didn't mean to wake you."

John says, "I wanted to talk to you. I wish I was holding you right now."

KD says, "That's sweet, John! By the way, I miss you, too!"

John says, "That's music to my ears. How was your day?"

KD says, "Usual, how about yours?"

John says, "Same!" John says in a seductive tone, "I wish we were kissing right now! Do you like my kisses?"

KD answers, "I enjoy myself."

John says, "I love your kisses, your soft lips, being close to you, touching you, the smell of your hair, and the way you hold on to me. There's so much passion in our kisses. Have you noticed we don't kiss like we just met?"

KD listens to John talk about their kisses and it sets her body a blaze. Her body fills with desire thinking about their last kiss. John stopped by early in morning a few days ago, and they ended up on her couch, kissing. John kissed her so deeply that his tongue excavated her throat while his hands explored her body. John laid her on the couch and wrapped her legs around his waist. Before he left, John held her face in his hands as he kissed her soul deep.

The thought of John's hands softly caressing her body makes her bite her finger. KD remembers the feelings she felt with John between her legs, laying on top of her. She plays in her hair and puts a pillow between her legs, remembering how excited her body was in the moment. She could feel John's muscular body through their clothes. John couldn't get close enough. The pressure of him moving his body against hers made her want him.

She holds the phone and her forehead, thinking about their last kiss. She licks her lips, remembering how John kissed her before he said, "Ladybug, I have to go." John had to pull himself away because he didn't want to leave. She walked him to the door. He backed her against the wall. He stared in her eyes. He took one last kiss before exiting the door.

She finally works through her emotions to speak; she says, "I noticed!"

John asks, "Do you feel it, too, the passion between us?"

KD says, "Yes!"

John asks, "Do you think you want to be with me in that way one day?"

KD answers, "Yes!"

John says, "I accomplished something great!"

KD says, "What's that?"

John says, "I made it to date three. I managed to get your attention."

KD says, "You did. That's big!" She shyly giggles.

John says, "Maybe, I can get a fourth date?"

KD says, "Definitely!"

John says, "You can choose. I'll take you anywhere you want to go, and we can do whatever you want."

KD says, "I'll cook for you."

John asks, "You can cook?"

KD says, "Yes!"

John says, "You're that beautiful, can sew and cook. That's unbelievable!"

KD says, "My mother is a southern belle. She taught me how to cook."

John says, "I'm impressed!"

KD says, "I'll cook whatever you want. You create the menu with an appetizer, an entrée, sides, and dessert."

John asks, "When?"

KD says, "Friday, I get off at 3:00 p.m. I can come home and be ready by the time you leave your office."

John asks, "Your place or mine?"

KD says, "Will you pick me up on your way home?"

John says, "You know I will!"

KD says, "Your place."

John asks, "Will you stay the weekend with me? I'll be a respectful gentleman. And, know this is a safe space. You can be comfortable in my home."

KD says, "I can stay if you're sure that's what you want."

John says, "I want you to stay with me. I want to fall asleep and wake up with you."

KD says, "Somehow, you always find the sweetest things to say."

John says, "I'm speaking from my heart."

KD says, "May, I ask a favor?"

John says, "Always, anything!"

KD says, "Would you always speak to me with that much kindness?"

John says, "Listen to me, I will always be thoughtful, kind, and caring in regards to you."

KD says, "You promise?"

John says, "I promise!"

KD says, "Have you thought of what you want me to cook for you?"

John says, "I'm thinking. The only woman whoever cooked for me is my mother. I miss her cooking, especially her chicken and dumplings."

KD says, "I can make chicken and dumplings for you. My grandmother taught me her recipe. I used to make it all the time for my daddy."

John says, "Apple pie?"

KD says, "With vanilla ice cream!"

John says, "You can bake and cook?"

KD says, "If you don't enjoy my cooking, I'll massage your back and let you kiss me."

John says, "Oh, wee! I like that proposal."

KD says, "You're going to like my cooking as much as my kisses."

John says, "I look forward to that." He pauses before saying, "Getting to know you has been a pleasure. You're so adorable and kind. We have the most interesting conversations. I'm enjoying learning about you. I want to know more."

KD says, "Like what?"

John says, "Tell me something, anything you've never told anyone."

KD says, "God, you're making me think at two-thirty in the morning. Something I have never told anyone. That's hard."

John says, "I'll go first. I was afraid of the dark until seventh grade, so I slept with a night light. My brothers made fun of me. They would play tricks on me, scare me, and beat my ass in the dark. They were rough, but they made me tough. I learned to face my fears."

KD says, "Big brothers are rough! I had to survive my own, so I empathize with you. Okay! I thought of something. I was walking home from Mena's house when I found this lighter. I cut between two vacant houses surrounded by bushes. I swear I did not mean for it to happen. When I flicked the lighter, one of the bushes caught fire. Next thing I know, the fire spread to all the bushes and the two houses. I ran into the ally, threw the lighter in the sewer, and ran home. I was so scared. I thought I was going to jail, so I didn't tell anyone."

John says, "Did the houses burn a little or were they destroyed."

KD says, "They were destroyed. If my parents knew I did that, my mother would have killed me. She can never find out."

John says, "I don't know if I should be scared or intrigued that you play with fire."

KD says, "It was a one-time thing. I learned my lesson, I swear."

John asks, "Do you have other secrets? Tell me something about you that your ex-husband doesn't know."

KD says, "You really have me thinking this morning. Something he doesn't know about me…let me think. He doesn't know all his friends, brothers, uncles, and cousins hit on me whenever he wasn't paying attention. They would pinch me, touch me, and try to kiss me whenever he wasn't looking. It made me so uncomfortable. I hated going to his family functions. I would literally walk around with my daughter on my hip. She was the only thing that would discourage them."

John says, "Shit, KD, that's deep! Why not tell him?"

KD says, "I didn't want to start anything, so I didn't tell him."

John says, "If anyone makes you feel uncomfortable, tell me. KD, I will believe you."

KD says, "They were hitting on nineteen- and twenty-five-year-old me."

John says, "Don't do that! Don't downplay KD right now. KD is fine and sexy at forty-nine."

KD says, "After the divorce, his brothers started texting me, pretending to be comforting, which quickly escalated to pictures of their man meat. Not one checked on their nephew, so I blocked them all."

John says, "Your friend's, cousin's, brother's girl and absolutely your nephew's girl is off-limits even after the break-up. They all violated the code."

KD says, "Tell me something about you that neither of your ex-wives knows."

John says, "That could take all week. There's so much they don't know."

KD asks, "Did their friends get at you?"

John says, "Friends, sisters, cousins, co-workers, I think my mother-in-law was trying to get at me one time. I thought about it for a second because she was fine, but I regained my sense and got the hell out of there."

KD laughs and asks, "John, you know you are a dog, right?"

John says, "I was a dog. I calmed down a few years ago."

KD says, "I'd like to know what calmed you down."

John says, "Getting older, having grand girls, empty, lonely mornings and nights, and I realized I really didn't have anyone to share my wins with. One day, I had a good day and no one to call to share my emotions with."

KD says, "I can relate to that."

John says, "I thought about something my ex-wives don't know. It's a good one. They don't know about Mandy."

KD says, "Who is Mandy?"

John says, "When I was sixteen, I went on a Caribbean vacation with my parents. I went swimming on our first day on the island. When I came out of the water, this beautiful woman was sunbathing on the beach. She smiled at me as she watched me walk out of the water. She was with her man, so I didn't think much about it. The next morning, before the sun came up, there was a knock on my door. When I opened the door, she walked into the room, handed me a box of condoms, and kissed me.

"Over the next two weeks, whenever she could get away from her man, she would find me. We were going at it all over the island. I called her Mandy, but I never knew her name. All I know is they were rich. She seemed about thirty-two. She wore a necklace with an M charm, so I made up a name."

KD says, "As a mother, I don't like that she took advantage of you."

John says, "Young males benefit from those experiences. That's how we learn how to, you know."

KD says, "Her husband could've killed you."

John says, "That's what made it fun and exciting."

KD says, "Your feelings could've been hurt."

John says, "Although we didn't talk, it was loud and clear what was up."

KD says, "Did you get with other older women?"

John says, "Absolutely! One of my professors, a few family friends, one of my mother's friends, one of my friend's mothers, my doctor after I hurt on my knee, and when I was fourteen my tutor let me get to a few bases, but she didn't let me hit the home run."

KD laughs. She says, "John, you were a bad boy. How did you get with the doctor? How old were you?"

John answers, "I just turned eighteen. She was checking out my knee, and I was checking out her blouse. You know a teenage erection happens quickly for the slightest thing. She saw it rise, and next thing I know, I was between her thighs."

KD says, "What happened with the professor?"

John says, "She wrote 'See me,' on my paper. I went to her office after class. I just remember having her against the wall, beating it like Sheila E on the percussions."

KD asks, "Which did you prefer older or younger women?"

John says, "I loved being with beautiful, Black, intelligent, classy, sexy women."

KD says, "Apparently, they loved you, too!"

John asks, "Do you have any sexual skeletons in your closet?"

KD says, "Well!"

John says, "I knew you did. Quiet girls are sneaky. Spill the beans, Ladybug, tell me what happened."

KD says, "It happened before we were married, so don't think I'm a bad person."

John says, "No judgment."

KD says, "I always had the biggest crush on this guy from my neighborhood named Dash. He is my brother's friend. My brother would have killed me if he known I liked Dash, so I never mentioned my crush to anyone. I was out with my Mena and Tri one night, and we ran into him. We had a few drinks. After we talked for a bit, he convinced me to leave my friends to go hang out with him. You know the rest of the story. It only happened that one time."

John asks, "Was it everything you thought it would be?"

KD says, "It was incredible!"

John says, "I'm glad he didn't disappoint you. How did you resist seeing him again?"

KD says, "I felt incredibly guilty about given myself to another man. Although Dash was cool, I loved my ex, and I didn't want him to find out and leave me. I also didn't want my brother to find out."

John says, "Did your brother ever find out?"

KD says, "He has never said anything, so he must not know. He still hangs with Dash. When Dash comes around, we can't look each other in the eye."

John asks, "Are you still attracted to him? Has he ever tried to get back with you?"

KD says, "No, Dash is happily married. Those feelings are long gone."

John says, "You know what that says to me?"

KD asks, "What?"

John answers, "God saved you for me! I'm in this, so he and all the other man looking, watching, wanting are all about to lose."

KD says, "You're that sure?"

John says, "I'm positive! I know you have at least one more secret to tell. Come on, tell me more."

KD says, "My ex and I were arguing about him cheating. I ran into Justin. Justin was fine. I really didn't like him. I just wanted to, you know, as revenge. Once I got it, I was over Justin. Justin, Dash, and the ex-husband are all the people I've been with."

John asks, "So your ex-husband was your first?"

KD says, "Yes, we were each other's first."

John says, "You were a good girl, KD."

KD says, "I hope I was."

John says, "Good girls have a naughty side. I can't wait to get to know your naughty side. If you had to name your naughty side, what would you name her?"

KD says, "Anya or Nadia, something with an 'a'."

John says, "Those are sexy choices, but there's something about KD that gives me a sweet and sexy vibe. I bet that side of you is incredible."

KD replies, "You think so?"

John asks, "Yes!"

KD says, "I guess you'll have to do your research."

John says, "Oh, I plan on doing a dissertation."

KD says, "I can't wait to hear your findings!"

John says, "Oh! I'll definitely let you know. What's some of your favorite childhood memories?"

KD says, "In the kitchen with my mother, at the sewing machine or in the salon with my grandmother, hanging with my aunts, riding in the car with my daddy, playing outside in the summer with Tri and Mena. What about you?"

John says, "Before my brothers died, we would visit my maternal grandparents in the south every summer. I loved hanging with my granddad. He taught me how to shoot. We hunted, fished, swam, worked on the farm, rode three-wheelers, went on boat rides, sled down the dirt hills, and raced our dirt bikes. We had good old country fun."

KD says, "That's where your adventurous side comes from."

John says, "I think so. It was never the same after my brothers died."

KD says, "Things are never the same after we lose loved ones."

John asks, "My favorite colors are red, black, and white. What are your favorite colors?"

KD says, "I like purple and gold."

John asks, "Do those colors have a special meaning?"

KD says, "Purple is vibrant and royal. Gold makes me think of something valuable."

John says, "Red, black, and white were the colors of my middle and high school team's jerseys. I feel like that was a good time for me. That's when I met my friends. Dealing with the death of my brothers helped me learn to press through pain. My parents didn't want me to go to a public school, but they had the best team. It was a good experience for me.

"I knew it wouldn't be easy to make either team, so I worked very hard to be a good athlete. Everyone judged me for coming from a rich family. I had to fight just about every day. I had to prove myself every day, all day. I learned to survive and endure whatever comes my way. I understood why my brothers were so hard on me. They were preparing me for what was coming."

KD says, "That's really inspiring. John Michael King, I like the man you've grown to be."

John says, "Thank you! I like the woman you are. Name one thing you cannot do that you wish you could."

KD answers, "Swim! I love the water, but I do not know how to swim."

John says, "I could teach you to swim. You'll be safe. I wouldn't let anything happen to you."

KD says, "I will take you up on that offer. What about you?"

John answers, "One time, I went on vacation with some friends to a ski lodge. I thought skiing would be something cool to try. I got to the top of the slopes. I looked down, and was like shiiidddd. I got my ass off that mountain so damn fast. I understand why a lot of Black people don't ski. The slopes are intimidating." KD and John laughs.

KD says, "Yeah, I don't think I could do it either."

John says, "Tell me your naughtiest sexual fantasy."

KD replies, "I don't really have one."

John says, "No curiosities or interests?"

KD shyly answers, "Well, it is not a fantasy, and I would never do it, but I wonder how stimulating it would be to have two men all over me. I would never do that. I feel dirty and bad just saying it. I think God would smite me to hell."

John says, "I glad you never need that because once I get you, I will not share you and I'm never letting go of you. I will be all over you with the energy of eight men. I will get every part the way you want. I'll get it in every position humanly possible. I'm going to learn every part of your body, and nothing will be left chance. I'll be intentional, methodical, consuming, thorough, and lasting every time. Whatever men did in the past won't compare."

KD is so turned on by his words that she stutters, she says, "I…I…I…you…uh"

John smirks and cuts her off, he says, "Before you ask, I have done everything possible in every way possible with a woman more than ten times, but I have a list of things I want to do to you that'll make my life complete. I can see us in my mind enjoying each and every one of my desires. I am going to take my time and enjoy living out each of my fantasies of you."

KD curiously asks, "What's on the list?"

John doesn't answer. KD repeats, "What's on the list?"

John asks, "Do you think about being with me?"

KD says, "So you're not going to tell me what's on the list?"

John replies, "I rather show you than tell you. KD, just know, I am interested in you personally, sexually, and intimately, only you. Is that sufficient?"

KD answers, "Yes! Those feelings are mutual."

John says, "I'm glad to hear that."

It gets quiet for a moment. KD breaks the silence, she calls his name.

John replies, "Yes, KD."

She answers, "In those moments, I want to be everything you need me to be. I want to do all the things you like, the way you like. I want the reality of me to be better than the fantasy."

John is at a loss for words. He wasn't expecting her to say that, but it intrigues him and appeals to him.

John says, "I feel the same way, KD!"

KD says, "Well, we have a lot to look forward too!" John agrees.

John says, "Pick one movie or book title that represents your life in some way."

KD says, "*What's Love Got To Do With It* says it all."

John says, "That's deep. Why?"

KD says, "To make a long story short, I put my daughter's needs ahead of my own for a long time, and the day came when I had to put myself first."

John says, "For me, it would be *The Pursuit of Happyness*. Despite his living situation I feel a connection to the father's story: the bond between father and son, surviving, and working hard as a father to raise my kids without their mothers."

KD says, "Few people have the capacity and capability to raise six children alone. I respect you as a parent, a man, a father."

John says, "Thank you! Is there anything you want to know about me?"

KD says, "There's a lot I want to know about you, but I will learn it organically as we interact. A man's actions speak louder than his words."

John says, "I respect that. May I ask a big favor of you?"

KD says, "What's that?"

John says, "Don't judge me based on my past with women. I've been honest with you. I'll always be honest with you. Don't let my past behavior with women discourage you from pursuing a relationship with me, please. I know I've been a piece shit to women, and don't deserve a fair chance from you. And, know that I have learned from my behavior. I recognize my faults, I take responsibility for my failures, and I got that player shit all out of my system. I am ready. I've grown up. I'm not trying to play any games. I'm ready to be serious with you."

KD says, "I get it. People grow and change."

John says, "Do you believe me when I say, I've changed?"

KD says, "I have no reason to doubt you."

John says, "I have an even bigger favor to ask of you."

KD says, "Ask your favor."

John says, "Please, don't see any other men. I want a fair chance to court you, only you."

KD says, "If you can agree to do the same."

John says, "I've already made that commitment. I don't want anything to come between us. I purged my phone, my home, my cars, my life of all traces of women. I like you, KD, I'm not trying to mess this up."

KD says, "The last four years of my life have been so peaceful and calm. John, I like you, but I can't go back to the chaos of a cheating and lying man."

John says, "I know you just met me, and you have every reason not to trust me. I wouldn't ask you to focus on me if I wasn't serious. Do you think you can take a chance on me?"

KD says, "I will take a chance. I won't see other men, and I will trust you."

John says, "I won't disappoint you! I won't let you down!"

KD says, "You promise?"

John says, "I promise! It's three-thirty, I better let you go to sleep."

KD says, "You'll call me tomorrow?"

John says, "You know I will!"

KD says, "Okay!"

John says, "Think about me!"

KD says, "I will! You do the same!"

John says, "I will! Rest well!"

KD says, "You too!

John knocks on KD's door, anxious to see her. When she opens the door, she hugs him and kisses his cheek. John says, "I missed you!" John grabs her overnight bag and the food that KD has prepped to cook.

KD says, "I missed you, too!" KD locks her door before they walk to the elevator.

When they get to John's house, John goes to take a shower and KD goes to the kitchen to cook. After his shower, John watches sports news before checking on KD in the kitchen. He smiles at her; he says, "What a sight to see!"

KD says, "It's a wonderful view from over here."

John says, "It smells good in here." KD winks at him. John says, "Let me help you!"

KD says, "Go relax! I'm cooking for you!" John smiles and walks out the kitchen.

After KD is done cooking, they sit at the dining room table. KD says grace. John takes his first bite. He could float away. He says, "KD, this is so good!"

KD says, "Thank you!"

John says, "You can cook, Ladybug. This taste just like my mother's."

KD says, "I'm glad you like it."

After they eat, they wash the dishes together as they talk. When they are done with the dishes, they sit down on the couch to watch television. John finds a movie. John lays on the couch. John reaches out his hand and says, "Would you lay with me? I'm so tired!" KD takes his hand and lays in front of him. He rests his arm on her waist. KD feels the heat of his body pressing against hers, and it's making her body react. As they watch the movie, John plays in her hair and kisses on the back of her neck. John says, "I love your hair! It always smells so good."

KD says, "Thank you!"

She's enjoying John's affection. His body heat, the heat of his soft lips lightly pressing against her skin, his hand on her thigh, and his fingers in her hair are making her delightfully comfortable. KD can feel John becoming bold and engorged against her. She wants to turn over to kiss him, but she cautions herself.

About an hour into the movie, John is quietly asleep cuddled against KD's back. She relaxes and soon falls asleep. The music during the movie's credit wakes John. John wakes KD. When she opens her eyes, he says, "Ladybug, let's go to bed. We are going upstairs, I'm going to be a gentleman, we are going to cuddle, and go to sleep. That's it!"

KD says, "Okay!" John holds KD's hand as he leads her to his bedroom.

John grabs her bag and shows her to the female master bathroom, and he goes to his bathroom. John uses the restroom and brushes his teeth. He takes off his shirt and shorts and climbs into bed.

KD brushes her teeth, uses the restroom, and changes into pajamas. She goes into the room to see John is asleep. She eases into the bed. She settles close to the edge as she pulls the cover over her. John opens his eyes; he says, "Why are you so far away?"

KD says, "I thought you were sleep."

John says, "Come over here, so we can cuddle." John lifts his arm. She scoots right into John's embrace. He relishes in the comfort of their contact.

He says, "We didn't say our prayers. Pray with me!" They get on their knees in the bed and bow their heads.

Just when KD settles in the bed, John says, "Give me a goodnight kiss!" KD turns to face him. John's hands rub up her thighs to her butt. He says, "Hold me as you kiss me, Ladybug." They look at each other. Their faces slowly move toward each other. KD wraps her arms around him. John closes his eyes as their lips meet. John holds her body to his as his hands rest on the small of her back. The kiss scorches like the heat of the sun. He kisses KD's forehead. He says, "Goodnight, Ladybug!"

KD says, "Goodnight!" KD rolls back over.

John cuts off the lights and snuggles against KD's back. John says, "Ladybug, would you take off your bottoms, so I can feel your skin. I promise I just want to cuddle with you." KD takes off her pajama bottoms, folds them, and sits them on the nightstand. John puts his legs against hers.

John relaxes; he says, "Oh! Ladybug, your legs are so soft."

KD asks, "Why do you call me, Ladybug?"

John asks, "Do you hate it?"

KD says, "No, I think it's cute. I was wondering if it was significant to you."

John says, "You are beautiful, quiet, pleasant, and a sign of good fortune just like a ladybug."

KD says, "That is the sweetest thing anyone has ever said to me."

John says, "You don't mind being my ladybug?"

KD says, "I'll always be your ladybug." John kisses the back of her neck.

John says, "Sweet dreams, Ladybug!"

KD says, "Sweet dreams, John!" The feel of her soft skin soothes John to sleep. KD looks back at John, who is sound asleep, and she can't believe he was telling the truth. She's impressed that he didn't try anything, but at the same time she's disappointed that he didn't try anything. She thinks, damn, he wasn't lying, he is really making me wait for it.

When KD wakes, she goes to take a shower and brush her teeth. When she comes out of the restroom, she can hear John working out in the next room. She goes into the room to see him bench pressing. She says, "What a beautiful sight to wake up to!"

John says, "Good morning! How did you sleep?"

KD answers, "Like a baby!"

John says, "You look cute!"

KD replies, "Thank you, but you're the one to keep an eye on."

John sits the weights on the rack, he says, "Come here." As she walks towards him, he gets up to meet her half way. She walks right into his arms. He quickly lifts her up, and she wraps her legs around his waist. She tightly hugs his neck. He kisses her with so much passion that she melts and clings to him like cheese on cooked pasta. John walks until KD's back is against the wall.

John grips her body with both of his hands as he kisses her with so much intensity that she moans. She is so hot that John can feel the steam from her body on his. John can tell she's yearning for more, but he stops. He puts her down, smacks her butt, and walks out of the room with a smirk on his face. She leans against the wall trying to calm her body down. She moves her hair behind her ear. John knew exactly what he was doing with that kiss. KD thinks to herself, that man is fucking with me.

That night, they go to dinner and a movie. Sunday morning, John gives her a key to let herself back into the house after church. When John comes home from his grandsons' game, he says, "I love coming home to you already."

She smiles and says, "I loved being here when you walked through the door." They hug and kiss. She hands him the key, but he tells her to keep it. She asks John, "Are you sure?"

John tells her she's always welcome in his home and no other woman will ever be in this house except his daughters and granddaughters. She puts the key on her key ring next to her apartment key. They eat and spend the rest of the day snuggling.

John sits at his desk, thinking about KD. John is frustrated with her limited time. He checks the calendar they share on their iPhones to keep each other abreast of their schedules. John sees she's working five nights in a row and is disappointed. John wants more of her time and attention, but he can't come out and ask. He thinks for a moment, and an idea pops in his head: if the tuition was no longer an issue, she wouldn't have to work so much.

John calls his assistant, Jayme. Jayme comes into his office to acquire his needs. John tells Jayme he needs her to research a way to anonymously pay a student's tuition. John shows Jayme the school's website.

John says, "His name is Daniel Jacobs. I saw trophies and awards from this school with his name on it. I need to figure out a way to pay his tuition, but no one can ever know it was me." Jayme writes down the information and assures John she is on it. John thanks her, and tells her this top-secret mission is the number one priority.

Later that morning, Jayme tells John about a scholarship program the school has in which one student is selected each year by a committee. A group of donors pays the student's tuition until they graduate.

Jayme adds, "We can contact the committee to try to persuade them to select him or we can create our own scholarship. We can set the criteria, ask for a list of candidates, and select who we want from the list."

John says, "What would it take to do that?"

Jayme says, "Just a check."

John says, "Let's do that! Tell the school we want to anonymously pay the tuition and all extra-curricular activities fees of five African American boys in the fifth grade from single-parent homes who are active in sports, science, and technology with a high G.P.A."

Jayme says, "I'm on it!"

John says, "I appreciate you! Remember, Daniel Jacobs and no one can ever know it was me." Within a few hours, Daniel and four other male students who fit the criteria receive a full scholarship.

On the first of May, KD sits down to pay her bills. She logs into Daniel's school account to pay the bill, but the balance is zero, which is strange. KD calls the receptionist of the accounting office, who explains Daniel received a scholarship from an anonymous donor, which paid for the rest of the year, three years of middle school, and four years of high school including all activities fees.

When KD calls to ask Daniel if he applied for a scholarship, he is clueless. KD immediately knows who's responsible. KD calls John. When he answers, she says, "I appreciate you, but that's a lot of money, and I cannot pay you back."

John asks, "KD, what are you talking about?"

KD says, "Daniel's tuition."

John says, "What about it?"

KD says, "Daniel received a scholarship from an anonymous donor."

John says, "That's good. I'm happy for Daniel."

KD says, "I thought maybe you pulled some strings. I really appreciate you looking out for us, but that was a lot of money."

John says, "I'm happy for him. He seems like a hardworking kid, so I'm sure it's well-deserved. A scholarship is a huge blessing." John chooses his words carefully. Jayme walks in his office to tell him the meeting is starting. John is saved by the bell. He is so uncomfortable not telling KD the truth.

John asks, "Ladybug, can I call you later? I have a meeting to get to."

KD says, "Of course!"

John says, "I want to finish this conversation. We can celebrate."

KD says, "Okay!"

John says, "I'll talk to you soon, okay."

KD says, "Okay!"

She noticed he didn't deny that he was the donor, but she figured he had his reasons for not being forthcoming with the truth. She appreciates his support, but she worries how such a large debt will affect their budding romance. Even though she thinks about it and feels so much gratitude for him, they never bring it up again.

KD stands in front of her building stretching with her earbuds in her ear when John taps her on the shoulder. KD turns to see John and smiles as she takes out her earbuds. John, dressed in workout gear, hands her a smoothie. He says, "It's strawberry, kiwi, watermelon, pineapple with a little spinach and kale."

She says, "Very thoughtful! Thank you! What are you doing out here this early?"

John says, "I wanted to spend a little time with you."

KD says, "That's sweet, John!"

She sips her smoothie; she says, "This is good!"

He winks at her. KD says, "How are you this morning?"

John says, "I'm good now that I'm with you."

KD says, "Cute! I must admit it's a pleasant surprise to see you this morning."

John says, "Really, because you didn't hug my neck or kiss me like you were happy to see me!" She pulls him into her arms. She wraps her arms around his neck and kisses him.

John says, "There's nothing like KD's sweet, tender kisses." She smiles at him. He says, "That's how you hug and kiss me every time you greet me."

KD says, "So, that's how you like it?"

John says, "That's how I need it."

KD says, "I got you!"

John asks, "You got me?"

KD says, "John, baby, I got you!"

They jog along the river until KD's smartwatch's alarm goes off. She says, "I hate to leave you, but I have to get ready for work."

John says, "I'll call you later!"

KD says, "Okay," as she jogs toward her apartment.

John watches her jog away, admiring everything about her and hating that she had to leave. As KD passes another jogger, they speak. When the male jogger passes KD, he turns to stare at her butt. The man jogs in John's direction.

When the jogger reaches John, John says, "You checked out my girl right in front of me."

The jogger says, "My bad! It makes you look."

John laughs. He says, "I can't even be mad at you."

The jogger says, "I've been out here trying to get her for a few years. How did you swoop in and get her?"

John says, "By God's grace!"

The jogger says, "Man, you know how many men are out here daily, shooting their shot. She shoots our asses down every time. No one gets any play, just a smile and wave."

John says, "It's like that."

The jogger says, "Hunt her like prey! Now that I know she has a man, I will respect the relationship. Just know, a myriad of men is hoping to catch you slipping."

John says, "I'll stay focused. Trust me!"

The jogger says, "Congratulations, lucky motherfucker." John laughs as the man jogs away.

After coming home from work and getting ready for bed, KD sits on her bed to call John. Before she can dial his number, her phone rings and it's him.

She answers, she says, "I was just about to call you!"

John asks, "What are you wearing?"

KD laughs, she says, "A t-shirt and some shorts, why?"

John says, "Come outside."

KD says, "Are you serious?"

John says, "Meet me in the back of the building."

When KD walks out of the back door, she sees John standing in the courtyard wearing a t-shirt, jeans, a baseball cap, and gym shoes. She thinks to herself: he looks so good.

KD says, "Hey, you," as she walks over to hug and kiss him.

John says, "You remembered!"

KD says, "I'll never forget."

John says, "Come take a ride with me," as he leads her to rail. He hops over. He reaches over the rail. She braces herself on his shoulders as he lifts her up and over the rail.

KD says, "What are you doing out on your boat this late?"

John says, "I couldn't sleep thinking about you. I thought we could talk for a while under the moonlight," as he helps her get on the boat.

As they slowly sail, they listen to music and talk about their kids. KD says, "I love the relationship you have with your kids."

John says, "I bet your kids love you!" KD says, "We are very close."

John says, "Hopefully, you will allow me to meet your kids one day. When the time is right and you feel comfortable."

KD says, "I'll keep that in mind."

John says, "When you're comfortable, I would love to introduce you to my kids."

KD says, "I'd love to meet them."

John looks at KD under the moonlight and says, "You're so beautiful."

KD looks at him; she says, "You are!"

John says, "I find everything about you very attractive. You are perfect in my eyes."

KD says, "John, I think the same thing about you."

They sail back to John's house where he docks the boat. John pulls her close. He picks her up and walks into the cabin of the boat as they kiss. He sits her on the table. He stands between her legs as he kisses her. He wants her so badly that his body hurts. However, John is intent on showing restraint.

KD wants to touch his skin, so she pulls his shirt out of his pants. John pulls the shirt over his head. He throws the shirt on the bench and goes back to kissing KD. KD's hands rub up and down John's back. John's hands are on KD's cheeks as he gets lost in her kisses.

John's hands find their way to her calves and slowly moves up to her thighs. Before his fingers move up to her shorts, John stops. As his fingertips press into her thighs, he steps back and stares in her eyes.

John says, "KD, I didn't bring you out here for that, so don't think that. It's hard to be near you and not want to touch you and kiss you. I don't want you to think that's all I want because it's not like that."

KD pulls him close to her. She wraps her legs around his waist, she wraps her arms around his neck, and she kisses him again. She kisses his neck as she rubs his arms with her fingertips. She admires his golden skin with her lips and tongue from his neck to his shoulder to his chest. John closes his eyes and enjoys her kisses and her touch. She gently puts her lips on his. KD leans back pulling John on top of her. They kiss. John stops. KD whispers, "Please, don't stop!"

John looks at her and says, "Ladybug, I'm trying to have self-control. I want to wait until the time is right."

KD rubs her thumb over his lips as if to say you're right. She asks, "Why are you so fine, Mr. King?" KD lets him go, but she didn't want to.

John answers, "God made me to attract you. I was made for you, and you were made for me. KD, being with me is a part of your destiny." She looks at him with wanting eyes as her hands slowly touch all over his chest and abdomen.

KD says, "If this is my destiny, God favors me." She hugs him.

John hugs her. He says, "God does favor us." He kisses her forehead. She kisses his lips.

He takes her hand; he says, "I'll take you home." Standing at the apartment's main door, he says, "I'll call you."

KD says, "You better!"

As they kiss, the mysterious black Benz lurks in the darkness across the street from the apartment building. The dark car blends in with the parked cars, so neither John nor KD are aware that they are being watched.

John gets in his car to drive home. The black Benz is careful to stay out of John's line of sight. John makes it back home and pulls into his garage, never knowing he was followed. He goes into the house to call KD. They talk until they fall asleep.

KD has the night off, so John takes KD out for date night. They go to the movies and have dinner at John's favorite restaurant. After they eat, John goes to the restroom. Just as John turn's down the hall, he almost bumps into Raina. When Raina and her friends realize it's John, they all frown and stare at him as he walks into the men's room.

John prays Raina won't start any drama with KD while he's in the restroom. John couldn't get out of the restroom fast enough. When he gets back to the table, KD sees he is agitated. She asks if he is okay. He swears everything is cool. When he realizes KD is calm, John settles down. He is so relieved that Raina didn't say anything to KD.

KD has been calling and texting every day and every night, so John panics when he can't get a hold of her throughout the day. He tries to call again when he knows she should be home. When she doesn't answer the phone, John rushes to her apartment. John knocks on her door. There's no answer. He pulls out his phone to call her as he knocks.

The ringing and knocking wake KD. She hops out of her sleep to grab the phone. When she answers the phone, John tells her he's at the door. She takes a second to compose herself. She runs to her bathroom to gargle with mouthwash and wash her face. She rushes toward the door. When she remembers she has a wrap scarf on her head, she snatches if off and fixes her hair. She stuffs the scarf in the couch between the seats before she opens the door. When the door opens, John is intrigued by her exposed body only shielded by a black lace bra, matching panties, and a short, sheer robe, but he stays focused on confirming her safety.

He says, "I've been calling you all day. Is everything okay??"

KD pulls him in the apartment and closes the door. KD hugs him as she apologizes; she says, "I stayed a little too long at the gym this morning. I was rushing, and I left my phone at home. I intended to call you, but I fell asleep at the kitchen table."

John says, "I was so worried about you. I had to see if you were okay."

KD says, "It's so sweet that you came to check on me, thank you."

She adds, "How was your day?" as she walks into the kitchen.

John says, "Better, now that I know you're okay," as he follows her into the kitchen.

She says, "I'm so sorry. I didn't mean to worry you."

John replies, "It comes with the position. I'm just relieved you're okay." His concern turns into preoccupation with her smooth, luminous, silky skin.

KD asks, "Position?"

John says, "As the man in your life, it's my obligation to worry about you and make sure you're good."

KD says, "So, I'm obligated to worry about you, right?"

John says, "You don't worry about me. You focus on making us happy. I'll do the worrying. I protect and provide. You care and love."

KD says, "Oh! I got it! I like that!"

John says, "I can handle my position. Can you handle your role?"

KD replies, "I can love and care for you with my eyes closed and hands tied." John smiles.

John asks about her day. John listens, but his mind is on the shimmer of her glowing skin covered in oil, her breasts sitting in her black lace bra, her butt bulging out of her panties, the sexy, sweet scent radiating from her, and her colorful toenails. As KD throws away the food she was about to eat and washes the dishes, John sits in the chair watching her body move. He asks about her kids.

She says, "Daniel is with his dad. His team won their game today. He video-called me with a huge smile on his face. Kelly has a few more weeks of her internship, but my college graduate is doing well. Thanks for asking." She asks about his family. John tells her everyone is good.

She asks if he is hungry or if he would like something to drink. He says no. She sits at the table with him. She asks if he's sure he wasn't hungry. He says, "No, thank you, but thank you."

They look at each other. Before she could say anything else, he says, "Turn off the lights." She thinks that's a strange request. Puzzled, she walks over to the switch and turns off the lights.

John says, "Come here!" She walks back to the table.

John says, "Sit down," he gestures for her to sit on the table.

She says, "I can't sit on the table. My son eats at this table."

He says, "I'm trying to eat at this table."

She says, "I thought you weren't hungry."

He stares in her eyes and says, "Not that kind of hungry."

When she comprehends what he meant, she says, "Oh!"

He says, "Sit down!" She sits on the table next to him. He pulls her directly in front of him.

John says, "Hug my neck and kiss me like you missed me." She leans over to hug and kiss him.

John says, "Damn, Ladybug, the way you kiss me!"

KD says, "The way you kiss me!" John kisses her thighs as she caresses his face.

He asks, "Do you mind me kissing you this way?

KD says, "Never!"

He says, "Your skin feels like silk. Lay back for me." KD lays back on the table as John caresses and kisses her thighs. He moves her panties to the side with two fingers. He kisses all over her stomach.

He deeply inhales, he says, "You smell so good."

He stares at her as his fingers softly roll over and inside her; he says, "You're so sexy!" John kisses her thighs as he plays with her until he finds her spot. The feel of his fingers moving over her spot causes the rhythm of her breathing to change.

KD looks at the ceiling, biting her lips and anticipating John's next move. He slowly kisses her legs as he softly caresses her thighs and butt making her feel wanted. She lies on the table in disbelief that John is touching her in this way. Finally, the moment has come for her to find out if John could live up to his reputation.

When she is slippery wet, he pulls her closer to him. John says, "Look at me!" When she looks at him, John closes his eyes and takes his first taste, and it brings KD so much pleasure. He says, "You taste so sweet," before he tastes her again. KD runs her finger through her hair as the softness of John's lips and tongue touch all over her.

John hears her feminine cries of passion and feels her trembling in his hands. He wants her to react more, so he sets his mind to suck her soul out of her body. His hands take a hold of her breasts as his mouth covers all of her. She is hairless, so his lips firmly grip all of her. He moves his head side to side as his tongue soars all through and over her. One of her hands gently caresses his head as she melts from the feel of his soft lips and tongue. John says, "Mm," as she melts in his mouth.

KD holds onto to the table with her other hand, breathing heavily, she whispers, "Oh my God, John, baby," as pleasure pulsates throughout her body from her scalp to the bottom of her feet. The sound of his lips and tongue sucking and licking her has her high and hot. John can feel the desire in her growing by the way her body is moving, the sounds she's making, and the way she is rubbing his head.

John's hands slowly slide down her body to her thighs. His hands tenderly caress her thighs as his tongue and lips seductively sway up and down then side to side before going round and round. She moans as John proves he is worthy of his reputation. Her chest quickly moves up and down. John looks at her as he gives her unbounded pleasure that makes her mind spin and renders her body powerless.

When KD begins to throb against his lips, John gently kisses her before he sucks her so firmly and deeply that his lips touch and pull her spirit. She holds on to his head as her body fills with a surplus of pleasure. John doesn't let her move or run from the overwhelming sensation. She's forced to experience the entire orgasm.

John lifts her from the table and carries her to her bedroom. He sits her in the bed. She takes off her robe and lays down. John takes off his clothes then attempts to get in bed, but KD pushes him back with her knee. John stops and looks at her.

KD asks, "Do you see other women?"

John says, "There's no one else."

KD asks, "When was the last time you were with a woman in this way?"

John answers, "A few days before I met you, but I ended that." KD stares in his eyes as he sits on the edge of the bed.

KD asks, "Are you still interested?"

John turns to face her; he says, "I don't want or need anyone else." He gets in the bed and kneels between her thighs. He rubs her legs.

She touches his chest and says, "Don't hurt me, John!" KD wants John just as much as John wants her.

He leans over as he softly caresses and kisses her body, he says, "KD, I'm not playing games. I'm not going to hurt you."

KD says, "Don't lie to me, John! I'm asking for the truth, not what you think I want to hear. If you're seeing someone else, this is the time to tell me." She wants him more than she wants the truth, but she insists to know the truth before she gives in to her desires.

John looks her in the eyes; he says, "I was seeing someone for about a year. She made some moves I didn't like. I was done with that situation, but I was weak, and I saw her one last time a few days before I met you. When I met you, I cut all communication with her. She was the one calling during our first date, but I made it clear it's over. I'm not trying to mess this up. Since I met you, I haven't seen or talked to any other women, and I don't want to. I wouldn't lie to you."

KD asks, "Are you sure this is what you want?"

John answers, "You are all I want and need."

KD says, "Will you always be honest with me even if you think the truth will hurt?"

John says, "I have been and will continue to be honest. Can you promise the same thing?"

KD says, "Yes, I can!"

He kisses her neck and whispers, "I don't want anyone else. Do you want anyone else?"

KD says, "No!"

He kisses her breasts; he says, "Tell me you are all mine!" He kisses her navel as he slowly pulls her panties off and sits them on the bed.

KD looks in his eyes and says, "I'm yours!"

He asks, "Do you want to be with me?"

KD says, "Yes!"

John says, "I really want to be with you." John slides on a condom. He says, "You are all I want, Ladybug, just you. Tell me, you want me."

KD looks in his eyes; she says, "I want you, John, more than anything."

John asks, "Do you mean that?"

KD says, "More than you know!"

John takes that as his cue. He slowly slides into KD. They instantly feel insurmountable pleasure. The first stroke lets John know he found his sexual home and his facial expression says it. They hold hands and make clamors of pleasure in each other's bodies. They look at each other astounded by how good the other feels. KD is so tight that John can feel every ripple and ridge of her squeezing him as he slides in and out of her.

John watches himself going in and out of KD, and the sight turns him on even more, making him want her more.

John looks at her. He leans overs to whisper in her ear as he holds and strokes her body; he says, "I'm yours, KD! I'm committed!" He kisses and sucks her neck. He whispers in her ear: "KD, baby, I won't lie to you. I won't hurt or betray you. We're in this together. For real! Say you're with me, Ladybug!"

John feels so good moving so deeply inside her that she would say anything to please him. KD says, "I'm with you, baby," as she feels John moving and pushing her muscles.

John whispers in her other ear as he nibbles on it, "Tell me you're committed to me."

KD says, "John, I'm committed to you." John goes so deep inside her that he disrupts her heartbeat. KD's fingertips and nails grip onto John's back.

John says, "That's all I want: you with me."

KD says, "I want that, too!"

John says, "It feels so good inside you. Do you like it?" KD nods yes, biting her lip. John says, "Let go and say whatever you feel. I want to know how you feel. I want to know you are enjoying me." KD stares at him in a way to let him know: oh, baby, I'm enjoying myself. John asks again, "Do you like it, Ladybug?"

KD says, "Yes, baby, I love it!"

John asks, "Do I feel good?"

KD says, "You feel amazing!"

John says, "You feel amazing." John whispers in her ear: "Ride me, baby!" He lays on his back. She sits astride him. She takes a hold of him as she slowly slides down his manhood. She rubs him as she begins to move. She rubs his chest with the other hand. John looks at her hair.

He touches her hair. He says, "I love your hair, Ladybug! It's as soft as silk. It's so sexy."

She says, "Thank you," as she moves her hair out of her face. He rubs her thighs as she makes circles up and down him. She feels so good that he looks at her with amazement on his face. She squeezes him with her muscles making him move around inside her. John loves how it feels. She grips him so tightly that it feels like she's sucking him.

He says, "Shit, Ladybug, you ride like a champ!" KD moves with ease as she rolls with every inch of John inside her.

John grips her hips and holds her in place while he makes her bounce on top of him. He hits her spot at the right time with the right stroke. KD moans as her cum drips down John, and it feel so good to John. John grabs the back of her thighs. He lifts her thighs up to her chest. He slides her up and down him. He looks in KD's eyes and says, "Oh my God, you feel so good!"

He wants to make it last, so he needs to switch positions again; he says, "Let me get it from the back." When KD assumes the position, John admires her body as he slowly makes his way inside her; he says, "Damn, Ladybug, you're so sexy."

John is a force of nature moving through KD. KD moves her body on him to put him exactly where she wants to feel him. John feels so good inside her that she moves faster. The speed and force of her body hitting against his causes her ass to recoil and ricochet against him as she squeezes him with Kegels.

John places his hands on the small of her back and guides her movements; he says, "Fuck me, baby! Ladybug, you feel so good!"

John wants to impress KD, so he takes control. He wants to make her feel good, so he puts his all into getting every part of her. He grabs her hips and quickly gets to the bottom of things. John is amazed by KD, her femininity, and her sexuality. He is so turned on that he can't get deep enough inside her. KD expresses her feelings just as John wants, which turns him on even more.

John can tell that KD is on the verge of an orgasm by her movement. He loudly moans as he encourages her. He says, "Fuck me, baby, just like that. Ah, baby! Yes! Keep giving it all to me 'til you cum."

He smacks her butt just to see her skin turn red. As the rush of heat and pleasure flood her body, she fights the urge to stop moving. John knows it's coming. He rubs her back. He says, "Ladybug, keep giving it to me." KD's body begins to shake, but she keeps giving it to John the way he wants it. John says, "Ladybug, you amaze me!" KD reaches back. John takes ahold of her hand and caresses her back as the pleasure radiates throughout her body. She squeezes his hand as her body lightly trembles.

He looks at the reaction on her face, and he is in love. John can't wait to give her that reaction again. John lets her relax and enjoy her orgasm as he softly kisses her hand then up the middle of her back to her neck.

When she lets go of his hand, she begins to move on him. At this point, John is approaching his zone of culmination. His fingertips roll over KD's scalp. He tightly grips her hair. John is quiet and focused. He tightly holds KD by her hair as he works his body to fulfill his desire, and impress the hell out of KD. John's eyes roll in the back of his head as he continues to take goal-oriented strokes; he says, "KD, baby!".

John pulls her face to his. He kisses KD to let her know he wants more. KD kisses him back to let him know she doesn't mind. John loves KD again and again with each time being better than the last time until his appetite is satisfied.

John lays next to KD trying to catch his breath. They gently comfort each other. KD takes the condom off John. She goes into the bathroom. She returns to the bed with a warm towel to tenderly wipe the sweat and wetness from John's face and body. John says, "Thank you, Ladybug!"

John loves how KD cares for him. The attentive care she shows him is another way KD sets herself apart from the females in his past.

KD says, "You're welcome," as she takes the towel back into the bathroom. When she returns, she finds her panties and bra in the bed and slips into them. She lays next to John. She rolls onto her side. John moves closer to her. He rolls his fingertips up and down KD's side.

John spoons KD as he says, "That was amazing, Ladybug!"

KD smiles and looks at him; she says, "It was amazing!"

John whispers, "KD, you're so sexy," as he caresses her hips. He kisses her shoulder.

She says, "You are!" John reaches for KD's hand; he says, "I wanted this since we met, but I didn't want to send the wrong message. My intention was to wait until you felt more comfortable, but that black lace lingerie made me lose my good sense. I had to have you. Our relationship is more than sex. I hope you know and feel that."

KD says, "I do."

John kisses the back of her neck; he smiles and says, "Sweet dreams, Ladybug!"

KD says, "Goodnight, John!"

After a couple hours of sleep, John wakes up. He wakes KD with soft kisses all over her body. He reaches for one of the condoms on the nightstand. John slips on the condom as he covers KD with kisses. His fingers play in her panties, making KD hot and wet. She smiles and says, "Good morning, Mr. King!"

John doesn't respond because he's focused on what's about to happen. He replaces his fingers with his manhood. KD, laying on her side, moans as John, laying on his side behind her, tightly holds her and deeply delves inside KD's love.

She whispers, "Ah! Baby," and rubs John's head. John controlled strokes hit KD exactly where she wants them. The entire room is full of the sound of his body smacking against hers. John is forceful. It isn't that he is being insensitive. His maleness had to have her this way. The sound of John breathing in her ear and the feel of him kissing on her neck turn her on even more. John fulfills his needs never speaking a word.

KD looks back to watch his eyes roll in the back of his head. KD feels his body gently shake. John squeezes and kisses her a million time before he says, "I hate I have to go, but I have some important meetings today."

KD asks, "Do you want breakfast?"

John says, "No, Ladybug, go back to sleep." John gets out of the bed and goes to the restroom. He returns to put his clothes on.

KD asks, "Can I bring you lunch?"

John says, "I would love that. Is two o'clock good for you?" KD wanting to cook for him makes John feel cared for. He has never had a woman to truly care for him, so her wanting to do things for him means so much to him.

KD says, "Yes!"

John says, "Ladybug, I'll see you later. Try to go back to sleep." John kisses her hand and forehead before he leaves to go home to get ready for work.

When he gets to the office, he is in a good mood. His daughters ask why he is so happy; he says, "I'm always happy!" They continue to question him, but he swears nothing is going on. They look at him with untrusting eyes. He says, "What? Why are you looking at me like that?"

In unison they say, "You're lying." He laughs.

John says, "I am always happy when my girls are around." They smile, but they do not buy his excuse.

At two o'clock, KD calls to tell him she has arrived with his lunch. He tells security to let her into his private parking area. He directs her to the entrance that leads right to his office. He opens the door to see her standing there in a short, tight dress, sandals, and sunglasses.

He admires her beauty; he says, "Good God! Ladybug, you're gorgeous!" He tells her, "Hug my neck!"

She wraps her arms around his neck. They kiss. She hands him his lunch. He says, "Come, talk to me while I eat." She follows him up the stairs.

He sits at his desk with his lunch. John opens the dish and says, "Ladybug, this smells and looks so good!"

KD says, "I hope you like it," as she looks at the pictures on his desk.

John tastes the stuffed chicken breast and vegetables; he says, "I love it!"

She asks, "These are your grandchildren?"

He says, "Yes, these two over here are my heart and soul: Lourdes and Langley. They are Kimma's daughters. Kimma is my oldest."

KD says, "John, they are gorgeous. Lourdes has your eyes. Langley has your nose and lips."

John adds, "And over here are my grandsons, Yasir and Yavay. They are Kenna's sons. This is David. He is Isaac's son. Alec and Alan are Alex's sons. Isaiah and Kera don't have children. Isaac and Isaiah are twins. They and Kimma are from my first wife. Kera and Kenna are twins. They and Alex are from my second wife."

KD says, "You have a beautiful family. Everyone looks just like you."

John says, "Thank you! I love having grandkids. It's better than having kids because you get all the love with no responsibility."

KD sees more pictures. As she looks at the photos of his children, John sticks his hand under her dress, putting his fingers in her thong. John says, "Damn! You're soaking wet!"

KD taps his arm; she says, "Get out of there!"

John asks, "Is that from this morning?"

KD says, "No!"

John corners her between his body and the desk. John says, "Ladybug, what's up?"

She says, "John, I'm going to go." KD eases out of the tight space.

John asks, "Why are you so wet?" as KD aims for the door.

John follows her; he says, "You can tell me, Ladybug, no judgment." KD begins walking down the stairs. John grabs her arm to pull her back.

KD says, "John, go eat your food."

John says, "I'll eat you, come here," as he moves to block her path.

KD says, "John, I'm going to go! Move!"

John says, "Tell me what's up."

KD says, "John, you're embarrassing me."

John says, "I'm your man. You don't ever have to feel embarrassed with me. You can always tell me how you feel or what is on your mind. [John moves closer to her.] Now, tell me how you feel and why."

KD says, "John, baby, we had a moment. Okay!"

John says, "I want to know what turns you on."

KD does not want to tell him, but she does to get him to leave her alone. She says, "We kissed, we talked, we were close, I like you, I like to be near you, and I like to talk to you. It happens when we're close, or we talk on the phone late at night. Now, can we end this embarrassing conversation?"

John hugs her; he says, "Your smile, legs, and that ass get to me every time I see you. That soft, silky skin, those pretty eyes, and that beautiful face make my heart skip a beat. When I'm close to you, it takes all my strength to maintain my self-control. I have those moments, too. You have the same effect on me. I'm fortunate that we have this connection. For the first time in life, Ladybug, I'm happy, comfortable, and confident in a relationship. You make me so happy. Are you happy with me?"

KD says, "Yes!"

John says, "We've had a good relationship thus far. You are such a special and remarkable woman. I like the person I have gotten to know. I have gotten to know your mind and your heart. Last night, we just began a new phase in our relationship. I'm getting to know your… [John pauses. They laugh.] It's exciting, getting to know you more intimately."

KD says, "I am very fortunate to get to know you more intimately." She smiles.

John kisses KD then he says, "Come talk to me while I eat my lunch." She follows him back into his office. She sits down on the couch. He offers her some of his food. She declines because she ate before she came. He sits next to her. John asks, "What's your plan for the weekend?"

KD says, "Church with my mother on Sunday is about all I have planned."

John asks, "What church do you go to?"

KD answers, "St. Paul Baptist."

Just as KD finishes her statement, Kimma walks through the door; she says, "Mr. King…."

She pauses when she sees KD; she says, "Oh! Hello!" KD greets Kimma with a smile.

John says, "KD, this is my daughter, Kimma. Kimma, this is my girlfriend, KD. Just the capital letters K and D together, no periods, no space."

They shake hands. KD says, "It's very nice to meet you. Kimma is a beautiful name."

Kimma says, "Thank you! It's nice to meet you, too."

KD says, "Your dad lovingly talks about you all the time. He's very proud of you."

Kimma says, "Ms. KD, would you excuse me? Wait, right here! Please, don't leave!"

KD confusedly says, "Okay!" Kimma leaves the office in a rush.

John says, "I hope you're ready for this."

KD asks, "What?"

John says, "She went to get her sisters. I haven't told them about you. They are about to be all in your business."

KD asks, "Are you ready for this?"

John answers, "I'm not the one about to answer a thousand questions."

KD says, "That's not what I meant. I'm asking, are you ready to be public with our relationship. It's been our little secret."

John says, "Ladybug, the secret is out." After a minute, Kimma returns with her sisters, Kera and Kenna, to find John and KD laughing. When his daughters walk into the office, he gets quiet and goes back to eating his lunch. He doesn't even look up.

Kimma says, "Mr. King, introduce everyone."

John stops eating; he says, "These are my twin daughters, Kera and Kenna. This is my girlfriend, KD!" John goes back to eating. Kera and Kenna are astounded.

Kimma says, "Yes, John's girlfriend, KD! Just the two capital letters KD. No space or periods!"

Kera walks over to touch his forehead; she says, "No fever!"

Kenna asks, "Daddy, your what?"

John says, "Girlfriend!"

Kimma asks, "How long have you been dating?"

John says, "We've been in a relationship for two months." Kenna fakes like she fainted.

Kera says, "Ms. KD, don't mind us. We've never known our father to be associated words like girlfriend and relationship." Kenna and Kera shake KD's hand.

KD says, "It's nice to meet you, Kenna and Kera."

Kenna says, "It's nice to meet you."

Kera says, "So, you're behind the smile." KD and John smile at each other.

Kera asks, "KD, did you cook for him?"

KD says, "I did!"

Kenna says, "She cooks for you! Daddy, you have a girlfriend who cooks!"

John says, "It's good, too, so would you all, please, let me eat."

Kera says, "Dad, she's gorgeous." KD smiles and thanks Kera. KD tells John's daughters they are beautiful. They thank KD for the compliment.

John says, "She is beautiful, kind, caring, smart, hardworking, fun, and a good mother." KD smiles at John. She touches his thigh and tells him thank you.

Kimma says, "Ms. KD sounds like an incredible woman."

John says, "She is!"

KD says, "Awe! Thank you!"

Kenna asks, "Ms. KD, how many kids do you have?"

KD says, "Two! My daughter, Kelly, just graduated from Michigan. My son, Daniel, is ten."

Kera asks, "Dad, have you met her kids?"

John says, "No!"

Kera says, "Memorial Day is coming up. Let's have a cookout at your house. You and the guys can grill. Kimma can make the sides and desserts. We can take a ride on your boat. KD can bring her family, so we can get to know each other. How does that sound, KD?"

KD says, "It sounds nice. [She turns to John to ask] I'm in if you are?"

John says, "It's a date."

Kimma says, "I'll bring my husband and girls, so KD can meet her step-granddaughters."

Kenna says, "I'll bring my husband and boys."

Kera says, "I'll invite my brothers, their spouses, and their kids because I don't have either."

Kenna asks, "Ms. KD, What do you do for a living?"

KD says, "I'm a RN." The girls are impressed.

John says, "My girl is educated, makes her own money, and don't need a man for anything." His daughters and KD laugh.

Kimma says, "Ms. KD, we look forward to getting to know you better. We are going to go and let you enjoy your lunch date."

John says, "Thank you, Nosey 1, 2, and 3."

Kera says, "It's our duty to look out for you, Daddy."

Kenna says, "And, we love you!"

John says, "I love you, too. I appreciate your diligence. Now, get out!" His daughters say bye to KD before they leave.

KD says, "John, this is a big step. Are you sure you're ready to take that step?"

John says, "You said you were in this with me. My kids and grandkids come with me. Your kids and your mother come with you."

KD says, "But your kids are grown. I have a young child. It's different."

John asks, "Have you told your kids you're seeing someone?"

KD says, "No! I was waiting until things were cemented."

John says, "You should be asking yourself if you're ready, not me?"

KD says, "I guess I'm saying my kids come with more responsibility."

John says, "That doesn't scare me, not even a little bit. I was fully aware of what I was getting into when I decided to pursue you. We're in this together, right?"

KD says, "Yes!"

John says, "I accept the responsibility. I'm so serious about this relationship, KD."

KD says, "I am, too!"

John says, "Then, there's nothing else to say. Hug my neck and kiss me, so I can get to this meeting."

KD wraps her arms around his neck and kisses him. He says, "If you don't leave right now, I'm not going to make it to this meeting." KD kisses him again. John asks, "Can I come by tonight? I'll cook dinner."

KD asks, "You're going to cook yourself?"

John says, "I can cook. I can stay the whole weekend and cook every night."

KD says, "I'd love that!"

John says, "KD, thank you for lunch. It was so good! Kiss me again before you go."

KD kisses his cheek; she says, "See you later."

John says, "I can't wait, Ladybug!"

After work, John goes to the gym before going home. He packs enough to have extra clothes and toiletries at KD's apartment. He showers before he leaves to go the market. He is cooking KD's favorites: crab legs, filet mignon, pasta, and salad. He gets his favorite seasonings and spices, candles, expensive champagne to set the mood, and a dozen red roses in a crystal vase.

When John gets to KD apartment, he runs her a bath and puts lit candles around the tub. He pours his special milk and honey into the tub. He tells her to soak and relax while I cook. When KD is done with her bath, she comes to the kitchen. John admires KD's body in her tank top and shorts. KD says, "Let me help you."

John says, "I got this! Go relax!"

KD says, "Are you sure?"

John says, "I'm sure! Go relax!"

When John is done cooking, he walks into the living room to lead her to the kitchen. KD sees the table set with lit candles, roses in a vase, and filled champagne glasses.

She smiles. She says, "This is so lovely."

John says, "Anything for you," as he leads her to the table.

He pulls out here chair and helps her sit. KD says, "You're going to spoil me."

John says, "That's the objective. The goal is much bigger."

KD says, "I wouldn't expect the King to have small goals."

John winks at her. He sits down and says, "Bless the food, Ladybug!"

KD prays over the food before they eat.

After eating and washing the dishes, they cuddle on the couch to watch a movie. John's lips nibbles on her neck and ear as he caresses her thighs.

KD says, "I talked to my daughter today."

John kisses her hand; he asks, "How did it go?"

KD says, "Very well. She said she will gladly hang with us, and she's happy I met someone and she's looking forward to meeting you."

John says, "That's a good thing, right?"

KD says, "It is!"

John says, "Am I rushing you? Am I asking for too much too fast?"

KD says, "No!"

John says, "For the first time ever in life, I know what I want. I have no doubts, but I realize I can't expect you to feel the same way."

KD asks, "How can you be so sure?"

John says, "Because of you."

KD says, "That's sweet!"

John says, "It's real!"

John's fingers are interlocked with hers, as he kisses on her neck while they talk. KD says, "John, I want the same thing, maybe I'm scared."

John says, "Did I rush things last night?"

KD says, "No! What scares me is the thought of falling in love with you, and you don't love me back or you leave."

John says, "That's not going to happen. Your heart is safe with me, and I know that's not easy to believe in a man, but I will prove my sincerity every day. Last night, did you enjoy yourself?"

KD says, "It was pleasurable!"

John says, "Our first time wasn't supposed to be like that. I'm sorry."

KD says, "I have no complaints."

John says, "I was supposed to lay you down and make love to your whole body."

KD says, "Is that the rule?"

John says, "More like a standard: the gold standard."

KD says, "Damn! I got cheated last night, so you owe me."

John says, "I'll spend my life making it up to you."

John picks her up and carries her to the bedroom. He lays her in the bed and takes off her shoes. John kisses around her ankle as he massages her foot. He slowly kisses down her calf. His hands stroke her calf as he affectionately sucks her toes. KD bites her thumbnail as she coyly looks in his eyes. His soft tongue tickles her toes.

She asks, "Is this how you're making it up to me?" He winks at her. He does the same thing to her other foot and leg.

He tenderly kisses her thighs as he stares in her eyes and rubs her legs. He takes off her shorts and shirt. He slowly caresses every inch of her entire body. KD undresses John. She slowly massages his shoulders and arms as she kisses down his chest. She licks up his chest to his lips. She kisses his lips before she licks them. She says, "John, you are the finest man I've ever seen."

John says, "Is that so?"

KD says, "It's so!"

John says, "I'm happy you like what you see."

KD says, "I like more than that!"

John says, "I'd like to know what exactly it is you like."

KD says, "I like everything about you, John."

John says, "The feeling is mutual, Ladybug!" They kiss. John gets on top of her. He gets so close to KD that even air can't get between them. John kisses KD with so much desire that she feels adored. KD's hands hold on to John's back as she is smothered in John's kisses.

John lays her on her stomach, so he can massage her back. KD closes her eyes and relishes in the heat of John's hands, which relaxes her. He softly kisses down her back. He kisses from her shoulder blade to her hand. When he gets to her fingers, he sucks her index and middle fingers so softly that it makes every part of her want to feel him. As his tongue and lips rolls softly over her fingers, she smiles at him.

John rolls her on her back. He slowly, passionately kisses from her neck to her navel. He slowly kisses lower and lower until he gets to her panties. He slowly slides her panties down her leg. He lays flat on his stomach. He stares in her eyes as he lays her thighs over his shoulders. He pulls her closer to his face.

He softly kisses her again and again as he stares in her eyes. He spreads her thighs a little more. He closes his eyes as he licks her. That first lick feels so good that she bites her bottom lip. He holds her thighs tightly to prevent her from moving. John licks every part of her. John covers her with his mouth and sucks her until he can no longer hold his breath. He takes a breath and goes right back to sucking her. KD can feel his tongue rolling against her as he sucks her so tightly that he tugs and yanks the passion embedded in the inner core of her being.

KD closes her eyes and breathes as she processes the pleasure John is giving her. John has KD so wet that his hands and face are coated with her essence. She delicately holds John's bald head in her hands as she moans.

He pushes her thighs together and pushes her knees to her chest. John fucks her with his tongue. He can tell its driving KD crazy. He sticks his tongue in her and pulls her back and forth on his tongue until she cums. The pressure from his tongue during the orgasm immediately leads to another orgasm. She says through labored breathing, "Oh my God! Baby!"

John wants to give her more pleasure. He covers all of her with his mouth and sucks, making her call his name. The way she calls his name lets John know she is submitting to his will. John switches position. He puts her on top to prove he is worthy of his title and reputation. KD rides his tongue, making it touch the exact spot that she needed touched.

She leans over to take a hold of him. She softly caresses John with both hands. KD is so turned on that she moans in a way that lets John know she needs him. John calls her name. She answers yes.

John asks, "Do you need it?" She answers yes.

He says, "Tell me you need me."

KD says, "Baby, I need you!"

John says, "Come here, Ladybug. You can have all of me. There's no limit." John sits up and KD crawls into his arms.

John lays her down, gets on top of her, and puts on a condom. He pins her thighs back. They kiss as John slowly pushes into KD. KD wraps her arms around his back. Once John is inside her, he goes to work, giving her all of him with each stroke. KD moves with John, letting him feel all of her. John is impressed by KD's ability to take all of him. She doesn't run or back away. She moves with ease with all of him inside her. Last night she let him control her body, but tonight she's fucking him back.

No matter his tempo, she fucks with him. She gives as good as she takes. KD is not shy tonight. She lets him know she loves every minute of his love. Tonight, she matches John's energy. She matches John's intensity. She matches John's stamina. She matches John willingness to please.

John has KD all over the bed in many different positions all through the night. John moves her with ease, switching positions fluently. Sometimes he's gentle and other times he's aggressive, and KD enjoys his every mood.

In the morning, John wakes up first. He brushes his teeth and takes a shower. John makes KD breakfast in bed. When KD gets out the shower, she brings snacks to the bedroom to keep them company throughout the day. They stay in KD's bed all day laughing, playing, and bonding, never touching their cell phones. John makes dinner again as he promised. After dinner, John and KD listen to music and dance in KD's bedroom. They fall asleep in each other's arms.

On Sunday morning, KD quietly gets ready for church while John is still sleeping. KD goes to her mother's house to eat breakfast before going to church. KD and Mrs. Daniels sit in their usual spot near the front at the center end of the pew.

KD and her mother are talking when John walks into the church impeccably dressed. His eyes scan the sanctuary until he sees her. As John walks through the church, people recognize him. People greet him with handshakes and smiles. He is cordial, but focused on getting to KD. People wonder who John King is visiting. One man asks if he needs help finding someone. John answers, "No! I see her."

The center aisle is blocked, so John must go to the opposite end. John says, "Excuse me!" People stand up to let him get by. As he makes his way to the other end of the pew, one of the elders of the church, says, "Young man, you're on a mission."

John says, "I'm trying to get to my lady."

The man asks, "Your lady goes here?"

John says, "Yes, KD Daniels."

The man says, "Lil' Daniels is your lady?"

John says, "Yes! KD is my lady!"

Another elder hears the conversation, he turns around to shake John's hand; he says, "Oh, you've got a good one."

The first man says, "Yes, sir, you've done well for yourself. KD is a good woman. I've known her all her life."

The second man says, "Every single man has been after her for years. Make sure you lock it down. [The man clutches a tight fist.] You don't want someone swooping in and snatching your prize. She's a queen fit to sit by the king's side. You get what I'm saying?"

John says, "I'm very blessed! Amen!"

The first man says, "Don't mess up! There's a hundred men waiting to take your place."

John says, "No, Sir, I won't mess up."

The second man says, "I pray your union is blessed."

John says, "Thank you both."

The people sitting near the elders talking to John overhear the conversation, and turn to stare at KD. KD notices everyone in the area is staring at her. She looks up to see John standing over her. She is shocked. She says, "Hey!" John speaks as he scoots between her and the person beside her. He sits and introduces himself to her mother.

John says, "It's nice to meet you, Mrs. Daniels. I'm KD's boyfriend, John."

Mrs. Daniels is taken off guard, but she says, "I'm pleased to meet you, John. Welcome to St. Paul Baptist Church!" John thanks Mrs. Daniels. Mrs. Daniels smiles at KD.

KD whispers to John, "What are you doing here?"

John whispers, "Couples go to church together." KD lifts her eyebrows. John wraps his arm around her shoulders. Everyone in the church looks at KD and John as they whisper.

KD whispers, "I didn't think you would want to come to church."

John whispers, "I want to be wherever my girl is. Besides, the men in here need to know you have a man."

KD whispers, "No one is thinking about me."

John says, "I already got the scoop from the two gentlemen down there. Apparently, you're prime for the pickings and I need to watch my back."

KD looks to see who John is talking about. The two elders' wave at her, and raise a fist to John. John nods. KD and John look at each other and laugh.

John whispers, "Are you mad that I'm here?"

KD whispers, "No! I always want to be with you. I'm shocked that you came to church."

John whispers, "I grew up in church. I'm a sinner, but I'm not a heathen. So, we're good?"

KD says, "Yes, always!"

They smile at each other. She kisses his cheek. Mrs. Daniels looks at the happiness on her daughter's face. Mrs. Daniels is happy to see her only daughter happy.

The deacon starts the service with a song. Some of the congregation stands up to sing with the deacon. Mrs. Daniels and John stand up to enthusiastically sing along. John and Mrs. Daniels are all smiles, while KD sinks down in the pew slightly embarrassed by her mother and boyfriend. When the pastor says hug your neighbor, John pulls KD to her feet. He embraces KD in a way to let every man in the sanctuary know he's permanently in the picture. He holds KD until the pastor begins his sermon, never letting her talk to anyone else.

At the end of the service, the pastor walks down the center aisle. He stops to shake John's hand; he says, "I love your enthusiasm. God bless you! Welcome to St. Paul Baptist." John thanks him and compliments the lively, spirit-filled service.

As they exit the church, John walks arm in arm with Mrs. Daniels. KD walks behind them feeling horrified and embarrassed because Mrs. Daniels introduces John as her son-in-law to everyone they walk past.

Mrs. Arlene Gable is standing with a group of women at the door of the church. Mrs. Daniels speak to the women. She says, "Deaconess, this is John King, my son-in-law." The women smile and says hello.

Mrs. Gable says, "So you're the blessing. It's good to finally meet you," she reaches out her hand. John takes and shakes her hand. John tells Mrs. Gable it was a pleasure to meet her. KD can't believe her mother. The thought of having to face the congregation if the relationship doesn't work is already embarrassing. When John and Kathy walks on, the women say hello to KD. KD says hello as she follows her mother and John.

Mrs. Gable stops her; she says, "I recognized his cologne. You look happy; I'm happy for you." KD thanks her.

Mrs. Gable says, "I prayed about it. Have you?"

KD says, "Yes, Ma'am!"

Mrs. Gable lays hands on her shoulders; she says, "God has his hands on this, on you. Be blessed and mindful of his work. Walk in faith. Everything is in divine order." They hug and KD thanks Mrs. Gable for her encouragement.

John walks Kathy to KD's car. As John opens the passenger door for Mrs. Daniels, she invites him to her house for lunch; she says, "After church, we always have lunch at my house. My son comes over with his family and a few of our friends join us. I would love for you to join us."

John says, "I would love to join you. Thanks for inviting me."

Mrs. Daniels asks, "Are you sure you're not too busy?"

John says, "I'm never too busy to spend time with the Daniels women."

Mrs. Daniels says, "Aren't you charming!" John smiles as he closes the door.

John walks KD to the driver's side door. He closes her door before running to his car to follow KD's car to Mrs. Daniels' house. As KD drives, Mrs. Daniels pries for information about their relationship; she says with a smiling face, "You didn't tell me you were dating John King."

KD says, "Momma, I was going to tell you today after church."

Mrs. Daniels is unconvinced; she says, "Yeah, I believe that."

KD says, "I was, for real! I just told Kelly. She was cool, so you were next, I swear."

Mrs. Daniels asks, "How did you meet him?"

KD says, "I was jogging one morning and he stopped me to talk."

Mrs. Daniels says, "Why did you keep it a secret?"

KD says, "I was waiting for the right time besides I didn't think you knew who he was."

Mrs. Daniels says, "The whole city knows who he is."

KD says, "I didn't recognize him when I first met him."

Mrs. Daniels says, "You don't watch the news much, do you?"

KD says, "Never!"

Mrs. Daniels says, "When did you start dating him?"

KD says, "We have been dating for about two months."

Mrs. Daniels says, "Two months? I'm just now hearing about this."

KD asks, "Momma, are you mad?"

Mrs. Daniels says, "He said he's your boyfriend."

KD says, "I heard him."

Mrs. Daniels asks, "Do you like him?"

KD says, "I do."

Mrs. Daniels asks, "Is he your boyfriend?"

KD says, "I'm too old to have a boyfriend."

Mrs. Daniels says, "No, you're not. I have a boyfriend."

KD says, "Momma!"

Mrs. Daniels says, "What! My husband died, not me. You have a whole lot of life ahead of you. You shouldn't spend it alone because that man left. King seems to like you, and you seem interested in him. Baby, you do what's best for you!

"I know you don't like to talk about your relationships, but there's nothing wrong with you spending time with John, and you know [Mrs. Daniels says with a sassy tone.]. You're single and well past grown. Your daughter is out of the house, and Daniel needs a man around. If John is in the position and desires to be exclusive with you, you should go for it. At the least, have fun, you deserve that. He does want to be exclusive with you, right?"

KD says, "Yes, Momma, we are exclusively dating."

Mrs. Daniels says, "I'm happy for you. God Bless!"

KD says, "Thank you, Momma!" KD pauses and thinks for a moment; she asks, "You have a boyfriend? Who is he?"

Mrs. Daniels says, "You have your secrets, and I have mine."

KD says, "Momma, you're really not going to tell me?"

Mrs. Daniels says, "I'm the mother, you don't get to be all in my business."

KD says, "Momma, you were all in my business."

Mrs. Daniels says, "Because I'm the mother. I'm entitled to know everything you do, but a mother gets to keep some secrets from her daughter."

KD says, "Momma, I need to know who you're spending time with for safety reasons."

Mrs. Daniels says, "All you need to know about me is that I am safe and satisfied. You need to know what Mr. King is doing. Don't worry about what I'm doing!"

KD says, "Momma, you are a trip. Did you just tell me to mind my business?"

Mrs. Daniels says, "Well, I tried to be polite." KD laughs.

KD says, "Momma, why did you just tell the whole church that John is your son-in-law?"

Mrs. Daniels says, "I couldn't help myself. Sheila Patterson, Marva Stevens, and their crew are always bragging about their rich sons-in-law. John King is a million times richer and a trillion times more handsome than all their sons-in law put together. When you and that man got a divorce, they took dig after dig. John showing up today was the Lord getting revenge."

KD says, "Momma, what's going to happen if John and I don't make it."

Mrs. Daniels says, "Nope, I don't see that. I hear wedding bells and I see them at the wedding watching with jealous eyes."

KD says, "Momma, John doesn't seem like the settle down, marrying type."

Mrs. Daniels says, "John King has never had a woman like KD Daniels. You're my daughter. You're a remarkable woman. You're a queen fit for that King. Don't you dare let that ex-man of yours make you doubt that. God removed that man from your life for a reason. Some relationships aren't meant to span a lifetime. They come for a reason in a season, and they go so God can manifest a new reason in a new season. KD, this is the beginning of a new season."

KD says, "John says he is serious about our relationship. He says there's no other women in his life. He has been extremely good to me, and he makes me feel so incredible. We have so much fun just doing simple things. He is so kind and generous. Everything he says and does is so sincere that I believe him, but John has been a player all his life. I have my guard up."

Mrs. Daniels says, "It's wise to be guarded and protect yourself. Just because John is a man doesn't mean he can't have a new season. Good love is a blessing for men as well. A good man needs good love just as much as a good woman. Have you prayed for wisdom and discernment?"

KD says, "I have!"

Mrs. Daniels says, "Well, Little Girl, seems like God is working. All your life you've embodied every fruit of the spirit. Since the moment I laid eyes on you, all through your marriage, and even going through your divorce, you've been so full of love, joy, peace, patience, kindness, goodness, faithfulness, gentleness, and temperance. Maybe, just maybe, the Lord is letting you reap the harvest from the good seed you've sown."

As KD pulls into the driveway, she says, "Thank you, Momma!"

Before Mrs. Daniels gets out of the car, she grabs KD's hand, she says, "Daughter, my sweet, precious daughter, your happiness and peace mean so much to me. Your relationship with John is your business. This isn't me prying, and you're way beyond needing my advice. As your mother, I will always share my wisdom. As my daughter, you will always be my prayer. I will always support you in whatever you do. Know this daughter, I pray for you every morning, noon and night. Something in my spirit is settled, calm, joyous at the thought of you with John. Whatever this is, whether fun or a serious relationship, I support you, KD! Okay?"

KD replies, "Okay, Momma!"

Mrs. Daniels says, "That man loves you. Look at him!" KD looks at John walking up the driveway in the rearview mirror. Mrs. Daniels adds, "Go kiss your man, while I go set the table." Mrs. Daniels smiles as she gets out the car and walks into the house, watching KD walk to John and into his embrace. They kiss.

KD says, "I hope my mother didn't embarrass you too much."

John replies, "I will never be embarrassed by being called KD's man or Mrs. Daniels' son-in-law. It's an honor to be both."

KD says, "Are you sure, everything is cool?"

John says, "We're always good!" KD kisses his cheek as a sign of gratitude.

KD wraps her arm in John's as they walk into the house. John asks KD, "Is this the house you grew up in?"

KD answers, "Yes!"

John asks for a tour, so KD shows him around the house. When they get to her old bedroom, John looks around at her old dolls, posters, and pictures on the wall. John sees a picture of KD as a teenager with Mena and Tri.

He says, "KD, you are gorgeous. Look at you looking all fly with your friends!"

KD says, "Thank you!" (Pointing to her friends in the picture as she says:) "That is Tri and Mena."

John looks at more pictures. He says, "You've been fine all your life. Damn, favor isn't fair! You stay killing it!" KD thanks him.

He asks, "Did you ever sneak boys in room to make out?" He walks over to her. He wraps his arms around her waist.

KD says, "No, my mother would've killed me." He kisses her. She kisses him back.

John says, "What do you think would have happened if sixteen-year-old KD had eighteen-year-old John in this room while her parents were at work?" John kisses on her neck.

KD says, "Probably something magical and unforgettable!"

John says, "We can make magic, right now!"

She smiles and says, "You're a bad boy!"

John says, "You know you like that bad boy in me!"

KD whispers, "I love that bad boy in me" She kisses him.

John says, "Ladybug, you're so nasty!"

KD whispers, "You didn't mind last night!"

John says, "Give me fifteen minutes to refresh my memory." She grabs his hand to lead him out of the room. They laugh as they walk out of the room.

While eating lunch, John is charming. He keeps everyone laughing and engages everyone in conversation. Of course, John and KD are asked a million questions about their relationship, and KD lets John do all the talking. John ensures Mrs. Daniels and Keith Jr. that his intentions and feelings toward KD are pure and good.

When it is time to leave to go to his grandsons' game, Mrs. Daniels sends KD to the kitchen to make John a plate to take with him. John follows KD into the kitchen. When KD hands him the plate, he kisses her goodbye. Mrs. Daniels sees them kissing. She smiles at them.

Mrs. Daniels says, "It's something burning in the kitchen!"

Keith Jr. turns to look. He says, "It's definitely hot in there!"

John and KD stop kissing and smile. KD says, "I'll see you later."

John replies, "Keep that fire burning and I'll put it out later!" KD winks at him.

Mrs. Daniel calls KD's name and ask her to come here when she's done. KD says, "I'm coming, Momma!"

John replies, "You could be if you let me take you to your old room!"

KD says, "The boys are going to be mad if you miss kick-off."

John says, "See you later, Ladybug!"

KD says, "See you, later, John."

Mrs. Daniels walks John to his car. She tells him she enjoyed his company and she hopes to see him again soon. John invites Mrs. Daniels to the Memorial Day cookout. She gladly accepts. By the time John leaves, Mrs. Daniels loves him. She officially nicknamed him Son, and told him to call her Kathy.

KD has been working overtime, so she and John haven't seen each other in the last few days. They talk on the phone and text as much as possible, but conversation isn't enough to feed John's need to be near her.

John goes into the security office at hospital. He talks to Trevor and Fordham. They are happy to see him. They laugh and joke before John explains his girlfriend is working on the eighth floor and he wants a quiet place to talk to her during her dinner break, which starts in fifteen minutes.

Trevor, a guard that has known John for a few years, says, "There's a small, empty security office on the tenth floor in the north stair well. No one goes in there ever. All the surveillance equipment has been removed."

Trevor hands him his key card. Trevor adds, "Press two-three-six and touch the access pad with the key card as soon as you press the six."

The second guard, Fordham, says, "We will cut the camera feed in the stair well on that floor to give you and your girl enough time to get in and out of there." John thanks them and hands each of them a few folded hundred-dollar bills.

Fordham says, "Take the security elevator up to the tenth floor. No one will see you. Come on, I'll take you to the elevator."

John calls KD. When KD answers the phone, John tells her to come to the tenth floor and use the north stairs. When KD gets to the tenth floor, she sees John standing in the corner. KD hugs and kiss him. John puts the code in the key pad and opens the door.

She asks, "What are you doing?" He pulls KD into the security office.

John makes sures the door is locked; he answers, "I need to kiss you, touch you. Ladybug I missed you so much." John wraps his arms around her.

She hugs him back, and says, "I missed you, too."

John sets a thirty-minute timer on his watch before he kisses her. They kiss until the timer goes off.

John says, "I'm going to go."

KD looks at her watch while she has him in her embrace; she says, "Baby, don't go. I have thirty more minutes." She says, "Baby, I need another kiss," before she kisses him.

John says, "I will always give you what you need."

KD whispers, "Thank you, baby, I appreciate you." Thirty minutes later, KD enjoys the final kiss of the night.

John says, "Call me when you get home."

KD says, "I will."

John says, "Have a good rest of your work day."

KD says, "Thank you, baby! Drive safely and rest well tonight!" KD leaves and goes down the stairs. John closes the door and goes back to the security elevator. He returns Trevor's key card and leaves the hospital.

John hasn't seen KD since the night at the hospital, so he is missing her, and she is missing him just as much. They both are excited as they prepare for the Memorial Day family dinner. Kelly picks up Daniel from Bradley's house before picking up their grandmother to go to KD's apartment. Before going to John's house, Kelly and KD sit Daniel to tell him about John.

KD says, "Son, sit down; I need to talk to you."

Daniel says, "Okay! Momma, what's wrong?"

KD says, "Nothing is wrong. I need to tell you something."

Daniel says, "What's up, Momma?"

KD says, "I've been dating someone. His name is John. He wants to meet you today. I would like for you to meet him, but only if you're comfortable."

Daniel says, "Mr. King wants to meet me. Okay, I'll meet him." KD has no clue how Daniel knows John's name.

Daniel says, "I saw a strange number in your call log, so I reversed looked it up. I need to know who's calling my mother." KD looks at her mother as if to say, see.

KD says, "Oh! How do you feel about me dating?"

Daniel says, "I'm cool with it!"

Kelly says, "DJ! This is serious! Momma has never introduced us to a man before. It's okay if you have questions or concerns."

Daniel says, "It's cool! Momma, you deserve someone. Bradley has someone."

KD says, "Your sister told you to say that?"

Daniel says, "No, I want you to be happy. Does dating John make you happy?"

KD says, "You make me happy. Nothing or no one comes before you."

Daniel says, "I know that, and I love you, too! I want you to know I support you dating Mr. King if you like him, he's nice to you, and treats you well. Is he nice to you, Momma?"

KD says, "Yes, baby, he has been a total gentleman."

Daniel says, "That's good, Momma. I am happy for you."

KD hugs her son; she says, "I love you so much!"

Daniel hugs his mother back; he says, "I love you, Momma!"

Mrs. Daniels says, "Seems to me, the boy is fine with it, so you have no excuses, KD."

KD looks at her mother. Mrs. Daniels says, "I'm just saying."

Kelly says, "Grandma is right, Momma, don't try to use us as an excuse to chicken out."

KD says, "Really, Kelly!"

Kelly responds, "All I'm saying is give it a chance!"

Mrs. Daniels says, "It's not every day that you get a chance to date someone who is as fine, charming, and rich as my future son-in-law. I think you would be crazy to pass on this relationship."

Kelly says, "No single woman in her right mind would give up the chance to date a man like King." KD looks at Kelly.

Kelly says, "Mommy, I mean, you should see where things go. I can tell you like him."

Mrs. Daniels says, "I can see it too, Kelly," with a smirk on her face.

She adds, "I hear wedding bells."

KD says to Daniel, "Let's go, Son."

Mrs. Daniels says, "Kelly, we must be telling the truth. The truth always makes people uncomfortable."

Kelly says, "Why are you rushing to get in the car, Mommy? Don't forget your overnight bag and purse, Momma."

Mrs. Daniels says, "Hmm! Must be spending the night!"

KD walks to the car followed by Kelly and Mrs. Daniels talking about how John would make the perfect husband for KD. KD gets in the backseat with Daniel to avoid talking to her mother and daughter. Mrs. Daniels talks about John all the way to his house. Kelly is all into the conversation. KD says nothing.

When they arrive at John's house, it is lively with his family. John, his sons, and sons-in-law spent all morning grilling. John's daughters and daughters-in-law spent the morning preparing sides and desserts. John greets Mrs. Daniels first before he smiles and walks over to greet KD. John takes her bag and purse.

KD introduces John to Kelly and Daniel. John shakes each of their hands and says, "Nice to meet you! Welcome to my home. Make yourself comfortable. Let me know if you need anything."

John introduces KD, Kelly, Mrs. Daniels, and Daniel to his family. Everyone politely greets each other.

Kimma says, "Kelly fits right in with the daughters. All our names begin with a K. Welcome to the sisterhood, Kelly." Kelly thanks her.

Kelly says, "I'm going to enjoy having big sisters."

Kera says, "Finally, I'm not the baby anymore."

While Kelly and Mrs. Daniels get acquainted with Kera, Kimma, and Kenna, John takes KD and Daniel to meet his grandsons who are playing video games in the basement.

Daniel asks John, "May, I play with them?"

John says, "Yes, you can! G-sons, be cordial to our guest. Make sure DJ gets a turn!" The boys welcome Daniel and hand him a controller.

John takes KD to the great room where his granddaughters are watching TV. When Lourdes sees John, she says, "Pop! Pop!" Langley turns to see John.

Langley says, "Granddad!" They run over to hug him. John picks up his granddaughters.

He says, "Grandgirls, I want to introduce you to my girlfriend. This is KD! KD, this is Langley and Lourdes."

KD says, "You two are beautiful! It's such a pleasure to meet such beautiful, precious girls."

Lourdes reaches for KD; she says, "KK!"

KD reaches out her hands to take Lourdes from John. KD says, "Aww, she's trying to say my name."

Langley says, "Nice to meet you, KD. Granddad, your new girlfriend is very pretty!"

John says, "Thank you, Grandgirl!" John kisses Langley's forehead before putting her down and taking KD's bag and purse to his room.

KD says, "Aww, thank you! You're very pretty!"

Langley says, "Thank you!" Langley and KD hug.

Kimma, Audrey (Alex's wife), Jayla (Isaiah's wife), and Isaac's wife, Tionna, set the table before Kimma calls everyone to the dining room to eat.

John says, "Langston, you're at the head of the table. As the head of the table, you say grace." Kimma sits across from Langston. John sits next to KD.

After Langston blesses the food, Lourdes crawls over to KD. Lourdes says, "KK!"

KD picks her up, hugs her, and says, "You're such a sweet baby!" Lourdes hugs KD's neck.

Kera asks, "Dad, how did you meet, KD?"

John says, "I was on my way to the office. I saw her jogging. I stopped to talk to her."

Kimma asks KD, "Did he give you some corny line?"

KD says, "He came out of nowhere, checking my pockets, talking about I stole his heart." Everyone laughs.

Kera says, "Really, Dad! Stole your heart. You couldn't come better than that?"

John says, "What? I got her attention!"

Kenna says, "I doubt that line got her attention."

Kelly asks, "What was it, Mother, that got your attention?"

KD says, "I didn't know who he was, and I didn't fall for that line. His handsome face and cute smile initially attracted my attention, but the intensity in his personality sustained my attention."

Isaac says, "Dad, you met someone in Detroit who didn't know you, had to be a first."

John says, "It was cool! We sat down to share a nice meal, enjoyed an engaging conversation, and played a little pool. I was an ordinary man, and she was this extraordinary woman I was trying to get to know." KD smiles at John. He winks at her.

Isaiah asks KD, "Ms. KD, are you from here?"

KD says, "Yes, I am!"

Kelly asks, "Momma, how did you not recognize Mr. King? Everyone in Detroit knows who he is and what he does."

KD says, "I've spent the last twenty-eight years in the hospital. I don't know what goes on in the world. After we talked for a while, I started putting things together and I figured out who he was. Briefly, I thought I shouldn't get involved him, but by the time I figured out who he is, I already liked him."

John says, "I'm glad you didn't give up on me." John rubs her thigh.

KD says, "I will never give up on you." KD rubs his hand.

Kera says, "Aww! You two are so cute together."

Mrs. Daniels listens to the conversation smiling. Kelly says, "I agree!"

Kenna tells her brothers, "KD's a nurse."

Alex says, "Dad, she's smart and beautiful. You chose well for yourself."

John says, "I did!" John kisses KD's hand.

Lourdes points to KD's plate and says, "Eat! Eat!" Kimma attempts to take Lourdes as she tells Lourdes to eat her own food. Lourdes cries and buries her face in KD's chest.

KD says, "Aww, let her stay. We can share." Kimma lets Lourdes stay with KD, which makes Lourdes smile.

Kelly says, "Momma, you've made a new friend."

KD says, "I think so. She's so adorable."

After they eat, the boys go back to the basement to play video games. The adults and the two girls go for a ride on John's boat.

Alex steers the boat while everyone enjoys the breeze. John touches KD's legs as they talk. She whispers in his ear, "You look and smell so good, Mr. King," as she touches his face.

He smiles; he whispers, "Thank you, Ladybug, but don't think I didn't notice you in that dress. I hope you let me take it off later."

KD lowly responds, "If you're a good boy, I'll think about it."

John whispers, "What if I'm bad?"

KD whispers in his ear, "Oh! I'm definitely letting you take it off." They laugh. John kisses her cheek.

John whispers, "I've missed you so much."

KD whispers, "I thought about you day and night."

John whispers, "Is that right? Tell me what you were thinking about as you hug my neck."

KD hugs his neck and whispers, "Your smile, your eyes, your heartbeat, your lips, your kisses, your…." as she sneaks a kiss.

John whispers in her ear. "Don't start! I haven't seen you. Plus, you have that dress you on. Mess around and get it tonight."

KD says, "Maybe that's the goal!" KD seductively kisses his lips.

John says, "You're making it so hard for me. [KD kisses him again.] Your mother is looking at us. You better stop kissing me."

KD rubs his beard and says, "But I don't want to stop." She kisses him again.

John says, "I don't want you to stop, but your daughter is looking at us, too."

KD whispers, "It's so hard to stop," as she sneaks one last kiss.

Mrs. Daniels says to Kelly, "Those two are like teenagers."

Kelly says, "KD is undeniably in love."

John says, "Look what you did."

He motions for her to look down with his eyes. She sees the print of his bold manhood through his shorts.

He says, "Your fault! You know what your kisses do to me."

KD and John laugh; she says, "I'm sorry!" John puts her legs across his lap to hide his engorged manhood. He massages her calves as they talk.

John says, "So, I'll see more of you starting next month?"

KD says, "Yes, I'm so happy. I needed more time with my son and more time with you."

John says, "I can't wait. I can't believe I get to see more of you."

John kisses her forehead. John's family notices how affectionate he is with KD.

Kera says, "I'm sorry, KD, but I have to ask. What did you do to our father?"

KD says, "I haven't done anything to him."

Kenna says, "We have never seen him so affectionate or giddy with anyone."

John says, "Don't embarrass me."

Kimma says, "Dad, you seem happy, and we are happy that you are happy."

John, still massaging KD's leg, says, "I can relax and be myself with her. She's everything I want in a life partner, lover, friend. I can't get enough of her. I can't help myself. This is it! KD's the one!"

Everyone freezes in shock and silently stares at KD and John. KD smiles and touches his face. John kisses her thumb as she caresses his face.

Kelly whispers to Mrs. Daniels, "Did you hear that?"

Mrs. Daniels whispers to Kelly, "I surely did! I hear wedding bells!"

Isaiah says, "What the hell did you say?"

John looks in KD's eyes; he says, "KD is the woman God made for me. This is it for me. She's the one. My soulmate. I'm happy."

KD smiles and says, "Aww, John!" She kisses him.

John kisses her back and says, "I mean that!"

KD says to him, "I feel the same way!"

John asks, "You do?"

KD answers, "I do!" They kiss.

Tionna says, "Pops, I'm happy for you!" John thanks her.

Audrey says, "That's so sweet! Pops, I'm happy for you, too!" John thanks Audrey.

Kimma says, "Daddy, I've never heard you talk like this."

John says, "I never felt like this."

Jayla smiles and she says, "I wish you two all the best." John and KD thank her.

Kera says, "Daddy is in love!"

Lourdes crawls over to KD. Lourdes reaches out her hands. KD picks her up. KD rubs Lourdes' back as Lourdes lays on KD's chest. John watches the interaction with a smile on his face, still massaging KD's legs. It warms his heart to see KD lovingly hold Lourdes.

Kenna says, "He's not the only one."

John says, "Children are great judges of character. My grandgirl knows my girl has a good heart." Lourdes spends the rest of the day in KD's lap. KD is Lourdes and Langley's best friend by the time everyone goes home.

KD and John sit on the deck of the docked boat alone under the stars and moonlight. Kelly is spending the night with Daniel, so KD can spend time with John.

John says, "I appreciate you texting and calling every night, but I missed seeing your face. That night at hospital, KD, girl, you are unbelievable." KD smiles and winks at him.

KD says, "It's been torture not seeing you these last few nights."

John says, "I want any and all your free time not dedicated to Daniel."

KD says, "Definitely!"

John asks, "Did you miss me?"

KD says, "I did, so much!"

John says, "Hug my neck and kiss me liked you missed me."

After they kiss, John says, "Aww! Ladybug, your kisses drive me crazy."

KD says, "Yours have the same effect on me."

John kisses her again before he says, "Today went well. I think our families will get along well. Our girls are already like sisters."

KD says, "The thought of everyone getting along does make things easier."

John says, "Daniel and the grandsons made friends quickly, and that's really a relief."

KD says, "Yes, it is. Daniel needs some males in his life, so this is good for him."

KD looks for her phone. She says, "I left my phone on the table. I'm going to go get it." As she walks toward John looking at her phone, John blocks the exit. She looks up. They smile at each other.

John asks, "Have you ever made love on a boat?" John walks into the cabin.

KD says, "No," as she backs away from him. John chases her and catches her. He picks her up and sits her on the table. He stands between her legs. KD wraps her arms around his neck.

John says, "I've been longing to touch you, Ladybug!"

KD moves close to kiss him, but her phone rings. She looks at the phone; she says, "Wait a minute, baby, It's my son." She answers the phone, "Hello, Son!"

Daniel says, "Hey, Momma, are you still with Mr. King?"

KD answers, "Yes!"

Daniel says, "May I speak to him?"

KD hands John the phone; she says, "It's for you!"

John looks concerned as he takes the phone; he says, "Hello!" John leans on the table next to KD. KD curiously watches John as he talks on the phone.

Daniel says, "Hello, Mr. King!"

John says, "What's up, Little Man?"

Daniel says, "Thank you for inviting me to your home. I had a lot of fun."

John says, "It was my pleasure. You are welcome here anytime!"

Daniel says, "Thank you, that means a lot to me! I know your time is limited, but I was calling to invite you to my game tomorrow. It's at my school at six o'clock. My mother is coming. If you're free, you can come with her."

John says, "I'll be there!"

Daniel excitedly says, "Really? You will come?"

John says, "I'll be there, for sure!"

Daniel says, "Would you tell my mother that Kelly and I said goodnight?"

John says, "Sure!"

Daniel says, "Thank you, Mr. King!"

John says, "You're welcome! Please call me John."

Daniel says, "OK! Goodnight, John, but please don't tell my mother I called you John. She wouldn't like that."

John smirks and says, "It'll be our secret. Goodnight, Little Man!" Daniel hangs up the phone.

John smiles and hands KD her phone. KD asks, "What did he want?"

John says, "He thanked me for having him over and invited me to his game tomorrow. He also told me to tell you that he and Kelly said goodnight. He's such a good kid. You're a great mother!"

KD says, "Aww! Thank you! You're a great father."

John says, "I wonder how different life would have been if I met you thirty years ago. Twenty-year-old me with you would've done great things."

KD says, "We will do great things!"

John says, "You think God brought us together now because we're both ready for this relationship?"

KD says, "That sounds like him."

John says, "I know I'm ready. Are you ready for this relationship?"

KD says, "If I'm not, I'm sure you'll help me get prepared."

John says, "For sure!"

John puts his head down. KD asks, "Are you okay?" John shakes his head no.

KD asks, "What's the matter, baby?"

John says, "Your son got in my head. I'm thinking of you as a mother, and I'm feeling guilty for wanting to do the things I want to do to Daniel's mother."

KD says, "Let's just go in the house, relax, and if something happens between KD and John, it happens. If not, it's okay. It's gratifying just being near you."

John says, "I had plans for you on this boat, though. When the wind blows, the boat rocks."

KD reaches out her hand; she says, "Another day! Let's go!"

They go into the house and up to John's room. KD grabs her overnight bag and goes to take a shower. John comes into the shower with her. KD immediately covers her breast with her arms.

John says, "I'll wash you, and you wash me."

KD says, "Baby, get out of here."

John says, "Why are you acting shy? I've seen all of you."

KD says, "Only in the dark."

John says, "I love your body. You never have to feel shame or insecurity. I look at you, and I see a pot of gold."

KD says, "You're used to twenty and thirty-year-old women. I'm almost fifty with a c-section scar and I've breastfed two babies. I can't compete with the young, flawless women you're accustomed to dating."

John says, "You can't compete because there's no competition. You are flawless! Feeding and birthing two beautiful children are not flaws. They're blessings. In my eyes, you are perfect just the way you are. Come here!" He wraps his arms around her.

KD leans her head on his chest, still covering her breasts with her arms; she says, "You're perfect!"

He says, "KD, if one of us is unable to perform self-care, the other one will have to feed and bathe the one in need. I will wipe your ass covered in shit, and I still would see you as the most beautiful and attractive woman I ever met. This is not a superficial relationship, so you need to get totally comfortable with me. You get what I'm saying?" KD says yes.

John takes her soapy loofah sponge and says, "Turn around so I can wash your back and that ass." KD keeps her arms over her breasts as she turns around.

John says, "You're so beautiful, Ladybug, relax!" as he rubs her with the towel.

KD says, "I knew you would make sure I'm prepared."

John asks, "What do you mean?"

KD says, "You push me past my comfort zone, but you always know what to say and what to do to make it okay."

John asks, "Are you okay with me being in here with you?"

KD says, "No, but I don't want you to leave."

John says, "Good because I don't want to leave." He kisses her neck; he says, "My turn, Ladybug!"

KD grabs her wash cloth. She washes his whole body. She tells him, "You're so sexy!"

John says, "I'm glad you think so!"

KD and John kiss as they stand under the water. John tells KD, "I'll leave, so you can finish your business. When you're done, meet me in the bedroom."

KD says, "Okay, baby! See you in a minute!" With him gone, KD can relax and finish her beauty routine.

John dries off and wraps a towel around his waist before he goes to his bathroom to brush his teeth. John shampoos his beard and head before washes his face. John looks at himself in the mirror, making sure he looks good for KD. He rubs moisturizer on his face before he leaves out his restroom. He puts a little Vaseline on his lips. John puts on lotion and a pair of underwear. He lays on his bed and turns on sports news.

As John awaits KD, the doorbell rings. John looks at the doorbell's camera feed to see Raina who is drunk. John's heart skips a beat as he rushes to put on a t-shirt and a pair of jogging pants.

Raina bangs on the door and repeatedly rings the doorbell. John is furious. He doesn't want KD to hear Raina at the door.

John opens the door and asks, "What the fuck are you doing here? You need to take your ass home." KD hears the chaos and sneaks out of John's bedroom door. She hides behind the wall at the top of the stairs to listen to the conversation.

Raina says with an attitude, "You won't answer my call, and I know you know it's me calling. You're ignoring me because you're too busy being in love with your new bitch. You never ignored me before. What's so special about her?"

John says, "We're in a relationship, a committed, faithful relationship. I'm not answering the phone for some bullshit."

Raina says, "Bullshit! John, that's what I am to you, now? Was I bullshit when you were calling to ask me to come fuck you? I can't believe you're happy with some simple, old bitch. She has nothing on me. I look better than her. I make more money than her. I know she can do what I do."

John says, "Girl, you have lost your mind! My girl is a bad, bad bitch. She obviously has you feeling a way because you're worried about her, and she gives no fucks about you. My girl is lacking in nothing, and in no category does my girl come second to you. I don't have the time to tell you all the ways my girl is ahead of the game. But I'll tell you what she's not, and that's a sack-chasing, money-hungry, evil, lying, manipulative, dingy bitch. Take your irrelevant ass home, so I can get back to my incredibly fascinating, beautiful woman. And trust she does that way better than you."

Raina says, "That's what you think of me after the year we spent together, John? We were so good together. I miss you. I can't stand living without you. Don't you miss me?"

John says, "Raina, I'm sorry you're hurting, but I'm happy in my new situation and I am not looking back, left, or right. Coming here only aggravates your pain. You need to leave."

Raina starts crying; she asks, "How could you toss me aside as if I meant nothing to you?"

John says, "Raina, you made this happen. You made deceitful moves."

Raina says, "You still love me. You may think you love her, but you don't."

John says, "First, I never told you I loved you. Second, I do love her, and there's nothing anyone can do to change that. Third, she's my woman. You were someone I fucked."

Raina says, "I know you love me, John. There's no doubt about that."

John says, "You make shit up in your head. We were cool. We had a nice time, but it's over."

Raina says, "She's here, isn't she, John?"

John says, "Yes, she lives here! This is her home, so you need to take your drunk ass home."

Raina says, "Tell her how you used to make love to me day and night for a year in that bed. Tell her all the things you said to me. Tell her how good I made you feel, and how much you loved being with me."

John says, "Raina, I'm in love with someone else. She's who I want to be with. The first time we were together, you said you understood there was no commitment and we were just friends. I'm in a committed relationship now, so the thing we had is over."

Raina says, "John, I'll tell her then." Raina screams, "Katie, John is my man, so don't get too comfortable."

John looks perplexed when Raina says Katie. It wasn't quite right, but it was too close for comfort. He knows Raina has been lurking.

Raina says, "Oh, yes, I know her name. I know she's a nurse. I know which hospital she works at. I know she drives a black Audi."

John tries with all his might to remain calm; he says, "Raina, your lurking, nosey ass needs to leave before you upset my girl."

Raina says, "Damn, you care that much about her feelings in just a few months? We spent every day together for a year, and this is how you're treating me?"

John says, "I'm not trying to hurt you, but I have to take care of my home and make sure my girl is happy. She is innocent. She had nothing to do with our friendship ending, so it would be unfair to upset her."

Raina says, "I don't give a fuck about upsetting her. What the fuck are you saying? John, why should I let the best man I've ever had go to make another bitch happy? Fuck that! You belong to me. You are supposed to be with me."

John is done being cordial. John says in a harsh tone, "I'm not about to stand here and engage in this dumbass conversation with your drunk ass. I don't know how else to tell you I don't want you. You don't have to go home, but you need to get the fuck away from here, so I can go back to enjoying my woman in our home."

Raina says, "Damn, that's how you talk to me, now? She got you that in love?"

John says, "Yes, she does! [John is frustrated with Raina. His tone becomes forceful.] Now, take your drunk ass home."

Raina says, "Damn you, John! Fuck you! Fuck your bitch! Fuck your relationship!"

John says, "Go home!"

Raina says, "John, you're a piece of shit. Karma is a bitch, and she will get your ass for this. This is not over. You cold-hearted son of a bitch.

You're right, I loved you, but you never loved me." Raina goes to get in her car.

John says, "Exactly," as he waves goodbye with a smile on his face.

He yells, "You drunk driver. I hope the police pull you over." John eases into the house. He slowly closes and locks the door, making as little noise as possible.

When KD hears the door close, she rushes into the bathroom. He quietly rushes upstairs. John undresses and eases into bed, hoping KD didn't hear any of that. KD peeks out the door to see him lying in bed, watching TV. She looks at herself in the mirror before going out of the door.

When KD walks out of the bathroom, John turns off the TV and sits up; he says, "Girl, get your fine ass over here." KD crawls in the bed and onto John's lap.

John says, "Ladybug, you look like an angel in all that white lace. He hugs her. You smell so good." She wraps her arms around his neck; he says, "Kiss me, baby," as his hands rub her thighs and butt.

Although KD heard the entire conversation between Raina and John, she subtly asks, "Who was at the door?"

John is disappointed that she heard that; he answers, "An unwanted, uninvited guest."

KD asks, "A female?" John pauses. KD says, "It's okay, baby, you can tell me!"

John says, "Yes!"

KD asks, "What's her name? Who is she?"

John says, "Her name is Raina Rhimes, the morning news anchor."

KD says, "And?"

John says, "Nothing!" KD's facial expression says, I want to know more.

John says, "Look, Ladybug, I don't fuck with her anymore. She was drunk, in her feelings, but I let her know it's you and me."

KD asks, "Did you love her? Were you two serious?"

John says, "It was casual. We were friends."

KD says, "Ending a relationship can be hard. Are you okay? Do you need to talk about it?"

John says, "About what?" KD looks at him.

John says, "KD, I'm not thinking about her. I haven't been communicating with her. Things happened before I met you that caused the end of our friendship.

"I should've stuck to my first mind when I cut off communication. I was wrong for having sex with her that last time knowing I didn't want to mess with her anymore. I never led her to believe we were more than friends. For me, it was just sex and companionship. We were cool, but she has some ways I don't like.

"When I met you, I ended all communication with her. Do not think I strung her along or was seeing both of you. The minute I met you, I totally committed to pursuing you. You are who I want. I want you, Ladybug, no one else. Don't let her get to you, Ladybug. We had a really good day. Let's get back to enjoying our day."

KD says, "John, you are who I want. I never want to bring drama or stress to your life. I don't want to come between you and other obligations and commitments. Are you sure you're not committed to her or still desire to be with her?"

John says, "We hung out for a year, but there was never a commitment or deep feelings. Ladybug, it is over. I do not want to be with her."

KD says, "If you can look me in my eyes, and tell me with all sincerity that you are committed to me and there's no other woman in your life, we never have to have a conversation about other women again. I trust you, John. I believe you when you say you've been honest."

John looks in KD's eyes; he says, "There is and will be no other woman. I have kept it real with you since day one. I want to be in this committed relationship with KD Daniels."

KD looks in John eyes; she says, "John, I appreciate your honesty and openness. I believe you have been honest with me. To be fair, I will reciprocate your pledge. I have been honest with you. There is and will be no other man because I am totally committed to you."

John says, "Ladybug, I appreciate that. I trust you, and I am happy that you trust me."

KD extends her pinky finger; she says, "We never have to have this conversation again." John locks pinky with hers.

John says, "I promise cheating and lying are not and will never be issues for us." KD promises the same thing.

KD says, "Remember the kiss you asked for?"

John smiles and says yes. She kisses John with so much passion that he immediately falls under her spell and forgets all about Raina. KD's hands touch all over John as they kiss for an hour. John holds her close, making sure she knows he doesn't ever want to let her go.

They are so in need of each other and so full of emotions that neither can take another minute without feeling each other. John reaches for the condoms on his nightstand. They kiss as John puts the condom on. John rolls KD on her back.

She watches him in the mirrored ceiling kiss across her lower abdomen as he removes her panties. He slowly kisses up her side. She jumps and says it tickles. He slowly sucks from just below her breast to her hip to tickle her even more. She giggles as he leaves small passion marks on her side before he kisses up to her ear.

John whispers in her ear, "I want to do things to you in a way they've never been done to make you feel better than anyone has ever made you feel. Is that all right with you?"

KD says, "Yes!"

John says, "Hold me, baby! Don't let me go!" She tightly wraps her arms around him. He adds, "Kiss me, baby!"

As they kiss, John slowly slides into KD. He wraps her legs around his waist. John takes slow, deep strokes to engage all KD's nerves. The sound of KD moaning and breathing in his ear encourages him to give her more pleasure.

John softly touches and kisses all over her as he repeatedly glides all the way to the end of her. KD feels him all through her inner being, and the feel of him feels so good that she can barely stand it. She watches John move in the mirrored ceiling and it turns her on even more. She whispers, "John Michael King, you are majestic," to express her gratitude.

While KD and John are preoccupied with love, John's neighbor, Jack Smith, comes in late from a date. Movement on John's boat catches his eye. Jack calls out, "Hey!" startling the two invaders dressed in all black with their faces covered in black ski masks. The two intruders take off running. They aren't carrying anything, so Jack assumes he stopped a burglary. Jack goes into his house and forgets about the incident.

The next morning, KD is curious about Raina Rhimes. She pulls out her phone to look her up. KD sees professional images of Raina used for news promos. KD is impressed by her youthful beauty. Nanette walks over to KD and ask what she is looking at. KD explains what happened when John's ex popped up last night. Nanette says, "If you want to find out about someone, look at their social media pages."

Nanette pulls out her phone and searches for Raina social media pages. Nanette gives her phone to KD, she says, "Here's everything you need to know." KD looks through pictures and the pictures trigger memories. As KD looks through the pictures, she remembers seeing Raina at the skating rink. She also remembers Raina bumped into the table at the restaurant while John was in the restroom. KD now knows that Raina has been lurking.

KD scrolls to pictures of Raina and John. She looks at the dates. The pictures of Raina and John align with the dates John said the relationship started and ended. It's hard to see John cozy and close to another woman, but KD remains level-headed. Nanette says, "Don't let her bother you. We all have a past. He likes you and she popped up because she knows he likes you."

KD closes the app and hands Nanette her phone. KD says, "I told John I trust him, so I'm going to trust him."

Nanette is impressed by KD loyalty. Nanette says, "Oh, you really like him,"

KD says, "I do! That's crazy right!"

Nanette says, "No, it's not crazy. John likes you too. It's a good thing. Besides, what is not to like about him."

KD says, "The man is perfect!"

John makes it to Daniel's game as promised. As the team warms up, Daniel looks to the stands to see John sitting with his mother and grandmother. Daniel smiles from ear to ear as he waves at them. They wave back at him. Daniel's coach has the team take a knee for a pregame pep talk. Daniel listens to his coach, but he is more concerned with impressing John. He knows he must play hard to impress John.

Daniel's team wins the kick-off. The ball rolls in Daniel's direction. Daniel kicks the ball to a team mate who makes the first goal. John is the biggest cheerleader in the stands. John's loud cheers inspire Daniel to play harder. John tells KD, "Little Man is good!"

KD says, "He's happy you're here!" By the end of the game, Daniel has three assists and two goals. Mrs. Daniels and KD hug and kiss Daniel. John and Daniel high-five.

After the game, John walks Mrs. Daniels to her car. Mrs. Daniels hugs John and thanks him. He opens her door, helps her in the car and tells her to drive safely. He says, "Call KD to let us know you made it home safely."

Mrs. Daniels says, "OK, Son, see you later." She waves at KD and Daniel before she pulls off. John gets in the car with KD and Daniel.

As KD drives, Daniel asks John if he would like to go to the arcade to eat pizza and ride the bumper cars to celebrate the win. John says, "It's up to your mother!"

Daniel says, "Momma, would you please drive yourself home and let us use your car to go to the arcade, so we can get to know each other? You know, have guy time."

KD says, "Well, Son, will you at least bring your mother a slice of pizza?"

Daniel says, "Ask Mr. King to bring you a hamburger and fries. He's your boyfriend. I'm just a kid." John laughs.

KD says, "It's like that, Son!"

Daniel says, "I'm just saying, he's your boyfriend, so he's responsible for you!"

John says, "He's right! You're my responsibility. I will bring you something to eat."

Daniel says, "Mr. King, my momma will eat pizza, but it's not her favorite. She prefers burgers and fries. Pizza is my favorite."

John says, "Thanks for the information. Please, Little Man, call me John."

Daniel says, "My mother would not like me calling you by your first name."

John looks at KD. He says, "Tell Daniel it's okay to call me John. We are passed the formalities stage."

KD says, "Daniel, John says you can call him John, so it's okay to call him John."

John says, "It's cool, Daniel, I promise your mother won't get mad."

Daniel says, "Okay! John, do you feel like hanging out with me?"

KD asks John, "Do you have time to hang with him?"

John says, "I do!"

KD says, "Are you sure?"

John says, "Yes, I am sure. I'll come through and hang with you tonight."

KD says, "All right, I'll drive myself home."

Daniel says, "Yes! We are going to have a lot of fun."

John says, "You know it, Little Man!" They fist-bump.

KD drives herself home; she says, "Have fun and be safe!"

In unison, John and Daniel say, "We will!"

KD says, "Daniel James, mind your manners! You have money, so don't ask John for anything."

Daniel says, "It's my treat!"

John says, "KD, don't worry. We will be safe!"

KD goes upstairs to her apartment and soon falls asleep on the couch. A little peace and quiet give KD exactly what she needed: rest.

Daniel and John talk about sports and school as they eat pizza. John tells Daniel he has talent. Daniel says, "I'm hoping sports will help me earn scholarships, so my mother won't have to work so hard to pay for college. My father will not help her pay my college tuition. I want to be an engineer, a scientist, or a doctor. I'm not sure yet. My sister says if I become a doctor, I will get a beautiful girlfriend because beautiful girls like smart guys."

John says, "She's right."

Daniel says, "That's why I have to go to college, so I can get a lot of girls."

John says, "Don't worry about your mother struggling to pay for college. You focus on being the best student and athlete you can be, and everything else will fall into place."

Daniel asks, "So you like, like my mother? Is she your girlfriend or are you two just friends?"

John says, "Our relationship is more than friends. She's my girlfriend. Are you cool with that?"

Daniel says, "As long as you're good to her and make her happy, I'm good. She deserves a good man to provide for her and protect her. She's a good woman. Does she make you happy?"

John says, "She does!"

Daniel says, "As long as you're both happy, I'm happy."

John says, "Thank you for being supportive, and you're right, your mother is a good woman."

Daniel says, "You seem like a good dude. You deserve a good woman. My mother is a good spouse. She is loyal, kind, and nice. She cares about people and their well-being. She's a good listener. She keeps the house clean, she cooks very well, and takes care of herself. She can't play video games to save her life, but I guess no one has it all.

"My dad always complains how his girlfriend doesn't do anything as well as my mother. He always tells me: [Daniel mocks his dad's voice.] 'Boy, be careful chasing a pretty face and nice body. I left my good wife for her. She can't cook for shit, she doesn't clean shit, and she let her body go to shit. When I met her, she was shaped like an hour glass. Now, she is shaped like a linebacker.

"Your mother made three meals every day. I always came home to a clean house. Your mother is thick in the hips, and got that dip. [Daniel moves his hands to outline a woman's curvy body.] She's just thick. Thick all over, her face, neck, arms. It's not what I signed up for, Son.' John laughs.

"My mom is super smart. She even understands the metric system, fractions, decimal numbers, and geometry. When I was in the third grade, the whole class got an F on the homework except me because their mothers couldn't add fractions with unlike denominators. The more you get to know my mother, you'll see she's perfect except her video game skills. I'm not saying that because she's my mother. It's all true."

John says, "She is perfect. I can see that already."

Daniel says, "My sister thinks you two are the perfect couple."

John says, "I'm glad you and your sister accept our relationship."

Daniel says, "Even though my mom works all the time, I could tell something was going on. She was smiling more, sneaking out in the middle of the night, and on the phone well into the morning. I wanted to know who she was talking to so much. I figured out her code a long time ago. It's 0901. That's my birthday.

"She left her phone on the table one day. I read your text messages. I'm sure I wasn't supposed to read some of them, but I couldn't help myself. Did you know she keeps all your text messages?" [John smiles.]

Daniel continues, "Really! She has never deleted one, but, please, don't tell her I read the racy messages, she would not like that." [John apologizes for the racy messages.] Daniel adds, "It was my fault. I shouldn't have been snooping. She's an adult. Of course, she's going to use adult words and have adult feelings. I had to look up some things to understand what you two were saying."

John thanks him for being understanding. Daniel explains, "I got your number from her call history. I reversed looked up the number, got your name, and did a deep social media dig. I had to make sure you weren't a psycho."

John says, "Did you approve of what you read?"

Daniel says, "I read a lot of vulgar yet complimentary posts from women. I read that you're a player, and you have a ton of women. That made me concerned, but I understand it's complicated being a man and men struggle with temptation.

"When you changed your status to in a relationship, I felt better. When a man posts about a female, it's serious. You publicly made a statement that you are taken when you posted her name and picture. When I met you, you were way cooler than I expected. That made me feel even better. I like that my mother has you to take her out and show her a good time."

John says, "Am I encroaching on your quality time?"

Daniel says, "No! I like that she has something to make her smile. I like you, and I'm glad it's my mother that makes you smile."

John thanks him and asks, "Do you have a girlfriend?"

Daniel says, "Yes, but the girl I really like is in the seventh grade. Her name is Breonna. She is so fine, but I know she'll never talk to a fifth grader. My girlfriend is Naomi. She's cute and all, but fifth grade girls are immature. I like middle school girls. The way they wear their hair, paint their nails, their bodies are so curvy, they're uniform skirts are so short that you can almost see everything, and they walk with so much confidence."

John says, "You are a mature, intelligent, young man. You should believe in yourself. If you want Breonna, you can get Breonna. You just have to get her to see you, not your age or grade. You need to get her attention. You can start by finding out what she likes, and talk to her about it. Once Breonna sees you, she'll be all over you."

Daniel asks, "Really? It's that easy?"

John says, "Girls want to feel special. If you show an interest in her interests, she will feel special to you. You're smart, talented, nice, and kind, so you have a lot working in your favor."

Daniel says, "We need to talk more often. My mother tries to keep me a baby, so she doesn't teach me about boy-girl stuff."

John says, "We will spend more time together. Let's hit the games and bumper cars before your mother calls to check on us, Little Man."

Daniel says, "This is going to be fun!"

John and Daniel have fun playing games and driving the bumper cars. By the time they make it back to KD's apartment, they are best friends. They walk into the apartment laughing. John has a burger and fries for KD from Coney Island. Daniel excitedly tells his mother how much fun he had with John as she eats her fries. KD smiles at her son's happiness. She thanks John for spending time with him.

With Daniel away for the weekend and KD having the night off, KD and John decide to have a date night. They go to KD's favorite restaurant.

While they're waiting on their food, John recognizes one of his father's best friends sitting across the room. John says, "Ladybug, excuse me for a minute. I see my father's best friends. I haven't seen him in a few years. I'm going to go over and say hi. I'll be right back."

KD says, "Okay," and she sips her wine. She watches John greet the man with a handshake and a hug. They seem very happy to see each other and their happiness makes her happy. She smiles watching them talk. Suddenly, she feels someone standing over her. She instantly gets a creepy feeling when a deep voice says, "KD Jacobs, it surely has been a long time." That voice sends a chill down her spine.

KD turns to look up and straight into the face of her nightmare, Dr. Rothman Segal. Her smile is immediately turned into a frown, and her happiness into disgust. She hates Dr. Segal with all her heart and mind. It could be that Dr. Segal resembles KD's ex-husband, or the fact that Dr. Segal sexually harassed KD for years. Either way, the sight of him repulses her. It's been seven years since the last time she seen him, and she still can't stand the sight of him. Dr. Segal has a way of making her feel uncomfortable, uneasy, and endangered. KD can't even fake a smile.

Dr. Segal says, "How have you been, Jacobs?"

KD begrudgingly says, "Hello!"

Dr. Segal says, "You look well!"

KD says, "I am." Dr. Segal gives her the smile she hates as he sits in John's chair. He scoots closer to KD. KD says, "My man is not going to appreciate you sitting there."

Dr. Segal says, "He won't mind if we chat a bit."

KD is very irritated; she says, "He's going to mind very much, so you should leave." John sees a man sitting with KD and he notices her irritated face. John is not happy about the way the man looks at her. Dr. Segal's lustful eyes scope KD from head to toe. John promises to check on his dad's friend soon before saying goodbye.

Dr. Segal sticks out his hand; he says, "Mrs. Jacobs, I'd like to apologize for the way things went the last time we saw each other. I didn't mean to offend you. I apologize for my actions."

KD looks at his hand; she says, "You should leave before my man gets back. He is very, very possessive, and he doesn't allow me to talk to other men."

John makes it to the table before Dr. Segal can blink. Dr. Segal is waiting for KD to accept his hand, but John pops out of nowhere, sticks his hand in Dr. Segal's hand, and firmly shakes it.

KD sips her wine and says, "I told you!"

John says, "I'm John, KD's man, and you are?"

Dr. Segal says, "I'm an old friend."

KD's frown twists even harder. She mumbles, "We were never friends," as she sips her wine.

John says, "Well, Old Friend," as John squeezes Dr. Segal's hand harder. He adds, "I need to take my place at my table with my woman, and we need to be alone." John lets go of his hand.

Dr. Segal says, "Excuse me! I didn't see a ring."

John says, "You're too preoccupied with everything else to see her hand." Dr. Segal stands up. John asks KD, "Are you okay?"

KD says, "Now that you're here!"

Dr. Segal says, "Take care, KD!"

John says, "She is well cared for. I take damn good care of my woman."

Dr. Segal is irritated by John's presence. He leaves the table very disappointed. John swaps the chair Dr. Segal sat in with one from another table. John puts the new chair in the proper position. John asks, "Who was that?"

KD says, "He's a surgeon. He used to work at the hospital, but we were never friends."

John says, "What did he say?"

KD says, "He apologized for something that happened a long time ago."

John asks, "What did he do to you? Do you want me to fuck him up?"

KD says, "No, it was a long time ago. For years, he made my work life hell. The night he is referring to, he went too far. It was my turn to do inventory. I was in the storage closet by myself. He comes in pretending he was looking for something. He was talking. I wasn't listening. I dropped something. He bent down to pick it up. He said here you go. I reached out my hand without looking.

"What he sat in my hand did not feel like what I dropped. I looked and he was standing there smiling with his little thing in my hand. I jumped back so fast that I knocked over some shelves. Everyone rushed in just in time to see him hurrying to put his little thing away. I bleached my hand one hundred times that night. I felt so violated, disgusted. To avoid a big scandal, the hospital asked him to quietly leave."

John says, "That nasty, arrogant motherfucker."

KD says, "I don't know what he thought was going to happen. Maybe he thought I would be so enamored with him that I would leave my husband."

John says, "I'm going to let him know not to come near you," as he stands up. KD stops him.

KD says, "Baby, it's okay! I'm okay! It's not worth getting upset."

John says, "Your well-being is worth everything to me."

KD says, "You came and made him leave, that's enough. Besides, he is with his wife. He's not going to say anything else. Baby, please don't leave me. Sit down and let's enjoy our date night." John and Dr. Segal look at each other with grim sneers as John sits back down.

Dr. Segal can't stop staring at KD. KD feels his eyes on her, but she focuses on John. Dr. Segal's wife gets frustrated with his preoccupation with KD. His wife insists he stops looking in her direction. Dr. Segal tries to focus on his wife, but his attention is drawn to KD until she and John get into John's car to go to the club to hang with his sons.

CHAPTER TWO

It's the start of summer, and Detroit is heating up like John and KD's relationship. With KD having more free time, she and John have been spending a lot of time together.

KD arrives at the park to pick up John. John and his friends are deciding who will play on which team for the last game. The sight of KD captures John's friends' attention immediately. John turns around to see what has his friends mesmerized. He smiles and says, "Here comes my Ladybug!" John walks over to greet her.

KD says, "Hello, baby!"

John says, "I know I'm sweaty, but hug my neck." KD wraps her arm around his neck. John says, "Kiss me like you missed me!" KD kisses him while his friends watch. John asks, "How has your day been?"

KD says, "So far, so good!"

John says, "You are gorgeous. I love your hair. The curls are cute."

KD says, "Thank you!"

John says, "Ladybug, come meet my friends."

KD says, "Okay!" John grabs her hand and leads her over to his friends who can't take their eyes off her or her pretty, white dress.

John says, "Fellas, this is my girlfriend, KD. KD, these are my friends: Troy, Rocco, Castle, Samuel, Stanley, Warren, and Matthews. We've known each other since middle school."

They all say hello as they stare at KD. KD waves and says hello to everyone.

John says, "Fellas, I'm going to talk to my woman for a second." The men start shooting hoops, trying not to stare too hard at KD as she and John walk away.

John walks KD to her car parked adjacent the court, KD asks John, "What did you tell your friends about me?"

John asks, "Nothing, Ladybug, why do you ask that?"

KD replies, "Why are they looking at me like that?"

John says, "You think they are looking at you because they heard something. No, Ladybug! They are looking at all that ass, those thighs, and your titties sticking out of that little, pretty, white dress. The only difference between them and me is I know what it looks and feels like under that dress."

KD laughs. She says, "You're bad!"

John says, "Ladybug, is it okay if we play one more game?"

KD says, "I'll be your cheerleader."

John says, "I promise I'm done after that, and we can go carry out our plans for the day."

KD says, "Okay, have a good game."

John kisses her; he says, "Thanks, Ladybug!"

John runs onto the court. His friends immediately start mocking him. Troy says, "Girlfriend!"

Rocco says, "My woman!"

John says, "Don't mock my relationship!" They all repeat the word relationship. John says, "Yes, we are in a committed relationship. KD is my baby."

Troy asks, "Did she drug you? Are you in need of help? Blink once for no and twice for yes."

Rocco says, "She put something in your drink, right? You're talking crazy talk: girlfriend, woman, relationship. You don't use words like that."

Castle says, "You shouldn't play with her like that, King. She seems like a nice woman."

John says, "No one is playing. KD and I have something real."

Stanley says, "King, are you saying you're ready to settle down?"

Matthews says, "Hey, two age-appropriate single people find love. It's beautiful and natural. Don't be so judgmental."

Samuel says, "King, I'm proud of you. I am happy for you."

Castle says, "I'll believe it if it lasts more than a year."

John says, "Don't do me like that, Cas!"

Rocco says, "King, you're really retiring from the game?"

John says, "I'm out! I have my soulmate."

Rocco repeats, "Soulmate?" Rocco is shocked.

Troy says, "It's a sad, sad day! One of the greats is retiring."

Matthews says, "Leave the man alone!"

Rocco says, "Seeing her in that dress, I see why you want to settle down."

John says to Rocco, "Don't be disrespectful! Don't look at her like that."

Rocco says, "I didn't look intentionally. You can't miss her, King!"

John laughs and says to Rocco, "Don't objectify my woman."

Troy says, "She is fine as fuck, King. You can't help but notice her." They all turn to look at KD, sitting in her car. When she looks up from her phone, John smiles and waves.

John says, "I know, Troy! She is a wonderful sight to see."

Matthews says, "Get out of the man's business and let's play ball."

They start the game. KD claps and cheers every time John makes a good play. When Castle pushes John, making him fall, KD yells, "Hey! Don't push him," with a stern and concerned tone. KD asks, "Baby, are you okay?" John looks at her and smiles. John give her a thumb up.

Troy says, "Keep fucking with her man, and she's going to pop your ass."

Rocco says, "Looks like she is reaching under the seat."

Matthews says, "John, at least you know she'll have your back!"

John says, "I'm trying to tell you this is different!"

Castle says, "Get your lying ass up and let's play ball."

After the game, John gets in her car. Before they pull off, KD asks, "Why did Castle push you like that? I didn't like that. It didn't seem friendly. It seemed intentional and malicious."

John answers, "Cas has always been jealous of my wealth. He'll never see me or my work. When he looks at me, he only sees what he doesn't have."

KD says, "Baby, is that really a friend?"

John says, "It's a side effect of being a rich kid trying to fit in. I've accepted his jealousy as a part of our friendship."

KD says, "I don't like him."

John says, "Cas is harmless!"

KD says, "Something about the way he looks at you gives me an evil vibe. It seems like he wants to hurt you. Will you be careful around him for me?"

John says, "Anything for you!"

KD smiles at John. She pulls off and drives to John's house. As soon as they walk through the door, John grabs and kisses her. He says, "I'm getting sweat all over your white dress, but I can't help myself. You are so sexy." He lifts her up and kisses her; he says, "I'm going to go take a shower. You should go up to my room, take off all your clothes, get into bed, and let me make love to you until your body is too weak to take anymore. What do you think about that?" He puts her down.

KD takes off her shoes and starts walking toward the stairs; she stops and says, "Sounds like a plan, but your family is expecting you to come to dinner tonight."

John says, "Let me text them right now to let them know we aren't going to make it. I'll see them tomorrow for Father's Day." When KD makes it to his bedroom, he watches her undress. He says, "Damn, Ladybug, you have no idea what you do to me. KD, you are fine, girl. Damn! I can't." She smiles and winks at him.

After his shower, John comes back into the room wearing a towel around his waist. He gets in bed. He removes the sheet covering KD. He admires her body as he touches her thighs. He says, "The entire time I was in the shower, all I could think about is touching and kissing you."

He kisses all over her body starting on her forehead and working his way down. When John gets to the middle, he stares in her eyes and licks her so deeply that he tickles her emotions.

He says, "I have my dinner right here. I'm good."

She smiles at him. He softly sucks her as his tongue sails around her like boat gently sailing upstream.

He says, "It's like licking to the center of a Tootsie Roll Pop."

KD says, "Don't bite it, baby!"

John says, "I won't bite it, baby. I'm going to lick it, suck it, and fuck it until you can't take any more."

KD says, "I'm going to enjoy that!"

John comes up, shyly smiling; he hesitantly asks, "Ladybug, may I ask you something?"

KD says, "Yes!"

John asks, "Do you still get your period?"

KD says, "Sporadically, why?"

John says, "I want to feel you."

KD says, "What do you mean?"

John says, "The condom, Ladybug, don't make me put it on!"

John reaches for his phone; he says, "I had a physical last week. I got a clean bill of health." He opens his medical chart app. KD reads his test results as John says, "I won't be with anyone else. You aren't going to be with anyone else. We are in a committed relationship. Ladybug, I will be faithful, I promise."

KD gives John his phone back; she asks, "What happens if you don't keep your promise?"

John says, "In business when two people want something from each other, they negotiate and come to an agreement that they both can live with."

KD says, "You want to create a contract regarding my sex?"

John says, "So to speak!"

KD says, "What terms do you want to agree on, Mr. King?"

John says, "We are in a committed relationship. I trust you and I want you to trust me. What will it take for you to trust me?"

KD says, "That depends on what you want from me. Spell it out in plain English exactly what you want from me."

John says, "I want to engage in unprotected sex with you for the remainder of our relationship."

KD says, "Do you plan to pull it out or leave it in?"

John says, "Which do you prefer?"

KD says, "What do you prefer?"

John says, "Leave it in!"

KD says, "If I agree to give you what you want, how will I know you are keeping your promise to be faithful?"

John says, "KD, when I look at you, listen to you, touch you, talk to you, kiss you, or make love to you, I know I don't need anyone else. I hope you don't want anyone else."

KD says, "I'm the same person that was married, and I couldn't keep my husband faithful. What would be different with you?"

John says, "I'm not him. Ladybug, you and I are not you and him."

KD says, "Point taken!"

John says, "I've never felt this way before, and something tells me you haven't either."

KD says, "True, but John, you are a man, you know how quickly a man changes his mind."

John says, "Can we agree to talk before we stray outside the relationship? If you want someone else, you let me know before you make a move, and I'll do the same."

KD says, "I can agree to that, but what happens if you break the contract?"

John says, "Whatever you want."

KD says, "John, I don't want your money if that's what you're thinking. I want you. It's not that I don't trust you. It's not you, baby, it's me!" John feels the sincerity in KD's word. John knows KD means that and that's another way KD set herself apart from the other women seeking John's affection. With KD, it is never about his money.

John kisses her hand and up her arm; he says, "Ladybug, I get that. You have every reason not to trust any man, but it's on me to reassure you. I will prove my fidelity. All I need from you is a chance. I got the rest."

KD says, "John, baby, don't hurt me!"

John kisses from her neck down to her breasts; he says, "I'm not going to hurt you!"

KD says, "If you cheat, this is over. I can't go back to that life."

John continues to kiss her as he says, "Losing you is not something I want."

KD caresses his back as she says, "I don't want that either. John, promise you won't hurt or leave me."

John says, "I promise I won't hurt you and I am damn sure I won't leave you. Ladybug! Kiss me, baby!"

KD says, "You kiss me!" John moves toward her face. KD pushes his face away; she says, "Not those lips!"

John says, "I just!"

KD abruptly interrupts, "Didn't you ask me for a favor?"

John says, "You're right. I got you, Ladybug!"

KD says, "You always do!"

KD watches John taste her; she says, "You're so good to me, baby." John winks at her.

KD and John hold hands as his tongue conveys his closing argument. KD says, "Oh My God, John! Baby!" She squeezes his hands as the pleasure he is giving convinces her to let John have his way. She looks up to watch them in the mirrored ceiling.

John moans, "Mm-hmm," as he consumes KD making tears roll down her face. Her body shudders and folds from the overpowering bliss she feels.

John gently kisses her and asks, "Did I earn my favor?"

KD, catching her breath and wiping her tears, says, "Yes, you did!"

John moves close to her; he says, "I need to feel you, now!" John slowly enters her and immediately feels gratification from her tight, soft, warm, wet body snuggly surrounding him.

John says, "Shit! KD, baby, you feel incredible." John enjoys the feel of her for a moment. KD squeezes him to give him the full picture. John says, "That feels so good, Ladybug! Do that again!" She squeezes him with all her might. When she lets go, John begins to stroke. He says, "Do you feel me, baby?"

KD says, "Yes!"

John asks, "Do you like what you feel?"

KD says, "Yes, baby, I love it" as she holds onto his back, looking at the image of them making love in the mirrored ceiling.

John says, "Tell me what you like."

KD says, "John, don't make me say it. You know what I like."

John says, "No, Ladybug! I'm your man; feel free to tell me anything. I want you to tell me what you like and how you like it."

KD says, "I get so shy when I talk about sex."

John says, "Would you feel better if I go first?"

KD says, "Yes, tell me what you like?"

John says, "I love being with you. Like is not strong enough to describe how I feel about you. I'm addicted to being near you, inside you, and next to you. I love to touch your soft skin, your silky hair, and I love when I'm so deep inside you that I can feel your soul surrounding me. I love to hear you moan and the look in your eyes when you cum. Your eyes twinkle and dance while you climax. You have the sexiest reactions and expressions.

"I love when you're on top. You move so gracefully, but your energy is demanding and controlled. The curves of your body rolling on me is so sexy. You move and surround all of me with ease, and I feel every millimeter of you as you tightly squeeze me.

"You're a good girl, but you give head like a naughty girl. When you look up at me with those pretty eyes as your soft, pretty lips surround me, sliding up and down me while your tongue soothes me, my mind is blown. Baby, honestly, it's the best feeling in the world.

"I love the way you hold me and touch me. When you call me baby and moan in my ear, I try to beat your body with a vengeance and you take it. I love your femininity, how you carry yourself, the clothes you wear, your lingerie, the way you smell, and the way you taste. Most of all, I love the way you care for me. Now, look into my eyes and tell me what you like."

KD smiles and looks in his eyes; she says, "I love everything about being with you. I love your touch, your kisses, your stroke. Everything about you amazes me."

John says, "Be specific."

KD shyly says, "Look at your right hand. See where it is. I love it when you touch me there. I love your fingers on me and in me. Your hands are so strong yet soft, and they always touch the right spot at the right time, in the right way."

John says, "Got it! What else do you like?"

KD takes his left hand. She says, "I love when you kiss me here. [She makes his left hand rub the side of her neck.] There! [She makes his left hand touch her naval.] I love how you kiss these. I can never get enough of that. [She makes his left hand slowly rub across her breasts.] I love the attention you give my thighs, legs, and feet, but my favorite is when you kiss me here. [She makes his left hand touch her pelvic area.] I swear I have never felt anything like you."

John smiles and says, "I like that, too." KD says, "See where he is; go deeper, baby, right there! That spot right there, when he hits right there, it drives me crazy."

John says, "So, you like it right there?" KD says yes. John says, "Let me memorize that spot." KD squeezes him, so that he won't forget. John bites his lip. John says, "That feels so good!"

KD says, "I don't have any complaints. You are very skilled at what you do. I appreciate everything you do to make me feel good, and I love every way you give it to me. You always make me feel so good. But, oh my God, when you get it from the back, baby, you make category five hurricanes in my body."

John says, "Let me get it like that right now."

KD says, "It'll be my pleasure."

John says, "It's my favorite, too. I love the way you move when you give it to me!"

As KD turns over, John admires her body. John says, "Ladybug, you, your heart, your spirit, your body are so amazing! I have my own piece of heaven right here with you. KD, I don't want to ever lose this heaven!"

KD says, "I don't want to lose you." They kiss and John gets right back to the task at hand.

John grabs her by the throat while he bangs her body out. KD holds on to his arms as her body uncontrollably bounces.

KD says, "Pull my hair!"

John says, "Oh! Shit! Ladybug, you like that?"

KD says, "I love when you're aggressive, but I also love it when you're sweet and gentle."

KD's moans let John know he is giving her joy and pleasure. The more KD moans, the more John wants to break her shyness. John asks, "Is that too much?"

KD says, "I can take it, baby!"

John asks, "You can take it?"

KD says with a voice revealing the pleasure she feels, "Yes! Give it to me, baby, I can take!"

John says, "You never run, never quit, never scared! I love the way you give it to me."

John wants KD so entwined in his web that she won't ever want or need another man. John is telling her that he has everything she needs by the way that he is loving her. He is intent on wearing KD's body completely out.

By the third time John's eyes roll in the back of his head, John has accomplished his goal. KD lays on the bed shaking, out of breath, and exhausted. She and John look at each other. KD puts her hand on her forehead and rubs her fingers through her hair as she breathes heavily.

John kisses her. He asks, "Are you good, Ladybug?" She answers yes. John stares at her; he says, "Ladybug, what's that look on your face?"

KD says, "Nothing, baby!"

John asks, "Was that too much?"

KD's body is trying to regulate itself as she answers, "No!"

John is curious; he asks, "What's up? What's on your mind?" KD smiles at him. She touches his face and giggles. John says, "Tell me!" He lays on his side right next to KD, leaning on his elbow.

KD says, "Nothing," as she continues to laugh. She turns away from him. KD is exhausted and trying to rest.

John says, "What are you thinking, tell me?"

KD says, "Baby, sometimes a woman wants to keep her secrets secret."

John says, "Your secrets are safe with me. What's so funny? What's on your mind?"

KD says, "You really want to know?" John confirms that he wants to know. KD looks at him; she says, "I wasn't thinking. I was cuming too hard to think. Okay!"

John says, "That made you laugh?"

KD says, "All right, I'm going to explain it you. I laughed because my orgasm was so strong it made me high. Okay! Stop asking questions, baby, you're blowing my high."

John says, "Oh!"

KD asks, "Did you think it was something bad?"

John says, "I don't know what I thought, but I know I want to please you. I was wondering if I did."

KD says, "That look was the look of a blown mind. Hold me, baby, and let me enjoy my high." KD holds on to his arms as she closes her eyes. John kisses her before he closes his eyes.

On Sunday, KD and John go to church before going to John's grandsons' game. After the game, the family has a cookout at Kenna's house to celebrate Father's Day. When they get back to John's house, John talks KD into playing cards, which John quickly turns into a game of strip spades. KD has John down to his underwear while she is fully clothed. When KD wins another hand, he says, "You hustled me!"

KD says, laughing, "I never told you I couldn't play spades. You assumed you were better than me, so I went with it."

John asks, "Do you want my draws?"

KD says, "Keep your underwear for now, but later I might have to run them."

John says, "I want a rematch!"

KD says, "Baby, don't be like that. Don't be a sore loser."

John says, "Come here!" KD shakes her head no. KD knows what he wants. John reaches for her; he says, "Come here, Ladybug!" KD smiles. She pushes John's arm away. John tries to pull her to his side of the couch, but KD pushes back with her leg. John tugs at her leg, pulling her to his side of the couch.

John tickles KD. He says, "This is my payback." KD laughs as she tries to get away. When she manages to get free, she runs upstairs. John chases her. John catches her in his bedroom and throws her on the bed. John gets on top of her.

John continues to tickle her. KD says, "Okay, baby, you win." John keeps tickling her. KD says, "John, baby, I have to go to the bathroom. Stop! Babe!" John lets her up and she runs to the bathroom. As KD washes her hands, John comes in the bathroom. She looks at him. He doesn't speak. He lifts her up and puts her over his shoulder. He carries her out the bathroom.

KD says, "What are you doing?"

John says, "I'm about to blow your mind again."

They make love until they fall asleep. KD is awakened by a strange feeling in the middle of the night. She opens her eyes to see a shadow in the shape of a human near the bedroom door in the mirrored ceiling. When the shadow moves, KD quickly lifts her head to look. She doesn't see anything, but she feels like there was someone in the room. KD calms her racing heart beat with a deep breath. KD's movement prompts a sleeping John to reach out for her. KD settles in John's arm and goes back to sleep.

John calls KD as Henson drives toward Downtown. When KD answers the phone, John says, "Ladybug!"

KD says, "Hey, baby!"

John asks, "Will you hang out with me tonight?"

KD says, "Where are we going?"

John says, "Someone gave me tickets to a concert tonight. Are you down?"

KD says, "Of course! I'm always down to hang with you."

John says, "I'll pick you up at eight."

KD says, "All right...." Before KD could finish her sentence, there's a loud bump. After hitting a pothole, Henson immediately begins to struggle controlling the steering wheel.

As the SUV drifts toward the curb, John yells, "Oh! Shit!"

KD says, "What's wrong?" Henson loses all control. The car wobbles as the power steering goes out.

Henson presses the brakes, but a crash is inevitable. He says in a panic, "I can't stop the car!" Thump. Clink. Boom. The driver's side front axle breaks, making the car crash into a pole. Henson says, "Mr. King, are you okay?"

John says, "I'm fine. Are you hurt?"

Henson says, "No!"

KD asks, "John, is everything okay?"

John says, "Yes! We hit a pole." They get out the car to survey the damage.

KD asks, "Do you need me to pick you up?"

John says, "No, I'm good, Ladybug. You get back to work. I'll talk to you later."

KD says, "Baby, are you sure? I can take a break."

John says, "I'm good, I promise! Have a good day at work, call me on your lunch break, and I'll see you tonight."

KD says, "Okay, text me to let me know you made it to work. Be careful, baby."

John says, "I will," before they hang up.

Jayme picks up John. Henson rides in the tow truck to the repair shop. As the mechanic checks the car, he discovers strange markings near the ball bearing and axle. He tells Henson, "Someone has tampered with this axle." Henson calls John to tell him. John immediately thinks it's Raina.

John says, "Thank you for letting me know."

Henson says, "Do you need me to call the police?"

John says, "No, I'll handle it."

Henson says, "The car will be ready Monday morning. I'll pick it up."

John says, "Take the weekend off. Thank you for getting the car fixed. I'll be sure to reimburse you."

Henson asks, "Thank you! Are you sure you don't need anything?"

John says, "I'm spending the weekend with KD. That's all I need."

Henson says, "I will see you Monday, Mr. King."

John says, "Have a relaxing weekend!"

While John and KD enjoy the concert, a heavy rain pours over Downtown Detroit. By the end of the concert, an overflow of rain water floods the streets. John takes off his jacket. He hands it to KD to cover her head. KD says, "Do you want to get under here with me?"

John says, "Getting wet never hurt me!"

KD says, "I bet!" They walk out of the concert hall into the rain. KD asks, "Did you enjoy the concert?"

John answers, "Yes! She put on a good show!"

KD says, "It was lovely. She looked and sounded so great! Thanks for taking me!"

John says, "I wouldn't want to be with anyone else."

When they reach the corner, there is a puddle of water too large for KD to step over. KD is suddenly lifted without warning. John says, "I got you!"

KD says, "Thank you, baby!"

She puts John's jacket over their heads. John waits for the light to change. A few cars ride pass, avoiding the huge puddle of water. Just as the crossing sign indicates that John can walk, the mysterious black Benz rushes through the red light purposely splashing water all over John's pants.

John yells, "Hey! Motherfucker!" at the speeding car. He asks KD, "Did they get you?"

KD says, "I don't think so."

John says, "Ladybug, my pants are soaked!"

KD says, "I'm so sorry, baby!"

John says, "Ladybug, I need to go home to change my pants before we go to the club."

KD says, "Okay!"

When they pull into John's garage, KD looks at him. He smiles at her. He rolls down the windows before cutting off the car. He leaves the music playing. He opens the door to get out of the car, but she grabs his arm. John looks at her; he asks, "You need something?" She stares at him with a smiling face, still holding his arm.

He curiously asks, "Ladybug, what's wrong?" She doesn't answer. She shyly smiles at him. John says, "Ladybug, I'll be right back. I'll quickly change my pants, and come right back." John tries to get out the car, but she pulls his arm. John says, "KD, what's up with you?"

John asks, "Do you want to come in with me?" She shakes her head no. John says, "What's up?" KD looks at him with lust in her eyes. John sees the lustful look on her face. He knows what she wants. He licks his lips. He says in a low, sexy tone, "Tell me what you need." John gets back in the car and closes the car door. He repeats, "Tell me what you need." KD touches his face. John says, "Say it! Whatever you want, you know I will give it to you."

KD says, "I want you!"

John asks, "What do you want me to do?" KD kisses him.

KD says, "It shouldn't hurt, right! I mean, you're already wet, so some more won't hurt."

John says, "You want it, right here, right now?"

KD says, "What's the point of having a man who drives a Lamborghini if you can't ride in it?" KD kisses him as she gets into his lap.

John says, "Tell me what you want." He kisses her as her hands touch all over him. Now, John wants her. His hands rub her thighs. She kisses his neck and ear. He says, "I want to hear you say what you want."

KD whispers in his ear, "Make love to me, baby! In the car, on the car, then take me in the house and make love to me over and over again." They kiss as she unbuttons John's shirt.

John says, "Whatever you want, I will give it to you, whatever, whenever, wherever!"

KD asks, "John, do you know how I feel about you? How much I care about you? Baby, when I'm close to you, I feel an incredible way I can't verbalize. I love to see you come and hate to see you go. When I'm not with you, all I can think about is you. When I am away from you, all I want is to be back in your arms. I don't know what I'm trying to say, but do you understand what I mean?"

John says, "I get it. I feel the same way."

KD asks, "Am I ever too much? Do you ever get tired of being with me?"

John says, "Never! Why would you ask that?"

KD answers, "Because, I can never get enough of you. I want to be with you all the time, but I try not to monopolize your time."

John says, "Don't ever think that. I always want you with me. If you need me in any way for anything, I am going to show up for you. There are times I want you, but I don't say anything because I don't want you to think I come around just for that. I want you all day, all night, every day and every night. I can never get enough of you.

"And, to let you know I am so serious when I say whatever, whenever, wherever, I am going to fuck the shit out of you in this car, on the car then I'm going to take you in the house and fuck you from the kitchen to my bedroom. After tonight, you will know it's always okay to tell me what you want and trust I will give you exactly what you want the way you want it. Do you hear me, Ladybug?"

KD says, "Yes! I hear you."

John says, "I'm your man. It's on me to take care of you in every way."

KD says, "John, you take really good care of me and my son. I appreciate you so much."

She kisses him. John says, "I appreciate you!"

KD seductively says, "Baby!" as she nibbles on his ear.

KD is in heat and John can feel it. John leans his seat back knowing exactly what it meant when KD said baby. She kisses and nibbles on his neck as her nails rake over his chest and abs. Her hands slowly make their way to his pants. She unbuttons his pants as she sucks on his Adam's apple. Her hands take a hold of him and stroke him as she continues to suck his neck. John slides his hands up her dress into her panties. He pulls her panties to the side as they kiss.

John tightly holds her as he pushes into her. John asks, "Is this what you want?"

KD says, "Yes, baby!"

John says, "We're just getting started!"

John takes her from the front seat to the back seat, against the side of the car, and on the hood of the car before he takes her into the kitchen. By the time they make it to the kitchen, they are completely naked. John has her against the refrigerator, on the counter, and on the table before going to the living room where they make love on the couch. After the couch, they make love on the stairs. As promised, John makes love to KD from the car to his bed.

When John rolls over, KD is in a state of complete exhaustion. John pulls her to lie on his chest. By the time her head lands on his chest, she is sleep. John caresses her hair as he lays in the dark thinking about their relationship.

His phone rings. When he answers, Isaiah says, "Pops, I thought you and your girl were coming to the club! That's the second time you stood us up."

John says, "Son, my girl needed my full attention!"

Isaiah laughs before he replies, "All right, Pops! I get it. You had to take care of your girl."

John says, "That's what a King does!"

Isaiah says, "You taught us how to wear the crown and provide royal treatment. I love you, Pops!"

John says, "I love you, Son!"

Isaiah says, "Tell, Ms. KD, hello!"

John says, "She's asleep!" Isaiah laughs.

Isaiah says, "Oh, you gave her that royal treatment!"

John says, "Most definitely."

Isaiah says, "Well, in the morning, tell her we missed her last night."

John says, "I will!"

Isaiah says, "Go to sleep, old man! I'll talk to you later."

John says, "Be good, Son!" John hangs up the phone, kisses KD's forehead, and falls asleep.

KD is leaving the grocery store with bags of groceries in her hands after a long day at work. It's late, she's tired and anxiously trying to get home to Daniel and John who are at her apartment playing video games. A black SUV slowly rides beside her as she walks to the car.

At first, the SUV doesn't register on her danger radar. When the SUV continues to move abnormally slow, she speeds up to put some space between herself and the vehicle. KD makes it to her car. The lurking SUV parks next to her car. She pops the trunk to place her bags in the trunk. She hears the driver's side door of the SUV slam. KD closes her trunk and quickly moves to get into her car. The driver calls her name. When she looks up, she sees Dr. Segal smiling at her. Dr. Segal says, "Your boyfriend let you come out alone this late?"

KD is uninterested in having a conversation with him. Her face can't hide it. She says, "He is never far." KD is trying to get into her car before Dr. Segal can say something else.

Dr. Segal says, "I want to finish our conversation. You never said if I am forgiven."

KD says, "I really need to get home to my man, so I can't converse."

Dr. Segal says, "Five minutes, Ms. KD, I know you can spare five minutes." Before KD can respond, her phone rings. It's John.

KD answers the phone, "Yes, baby," ensuring Dr. Segal hears her. She says to Dr. Segal, "I have to go!" She rushes to close and lock the door. She starts the car and backs out.

John asks, "Where are you and who are you talking to?"

KD says, "I'm leaving the grocery store down the street. The dirty doctor."

John says, "I'm on my way."

John hangs up his phone without giving KD a chance to speak. John rushes to his car and speeds to the store. When he gets there, Dr. Segal is putting his bags in his car. John walks over to him.

Before Dr. Segal can get in his car, John calls out to him, "Old Friend, KD is taken. It's very disrespectful that you won't respect that. She doesn't want to engage in a conversation with you. Whatever you're reaching for, it's not there. Don't come near her. Don't look at her. Don't talk to her. Respect our relationship as you would like a man to respect your relationship with your wife. And, that incident that took place seven years ago better be the last time you disrespect my woman. She is my responsibility now. I'm not her ex-husband. I will protect mine. Do we have an understanding?"

Dr. Segal says, "I will not talk to her anymore."

John says, "Thank you!"

John walks back to his car and pulls off. John drives back to KD's apartment. When he walks through the door, KD is sitting on the couch talking to Daniel. John asks Daniel to take the groceries into the kitchen and put them away. Daniel says okay and takes the groceries to the kitchen.

John asks, "Are you good?"

KD says, "Yes!"

John says, "I had a talk with Old Friend. If there's a next time, I'm going to have to lay hands on him, and I'm not talking about the healing kind."

KD says, "I appreciate you looking out for me, but I don't want you to get in any trouble."

John says, "Let me worry about that. You focus on staying safe. What did he say to you?"

KD says, "Thank God you called. He didn't get a chance to say much. You saved me!"

John says, "I always will!"

They kiss as Daniel walks into the room. Daniel covers his eyes and says, "Woah, child in the room." They stop kissing.

KD asks, "Son, are you ready for school?"

Daniel says, "Dinner, check! Homework, check! Uniform, check! Bag packed, check! Lunch packed, check!"

KD says, "Good job, Son! Goodnight, Son!"

Daniel says, "Goodnight, Kissy Face KD! Goodnight, Kissy Face John!"

John laughs and says, "Goodnight, Little Man!"

John looks at KD; he says, "Kissy Face KD, let's go to bed!"

KD says, "Okay, Kissy Face John, but I'm going to check the kitchen first. I hate the way he put things in the cabinet and refrigerator."

John says, "He did a good job! Exactly the way you would do it."

KD says, "You haven't checked. How do you know?

John says, "KD, I have three sons. I've been a father for thirty years. Daniel and I do more than watch sports and play video games. Go look! If I'm wrong, I'll go fix it. If he did a good job, learn to trust me."

KD goes to check the refrigerator and cabinets. Everything is perfect. She goes back to John with an impressed expression on her face. She is speechless.

John says, "Kissy Face KD, can we go to bed, now?"

John reaches out his hand. KD walks over to take his hand. John leads her to her bedroom. She hugs him as they walk.

KD says, "John, you make miracles."

John says, "You are my miracle!" KD kisses him.

After their family barbeque on the Fourth of July, John and KD are left to clean up John's house. When they're done cleaning up, John and KD are so tired that they seek refuge in his bed fully clothed. KD takes off her shoes and lays across the bed. John kicks off his shoes and lays beside her.

KD says, "Baby, today was lovely, but I am so tired."

John says, "You and your mother threw down in the kitchen."

KD says, "Thank you, baby. You were the king of the grill, today. The ribs were so good, and I don't even like ribs."

John says, "I hate that Little Man missed today."

KD says, "I missed him, too! I'm thankful everyone had a good time, though."

John says, "You know what I'm thankful for, Ladybug?"

KD says, "What's that?"

John says, "You!"

KD says, "Aww! Baby, that's so sweet. [KD grabs John's hand.] I'm thankful for you, too!"

John says, "KD, you're so good to me!"

KD says, "You're so good to me!" John closes his eyes. KD rolls onto her side to get comfortable. KD breaks the silence by calling his name.

John answers, "Yes, Ladybug?"

KD says, "Tell me you love me!" John opens his eyes, but he doesn't speak. John smirks with a facial expression that says, where did that come from. KD says, "You heard me. Tell me you love me." John still doesn't say anything. KD says, "John, come on! I want to hear you say it. I know you do. You know you do."

John says, "How do you know?"

KD says, "I can feel it when you touch and kiss me. If you miss my call, you call right back. You could be anywhere in the world, but for the last few months, you're with me. You have this huge, beautiful house, but you're in my tiny apartment every night. You reach for me in your sleep, and hold me all night."

John says, "I reach for you in my sleep?"

KD says, "You're all over me in your sleep. I don't mind. It's cute."

John says, "I'm cute, huh?"

KD says, "You're adorable."

John says, "If you love me, tell me you love me."

KD says, "I do, but the man is supposed to say it first!"

John says, "I'm glad you know me and how I feel because I do."

KD says, "It's time for you to start saying it all the time. I want to hear you say it right now!"

John says, "I love you, KD!"

KD smiles and says, "I love you, John!" KD rolls over to hug him; she says, "Goodnight, John!" She kisses him.

John says, "Goodnight, Ladybug!"

After church, John and KD stop by KD's mother's house for lunch. While at her mother's house, KD receives a phone call. When KD answers the phone, Mena excitedly says, "Guess who's home!" While KD is on the phone, Keith Jr. walks in the kitchen with his friends, Dash and Vino. Keith introduces John to his friends. John shakes their hands and politely greets them. KD smiles and waves as she talks to Mena.

KD gets excited; she says, "You didn't tell me you were coming home! I've missed you, Mena. I'm so happy you're home."

Mena says, "I'm home for good, and I need to see my friends. Can you come by tonight?"

KD says, "I will. I can't wait to see you."

Mena replies, "Tri is coming at 7. Can you come around that time?"

KD answers, "I'll be there."

John discreetly monitors the energy between KD and Dash while they eat and talk. He notices they never look at each even when they talk, but when KD and John get up to leave, John catches Dash sneaking a peek at her body. When KD and John get in his car, John says, "Your old flame thinks you still got it!"

KD replies, "And, I'm going to give it all to you!"

John smiles, he says, "I can't argue with that!" They pull off to go to his grandsons' game.

KD and Tri pull up at Mena's house at the same time. They are excited to see each other. They hug each other. Tri says, "Where have you been? I haven't seen you or heard from you."

KD says, "At that hospital as usual. How have you been?"

Tri says, "You would know if you called me!"

KD says, "Tri, don't be like that." They laugh as they walk toward the house arm in arm. Mena opens the door, and they all break out screaming. They have a group hug before they walk into the house.

Tri says, "Mena, you were gone so long. We've missed you."

KD says, "It's so good to see you!"

Mena says, "We served our country with all we had, and it is time to reap the fruits of our labor. We are retiring. Troy is having a baby, and we want to be here for our grandbaby. We missed so much with our kids. We're not missing a moment with our grandbaby."

KD says, "Aww! I'm so happy for Leah and Troy."

Tri asks, "Where is Major?"

Mena says, "He comes home next month."

KD says, "I'm happy for you both! Congratulations on your retirement!"

Mena thanks KD before she says, "Ladies, I cooked! I have junk food and alcohol. It's about to be a good time."

Tri pulls an edible from her purse and says, "Work is on my nerves. My kids are on my nerves. My husband is on my nerves. I need to decompress. Let's get fucked up."

Mena says, "Let's go to the kitchen."

After they sit around the counter, Mena says, "K, you are glowing. What's up with you?"

KD says, "Highly unlikely. I mean, I couldn't be pregnant."

Tri says, "What has you so happy?"

KD says, "I'm in a good space. Work is good. My kids are good. My mother is healthy."

Tri says, "Bullshit!"

Mena says, "You're seeing someone!"

Tri says, "That would explain why I haven't seen her or heard from her in months."

KD says, "I text you all the time."

Tri says, "Not good enough! I need to hear from you at least once a week."

KD says, "I promise to call more!"

Mena says, "There's a man in your life. Look at you! K, you are beaming like you're in love."

KD says, "I've been eating right and exercising every day."

Tri says, "I bet you have been exercising!" Tri mimics sexual movement.

Mena says, "We're your girls. We've known you since the first day of elementary school. You're in love!"

Tri says, "No keeping secrets. Who is this mystery man?"

KD says, "All right, all right! I've been talking to a guy named John. We're cool. That's it."

Tri says, "Give me his full name and DOB. I can get his credit score and criminal history in thirty seconds."

KD says, "You don't need to do that. He's a decent guy."

Tri says, "I think you're holding back, but I'll wait until you're ready to talk."

Mena asks, "Do you like him?"

KD says, "I do. He's sweet."

Mena says, "Tell us about him."

KD says, "He's divorced, has grown kids, he's smart, and hard-working."

Tri says, "Have you met each other's kids?"

KD says, "Yes! Everyone is supportive of our friendship."

Mena says, "How long has this friendship been going on?"

KD says, "Almost four months," trying to conceal the seriousness of the relationship.

Tri says, "Your mouth is saying one thing, but your body language is saying something else."

Mena says, "It's more than a friendship, isn't it?"

KD smiles and says, "We're friends!"

Mena says, "You deserve to be happy. It's okay, whether it's serious or just little fun."

Tri says, "There's nothing wrong with you having a whole lot of fun." KD and Mena laugh.

Mena says, "That is true!"

Tri says, "So you haven't given John some of that thang, yeah right, KD who do you think you're fooling?"

Mena says, "Tri, you have to ease into the tea."

KD says, "We have great conversation and a lot of fun when we hang out."

Tri says, "I think she did; that's why she's so vibrant and shit. You aren't glowing and shit from his fascinating, fantastical conversation."

Mena says, "If you hadn't, do you want to? Have you thought about it?"

Tri says, "Look at her face! You did, didn't you?"

KD says, "Mena, give me some alcohol because I'm not about to have this conversation sober." Mena pours three drinks. She hands one to Tri and one to KD.

Tri says, "Mena, that's a yes! Come on, K, give us the details. What is this dude, John, working with?"

KD shakes her head. KD says, "I am happy. He is happy."

Mena says, "KD, where did you meet him?"

KD says, "I was jogging on the riverfront."

Mena asks, "You must more than like him if you let him meet your kids."

KD says, "I do like him!"

Tri says, "So you've let him get that?"

KD says, "I have!"

Tri says, "And?"

KD drinks from her cup. Tri and Mena await her answer. KD says, "Connoisseur! The man is a sex connoisseur. He gives me what I want exactly the way I want every time we are together. I don't have to ask. He reads my body like it's his favorite book. He has studied it cover to cover over and over. He knows every page, every paragraph, every sentence, and every word. He consistently and perfectly gets all the way to that part that needs to be got. You get what I mean?"

Mena says, "Oh my, the top of the bottom, that's dangerous territory."

Tri says with closed eyes, "Well, damn! I'm just imagining how that feels. KD, keep talking."

Mena says, "One day at a time. Don't overthink this. Enjoy it! You deserve it!"

KD says, "Thank you, I am."

Mena says, "Tri, how is Frank?"

The mention of Frank's name ruins Tri's daydream. Tri answers, "Bored! Boring! He works ten-hour days. I work ten hours a day. Putting three kids through college is expensive and draining. By the time we get home, we have no energy for each other. We aren't living that life KD is enjoying."

Mena says, "The pangs of aging and parenting."

Tri says, "Tell me about it! Can you believe one of us is about to be a grandmother?"

 KD says, "Uh! Don't remind me. It feels like yesterday, we were young and having babies. Now, one of our babies is having a baby."

Mena asks, "How are Kelly and Daniel?"

KD answers, "They are well!"

Mena asks, "Tri, how are the kids?"

Tri says, "Everyone is well! So, K, does Daniel like this guy you're seeing?"

KD says, "My kids adore him. Momma likes him. Even, Keith and his kids like him."

Mena says, "That's a good sign, K!" Mena pours more drinks. Mena also fixes each one of them a plate.

KD says, "I hope so!"

Tri asks, "So, let me process this. You've met his family and probably his friends. So, everyone is acquainted except us. Dammit, KD, how dare you leave us out!"

KD says, "It's not like that. I've told him all about my best friends. He wants to meet you."

Mena says, "We want to meet him, too. If you like him, we will love him."

Tri says, "She's right, K! We will welcome him into our family. You're our sister. We will support you, always! Now, tell us some more about this guy."

Mena says, "Tri, let the alcohol kick in."

Tri says, "I know what will get her to talk." Tri opens the edible. They eat and drink as the talk about old times. When the alcohol starts to kick in, Tri gets back on John. Tri says, "Describe John in three adjectives and I won't ask any more questions."

KD says, "Generous, unrelenting, and impressive," KD smiles thinking about John.

Tri says, "Are you talking generally or sexually?"

KD says, "Both!"

Mena and Tri are curious at her choice of words. Mena asks, "Impressive?"

KD says, "Impressive af!"

By the end of the night, KD is drunk and high. She lays on Mena's couch and calls John. When he answers, he says, "Ladybug, what's good with you?"

KD says, "Baby, I'm too drunk to drive."

John asks, "Are you safe?"

KD says, "Yes, will you pick me up?"

John says, "Text me the address. I'm on my way."

KD says, "Thank you, baby!"

John rushes to his car. When the text pops up, he uses his phone's GPS to guide him to Mena's house. John hops out the car and knocks on the door. Mena and Tri rush to the door, so they can get a look at John. When they open the door, they are both awestruck.

Tri says, "It's John King!"

Mena says, "Welcome to my home, Mr. King. Come in!"

John says, "Thank you, but please call me John," as he walks into the door. Mena and Tri introduce themselves. John shakes their hands. He says, "It's a pleasure to finally meet the infamous best friends, Tri and Mena. KD talks about you all the time, so I feel like I know you."

Mena says, "It's nice to meet you!"

Tri says, "We look forward to getting to know you." John thanks them before he puts on KD's shoes.

John picks KD up and carries her to the car. Mena and Tri follow him with her purse. Mena and Tri watch as John tenderly puts KD in the passenger seat, leans her seat back, and puts her seatbelt on. John puts her purse in the back seat. John thanks Mena and Tri again, and they say goodbye. John gets in the car and pulls off.

As they watch the car pull off, Tri says, "No question, he is hitting that. Did you see how fast he showed up? How he put her shoes on and carried her to the car?"

Mena says, "He is. I saw."

Tri says, "He is still fine. Fine and Rich! My girl hit the jackpot."

Mena says, "She did!" Tri puts her hand up and Mena high-fives her hand.

John takes KD to her apartment. KD wakes up long enough to walk into the building, but she falls asleep on the elevator. She falls right into John's arms. The other couple on the elevator strangely looks at KD and John. He smiles at the other couple on the elevator; he says, "Long night!" The couple get off the elevator first. John picks KD up and carries her to the apartment and straight to her room.

John runs a bath, helps her undress, and helps her in the tub. KD says, "John, you are so good to me," as he bathes her. She says, "I love you so much!"

John says, "I love you, too!"

She touches his face; she says, "You are so handsome."

He smiles and says, "Thank you!"

She says, "You do the sweetest things for me. You say the sweetest things to me. You support me and love me. When you make love to me, you make me feel young and beautiful."

John says, "You are young and beautiful, Ladybug."

Tears start rolling down her face; she says, "The dick [she pauses] the dick is so good!" She cries; she says, "It's the way you get that spot, for me!"

John says, "I'm glad you enjoy yourself." She continues to cry while she rejoices in her spirit.

He says, "Ladybug, you are drunk!"

KD says, "I'm drunk in love like Beyoncé," she laughs as she reaches for him. He helps her stand up. She says, "King of Detroit, that's what they call you right." John wraps a towel around her and picks her up and carries her to the sink.

She says, "If they knew how you fuck me, they'd call you King Ding-a-ling!" she laughs. She grabs the crouch of his pants. She laughs and says, "Pull out that thing, King Ding-a-Ling." John moves her hand.

John says, "Girl, what were you drinking? You're tripping!" John tries to conceal his amusement.

KD says, "I had a little taste of something brown, squid of something clear, but mainly we drank these fruity, frozen drinks. Tri had a brownie. Baby, I'm drunk and high at the same time. It's weird."

He brushes her teeth. He rubs lotion on her. He puts deodorant on her, dresses her in a t-shirt and underwear, and lays her down.

She says, "John, come to bed with me. I need you next to me."

John says, "I'm coming, Ladybug!"

John goes to take a shower and brush his teeth. He quietly puts on lotion and deodorant. He slips on a pair of underwear, and quietly ease into bed. When KD feels him in the bed, she pulls him by his underwear. She traps him between her legs and rubs on his chest.

John says, "KD, go back to sleep. We'll talk in the morning."

KD says, "I don't need to talk, John, I need you to fuck the shit out of me, so I can scratch your back. Come here, baby!"

John says, "Ladybug, you need to go to sleep."

KD says, "What I need is for you to pull that big, pretty dick of yours out of those Calvin Klein boxer-briefs!"

She slowly slides her hands down his underwear. She says, "There he is. John, it's so big. I'm going to call him The Yeti." She rubs him as she talks.

John says, "Come on, Ladybug, please, go to sleep!" He tries to move her hand. John says, "Sleep it off, and we'll talk in the morning."

KD says, "Just listen to me!"

John listens to pacify her. She puts her hands back into his underwear. John doesn't stop her. She rubs him as she talks.

She says, "When we are together in that way, I feel fireworks and waterfalls in my body. My heart beats to a whole new rhythm when you are inside me. You amaze me in every way. Baby, you move like a prodigy. I love when you tell me how you feel, what you're feeling, or what you like. It makes me feel sexy and desired.

"It turns me on when you tell me what to do. I want to give you exactly what you want, so I can hear you say just like that, KD, Baby, fuck me just like that. When you like what I'm doing, you call my name and you hold me. When it gets good to you, I can hear you moan in my ear and feel you breathe on my neck. The look on your face when you are loving me is so sexy, baby.

"I love it when you're all over me like you can't get close enough. You want more and more like you can't get enough. When we start, you are gentle. When you get into it, you become aggressive. You switch positions like it's nothing. You make me feel so light when you toss and turn me around with ease.

"When it gets good to you, you get quiet and zone out. I know the exact moment because you make this face that says I'm about to get it. And, you do, every time! Just before you cum, your eyes roll back in your head three times. Afterward, you hug me and say, KD, baby.

"It's so exhilarating to know I have you as my man and to think someone who is as fine as you is attracted to me. I'm thankful that you never disappoint me or leave me unsatisfied. I never quit on you or deny you. Even if it's too much and I can't take it anymore, I give it to you. I take it all for as long as you need me because I want to please you. I will always give it to you the way you want it because you deserve that."

She kisses him. John kisses her back. She pulls his underwear down. She leans over and seductively kisses the tip of him while staring in his eyes.

She says, "I will do whatever you want, whenever you want because you deserve the best of me, all of me." She licks all over him before she sucks him.

KD has John intoxicated with her words and seduction. The alcohol got her to speak freely. John loved everything she said.

John says, "Ladybug, I am touched by and appreciate your honesty, but Ladybug," she cuts him off.

She lays down; she says, "I need to feel you, baby." She pulls him on top of her. She rubs his shoulders and back as she kisses his neck.

She says, "John, please, baby, touch it to see how wet I am."

John trying to fight temptation, says, "I can't take advantage of you. Go to sleep, Ladybug, sober up and let's talk in the morning."

KD says, "John, don't you want a piece of my cookie?"

John says, "You know I always want you. You know that."

She takes him in her hand to rub him against herself. Immediately, John feels and hears the alluring assets of KD's love, and he is instantly filled with desire.

She says, "See, baby, I need you."

John is losing his will to resist. She slides him inside her; she says, "Ah! Baby! See how wet it is. I need you, baby, and I need you to need me." She repeatedly glides him in and out as she moans and calls his name. John's mind is blown by what is happening.

She says, "John, baby, don't you love me?"

John says, "You know I love you." John tries to remain neutral, but the scene is too sexy for him to resist.

KD says, "John, fuck me, baby, please!" She wraps her legs around him, and says, "I need you, right now. Don't deny me!" She kisses him, and he kisses her back. The kiss does it. John's will to resist is broken. She kisses him again. She whispers, "Come on, baby, give in. Don't deny me!"

John whispers, "I'll never deny you, you're my Ladybug. You will always get whatever you want from me."

KD says, "John, take control, baby, please, I need you!" KD opens her legs to signal to John that she wants him to go deeper. John sucks KD's neck as he pins her legs back. Now, John is into it, all the way to the bottom. KD cries out, "Yes, baby! Get it! Good boy!"

John whispers in her ear, "This is what you want?"

She kisses him and says, "Yes, baby, just like that." John went from zero to thousand in a matter of seconds.

John says, "I love you, Ladybug!"

KD says, "I love you, Baby. You feel incredible. Most women will live an entire lifetime and never feel anything like you." John loves the way she is talking. The energy of the moment is getting to him.

John says, "Hold up, baby!" John moves back to take a second to compose himself. John says, "Baby, I'm trying to make it last." She keeps moving. John says, "Don't chase it!" KD doesn't listen. John says, "If you keep throwing it like that, your cookie will be drenched with milk."

KD keeps moving, she says, "I want you to cum over and over and over."

John says, "You're about to get what you want."

In the morning, John wakes up and eases out of bed. He showers, brushes his teeth, and gets dressed. Henson picks him up and takes him to work. The entire morning, his mind stays on KD. He can't get over last night. As soon as he sits down at his desk after his morning meeting, KD calls. When he answers, KD asks, "Why didn't you wake me up? I would've cooked breakfast for you."

John says, "You needed to sleep."

KD says, "I can bring you something to eat."

John says, "You don't have to do that. I'll grab something. How are you feeling?"

KD says, "Like I drank too much last night."

John whispers into the phone, "You were in rare form last night. Do you remember what happened last night?"

KD says, "Did I make you mad?"

John says, "No! You got to me. You shouldn't say things you don't mean."

KD says, "I meant everything I said. I didn't have to be so vulgar. Baby, you know that I am a lady and that was the alcohol talking last night."

John says, "How can you be sure you meant it if you don't remember what you said?"

KD says, "I don't want you to leave me. I do love you and making love to you. You do make me feel incredibly good. You are the best thing to happen in my life outside my children. John, I meant everything I said last night. Did I offend you with my overtness?"

John says, "KD, I can't have this conversation right now. I won't be able to concentrate at all today. I've got to get off this phone. Have a good day. Try to get some rest. I hope you feel better. I'll see you, tonight."

KD says, "John, what's wrong? Why do you want to get off the phone?"

John says, "You have me in my feelings."

KD says, "That's a good thing, right?"

John says, "It's a great thing! Do you remember what happened last night?"

KD says, "Yes! My whole body remembers what happened. I can still feel you inside me. You were masterful. I remember every position, every stroke, every kiss, every touch."

John says, "KD, I have a lot to do today, but if you keep talking like that, I'm coming home."

KD says, "Bye, John, have a good day."

John says, "You, too, Ladybug!"

Before she hangs up, she says, "I love you!"

He says, "I love you more!"

John and KD sit at the bar of his son's club. John smokes a cigar as they chase shots with lime. John puffs his cigar as he stares at KD. KD gets shy. She says, "When you look at me like that…." She smiles and doesn't finish the statement.

John says, "What?" and gives her the look again.

KD shyly says, "Nothing!"

John says, "Say what's on your mind."

KD whispers, "I want to kiss you."

John gives her the look again. He says, "Do it!"

KD says, "What? I couldn't. We are in public. Everyone would see us."

John says, "Everyone is too busy enjoying themselves to worry about us. We should be enjoying ourselves, and not worrying about everyone else."

KD says, "There's always eyes on you. I can point out ten women watching you right now."

John says, "Let's give them something to watch."

He sits his cigar down. He grabs her hand and pulls her close to him. She puts her hands on his cheeks. He places his hands on her hips. She kisses him as if they were alone in her bedroom. Raina and her friend sit in the back of the club watching them kiss. KD sits back down. She smiles at him. He winks at her. He picks up his cigar.

She asks, "Your birthday is coming soon. What do you want to do?"

John exhales the cigar smoke. He gives her the look as he answers, "Make love to you over and over and over again."

KD says, "I'm not opposed to your plan and I can see your vision, but seriously, it's your special day. What do you want to do on your special day?"

John puffs his cigar. He says, "My birthday plans are to make love to you in Saint-Tropez. Kiss you as we walk through the streets of Sorrento. Every night, when we get back to the hotel, I'm going to make love to you all night. Is that all right with you?"

KD asks, "Are you serious?"

John says, "I already made the reservations. I know you have a passport. Kelly told me."

KD asks again, "You're serious?"

John says, "Remember we talked about the list of things I want to do to you? Well, that is on the list!" He puffs his cigar. He says, "You should kiss me again! Let me grab your booty. Make the gawkers madly jealous."

John turns to her and sits his cigar down. He pulls her to him. He grips her butt. He says, "Hug my neck, and kiss me." She kisses him again as she would if they were alone in her bedroom. That second kiss upsets Raina. She can't stand to watch their affectionate interaction. Raina's friend consoles her, and encourages her to get over John.

John and KD, encouraged by the alcohol, seductively dance before drinking more shots. By the time the bar closes, they are drunk. His sons walk them to the Range Rover waiting outside. As Henson drives them to his house, they passionately kiss in the back seat. The usually conservative KD doesn't even care that Henson is in the car. The mysterious black Benz rides alongside the Range Rover, but they are too into each other to notice the lurking car.

When they make it to John's bedroom, John says, "Ladybug, you got me drunk to take advantage of me, but you aren't getting none of this dick." They laugh.

She says, "Not even a little bit!"

John jokingly says, "Nope," with a drunken slur.

She says, "You are silly," as she walks to the restroom. When she comes out of the restroom, John is asleep, laying across his bed. She's just as drunk as him, so it's a struggle to lift him. She manages to take off his clothes and shoes. She undresses, grabs a blanket, and snuggles next to him under the blanket.

John wakes up an hour later. He looks at KD lying next to him. He lifts the cover to see her underwear and bra, which instantly fills him with desire. He touches her and kisses her. The feel of his hands and lips wake her. She opens her eyes to see him looking at her. He kisses her. She wraps her arms around him. John says, "May I, have you?"

KD says, "Always and forever!" Their drunken passion fueled by their deep emotions erupts throughout the rest of the night.

KD comes home from work to find a very quiet, fully-clothed John lying across her bed, looking at the ceiling in the dark. KD can tell there's something bothering him. She asks, "Are you okay, baby?" She undresses as she awaits his answers.

John says, "Ladybug, I had a bad day."

KD asks, "Do you want to talk about it?" KD lays next to him. She puts her hand on his chest and her head on his shoulder.

John says, "You know, I've been working with the investors for months. Today, suddenly, things started stalling. What if they want to back out? I could lose a lot of money. I mean a lot! I invested a lot of time and energy into this project. I'm not even sure what went wrong. I usually see things like this coming, and I'm able to keep things moving forward. KD, this time, I was completely blindsided. Losing this deal can set me back, big time."

KD kisses his cheek. KD says, "I don't know anything about business or dealing with a lot of money, but you know what I do know?"

John asks, "What's that?"

KD says, "I know you. John Michael King can do anything. He can make the impossible possible. You, all on your own, have carried on and expanded your grandfather's and father's legacies. No one knows what you do better than you. Mr. King, you are a legend. I love how you move, and I know I'm not the only one. People are drawn to you, John. Do you know why so many women are attracted to you, why I love you?"

John asks, "Why is that?"

KD says, "It's that killer smile, irresistible charm, the unyielding determination that make people do what you want them to do and make them believe it's their own desire to do it. You always know what to say and what to do. I think John can make this or anything else happen. I believe in John Michael King.

"In the morning, put on that smile, be your charming self, and have that unbreakable confidence surrounding you. Don't think for a minute that they don't recognize the benefits of being connected to you. They aren't backing out. Baby, they are busy making things happen." She kisses him; she says, "You got this, baby!"

John says, "And, this is why I love you. Thank you, Ladybug!"

KD says, "I know how I can help you get your confidence back."

John says, "How?"

KD says, "I'm going to go take a shower. When I come back, you can do anything you like!"

John hops up; he says, "Anything?"

KD says, "Anything, everything you want to do to me," as she walks into the bathroom. John starts undressing and follows her into the bathroom.

They flirt and play as they bathe each other, dry each other off, rub lotion on each other, and brush their teeth. When they are done, John stands behind KD. He softly kisses her neck. John tells her, "I've never had a woman like you in my life. I never had a woman who believed in me or cheered for me. Two loveless marriages and a bunch of meaningless sex are all I've known until you. Ladybug, it's fascinating to be genuinely loved and wanted by a beautiful woman. You are everything I ever wanted in a woman."

John kisses KD's neck as she says, "I hate that has been your experience because you are sincerely a wonderful person, and you deserve true love. Hearing you say that makes me love you more, and I am thankful that I'm the woman who gets to truly love you. The heartaches and pain in my past make me appreciate you even more. Thank God, we found each other."

John sits her on the sink to kiss her. John says, "Thank you, Ladybug, I was feeling bad, and you knew exactly what to say to make me feel better. You know what's about to happen, right?"

KD says, "I know," she smiles. They kiss.

John says, "Baby, you give me the energy I need. I love that about you!"

KD says, "Mainly because I want and need you just as much as you want and need me."

John says, "Your willingness to please me blows me away."

KD says, "I will be and do anything you want and everything you need!"

John kisses her and says, "I love you!"

KD wraps her legs and arms around him. She responds, "I love you!"

The night before John's flight, he and KD go to the club to have dinner and a drink with his sons and their wives. They leave the club with smiles on their faces. John opens the passenger door and helps KD get in the car. Just as John starts the car, he realizes he left one of his phones charging in his son's office.

He runs back into the club to get his phone, leaving KD waiting in his running car in front of the club. KD checks her cell phone patiently waiting for John. A black SUV pulls up next to John's car. The driver blows the horn. KD looks up to see Dr. Segal, smiling at her, immediately killing her good vibe.

Dr. Segal rolls his window down. He shouts KD's name and asks her to roll the window down. She tries to ignore him, but he won't leave. KD cuts off the car. She gets out of the car to go back into the club. She hides behind the door.

When John comes through the inner door, he sees KD peeking out the main door. John asks, "Who are you hiding from?"

KD says, "Dr. Creeper is out there! It's like he knows when I'm alone."

John says, "You don't have to hide from him. I'm about to fuck him up."

KD holds his arms; she says, "Baby, he is not worth getting upset, hurt or in trouble. If he doesn't leave in a minute, I'll call the police."

John says, "KD, I was nice, and he didn't respect that, so now, I'm smacking him."

KD says, "Baby, calm down, please. Are you actually about to tell your sons you're going outside to fight like a teenager? Baby, he'll leave in a minute."

John looks in KD eyes; he says, "Go back to the table and sit with the kids until I come back." They stare at each other. John's face says, I'm doing this. KD moves her hands and walks away.

John walks out the door. Alex, Isaiah, and Isaac are still at the table with their wives. KD rushes to ask John's son to please go outside to get their father. They confusedly ask what is going on. KD, with a frustrated face, tells them their dad is going outside to fight. Everyone rushes toward the door. The mysterious black Benz sits across the street watching the confrontation.

When John gets outside, Dr. Segal is leaning on his car. John says, "Motherfucker, get the fuck off my car!"

Dr. Segal asks, "Where is KD?"

John says, "For you to be a doctor, you're not that damn bright. What part of don't talk to my woman don't you understand?" John is getting closer to Dr. Segal.

Dr. Segal says, "I don't understand any of it because she didn't say it."

John is face-to-face with the doctor. John says, "I tried to be nice, but that wasn't explicit enough. Now, I'm going to whoop your ass! Maybe that will help you understand."

The driver of the mysterious black Benz senses an altercation on the horizon, so the driver pulls out a cell phone and begins to record the confrontation.

Dr. Segal pulls out a gun and points it at John. Dr. Segal smiles as he looks in John's eyes. John is emotionless. He moves so quickly the doctor doesn't even have time to comprehend what's happening. John takes the gun from Dr. Segal and starts beating him in his head and face with the gun. John chastises Dr. Segal as if he is a disobedient child, deserving punishment.

When John's sons and daughters-in-law make it outside, they see John has Dr. Segal on the ground repeatedly beating him with the gun. John's sons pull him off the doctor. Alex takes the gun from John and puts it in the back of his waistband.

Isaiah and Isaac pull John into the club. Alex stays outside to talk to Dr. Segal. Alex helps Dr. Segal get up. When Dr. Segal is on his feet, Alex checks to see if he is okay. When Dr. Segal says he is okay, Alex asks him to please leave to avoid another altercation. Alex helps him get in his car and asks if he can drive. Dr. Segal seems like he's on the verge of fainting, but he says he can drive. Alex helps him put on seatbelt and closes the door.

KD sees Isaiah and Isaac struggling with John who wants to go back outside to fight some more. KD rushes to the commotion. KD says, "John, baby, calm down, please!"

John looks at her worried face and immediately calms down. Isaiah and Isaac want to know what the fight was about. John says, "He disrespected my girl!"

KD asks, "What happened out there?"

John says, "I was cool. He pulled out a gun." KD looks at John's face and hands to see if he's hurt. John says, "He didn't get a chance to hit me."

Alex walks over to them and asks, "Who is that?"

KD says, "He's a doctor I worked with years ago. We ran into him at a restaurant a while back, and now, he keeps popping up."

Alex says, "He's gone now! I watched him pull off." Alex asks, "Pops, are you cool?"

John says, "Yes! I'm good, Son!"

Alex says, "Take Ms. KD home and chill. In the morning, I'll turn this [Alex shows John the gun] in to the police as if a customer left it."

Isaiah and Isaac encourage John to remain calm. John agrees to chill. Everyone walks John and KD to his car. Alex knows his father is a hothead. Alex says, "You're taking Ms. KD home, and chill with her for the whole night, right, Pops," as John puts KD in the car.

John says, "Son, I promise, I'm chilling with my girl for the whole night." Isaac, Isaiah, Alex and their wives hug John before he gets in the car.

As John drives, KD says, "You really had a fight tonight?"

John asks, "Are you mad at me?"

KD says, "No, baby, I get why you were angry, but we could've called the police like we said we would if he came back around."

John says, "It's a man thing, Ladybug. I can't let that shit slide like I'm a bitch. I had to hit him. That's how men are taught to handle conflict. Violence is how we solve our problems."

KD says, "Baby, that makes sense when you're eleven and on the playground with bullies, but we are mature adults. We handle things with a higher level of maturity."

John says, "I didn't make the rules. I just follow them. I learned early to hit first and hit harder."

KD says, "Baby, what did you do when he pulled out the gun?"

John says, "I took the gun and beat his fucking face and head with it. It happened so quickly; he couldn't even brace himself for the hit."

KD says, "Baby, that was so dangerous." She put her hand on the side of his face; she says, "I love that you love me and want to protect me. I appreciate that, but, baby, I can't stand the thought of you getting hurt. I'm not saying don't be yourself or don't be a man. Baby, please make better decisions. I can't lose you, especially over something and someone so trivial. That man is not important. Promise, me you will think before you act and always be safe."

John says, "I promise!"

KD says, "But, it's sexy to know you were fighting for me."

John asks, "How sexy?"

KD replies, "Very sexy!"

John asks, "Sexy enough that you want to, you know?" KD smiles and winks at him.

When they get to John's house, KD says, "Mr. King, you have a meeting in the shower followed by a meeting in your bedroom." She pulls her dress over her head.

John looks at her and says, "Lead the way, Ms. Daniels." He follows her to the bathroom.

The next morning as John is preparing to leave for his flight out of the country to meet with the investors, he tells KD to be safe. He instructs her to call the police or one of his sons if the creepy doctor comes anywhere near her. John gives her a stack of money and tells her this is to handle any emergencies that pop up. He also hands her his car keys.

KD says, "Does this mean I can drive your car?"

John says, "I drive your car all the time." KD smiles with an unbelieving smirk.

She replies, "Boy, you know you don't want me to drive your Lamborghini. I'll keep your keys, but I won't drive your car."

John says, "Drive the car! Let everyone see you, so everyone knows you're John's girl."

KD says, "Do you really want everyone to know that?"

John says, "I want the whole world to know KD Daniels is my woman."

KD says, "Have a successful trip and be safe!" She smiles at him.

John says, "Thank you! I miss you already!" They kiss and tell each other I love you before John leaves out door.

With Daniel at camp, KD is alone and feeling lonely when a frantic Kimma calls to ask if the girls could stay with her for the night because her husband must have emergency surgery. KD rushes to the hospital. KD takes the girls to John's house because they have their own room and clothes there.

The girls and KD play before she cooks for them. She gives them a bath, and they fall asleep watching movies in John's bed well past their bedtime. While they are sleeping, she takes a shower before she crawls into bed with them. John video-calls KD as soon as she gets in the bed.

KD whispers, "Hey, baby!"

John says, "Hey! Were you sleeping?"

KD says, "No! How are things going?"

John says, "Things are going well, but I can't wait to get home to you."

KD says, "I can't wait to see you. I miss you so much."

John says, "I miss you, too!"

Just as John finishes his sentence, Lourdes pops up and crawls in KD's arms. She rubs her eyes as she looks at the phone. Lourdes says, "Pop-Pop!"

John says, "Hey Lovebug, I miss you so much." Lourdes lies on KD's chest and falls back to sleep. KD cradling his granddaughter warms his heart. John asks, "Is Langley there, too?" KD shows him Langley sleeping in his bed. He asks, "What are you doing with my lovebugs?"

KD says, "Your son-in-law had to have emergency surgery, and your daughter is spending the night at the hospital with him. They wore me out, but we had fun."

He says, "Ladybug, thank you for caring for my girls while I'm away."

KD says, "Of course, I got you, always!"

John says, "You know I love you, and the fact that you love and care for my girls makes me love you even more."

KD says, "I love them and, you know, I love you."

John looks at KD, holding Lourdes and rubbing her hair; he says, "I wish I was there snuggled up with my girls."

KD says, "We wish you were here, too!"

John says, "Get some sleep, Ladybug, I'll check on you and the girls tomorrow."

KD says, "Okay, baby!"

They both say, "I love you!" before they hang up.

In the morning, KD prepares breakfast for the girls before she dresses them and combs their hair. When Kimma comes to get the girls, they cry because they want to stay with KD. KD convinces Kimma to let the girls stay another night, so Kimma can take care of her husband.

John is supposed to fly directly to California, but he misses KD so much that he flies home to spend a few hours with her. He unlocks her door. When she sees him walk through the door, she is so surprised. He takes KD in his arms for a kiss. He carries her to her bedroom. With little time to spare, John gets right to loving KD.

Kelly comes to surprise KD with some mother-daughter time, thinking KD was bored and lonely. The apartment is quiet and dark. Kelly sees her mother's purse hanging on the closet doorknob, so she knows she's home. Kelly sees light coming from the kitchen, but no one is there. She goes toward her mother's bedroom door.

Just as she's about to open the door, she hears John's voice saying, "Ladybug, baby, yes, fuck me. You feel so good, KD, Baby, I love you."

She hears her mother moaning and their bodies clapping as John continually professes his love and admiration for KD. She carefully and quietly backs away from the door. Kelly proudly smiles as she quietly goes to the kitchen to grab a snack. She grabs a pillow and a blanket from the closet. She quietly makes herself comfortable on the couch. The television lowly plays as Kelly plays on her phone until she falls asleep.

Before sunlight breaks through the early morning sky, John and KD playfully walk out of the room. John walks backward as KD tries to kiss him. John catches a glimpse of Kelly on the couch. He quickly dodges KD's kiss, and says, "Baby Girl, it's good to see you."

KD is mortified that Kelly is in the apartment. She immediately feels shame. John grabs KD's hand; he says, "I will call you as soon as I land."

Kelly says, "Stepdad, I can cook breakfast if you want to eat before your flight?"

John says, "Thanks for offering, Baby Girl, but I have to go!" John and KD say I love you to each other before he leaves out the door.

KD says, "Be safe!"

John responds as he closes the door, "You, too, Ladybug!"

KD fixes her face to cover her shame as she turns to face her daughter; she says, "Kelly, baby, I didn't know you were here."

Kelly says, "You were busy when I got here last night, so I just crashed on the couch."

KD sits on the couch and hugs her daughter; she says, "If I knew you were coming…"

Kelly cuts her off; she says, "If I knew you were coming." KD's facial expression says, I am so embarrassed. Kelly says, "Momma, it's okay! Don't feel bad. You're an adult. I didn't call."

KD says, "Baby, I am so sorry."

Kelly says, "Don't be sorry! Mommy, you shouldn't feel ashamed for loving John."

KD says, "I don't want my daughter exposed to that part of my life."

Kelly replies, "It's not like I've never heard you and daddy before."

KD says, "What? When?"

Kelly responds, "When I was young, during the happy times."

KD says, "I always thought I was so careful."

Kelly says, "You were an excellent mother. Kids wake up in the middle of night."

KD says, "No, Kelly! Do not tell me that. Why didn't you say something?"

Kelly says, "Momma, at the time, I didn't know what was happening. I had a bad dream. I was coming to your room because I was scared. I heard some noises and I thought I needed to go back to my bedroom."

KD says, "You know I would never let last night happen if I knew you were here."

Kelly says, "Momma, I'm glad you have John. He is a cool dude. I love him. I respect him. I love you with him. Do you know he and I talk every day?"

KD says, "No! What do you two talk about?"

Kelly says, "Basically, how much he loves you and Daniel, his work, Daniel's games, his kids, what's stressing him out, and you. He is trying so hard to make Daniel and I feel like a part of his family. He wants this relationship to work."

KD says, "I know he's trying. Are you sure you are okay with this relationship? This is the first time you've seen me with a man that's not your male parent."

Kelly asks, "How do you feel about the way things are going with John? It seems like things are going well."

KD says, "They are, and it scares me."

Kelly says, "Mom, chill! If it works, it works. If it doesn't, at least you had an experience."

KD says, "I don't want to be hurt."

Kelly says, "I'm sure he doesn't want to be hurt. You do your part, he does his part, and that's all either of you can ask."

KD says, "Something about John makes me feel inadequate or undeserving. I feel like any day he will look at me and realize he can do better."

Kelly says, "Does he answer your calls? Does he show up when he says he will? Does he keep his word? Does he listen when you talk? Does he make you feel special and wanted? Does he check on you? Does he give you what you want and need? Do you have fun with him? Do you feel protected and safe with him?"

KD says, "The answer to every question is yes since day one."

Kelly says, "Momma, what else do you want the man to do? He can't walk on water. He's not Jesus! John loves you, and he's good to you. He's a multimillionaire with a huge house, but he's here every night in your two-bedroom apartment with your son because he knows how important your son is to you. He does more with the boy than the boy's real daddy. He's doing everything a man needs to do. Momma, don't you think he deserves a little break."

KD says, "I know you're right!"

Kelly says, "Look, who raised me. I know what I'm talking about."

KD says, "My girl is all grown up!"

Kelly says, "I can say the same thing. My girl is all grown, and she has it going on." Mocking John's voice, she says, "KD, Baby!"

KD says, "So embarrassing!"

Kelly says, "Momma, you're in love; that's not embarrassing. It's beautiful! You're a grown woman. You're supposed to let him know that you play no games." KD covers her smiling face.

KD says, "Do you think DJ is really okay with me dating?"

Kelly says, "Are you kidding, he loves John!"

KD says, "I'm glad you both accept him."

Kelly says, "Momma, I came over last night because I need to talk to you about John."

KD looks concerned; she says, "You can always tell me anything."

Kelly says, "Momma, it's not bad, relax."

KD says, "Okay, I'm listening."

Kelly says, "John has been campaigning for me to come work for him when my internship is over. He offered me a ridiculous amount of money. Momma, this will look so good on my resume, and the money is not something I can pass up."

KD says, "I love that John is looking out for you, and you two are bonding, but baby, what happens if he and I don't make it."

Kelly says, "The way you had him last night! I'm not concerned, at all!"

KD says, "Kelly, stop!"

Kelly says, "Mom, you're a woman! It's okay for you to be sexual. We're both adults. We can talk about this stuff."

KD says, "We can talk about you, not me."

Kelly says, "Momma, you are so happy with John. You're in love. He's in love. You needed a good man to give you good love after the break-up with Daddy. He needed a good woman to love and care for him. Momma, I am so proud of you and him for taking a chance on love. It's okay to share your happiness with me."

KD says, "I will support whatever you want. If you want this job, take the job. I don't think John would do anything to hurt you. If things don't work out, at least you will have gained some experience."

Kelly says, "Mommy, thank you!" Kelly hugs her mother.

KD says, "You're welcome, baby!"

Kelly says, "It's going to work out, I promise!"

KD says, "I trust your judgment. You know what's best for you."

Kelly says, "Mommy, I love you and Stepdad. I am so blessed to have you both."

KD says, "I'm blessed to have you."

CHAPTER THREE

KD spends the breezy, rainy September morning cleaning and doing laundry at John's house. John's flight is delayed due to heavy rain and thunderstorms, so she is not sure when he will be home. She starts upstairs in the bedrooms cleaning, dusting, and changing the bedding. She also cleans the bathroom and sweeps the floors.

When she finishes the top floor, she cleans the kitchen. Just as she finishes mopping the kitchen floor, she hears the dryer stop. She goes to the basement to fold the sheets. As she folds the sheets, she hears a bump like something fell. KD pauses. She stands still, listening. Soon, she hears another bump blended with the sound of the spinning washing machine. She quietly tiptoes to the basement stairs. She hears another sound, but it seems closer.

She grabs one of John golf clubs before she steps on the first stair. She hears footsteps in the kitchen. Her heart pounds as fear rises in her chest. She quietly moves up the stairs holding the golf club in the position to swing. The basement door opens. KD jumps. She grips the club preparing to swing it. John pops his head through the door. John says, "Ladybug!" She puts the golf club down.

KD says, "John, you scared the shit out of me. I thought you would be here much later."

John says, "What are you doing in the basement?"

KD says, "Folding the sheets. I wanted you to come home to a clean house."

John says, "You're so thoughtful." John comes down the stairs. John hugs and kisses KD. He says, "I missed you!"

KD says, "I missed you, too!"

John says, "I'll help you with the laundry." John and KD walk to the laundry room. He says, "You know I pay people to clean."

KD puts the golf club back. She says, "I like to take care of you." He tells her she's sweet. They talk about his business trip as they fold the sheets.

John says, "You know what's crazy?"

KD says, "What?"

John says, "I have so much fun doing the simplest things with you. I have never enjoyed folding laundry this much ever in life."

KD says, "I love being near you no matter what we're doing."

John asks, "Do you think you will say that in twenty years?"

KD says, "I'm positive that I will." John helps her finish cleaning the house. They make lunch and cuddle until it is time to pick up Daniel from school.

John rides with KD to pick Daniel up from school. Daniel is so excited to see John in the car. Daniel runs to the car and hops in with a massive smile on his face. He excitedly greets John. John is excited to see him.

Daniel says, "John, I wasn't expecting to see you."

John says, "We are going to hang out to celebrate your big win. I'm so sorry I missed the football game yesterday. Little Man, I really tried to make it back in town for the game. The weather delayed my flight."

Daniel says, "It's okay, I know you tried to make it. Where are we going?"

John says, "Where do you want to go?"

Daniel says, "Let's go bowling. We can eat pizza."

John says, "That's where we are going."

Daniel says, "Thanks, John, I appreciate you!"

John says, "I appreciate you! I heard you were great in the game yesterday."

Daniel says, "I used those move you taught me. No one could catch me."

John gives Daniel a fist bump; he says, "I'm proud of you, you know that, right?"

Daniel says, "Thanks, John!"

KD says, "Well, hello, Son, how was your day?"

Daniel says, "Hey, Momma, it was cool. How was your day?"

KD says, "It's going well. Thanks for asking, Son."

Daniel asks, "Were you with John all day?"

KD says, "I was."

Daniel says, "John is the best person to hang with. He always makes sure you have a good time."

KD smiles at John and says, "He does!" He winks at her.

KD asks, "Do you have a lot of homework?"

Daniel says, "Just have to do a few things, but I promise to do it before I go to bed."

John asks, "What did you learn in school today?"

Daniel says, "You know, the usual math, science, social studies, and English. But it's health week in P.E., so we are studying human health and development."

John says, "Sounds interesting."

Daniel says, "It's big words for sex. We are learning about sex and how babies come from sex. When girls hit puberty, they get their period, and you can get them pregnant. They're not teaching us how to have sex. We're just learning the basics and dangerous outcomes of sex. Are you two having sex? I really want a baby brother, so I can have someone to play with."

KD and John are aghast. KD holds in her laugh. John is silenced by shock. Daniel says, "Well, will one of you answer me? Can I have a baby brother?" John tries to produce speech but can't. John's mind is devoid of a response. He looks at KD for help.

KD touches John's arm to let him know she has it; she says, "Son, when women reach a certain age, they can no longer get pregnant."

Daniel says, "Women do it all the time! Maybe, you can, too!"

KD says, "God's blessings for one woman are not necessarily the blessings he will have for another woman. Besides, babies are a lot of responsibility. Raising a baby is time-consuming and financially draining."

Daniel says, "John is wealthy. He can afford a baby. Can't you John?" John can't answer.

KD says, "Son, you can't make John obligated to fulfill your desires. That's a lot of responsibility that requires a couple to think and plan ahead. Who would watch the baby while John and I are at work and you are at school? You know your grandmother is not about to deal a crying baby all day."

Daniel says, "John is a great dad. He wouldn't mind a baby, would you, John?" John can't answer.

KD says, "It's not that simple. You saw how hard things were with your dad and I. Responsibility causes stress in relationships."

Daniel says, "So, no little brother?"

KD says, "No!" Daniel is disappointed. John and KD look at each other. John's face says he's relieved.

After bowling, KD and John talk about Daniel's question in KD's bedroom. John says, "Ladybug, I was so tongue-tied! I didn't know what to say."

KD says, "I was shocked too."

John says, "Your response was perfect! What am I going to say if he brings it up again?"

KD says, "You're going to have to have the talk with him."

John says, "His father may want to handle that."

KD says, "His mother asked you to do it."

John says, "KD, I don't know. That's important to a father."

KD says, "It can't be too important, he hasn't done it yet."

John says, "What if he tells his father?"

KD says, "He doesn't tell his dad what goes on in my home."

John says, "If he brings it up again, I'll ask if he wants to talk to his dad or me."

KD says, "I vote for you."

John says, "Why me?"

KD says, "Because you do it better. He should learn from the best."

John says, "Aww shit! [He kisses her.] Maybe we can make that baby brother, after all!"

KD says, "I went through hell to get pregnant. Finally, I had my daughter. I was relieved, but he wanted a boy to the point he stressed me out. I had miscarriage after miscarriage. After five miscarriages, nothing for years. One day, I popped up pregnant. We had one encounter after a very long time of a sexless marriage. When I told him, the bastard told me to get rid of it after he asked me if it was really his."

John says, "KD, you didn't deserve that. I'm sorry that happened to you." John hugs and kisses her. Daniel knocks on the door.

KD says, "Come in, Son!" As Daniel walks in the room, John and KD are sitting up.

Daniel says, "Looks like I caught you two kissy faces at bad time."

John says, "It's okay, Little Man, come in."

Daniel says, "John, can you help me with my homework?"

KD says to Daniel, "Baby, I'll help you."

Daniel says, "I want John to help me."

KD says, "Well, if John doesn't mind."

John says, "Of course, I'll help. Give me a second to talk to your mom."

Daniel says, "Okay," as he leaves the room.

After Daniel leaves, John says to KD, "You shared something heavy, are you good? We can talk about it."

KD says, "I'm fine!"

John asks, "Are you sure?"

KD says, "Go see what the boy wants. I'm good!"

When John gets to Daniel's room, Daniel says, "I finished my homework a long time ago. I had to come up with an excuse to get you in here to play the game with me."

John laughs as he grabs the second controller; he says, "You're too slick, Little Man! Before I touch this controller, are you sure everything is done correctly?"

Daniel says, "I could've done that homework in my sleep."

John says, "My man!"

Daniel goes over to his backpack. He pulls out an invitation to the robotics competition. He hands it to John. John takes the card and reads it.

Daniel says, "I would love for you to see my robot, but I understand if you have pressing matters at work. I don't mention my competitions to my mother, so she won't feel guilty."

John says, "Things have changed. She doesn't have to do everything by herself anymore. We both will be there. We love you and we want to support everything you do."

Daniel says, "My STEM coach says my robot will be one of the top three. I put my all into my robot. The winner of the STEM competition always wins scholarships and gets opportunities to be in more competitions. If I win, I can build a bigger and better robot for the next competition."

John says, "I'm so proud of you, Daniel. That's incredible. You are the smartest person I have ever met. I'm sure your grandmother and sister will love to see your robot. From now on, you tell us about everything. We will make sure at least one of us is always there for you no matter what. I promise!"

Daniel says, "John, I will always be there for you, too, no matter what." They bump fists. Daniel is so happy that John is going to come to the competition. John and Daniel play video games until Daniel's bedtime.

When John returns to KD's bedroom, she says, "Did you have fun playing video games?"

John laughs. John says, "We did!"

KD says, "I knew he didn't need help with his homework. He thinks he's slick."

John says, "Little Man is way too slick!"

KD says, "He used to ask me to play, but I'm not good enough since you came around."

John says, "It's not that, Ladybug. He wants to bond with a man. Trust me, he loves you."

KD says, "So, that's what's going on?"

John says, "It's just male bonding."

KD says, "Come, bond with me!" John kisses KD before he shows her the invitation.

Johns says, "He didn't want to tell you because he didn't want you to feel guilty if you had to work. I told him you and I will be there and we would invite Kelly and Kathy."

KD says, "I can't imagine all the things I missed over the last five years."

John says, "Hey, don't feel bad. You provided well for your son all on your own. I'm here now, so it's not all on you anymore. Let's look to the future; it's two of us now. Let's promise that at least one of us will make it to every game, competition, parent meeting, whatever. Can we look forward and make that commitment to him and each other?"

KD says, "We can!"

John adds, "I am here for you and Daniel, always, no matter what. We are in this together, remember that. We are a family!"

KD says, "Thank you, baby."

John says, "I love you!"

KD says, "I love you!" John hugs KD to let her know he has her.

John picks Daniel up from football practice because KD is still at work. They go straight to the park to practice handling and shooting the basketball. John tells Daniel, "We better go home, clean up, and cook before your mother comes home." After they eat, John goes to KD's room to watch the game. Daniel comes to KD's room with his homework, so he can watch the game with John.

When KD enters the apartment, she hears them excitedly talking about the game. Daniel says, "John, did you see that? Can you teach me to do that?"

John says, "Of course."

KD walks into her room and says hello. Daniel says, "Hi, Momma!"

John says, "Hey, Ladybug!" KD asks how they are doing. They let her know all is well.

KD goes to her bathroom. As she showers, she hears them talking. Daniel sounds so happy and that makes her happy. Daniel excitedly says, "John, that was awesome. Did you see that?"

John says, "That was nice! We need to practice that move." John is so engaging with Daniel, and it warms KD's heart.

John asks, "How is that homework going?"

Daniel says, "I'm done!"

John says, "I'm proud of you! I had fun hanging with you today."

Daniel says, "I had fun too, John! I better go to bed before she gets upset."

KD peeks out the door with her toothbrush in her mouth; she says, "Go to bed, Son, no video games. You hear me, Son!"

Daniel says, "Yes, mother," as he rolls his eyes. He looks at John and says, "There goes my plan up in smoke!"

John is tickled. He says, "Goodnight, Little Man!"

Daniel says, "Goodnight, John! Go straight to bed, Kissy Face John, no kissing, Kissy face KD. I know that's what you're going to do as soon as I leave the room. You all get to have fun, but I'm banished to bed. So, under stimulating! Childhood is depressing."

John laughs as Daniel leaves the room. John's attention goes back to the game. KD comes out of the bathroom with wet hair and only a towel covering her body. John is totally preoccupied by the game. John never looks at her as she crawls in the bed.

With his eyes glued to the TV, he says, "How was your day, Ladybug?" She doesn't answer. She leans on her knees between his legs and slowly rubs up his thighs. John looks around her to see the TV. He asks, "You had a good day?" KD doesn't answer.

John is so into the game that he doesn't realize she is seducing him. KD lifts his jogging pants and underwear to expose his manhood. John, still looking at the television, asks, "What's up with you?" KD doesn't answer. She strokes his manhood as she bends over. She slides her lips over him. John immediately puts all his attention on KD. John is about to speak, but KD puts her hand over his mouth as if to say shut up and enjoy yourself.

They stare in each other eyes as KD sucks and strokes him with her hands. KD's magnificent performance makes John forget all about the game. She is entertaining all his senses in a way nothing else could. KD's lips, tongue, and cheeks delicately, yet strongly pull, tug, and glide over him as she seductively looks into his eyes.

John feels so good that he lays back and relaxes. She sees his eyes roll to the back of his head. She knows what's about to happen, but she doesn't stop. She gets up and whispers in his ear, "Make love to me!"

He quickly leans up; he whispers, "You don't have to ask me twice," as he unties the towel and throws it on the bed. She looks at him as he softly caresses her body. He pushes her body to the mattress. He slowly slides into her. The feel of her relaxes every bit of tension in John's body. The burst of tingles in her stomach makes her bite her lip. They look in each other's eyes, acknowledging the incredible sensation each one is giving the other.

John places one hand on her throat and his other hand presses down on her pelvic area. John sways her body in rhythm with his deep, long strokes. KD immediately feels a surge of pleasure as John works her body. KD begins to breathe heavily as an orgasm is on the horizon. She and John try to be as quiet as possible, so Daniel won't hear them. John covers her nose and mouth just for a moment to intensify her pending pleasure. The sensation makes her eyes water.

She looks at him with amazement on her face and gratefulness in her eyes, unbelieving of the miracle he is making. Her orgasm starts in her chest, taking her breath away. Her body begins to twitch as she holds on to John's arms. KD is overcome with pleasure. She bites her lips to keep from making a sound.

John whispers, "Ladybug, look at her." He repositions them so KD can see. KD lifts her head to peek at her body taking in John. John whispers, "Look at how she's taking all of me. Baby, it's a wonderful sight to see." John takes long, deep strokes.

He looks up into KD eyes; he says, "Listen! You hear how wet she is?" John strokes faster to make the swishing sound louder. John looks at KD with ecstasy in his eyes and pleasure on his face. He says, "Baby, you hear her?"

KD whispers, "Yes!"

John goes back to watching himself move in and out of KD. John says, "Ladybug, look at her cum on me." KD lifts her head to watch, which makes the sensation more intense.

John whispers, "Baby, she is talking to me." He asks, "What do you think she's saying?"

KD answers, "John Michael King, you feel like the first warm day after a long, cold winter. Just like the day we met. After a long, harsh winter, you brought the joy of summer."

John whispers, "I hope she knows I feel the same way!" John folds KD's body making her knees touch her arms. Her butt is lifted to his hips. He watches himself move through her like a train traveling through a tunnel. John whispers, "Turn over!" KD rolls over onto her knees. She stretches out her arms to arch her back. John takes a minute to enjoy the view.

John says, "You're so perfect!"

KD whispers, "You are!"

John lowly says, "You fuck me first!" John caresses her back and butt as she pushes him inside her. Once John is inside her, she begins to push her body back and forth. KD rolls her spine and hips encompassing all of John. KD looks back at him. The expression on his face says exactly how he feels. He bits his lip to refrain from moaning. He whispers, "Oh my God, baby, give it to me!"

KD whispers, "You can have it all, baby!"

John says, "You won't give it to anyone else."

KD says, "No, baby! Never!"

John says, "You promise?"

KD says, "I promise!"

John says, "Tell me!"

KD says, "It's yours, baby! I promise there will never be anyone else."

John says, "I get all this for the rest of my life."

KD says, "Yes!"

John says, "All of you belongs to me?"

KD says, "Yes!"

John says, "Let me enjoy my blessings!"

John adjusts her body. He says, "Keep that arch." She turns to look at him. He stares in her eyes as he deeply strokes inside her, making her body bounce on him. It's hard to be quiet, but she holds in her feelings. John is inspired by the expression on her face. Her eyes are rolling in the back of her head. He asks, "Right there?"

KD says, "Yes! Baby, stay right there."

John fulfills her request. The pleasure makes her break her silence. John sticks his thumb in her mouth to keep her quiet. John knows what the look on her face means. KD's entire body begins to tremble with tremors of pleasure. All she can see is a blinding white light as her body becomes weightless. She feels complete contentment as John kisses her.

John lays on his back. KD gets on top of him. She slowly lowers herself onto him. John lays back and relinquishes control. He says, "I'm just going to lay back and enjoy the ride." When John feels himself climaxing, he leans up, grabs KD by the throat, and pulls her face to his. John makes her body bounce on him as he strokes upward into her.

John says, "You are so beautiful when you feel that way, Ladybug."

KD says, "Thank you, Baby!"

John says, "Don't ever give that look to anyone else! Save it for me, KD, promise!"

KD says, "I'll save it all for you, baby, I won't be with anyone else."

John says, "I won't either!"

KD whispers, "I love you so much!"

John gets quiet. John keeps stroking as her next orgasm floods her body with pleasure. KD lowly whispers, "Bay-bee!" They hold each other as they both experience an incredible high.

John asks, "Are you good?"

KD answers, "Yes!"

John says, "Me, too!" He gets comfortable.

He asks, "Are you satisfied?"

KD answers, "Yes!"

John says, "Me, too!"

She gets under the cover and rolls on her side to get comfortable. She relaxes, preparing to fall asleep while John watches the end of the game. John lays there watching TV for a few minutes. Quickly, he begins to feel lonely. John moves closer to her.

He asks, "Can we cuddle?"

KD, she says, "Yes!"

John scoots behind her and wraps his arms around her. He kisses her shoulder. He says, "Goodnight, Ladybug!"

She says, "Goodnight, baby!" She closes her eyes. John lays holding her for a while. He calls her name. She says, "Yes, baby!"

He asks, "Do you want some more?" She turns to look at him. He smiles at her.

She looks in his eyes and asks, "Are you sure you don't want to watch the rest of the game? It's almost over."

John quickly says, "Fuck that game!" He realizes that wasn't the best response. He says, "I mean, I feel a need for you and was wondering if you need me."

KD smiles and says, "Yes!"

John asks, "Are you for real? I can have some more?"

She says, "Yes!"

John kisses and rubs her body as he talks to her; he asks, "You are so perfect! Your energy, body, appeal, voice, personality, and demeanor are everything I'm attracted to. You're my perfect woman. Tonight, don't get me wrong, you're incredible every time, but tonight that energy was turned up. What's up?"

She looks at him touching and kissing her as she listens to him talk. She thinks about how much she loves and appreciates him. She answers, "Tonight, I heard you and Daniel bonding, how supportive you are of him, and how you give him the love he has never had from a man. I don't have anything to give you other than myself to show you how much I appreciate you for loving my son. Thank you for loving us the way you do."

John says, "So this is what a real relationship is like, an equal exchange of love and appreciation!" He kisses her. He says, "You don't have to thank me. It's a pleasure and an honor to be your man. But if ever you feel inspired to be that nasty, girl, help yourself!" They laugh.

KD says, "You liked tonight?"

John says, "Honestly, I loved it. Remember, when we first started dating and I said you would be the best and you would bring out the best in me?"

KD says, "I remember!"

John says, "I knew then you had it in you. Every time we're together, you get more comfortable. Every day our relationship and love grow stronger. I know you think I'm talking shit when we're intimate and I say you're the best and I have felt nothing like you before, but, KD, I'm telling the truth, the honest to God truth. We have the most incredible sex.

"It's not just the sex. The way you treat me and support me makes the sex even better. Ladybug, you are incredible in every way. When I found you, I found the woman that completes me. You are who I've searched for all my life. Don't ever leave me!"

KD says, "John, there's no way I'm leaving you. I love you too much to live without you."

John says, "Honestly, I feel your love, and it relaxes me and brings me so much joy," they kiss. He says, "I am so in love with you and I mean everything I say to you."

They kiss again, leading to the deepest intimacy John has ever experienced. John has never been so open and vulnerable with a woman. John reveals his real emotions to KD and feels no apprehension. He feels safe with her. The safety and stability he feel in their relationship make the sex more incredible and intense.

The next morning, John is alone in KD's apartment. As soon as he steps out of the shower, there's a knock on the door. John wraps a towel around his waist and rushes to open the door. John doesn't recognize the man; he says, "May I help you?" The man is uncomfortable looking at John nearly naked with drops of water running all over his exposed muscular chest.

The uncomfortable man finally speaks; he says, "I'm Daniel's dad. He left his bag in my car. I thought I'd bring it here in case he needs it before Thursday." John reaches out his hand and says, "I'm John!"

The man shakes his hand and says, "I'm Bradley!"

John says, "I'm sure he'll appreciate you bringing it. I'll make sure that he gets it."

Bradley says, "Thank you!"

John says, "You look familiar. Have we met before?"

Bradley says, "Yeah, we've met a couple times. The company I work for did some contract work for your company back in the day."

John instantly puts the pieces together; he says, "Bradley Jacobs! [The energy immediately changes.] I didn't know you were Daniel's dad. KD doesn't talk about her past."

John conceals his hate with his cordial manners. John asks, "You've been good?"

Bradley hates John a million times more than John hates Bradley, but he remains cordial; he says, "All is well!"

John says, "You have an awesome son. I know you are proud of him. He does so well in school. He's a good person and talented athlete. I try to catch every game and competition." John intends to be demeaning because Bradley never comes to Daniel's school events.

Bradley says, "I'm proud of all my boys." Bradley wants to flex just a bit.

John says, "Daniel never mentioned younger brothers."

Bradley says, "Younger sister and two older brothers." That statement enflames John, but he remains calm and cordial. Bradley says, "I hope all is well with KD."

John says, "KD is always good! That's my heart. I'll always make sure she is well, but she'll appreciate your concern."

Bradley says, "You and KD take care!"

John says, "You, too!"

That afternoon, John thinks about Bradley having children outside his marriage. He calls Kelly to get more information. John says, "Your dad came by the apartment this morning."

She says, "What! He is never supposed to come into the building. I can't believe him."

John asks, "Why?"

Kelly says, "Something terrible happened one night when DJ and Momma still lived in our house; that's why Momma sold the house and moved into the apartment. That's all I can say. It would be inappropriate for me to share because it's not my story to tell. [That comment makes John think Bradley did something bad to KD.] What did he want?"

John says, "He left a bag claiming Daniel left it in his car, but I've never seen Daniel with that bag, and there was nothing in the bag."

Kelly says, "That doesn't sound right. I don't know why he would come there."

John says, "It's probably nothing. I don't want to start something over nothing."

Kelly says, "I will definitely tell him to never come back there!"

John says, "Don't mention it, please! Baby Girl, thanks for talking to me!"

Kelly says, "Okay! You're welcome, Stepdad!"

John asks, "Baby Girl, before you hang up, let me ask you something. Do you have a brother other than Daniel?"

Kelly says, "He mentioned them? Momma doesn't know, but Bradley Jr. is three years older and Brady is one year older than Daniel. We met them after the divorce. Dad begged us not to tell our mother about them or our little sister, Braly, who is four years younger than Daniel. We keep the secret because what good would it do to tell our mother that our father cheated on her with two women and fathered three kids outside their marriage."

John asks, "Who are the mothers of the three kids?"

Kelly says, "Bradley's mother is his co-worker, Heather Helms. Brady and Braly's mother is Camille Sims. He still lives with Camille."

John shakes his head. He can't believe Bradley had children with Heather and Camille.

John asks, "Is Camille nice to Daniel?"

Kelly says, "Camille is cordial, but not engaging. Dad only gets Daniel, so he won't have to pay child support. Dad and I are close, always have been, but he and Daniel don't care for each other at all."

John says, "Baby Girl, that's terrible."

Kelly says, "Honestly, Daniel hates Bradley."

John says, "Baby Girl, that explains a lot. Daniel never complains, but he is so sad every Wednesday night."

Kelly says, "Daniel is miserable, but he knows what will happen to our mother if she makes our dad mad, so he just goes to keep the peace."

John asks, "What do you mean what will happen to your mother?"

Kelly says, "I don't know if she would like me telling you. Stepdad, just know Daniel saw things he shouldn't have and even though he was young he knew what was going on, and he remembers everything."

John can't take any more of the conversation. He can't stand to know Bradley harmed KD, and he can't do anything about it because it would hurt Kelly. He says, "Baby Girl, thank you for taking the time to answer my questions."

Kelly says, "You're welcome, Stepdad. Talk to you later."

John hangs up and texts KD: You know I love you, right?

KD: I do! I love you, too!

John: You know I will never hurt you!

KD: Is something wrong?

John: No! Everything is right. I'm in love with you, and I want you to know it.

KD: I'm in love with you, and I will never hurt you.

John: Promise, you'll never leave me.

KD: I promise. Are you sure everything is okay?

John: Everything is fine. Ladybug, I'm going to my grandsons' game this evening with my sons. Be careful. Call me if you or Little Man need anything.

KD: OK! Are you sure everything is okay?

John: Everything is good! I'll see you tonight!

KD: See you later!

When John gets to KD's apartment, she is cleaning up the kitchen. Daniel is in his room playing video games. John goes to say hello to Daniel first. After talking to Daniel, John walks into the kitchen as KD washes the last dish. KD looks up and smiles; she says, "Hey, baby!"

John says, "Hey, Gorgeous!" John walks over to her, hugs her, and kisses her neck.

KD asks, "How was your day?" KD wipes her hands. She turns to hug and kiss him.

John says, "Work was work, but my day was strange. Your ex stopped by this morning."

KD asks, "My who stopped where?"

John says, "Bradley Jacobs was here!"

KD says, "Impossible!"

John pulls her to the table. He sits her in his lap. John says, "Tell me what really happened between the two of you."

KD asks, "Why would he come here? Are you sure?"

John says, "A man came to the door. He said he is Daniel's dad and he handed me a duffle bag that he claimed Daniel left in his car, but I've never seen Daniel with that bag. I opened the bag, and it was empty. It's the green duffle I put in the closet. He was probably just lurking."

KD says, "Why would he want to see what I'm doing?"

John says, "He found out a man is here. He wanted to see who."

KD says, "But why?"

John says, "Ladybug, he still cares about what you do! Be careful. Be watchful getting in and out of your car."

KD says, "Okay, but I can't imagine that he cares, and I, for sure, don't give a damn what he is doing." Looking to change the subject, she says, "Are you hungry?"

John says, "No, I already ate!" KD gets up and leaves the kitchen.

KD goes to her room, and John follows her. John says, "I'm not trying to upset you. I'm only trying to understand what happened between you and him." KD crawls into bed so embarrassed by her past that she can't look at John. John sits at her feet.

John says, "Something happened that you're not telling me. It's okay if you don't want to talk about it, but I'm here for you. If someone hurt you, I want to know." KD doesn't speak. John asks, "Can I be honest with you?"

KD says, "Yes!"

John says, "Only if you promise not to get upset."

KD says, "Okay! I promise I won't get upset."

John says, "With your ex stopping by, well, I needed to get in his head, so I called Kelly. She didn't say anything specific, so don't get mad. What she did say made me feel like you may need me because he did something to you, and no one protected you. No one checked on you. When beautiful women are vulnerable, men take advantage of that. You have someone now to listen to you, protect you, and check on you. That's what this is. I'm checking on you."

KD, still refusing to look at him, says, "He hated that I got to keep the house. When Kelly left for college, the peacemaker was gone. A year after the divorce, he came over one night, claiming he wanted to see Daniel. I knew that wasn't what he wanted, but I didn't have the energy to fight him anymore. I let them talk in the dining room, and I locked myself in the bedroom. I didn't hear footsteps or voices. All I heard was the bedroom door being kicked in.

"Our son sat at my bedroom door crying, begging him to stop. To know my son heard and saw him do that to me tears me up inside. Daniel called his sister, and she convinced him to leave. He promised to never come back if we didn't call the police."

John lays next to her and wraps his arms around her; he says, "I'm sorry that happened to you and Daniel. Neither of you deserved to go through that." John holds and kisses her as she cries.

KD asks, "Why would he come here?"

John says, "That's a good question." John consoles KD until she stopped crying. John says, "He will never hurt you again! I promise I will keep you safe."

KD says, "I know you will. I appreciate that about you!"

After the visit from Bradley, John worries about KD's safety, so he upgrades the building's security system, gets new security cameras installed throughout the building, and buys two brown and white Akita puppies. When John walks into the apartment with the puppies, Daniel rushes over to hug the puppies. The puppies love Daniel immediately. They jump and lick all over him.

Daniel says, "John, are these your puppies?"

John says, "If your mother lets us keep them."

KD hears the commotion in the front room. She comes to see what John and Daniel are doing. When KD walks into the room, John says, "The puppies are housebroken. They are training to be guard dogs. I would feel more comfortable knowing they are here when I'm not."

Daniel says, "Momma, please, may we keep them?"

KD says to John, "They are so adorable." She bends down to pet the puppies.

John says, "Their trainer is coming by tomorrow to teach us how to care for the puppies."

KD says, "John, that sounds expensive. Are you sure about this?"

John says, "The safety of my woman and little man is important to me."

KD says, "Well, I guess we have new puppies."

Daniel says, "Thank you, John, and thank you, Momma. They can sleep in my room."

John says, "They have a special diet because they are puppies. This is all they can eat for now." He grabs the bags dog of food, doggie bowls and toys, and takes them into the kitchen.

As John and KD shop for costumes, he explains the annual pre-Halloween social event sponsored by the club to raise money for breast cancer awareness. Dr. Segal intensely watches them from his car parked outside the store. The mysterious black Benz is also outside the store lurking across the street. John and KD are unaware that they are being watched.

John says, "We sell dinners, have a raffle, collect donations from Detroit-based corporations, and have a best costume contest. All the proceeds go to the Detroit Cancer Center's community outreach program. They provide free screenings and treatment to the under or uninsured in the community. Every year the party gets bigger and better. Last year, we raised a million dollars."

KD says, "Sounds like fun for a great cause."

John says, "Ladybug, our costumes have got to be lit. Last year, I lost to Isaiah and Jayla."

KD says, "What were you dressed as?"

John says, "We were Ike and Tina. I made her eat the cake and everything."

KD says, "What were they dressed as?"

John says, "They were Jay and Bey. I hate to admit it, but they were so cute."

KD says, "That sounds really cute, but at least you lost to one of your sons."

John says, "I hate to lose, especially to them. They throw it in my face when they beat me at anything and call me old. They make me think I am losing it."

KD sharply says, "John Michael King isn't losing a damn thing."

John says, "I love you, Ladybug!"

KD says, "I love you, too, baby, but we can do better than Ike and Tina."

John says, "I see now, that was a poor choice. See how you make me better."

KD says, "We need something more fitting of your personality. You're a hero, savior, baby."

John says, "You're right!"

The two lurkers watch KD and John buy their costumes and follow them to a Downtown restaurant where they have lunch. They laugh and affectionately talk as they eat. Both lurkers watch filled with jealousy. After eating, John carries KD on his back to his car. Their happiness disgusts the jealous lurkers so much that they leave.

The night of the fundraiser, John and KD arrive at the club dressed as The Punisher and Lynn Michaels from the Marvel comic books. The couple looks great and is happy as they enter the club. John's kids and their spouses are in attendance. John's friend and their wives are also at the party. John and KD greet everyone; John immediately begins to enjoy the party.

The servers sell raffle tickets for $100 per ticket. KD is smart. She buys ten tickets but she buys each ticket at different times and from different servers. The three prizes are $5,000 in cash, a $10,000 designer purse, and an expensive bottle of champagne. John spends nearly $6,000 on raffle tickets. Like everyone else, John is after the money, so the competitive spirit is thick in the atmosphere.

KD buys food. She sits and eats with a smile on her face watching John have fun with his kids and friends. Bella strikes up a conversation with KD. Bella introduces herself.

KD shakes her hand; she says, "I'm KD!"

Bella says, "It's nice to finally meet you. Do you need anything, a drink, wine, water?"

KD says, "What do you suggest?"

Bella says, "I know just the drink, I'll be right back."

KD says, "Okay!"

Bella comes back with a drink. Bella says, "You're going to love this. It's a favorite."

KD sips the drink; she says, "It's good!" KD smiles and says, "Thank you," as she tries to hand Bella a twenty.

Bella says, "It's on me. Anything for the woman that makes Bossman happy."

KD she says, "Thank you!" KD is delighted with Bella.

Bella says, "My father worked in the factory for many years, so we've known Mr. King our whole lives. Mr. King has been like a father to me since I lost my parents in a car accident when I was in high school. He has taken care of my siblings and me. He got us an apartment, a car, and every Christmas he literally dresses up like Santa Claus to bring presents for my younger siblings. He did everything to keep us together. He got us a lawyer. He went to court with us. He knew if we were put in the system, we would be separated.

"He paid for my big brother to go to school, and gave him a job after he graduated. My brother has bought a home and he is the guardian for my little brother and sister. They are so happy and well-cared for. He got me this job, and helped me get my own apartment. He keeps us all out of trouble. He's paying my tuition now, and promised me a job when I finish school.

"He is a good man. People don't know how much he does for people in the community. Everyone has opinions of him: oh, he's this and he's that. He is a lifesaver. He saved us. You came along, and you saved him."

KD's heart melts listening to Bella's story. KD says, "Thank you! Your story is so inspiring. You are an incredibly strong, young woman to survive and thrive after such a tragedy. I am so happy your family is doing well." KD reaches out to hug Bella.

Bella says, "I wish you and Bossman all the best. I hope you know how much he loves you. Don't listen to rumors. This is the happiest I have ever seen him and we are all happy for him."

KD says, "I wish you all the best. I know you have a bright future, and thank you for the advice."

Bella says, "Bossman introduced me to Kelly. She is lovely just like you. I can see why she is so pretty."

KD says, "Thank you! You're beautiful inside and out. Be blessed, Bella!"

Bella says, "If you need anything, let me know."

KD says, "It was so nice to meet you and talk to you. We have got to talk again."

Bella says, "Okay, Ms. KD!"

It's time for the raffle and the whole club is on edge. The first prize is the bottle of champagne. The host calls the number. A tall, beautiful woman with long blonde hair dressed as Cat Woman screams. Her friends clap for her as she goes on stage to get the champagne.

The highly sought after purse is up next. The club is silent as the host calls the numbers. KD is shocked when she realizes she has the winning number. The host asks, "Do we have a winner?" KD raises her hand. The host points at her and tells her to come to the stage with her ticket to get her new handbag.

John yells, "Congratulations, baby! That's my baby!" Everyone at their table cheer for KD as she goes on stage to get her bag. A lot of the women in the club show great disdain for KD, especially the one who won the champagne. KD feels the hate and sees the mean mugging. John sees it too, so he celebrates her win even louder.

When she gets back to the table, John kisses her. The gawkers watch, wishing it was them. John looks at her purse and tells her the purse is very pretty. Everyone at their table congratulates her. John kisses KD again. He says, "I love you, Ladybug!"

She replies, "I love you more!"

It's time to call the winning number for the money. John doesn't want the money; he wants the bragging rights. He bets his sons a thousand dollars each that he's going to win. John taunts his sons and friends with his tickets. The atmosphere is contentious as the whole club becomes silent again. John silently gloats, thinking he is going to win. Everyone has their tickets in their hands closely surveying the numbers as the host calls the numbers. Immediately after the host says the last digit, KD shouts, "I won!"

John looks at her ticket and says, "Baby! Congratulations!" He hugs KD and carries her to the stage. KD runs to the host. She jumps up and down as the host hands KD the envelope holding the money. John carries her back to the table.

When he gets back to the table, he tells his sons, "If my girl won, I won. Pay up!" Neither of them buys that argument. They order him to pay up. KD puts the money in her new purse. The whole club is salty because KD won twice. The host says, "She bought multiple tickets, so she can win multiple prizes." The crowd complains, but the host hushes the crowd when she says, "She's a blessed lady, what can I say!"

John yells, "That's right!"

John tells KD to take her new purse with the money in it to his son's office. John asks Nisha, one of the servers, to take KD to the office and lock her purse in the safe or desk drawer. Nisha shows KD to the office and locks her purse in the safe. Before going back to the table, KD stops at the bar to order another drink.

As she waits for the drink, she feels a hand move across her back around to her breasts. She feels a kiss on her neck as she is wrapped tightly in an embrace. At first, KD thinks it's John. KD picks up her drinks and sips it while she is in the embrace. The lips kiss her again. That second kiss doesn't feel right. She notices the scent of the cologne is not John's.

KD looks at the arm wrapped around her. The costume is the same as John's but the skin tone is nowhere close to John's. KD immediately jumps out of the embrace. She turns to see a familiar smile and eyes behind the same mask John is wearing. She throws her drink in the man's masked face. She throws the glass at him. She picks up a few discarded drinks from the bar and throws them at the man as well. The man grabs her arm, but she pushes him away.

KD says to the man, "Don't ever touch me! Stay away from me!" KD pushes the man again before she runs and locks herself in John's son's office. KD runs pass Bella so fast she didn't hear Bella asking her if she's okay. Bella watches KD run into the office. She immediately runs to tell John something is wrong with KD. Another server cleans the drinks and picks up the glasses KD threw.

KD paces the floor, shaking with anger and fear. John knocks on the door, and asks her what's going on. She tells him she's okay and to go back to the party. John says, "KD, open the door or I'll kick it in." KD opens the door. When she sees his face, she quickly wraps her arms around his neck. She squeezes him so tightly that he knows something is wrong.

John asks, "Ladybug, you're shaking. What's wrong?"

KD says, "I'm good, I just need a minute."

John says, "KD, what's up? Obviously, something scared you, talk to me." KD holds on to John like a scared little girl who had a nightmare holds on to her daddy. John sits her on the couch. He says, "Talk to me!" KD is visibly shaken as he consoles her.

KD says, "Can you hold me for a moment? After I calm down, we can go back to the party and talk about it when we get home?"

John says, "KD, look at me and tell me what's going on." KD gets in his lap.

KD says, "You're here! I am okay, now. Let's just go back to the party."

John says, "You stay by my side. Don't move unless I move. This conversation is not over." John wipes KD tears. He says, "I hate to see you cry. What happened?"

KD says, "We'll talk when we get home."

John and KD go back to the party. KD stays by his side for the rest of the night. John and KD win second place to Isaiah and Jayla who are dressed as Barak and Michelle Obama. John is pissed about losing to his son for the second time, but he congratulates Jayla and Isaiah. When they get in the car to go home, KD, holding her prizes, says, "Can we go to your house tonight?"

John says, "What's up, KD?"

KD says, "I want to spend the night with my man at his house. Something has to be wrong?"

John says, "Someone tells me my girl ran and locked herself in the office. I find you crying and shaking like you seen a ghost. Now, you want to go to my house. Yes, something is wrong."

KD says, "I don't want to talk about it. Let's just go to your house and forget about it."

When they make it to John's house, KD goes straight to his room and locks herself in the bathroom. She takes a shower. She brushes her teeth before slipping on one of John's t-shirts. She crawls under the covers still visibly nervous and scared.

John takes a shower and brushes his teeth. When John comes out of his bathroom, he moves the covers from KD's head. He sees she's crying.

John says, "KD, what happened?"

KD says, "Baby, don't get upset."

John says, "KD, what happened?"

KD says, "I was at the bar ordering a drink. You, well, someone I thought was you came up behind me, touched my back, my breasts, and kissed my neck. The touch and kiss were so familiar that for a second, I thought it was you. When the lips touched my neck a second time, my brain said those do not feel like John's lips. Then my brain said he doesn't smell like John.

"The person was dressed exactly like you, but the skin tone was very different. It became clear that it wasn't you, but I knew those lips, that touch, and that smell. The thought of him touching me. I couldn't believe he was standing there smiling at me. John, baby, I can't lie I was so scared. It shook me up, but it is over, so let's just forget about it."

John asks, "KD, who was it?"

KD says, "Baby, please let it go."

John says, "You don't have to fear anyone. Just tell me who touched you."

KD says, "Baby, maybe I was tripping."

John says, "We tell each other everything. No secrets, Ladybug. Who was it?"

KD crawls in his arms; she says, "Bradley Jacobs!" John hugs her. KD says, "He kissed me and touched me. When I turned and saw him smiling at me, all the feelings I had the night he raped me flooded my mind." John holds her as she cries.

John says, "Ladybug, I'm so sorry that happened to you. Why didn't you come get me, so I could handle him?"

KD says, "I don't want your kids to think there's going to be trouble every time I come around. Bradley's not worth your energy. Plus, he is Kelly's father."

John says, "That's the only reason he hasn't been handled. Baby, you are shaking."

KD says, "How'd he knows which costume you were going to be wearing tonight? Do you think he is stalking us?"

John says, "I think he is, so you need to be careful."

KD asks, "What does he want?"

John answers, "I think he's trying to break us up."

KD answers, "That's not happening. Do you think he is trying to get full custody of DJ?"

John answers, "He doesn't need to follow us or dress like me for that. What he did tonight doesn't seem like a child custody case."

KD says, "Would you get a gun and come back to hold me until I fall asleep?"

John says, "Ladybug, I don't like when you cry. I don't like that he puts this much fear in you. I'm going to be cool because he's Kelly's father, but I swear you don't have to fear him. I got you. I won't let Bradley hurt you again."

KD says, "Thank you for protecting me. I love you so much!"

John says, "Try to get some sleep, Ladybug. You are safe. You don't have to worry," he kisses her forehead. He adds, "I love you! Ladybug, sweet dreams!" John doesn't sleep until he thinks KD feels safe.

John tells KD to come take a ride with him. KD asks, "Where are we going?"

John says, "Ladybug, you're with me," KD grabs her purse and gets in the car without speaking another word.

When they arrive at the gun range, KD asks, "What are we doing here?"

John says, "You need to protect yourself when I'm not home. I need to make sure you are comfortable enough with a gun to pop someone trying to get in the house."

KD says, "Baby, I don't know if I can do that."

John says, "Stay in the car if you don't trust me, or think about Little Man and get out the car for him." KD gets out the car. John knew she would try it if he mentioned Daniel.

First, John shows her how to load the gun. He has her practice loading the gun a couple times. He put the goggles on her. He moves her body to show her how to stand. He put the gun in her hand. He whispers in her ear, "No one has the right to come into your home. You have a God-given right to protect yourself and your son. Whether it's Bradley Jacobs or some random person, it's on you to keep yourself and Little Man safe if I'm not there. Okay, Ladybug." She nervously shakes her head.

John says, "Relax," as he places her hand on the gun. He shows her how to hold the gun. He places her finger on the trigger. He says, "Squeeze." She jumps from the loud bang. He helps her hold the gun for the first few shots. He feels she is nervous, so he supports her. He says, "Keep your hand here, so you don't hurt your hand." He eases away his support of her hands.

He tells her, "Squeeze." She shoots. He says, "Squeeze!" She shoots. He says it again, "Squeeze!" She shoots again. He says, "Aim it at the center. Let loose, Ladybug." She rapidly fires until the gun is empty. He tells her to load the gun. She does it right. He says, "There you go, Ladybug. Let loose!" She repeatedly squeezes the trigger until the gun is empty.

Riding in John's car to Daniel's school for the robotics competition, John asks KD to connect his phone to the charger. KD opens the center console to get his phone charger. KD notices several pieces of crinkled paper next to John's charger. She moves the paper to get to the charger. She notices her name is written on the paper. KD plugs the charger into John's phone. Very curious, she decides to read one of the notes. KD mouth drops. So, appalled by the first one, she reads more. She says, "What the hell?" John looks to see what has her upset.

John says, "Ladybug, don't read that."

KD is livid. KD asks, "Where did these come from?"

John says, "I randomly find them on my windshield, but, Ladybug, I am not fazed by that."

KD says, "None of this is true. I have never and would never cheat on you."

John says, "I know. Someone is jealous. I only keep them in case this person escalates."

KD says, "John, who would say things like that about me? They know my name, what I do, what I drive, what I look like, and my son's name."

John says, "KD, our relationship is between you and me. What people think or the lies people tell have nothing to do with us."

KD says, "John, I don't like this. I don't like that someone is saying those things about me."

John says, "I'm your man! What matters is what I think, and what I know. Look at me! That shit doesn't matter to me. I know what's up. You know what's up. We trust each other. All right, Ladybug! Put that shit back in the console, and get back to enjoying your day."

KD looks at him about to give a rebuttal, but John cuts her off. John says, "It's you and me. I'm keeping my promises. You're keeping your promises. We are good!"

KD opens her mouth to speak, but before she could get a word out, John says, "We're good!"

KD concedes; she puts the notes back in the center console. John says, "Don't think about that shit. We are going to support Daniel. Your mother and daughter are going to be there. I can't have them thinking I upset you. Calm down and get back to being my happy KD."

KD says, "You're right, baby!"

John says, "Where's my smile?" KD smiles. John says, "That's my girl!"

After the robotics competition, Daniel begs to spend the night at John's house. Daniel really wants to play video games on large screen projector in John's basement. Being the first-place winner of the robotics competition, KD lets him have what he wants. They have dinner with Kelly and Mrs. Daniels before they go to KD's apartment to pack an overnight bag and get the puppies.

That night, KD is lying next to a sleeping John. KD takes his glasses off his face and takes his iPad from his chest. She places them on the nightstand. KD receives a text from her daughter.

Kelly: Momma, have you ever looked at John's social media pages?

KD: No, what's on them?

Kelly: You!

KD: What about me?

Kelly: Go look!

KD doesn't have social media, so she sneaks his iPad off the nightstand. John opens his eyes to see her taking the iPad and says, "The passcode is your birthday." KD sits the tablet back on the nightstand. She waits for John to fall asleep. She eases out of bed, grabs the tablet from the nightstand, and tiptoes into the bathroom.

KD sits on the edge of the tub and unlocks the tablet. She is shocked when she opens the first app and sees a picture of him and her on his boat as his profile picture with the caption: I found the love of my life. His cover photo is a picture of him with KD's sitting in his lap with the caption: Love of My Life #LOML. She is moved by the sentiment.

She reads his recent posts. Every word is about his grandkids, her, her son, or their relationship. She is shocked because she had no clue the John posted about her or their relationship. The next image is of KD with his granddaughters with the caption: She loves every part of me, and every part of me loves her. She scrolls to a picture of her, Lourdes, and Langley with the caption: My Ladybug #LOML with my Lovebugs #bestgrandgirls. She keeps scrolling to an image of her leaning on John's back with the caption: She has my back and my heart #LOML.

Next is a picture of John and Daniel with the caption: My little man is so smart and brave #proudstepdad. There's a ton of pictures of John and Daniel with the hashtag #proudstepdad. They are playing basketball, cooking, at the arcade, at sporting events, and fishing. John posted a ton of pictures of Daniel's all-boys birthday celebration. Daniel looked so happy in every picture and it makes teary-eyed KD smile.

She scrolls through his photos and videos to see John documented their trip to St. Tropez and Sorrento for his birthday. As she looks at the pictures and videos, she remembers the trip. KD remembers swimming and sunbathing on the beaches of St. Tropez. KD smiles when she comes across a video of her and John playfully singing to each other as they sail on the Golfe de St. Tropez.

She comes across a picture of her leaning on his arms on the train ride. That picture sparks beautiful memories. She bites her thumb as she thinks about the way John made love to her on the train. When she gets to the pictures they took in Italy, she remembers hugging and kissing him while they walked through the streets of Sorrento at night with music blasting and kissing in the cave of the Blue Grotto on Capri Island.

John posted pictures and video of him teaching her to swim in his pool. She watches a video of him cheering her on when she started to swim. He posted over fifty pictures of her in a bikini with her hair wet with the caption: From her head to her feet, she is beautiful! #LOML. He posted video on them kissing and hugging in the pool. She remembers what happened in the pool after the video stopped. She knew he took the pictures, but she had no idea he posted the pictures. Although she is a private person, she is flattered by his public display of affection.

John posted photos and videos of them with their kids and friends from the Fourth of July and Memorial Day. On the Fourth of July, John posted a picture of the women with a caption: All My Girls. There's a picture of John and her mother from Memorial Day with the caption: Moms. Next is a picture of KD hugging Kelly on his boat on Memorial Day with the caption My Favorite Girl #LOML and My Baby Girl #proudstepdad. Her favorite is of him and her kissing with the caption My Favorite Girl, My Favorite Thing #LOML.

She keeps scrolling until she gets to when he first posted about her. She sees he changed his relationship status from single to in a relationship the morning after they made love for the first time. The posts make KD smile. She switches to the next app. She sees John has chronicled their entire relationship. He brags about how good his woman and stepson are to him in most of his posts. KD kills the apps and locks the tablet.

She creeps over to the nightstand. She quietly and slowly tries to put the tablet back on the nightstand. She jumps when John says, "Did you find what you were looking for?"

KD says, "You scared me."

John says, 'That's what happens when you get caught snooping. Did you see what you wanted to see?"

KD says, "Yeah" with a sneaky smile.

He says, "It's cool! It's not like I haven't gone through your phone before," he grabs her arm and pulls her into the bed.

She asks, "You've been through my phone?"

John says, "A few times."

KD asks, "What did you find?"

John answers, "Absolutely nothing!" They laugh. John says, "I was so relieved!"

KD asks, "My life was pretty boring before I met you."

John asks, "How did you abstain? I mean, I didn't even see any dirty videos."

KD says, "After it's taken from you, you feel differently about giving it away."

John says, "That's understandable."

KD says, "When did you go through my phone?"

John says, "When we started to get serious. I had to make sure things were what you said they were."

KD says, "Oh!"

John asks, "What interested you in my tablet," as he wraps her in his arms.

She rests her head on his chest; she says, "My daughter texted me, telling me I was on your social media pages. I wanted to see what you posted."

John asks, "Did you see?"

KD says, "Yes!"

John asks, "Did you like what you saw?"

KD says, "John, everything you wrote was so sweet."

John says, "I tell you that stuff all the time."

KD says, "But that is public for the whole world to see. It's sweet that you speak so highly of my son and that you love him like your own. John, I appreciate that."

John says, "I love our relationship. I know him because of you, but I love him because of him. He is a great kid. KD, you've done a wonderful job."

KD says, "Thank you, baby!"

John says, "Can we go to sleep now or do you want my social security card, baby photos, and birth certificate. It's in the safe if you ever need it, and the code is your birthdate."

KD says, "My birthdate?"

John says, "If it is an emergency, I figured you would easily remember your birthdate. The passcode to everything is your birthdate."

KD says, "I feel so special."

John says, "Ladybug, I'm exhausted, so if you're done being Magnum P.I., I would love to go to sleep."

KD says, "Goodnight, John!"

John says, "Goodnight, Love of My Life!" He kisses her shoulder and closes his eyes. KD lays on his chest, thinking about what she read until she falls asleep.

John is deep asleep when a hand touches him. John jumps out his sleep to see Daniel standing over him. John looks confused because Daniel has his finger over his lips telling him to be quiet. Daniel waves for him to follow him out of the room. John eases out of bed, trying not to wake KD. Daniel points out his thumb and forefinger. John knows that means grab a gun.

Daniel is careful not to make noise, but he moves with urgency. John cocks the gun as he whispers, "What's up, Little Man?" Daniel holding a finger over his mouth waves, indicating to quickly follow him.

When they get to the kitchen, Daniel takes him to the window. He points out the window. There's a flashlight moving around in the backyard. John looks around the backyard and sees another flashlight. Daniel points to the puppies. John whispers to Daniel, "In thirty seconds, give the signal and let them out the door, then, go back upstairs to your mother." John rushes to the front door.

Daniel looks at his watch. When thirty seconds pass, Daniel opens the door and gives the puppies the attack signal. Daniel hurries to close door before he runs up the stairs. The puppies charge the two masked men making them flee from the backyard. The puppies manage to bite their ankles, but they aren't strong enough to stop them from escaping. John is posted with a gun waiting on the would-be intruders to make it to the front of the house.

As soon as they are visible, John shoots. John manages to shot one in the shoulder and the other in the arm, but they manage to keep running. John runs after them, shooting. He shoots each of the men again. The force of the bullet makes one of the men fall, but he hurriedly gets up. The fear of the bullets whizzing through the air motivates him to run despite the pain. John keeps shooting, managing to shoot each man again.

Despite being wounded three times, the men make it to a dark, running car awaiting them at the end of the driveway. A third masked person is in the driver's seat. They jump in the car and the driver pulls off at top speed. John empties his gun shooting into the car as he chases them. He shots out the back window and hits the dashboard and seats several times.

The gunshots wake KD. She hoops up and reaches for John. She panics when he is not there. She hurries out of the bedroom to see Daniel watching from the top of the stairs.

KD hugs Daniel. She asks, "Daniel, what's going on?"

Daniel says, "Two people were trying to break in, so John shot them."

KD says, "What? Oh my God!" John and the dogs come back into the house. KD says, "John, what is going on? Are you okay?"

John says, "Go wait in my room, Ladybug, take Daniel with you. I'll be up there in a minute."

Daniel and KD go back to John's room as Daniel tells her what happened: "I was sneaking back to the basement with the dogs to play video games because I couldn't sleep. Well, I could sleep, but I didn't want to sleep. I was getting some water when a light came through the window. I peeked out the window and saw two people holding flashlights looking into a basement window. I ran upstairs to get John as fast as I could. The dogs chased them to the front and John shot them."

KD says, "Were they trying to break in?"

Daniel says, "It looked like they were trying to get into a basement window."

KD says, "Come here, baby! Are you okay?" She hugs Daniel.

Daniel says, "I wasn't scared, Momma. I didn't panic. I stayed quiet and came straight in here to get John."

KD says, "You did the right thing, Son."

Daniel says, "The puppies were so brave. They bit them."

John comes in the room; he asks, "Are you okay, Little Man?"

Daniel says, "Yeah! I told Momma what happened."

KD and John look at each other. KD asks, "What happened out there?"

John says, "They got away, but they are both hit several times. The police are on the way."

KD says, "I can't believe you shot two people. This is unbelievable."

When the police arrive, they look for evidence. They get samples of blood from the specks of blood left from the dog bites and gunshot wounds. They also take DNA swabs from the dogs' fur and mouth. They take pictures of the footprints, they dust the basement window for prints, and get statements from Daniel and John.

When the police leave, Daniel and John give the puppies a bath to get the blood out of their fur. As they bathe the dogs, John tells Daniel he will always do whatever he has to do to keep him and KD safe. John apologizes for the craziness, but Daniel is unbothered. He thinks John is cool and brave for shooting the would-be intruders. After the dogs are clean, Daniel asks if he and the puppies can sleep in the room with KD and John. John says, "Of course!" John and Daniel get into the bed on opposite sides of KD.

KD cradles in John's arm. She asks, "Do you think they were trying to break in?"

John says, "I don't know what they were doing."

KD says, "Baby, are you okay? You shot somebody."

John says, "They weren't about to get in here with my woman and little man. I will protect you at all cost."

KD says, "Baby, the thought of tonight is so scary."

John hugs her tighter. He says, "I love you so much! I will always make sure you're safe. Try to go back to sleep." KD thanks him before telling him she loves and appreciates him.

Before Daniel falls asleep, he looks up at the ceiling. He says, "John, you must really love to look at yourself. The ceiling is completely covered with mirrors." KD and John look at each other and smile. John says, "It's just decoration."

Daniel says, "It's cute, a little vain, but cute." John and KD try to conceal their laugh.

KD says, "Goodnight, Son, I love you!"

Daniel says, "Good night, Mama! Good night, John!" John tells him good night.

The next day, John gets a new security system with outdoor cameras. He also gets new gun boxes installed throughout the house that open with his thumb print or a passcode. He and KD go to the range every day to practice shooting until John's next business trip. KD becomes more comfortable with handling the gun. John encourages her and affirms she can and will stop a threat because he can sense she is apprehensive.

Before he leaves, John tells KD, "Be watchful and careful. Call one of my sons if you feel uncomfortable. Call me every night as soon as you walk through the door." KD promises she will be safe. John says, "Don't be out late, don't open the door for any unexpected visitors. As a matter of fact, Henson drives you any and every where you need to go." KD promises she will be safe and comply with his list of demands.

When John returns home from a business trip, he stops by the office for a little while. Since KD is at work and Daniel is with his father, John decides to go home. He showers before relaxing on his couch to eat and watch sports news. KD texts him.

KD: Are you at home?

John: Yes

KD: Alone?

John: Yes

KD: What are you doing?

John: Watching sports news. How are you? How is work going? John gets no reply.

Darkness fills his house as he lounges on the couch watching television waiting on KD to text back. John hears a noise at his front door. John cuts off the TV and creeps toward the door. He approaches the door just as KD opens the door. She is dressed in black thigh-high boots, leather gloves, and a black satin trench coat.

John says, "Hey, you! You're supposed to be at work." KD doesn't speak as she closes and locks the door.

John reaches out to hug her; he says, "I missed you!" KD hugs him tightly. KD pulls off her gloves before pulling down his pants and underwear. John smiles and says, "It's good to see you, too!" KD smiles at him as she unbuttons and takes off her jacket.

When John sees her strappy lace bralette, the matching G-string thong with a lace garter belt and attached thigh-high lace stockings, he says, "Damn!" KD gets on her knees. Her attire, her hair, her quietness, and her energy have John mystified and intrigued. KD rubs him. John touches KD's hair; he says, "I like the braids. They're so sexy!"

KD rubs his butt cheeks. She slowly spreads them with her fingers. He says, "What are you doing?" Her finger slowly moves inward. He says, "Hey, get…." Before he could finish the sentence, she hits the spot instantly making him rock hard. He says, "What the…?" The rapid flow of blood from his brain and feet to his manhood slightly makes him lightheaded.

KD closes her eyes and opens her mouth. Her lips and tongue glide over him while she squeezes him with her hands. John says, "Is this your way of saying you missed me?" She winks at him. She wants John to feel how much she missed him. She escalates from gentle to intense. John says, "Be as nasty as you want to be!" She indulges so well that John's knees buckle. John says, "Oh! I love that shit! Keep doing that!"

KD keeps giving him what he wants. John gets quiet; his eyes roll in the back of his head. John leans against the wall vulnerable from the pleasure racing through his body. KD shows him her tongue before she swallows. When John sees that, he is immediately energized. John picks KD up from the floor and put her against the wall. He pushes her panties to the side to let her slide down on him. The feel of him entering her sends bursts of pleasure throughout her body. KD grips his shoulders as John's love gives her the feelings she desired.

As John carries KD to the couch, she looks in John's eyes and caresses his face. She feels hopelessly head over heels in love with him. She doesn't have to acknowledge her feelings verbally because John sees it in her eyes and feels it in her touch. KD has never been in love like this, and it scares her. While KD feels fear, John has never been so sure of a relationship.

He lays her down and takes a moment to look at her body. He says, "KD, this outfit! I love it. It's so sexy! You are so sexy!"

KD says, "Thank you, baby! You're incredibly sexy!"

John asks, "Did you buy this outfit for me?"

KD says, "I did!"

John says, "You knew what this was going to do to me?"

KD says, "Wishful thinking!"

John softly touches her cheek; he says, "I appreciate you, Ladybug."

KD says, "I appreciate you."

She rubs his arms as he admires her body with his hands. John leans over to kiss her neck. She touches his face as she watches him caress her body. He kisses her lips. KD instantly feels her love unleashed throughout her body. John touches a swollen area of skin. John asks as he reaches for his phone, "Did you hurt yourself?"

KD says, "It did hurt!"

John asks, "Ladybug, what's this?"

KD says, "Look at it!" John shines his phone's flashlight as he rubs her skin.

John asks, "Ladybug, that's my signature. Is that real?"

KD says, "Yes!"

John says, "Ladybug, you got my whole name tattooed on your girl spot."

KD says, "Yes, I did!"

John says, "Ladybug, I don't know what to say." John softly kisses the tattoo. He says, "KD, I can't believe you really did this. I'm honored. I mean, no one has ever done anything close to this. Ladybug, this makes me feel special and loved. When did you get it?"

KD answers, "A few nights ago."

John asks, "Ladybug, that's so cute! I'm touched! For real! I can't believe you got my name tattooed on you. What made you get a tattoo?"

KD answers, "I got two! Find the other one." John lifts her strappy bralette. He sees ladybug tattooed on her left breast over her heart. KD says, "I was hanging with Kelly and Kera. We were talking at dinner and next thing I know we are at the tattoo parlor. They were picking out tattoos when I reached in my purse to look for something. I pulled out one of your cards. I saw your signature. I was missing you, and imagining what it would be like to see you. I thought what better way to show my devotion and commitment."

John says, "KD, I love it. I love you!" He kisses her. He lightly rolls his fingertips over the tattoo. He says, "Ladybug, this is the most thoughtful thing anyone has ever done for me." John kisses her lips. He looks at the tattoo again. He says, "I can't stop looking at it," his index finger slowly rolls over it. He asks, "Kelly knows you did this?"

KD says, "Kelly and Kera saw it, but all our girls know about it."

John says, "What did they say?"

KD says, "They said it's cute. Are you sure you like? Is it too much?"

John says, "Seriously, Ladybug, I love it. I'm shocked, but I'm flattered!"

KD says, "I'm in love!"

John says, "You mean that, don't you?"

KD says, "I really do!"

John kisses her. He is unable to stand one more second without feeling her. John slides into her, making love flow through her body. She expresses her emotions, and John loves it. He takes in the scene auditorily and visually.

He asks, "You feel that, too?"

KD says, "Yes, baby!"

He asks, "What is that feeling?"

She answers, "Love!"

John says, "It feels so good to be loved by you!"

KD says, "I feel the same way!"

John bends KD over the back of the couch. John is so excited that he travels so deeply inside her that he hits a spot neither one of them felt before. They pause, she looks back at him, and he looks at her. They stare at each other for a moment.

KD says, "Where are you?"

John says, "You're the nurse! You tell me!"

KD says, "You felt that?"

John says, "I felt a part of you I've never felt before. Did I hurt you?"

KD says, "No! It felt weird."

John asks, "Are you good?"

KD answers, "I am!"

John says, "Let me see what happens if I keep hitting that deep!"

KD smiles at him. She says, "Just don't break it!"

John says, "I definitely don't want to do that to the best thing I ever had."

KD says, "You flatter me!"

John says, "Can I ask you something?"

KD says, "Go ahead!"

John asks, "Do I flatter and fuck you better than the men before me?"

KD answers, "You absolutely do! You're the best."

John says, "What is it that I do that makes me the best?"

KD says, "You want to talk about that right now?"

John says, "I'm not stopping. I can listen and perform, trust me. Baby, when you talk like that, it motivates me."

KD says, "You pay attention to me and what I like. You put your whole heart, mind, body, and soul into giving me what I need the way I like. No one has ever put so much into loving me and making sure I enjoy myself. Every time I think you've given me your best; you blow my mind with something new. Honestly, baby, the way you love me is so amazing."

John says, "Like this?"

KD says, "Yes, baby! Just like that!"

John asks, "Do you love it, Ladybug?"

KD says, "Yes, baby, I love it!"

John says, "Let me ask you something else."

KD says, "Ask your question."

John asks, "Am I the biggest?"

KD answers with no hesitation, "Yes, you are!"

John asks, "So you are completely satisfied with my sex?"

KD confidently answers, "I am completely satisfied with all of you."

John asks, "Is there anything you need that our relationship doesn't give you?"

KD says, "No!"

John says, "If you are wondering, I'm letting you know I am completely satisfied with everything in our relationship. I love you. I am in love with you. I love making love to you. You are amazing. Your sex is amazing. You make me feel amazing. You're my wonder woman."

KD says, "You're my superman! Being with you is like having six feet two inches, two hundred pounds of twenty-four-karat gold in my hands. You are incredible."

John says, "Ladybug, I have never wanted a woman or enjoyed a woman this much. You never have to wonder about my love, okay, Ladybug!"

KD says, "Okay!"

After John loves KD with all his might, KD quietly lays on his chest feeling him breathe and listening to his heartbeat as he sleeps. She hates to leave, but she must go. KD kisses John, waking him up; she says, "Thank you, baby! I needed that," before getting up to put on her coat and boots.

John checks his watch, he asks, "It's four o'clock in the morning. Where are you going?"

KD says, "I left my son home alone. He's never been home alone this late."

John says, "It's the weekend, I thought he was with his father?"

KD says, "He hasn't gotten Daniel for two weekends."

John asks, "Why?"

KD says, "No call, no show! I have never left him alone all night."

John says, "I'll come with you."

KD says, "Baby, you're tired. I'll be careful."

John says, "You better!" John attempts to get up, but KD says, "Go back to sleep, baby!"

KD kisses John. She says, "I love you," before she walks toward the door.

John says, "I love you! Ladybug, be careful! Call to let me know you made it home."

KD says, "I will!"

Before she walks out the door, John says, "Hey!" KD turns around. John says, "Happy birthday, Ladybug!"

KD says, "Thank you, baby," before she walks out the door. John lays on the couch physically exhausted. He lays there thinking: she fucked the shit out of me and left me worn out on the couch like a bitch. She's something else.

The next day, John sits on his bed, thinking about the night before. He calls KD, who is making her rounds at the hospital. When she feels her phone vibrating, she quickly reaches in her pocket to see if it is John. When she sees his name, she ducks in the stairwell. KD says, "Good afternoon, baby!"

John says, "Good afternoon! I missed you after you left. I'm not complaining, but I wanted more time with you."

KD says, "I understand. I hated to leave you."

John says, "You shouldn't have!"

KD says, "I hate the thought of him waking up alone."

John says, "That's not what I meant. I love you. I love your son. I want you and him around me all the time."

KD says, "We are around you all the time."

John says, "No, Ladybug, I want you and Little Man to move in with me."

KD says, "John, that's a big step."

John asks, "Do you love me?"

KD says, "I do!"

John asks, "Are you in love with me?"

KD answers, "I am!"

John asks, "Do I take care of you? Am I good to you?"

KD replies, "You do! You are!"

John says, "Do you believe I will provide for you and protect you?"

KD says, "Yes!"

John asks, "Do I satisfy you?"

KD answers, "Yes!"

John says, "I'm so happy with you. Are you happy with me?"

KD says, "Very!"

John asks, "Do you want to live with me?"

KD says, "Yes!"

John asks, "Could you happily spend the rest of your life with me?"

KD says, "Yes!"

John says, "KD, this is what we both want."

KD says, "I could take the chance if it were just me, but I have to think about DJ. What if we don't work?"

John says, "We're going to make it work because we want this family."

KD says, "John, you've done so much for DJ. I appreciate you, but I don't want you to feel obligated."

John says, "I am obligated as the man trying to be with you. I know what I'm getting into, and this is what I want. KD, this is what you want, so say yes!"

KD says, "If you sit DJ down to talk man to man and he says yes, my answer is yes."

John says, "I'm going to talk to Little Man. Tonight, we will all sit down together to have a nice dinner to celebrate your birthday and talk about our future. Okay, Ladybug?"

KD says, "Okay!"

John says, "Have a good day at work, Ladybug!"

KD says, "Okay!"

John says, "Happy Birthday, KD!"

KD says, "Thank you, baby!"

When they hang up, John sits on his bed looking at KD's birthday gifts. He calls Daniel who is at his grandmother's house to ask Daniel to have lunch with him. Daniel is always happy to spend time with John, so he's ecstatic to have lunch with John. John takes him to his favorite Italian restaurant so they can talk.

John says, "I want to have a very frank and honest conversation with you. I want us to put everything on the table, and this is a safe space so you can say whatever you need to and it stays between us."

Daniel eats as they talk; he says, "Okay!"

John says, "You know how I feel about you and your mother."

Daniel says, "Yes!"

John says, "I want us to be a family. I want us to live together. I want to ask your mother to marry me, but I need to talk to you first because you're the man in her life. I want your blessing." Daniel sits quietly. Suddenly, he seems sad. He stops eating to stare out the window.

John asks, "How do you feel about that?"

Daniel asks, "John, I love you, but if marrying my mother means you get to yell at her and hit her, I prefer you don't marry her."

John says, "I would never hit your mother. I love her."

Daniel says, "You can love her and still hit her."

John says, "I'm one hundred per cent man and one hundred per cent asshole. I guarantee you there will be times KD will be upset with me. Men have a way of making women mad that we don't understand. I know I can be selfish and self-centered, and she will get angry for those two reasons. She may cry, curse me out, or make me sleep on the couch. I promise you those times will come, but a man deals gently with his wife, and he has self-control.

"I can't promise that your mother will never be disappointed or unhappy, but I can promise you I will love her, take care of her, protect her even in those moments. I only want to love her, not hurt her. Will she get her feelings hurt? I guarantee she will, but it will never be intentional and, damn sure, it will never be physical."

Daniel says, "My mother has been through a lot. I can't watch her cry and get hurt again."

John asks, "You saw someone hit your mother?"

Daniel says, "My father used to hit my mother. He would yell at her and make her cry. My sister would rush me to my room, but I heard everything. Do you know what rape is, John?"

John says, "Yes!"

Daniel says, "When I was five, my mother and I were home alone. We were laughing and having a good time. Bradley came over, and my mother locked herself in her room. He pretended that he wanted to spend time with me, but I knew he didn't because he doesn't even like me. We knew he came to bother her. I don't know why he had to mess with her because he had a girlfriend. It wasn't the first time I heard her cry, scream no, and beg him to stop, but it damn sure was the last time, John, I can't live through that again."

John says, "Daniel, I never want to say anything against your father, so I'm attacking his actions and not him when I say this. That is not the behavior of a grown man, a husband, and definitely not a father. He should be ashamed of himself for exposing you and her to that trauma. Neither of you deserved that."

Daniel says, "He cheated on her. I never told her, but I saw him kiss Bradley Jr.'s mother while he was still married to my mother. He told me she was his friend like I hadn't just seen him kiss her with his tongue. John, I can't watch my mother be dishonored again. John, I love you, but if you hurt my mother, I won't love you anymore."

John says, "I'm going to be honest with you."

Daniel says, "Okay!"

John says, "I married way too young because I got a woman pregnant. I had no intention on starting a family with her. I didn't want to settle down. I knew that I wasn't ready, but I thought it was the right thing to do. A weak heart and good intentions don't create a good ending to any story. I married another woman for the same wrong reasons and got the exact same result.

"After the second divorce, I told myself no relationships, lying, or cheating. I convinced myself that the best thing for me was to stay single, so I could do what I wanted. I spent the next twenty years running through women like water running through a broken faucet. One day I looked at my life, and I was lonely even though I was surrounded by women. I needed something that none of them could give me, and to be honest, I didn't even know what I needed.

"I saw your mother and something drew me to her. We talked. I had to see her again. I got to know her, and she fulfilled the longing and loneliness I felt. When I entered a relationship with KD, I got something I never had before. You know what I got?"

Daniel says, "What?"

John says, "Love! No woman has loved me like KD loves me. I found the person I can call to share my good news with and the woman who turns my bad days into good days. I'm not letting anyone distract me from the best thing that has happened to me outside my children and grandchildren.

"Your mother is happy, and she makes me happy. We've found something in each other neither of us had before, and we're both old enough to appreciate and deserve it. Your father and I are in opposite situations. He had a good woman at a young age. That was all he knew. He got out there in those streets and ran into the wrong women. He took his frustration out on KD. He knew KD's weakness: you and your sister. He knew KD didn't want to upset her kids.

"The way your father treated your mother wasn't right, and it's not the way it should be. A man is supposed to honor and protect his wife, but sometimes men can make their good woman their foot stool, their enemy. They get arrogant and think their good woman is burden. I, on the other hand, had superficial relationships young. I didn't have a woman to have my back and stick by me through the storm and pressure. My experiences have taught me that my good woman is a blessing.

"I won't cheat, hit, or dishonor your mother. She has made it very clear that she will not put up with that, and your well-being comes first. KD is my best friend, she's my girl, she's the love of my life. She will never be my enemy. I have no desire to fight or hurt her. We have something real. She deserves that after all she's been through. She is happy with me. She's in love with me, and that makes me happy. And, I don't ever want to let you down or disappoint you. I want us to be a family. I'm not going to risk or ruin our family for anything."

Daniel says, "I want us to be a family, too, but only if you are going to be respectful and considerate to my mother emotionally, mentally, spiritually, and physically."

John says, "I promise your mother will be safe with me physically and emotionally. I'll make you a deal. We will find a new house together, all three of us. If I fail to keep my promise, I will leave. You and your mother can keep the house. Little Man, you have gotten to know me well. Can you trust me enough to take a chance on me?"

Daniel says, "I want a huge room, a king-sized bed, a Jacuzzi tub, swimming pool, and a basketball court in the backyard."

John says, "Deal!" They shake hands. John says, "Tonight we're going to have a family dinner to celebrate your mother's birthday. I'm going to ask her at dinner. Are you okay with that?"

Daniel says, "Honestly, I hoped for this for a while now."

John says, "I'm glad this is what you want."

Daniel asks, "Are you nervous?"

John says, "I am!"

Daniel says, "Don't be! She wants to marry you. I know my mother."

John says, "You think so?"

Daniel says, "I know so! My grandmother is going to church-lady shout. She's been waiting on this since she met you. She keeps saying, 'I love my new son. I hear wedding bells. I can't wait for him to ask KD to marry him.' My grandmother is so happy my mother has you. I'm glad, too!"

John says, "I'm glad she has you." John and Daniel fist-bump and go back to eating.

As John and KD dress elegantly for dinner, KD says, "Thank you for the roses."

John says, "What roses?"

KD says, "I got a dozen long-stem red roses and a card that said happy birthday, baby! I assumed they were from you."

John says, "I didn't send roses."

KD says, "I thought it was strange because you only call me baby when we are having sex!"

John asks, "I do?" He takes a moment to think about it. He says, "I do!" KD laughs. John says, "That's because you're my Ladybug!" He winks at her.

John asks, "What flower shop did the roses come from?"

KD says, "The roses were in a clear vase sitting on the counter with a birthday card. My name was on the envelope. I didn't see a delivery person or a logo on anything."

John says, "Throw all that shit away. Someone is trying to be cute."

KD says, "I will!"

Everyone shouts, "Happy birthday, KD" as soon as John opens the door to the private room of an elegant new restaurant in Downtown Detroit. The room is professionally decorated with roses and balloons. KD is honored to see their kids, John's grandkids, her brother and his family, her mother and her mother's boyfriend, Mena, Tri, Nanette, Laura, and Karen standing around the long table in the center of the room.

KD is overwhelmed with appreciation. KD greets everyone with a hug, and thanks them for coming to celebrate her birthday. They all tell her they wouldn't be anywhere else. When she greets her mother, she hugs her tightly. She says, "Momma, I didn't know you were coming."

Mrs. Daniels says, "Happy birthday, Little Girl!"

KD says, "Thank you, Momma!" John greets KD's friends and thanks them for coming before he leads her to a table full of gifts and a big, beautiful cake against the wall.

KD says, "You did all this for me?"

John says, "Of course, I'll do anything for you!"

KD hugs him and says, "Thank you, baby!"

Lourdes and Langley run to KD. They tell KD, "Happy birthday." She picks up Lourdes to thank her and hug her. She hands Lourdes to John, so she can pick up Langley to thank her.

KD sits next to her daughter. She smiles at her daughter before greeting her. She says, "Hey, daughter, I didn't know you were going to be here."

Kelly says, "John's been planning this for weeks."

KD asks, "What is he up to?"

Kelly says, "I don't know, but he is up to something."

Langley won't leave KD's lap. Lourdes sits on John's lap, so she can be close to KD. John's daughters jokingly try to figure out why Lourdes and Langley love KD so much.

John says, "They know their granddad loves her."

Kimma says, "Oh, that's what it is?"

John says, "Kids can sense good people."

The dinner party enjoys an engaging, light-hearted conversation while they eat. After dinner, KD opens her birthday gifts; she thanks everyone for the gifts. She adores the bracelet John gave her already.

When the candles on the birthday cake are lit, John stands up with Lourdes in his arms and says, "I want to thank you all for sharing this special moment with us." Everyone gets quiet and looks at him. Kimma, Kera, Kenna, and Kelly pull out their phones to record John's speech.

John turns to KD. He says, "KD, our time together has been amazing. You are an incredible woman, and you make me a better man. My days, my nights, my life have completely changed since you let me into your life. This is the happiest I've ever been. You are everything I could ever ask for in my life partner, friend, and lover.

"You make the sun brighter and my burdens lighter. When I have a bad day, you encourage me. When I have a good day, you celebrate me. I love you. I'm in love with you. I want to share my home, my life, and my world with you. I hope you feel the same. I asked our families and your friends to celebrate this very special moment with us."

Sensing something big was about to happen, Kelly takes Langley from KD's lap, and Kimma gets Lourdes from John. John turns KD's chair to face him.

John says, "KD, since we meet, I have a whole new set of dreams. I dream of growing old with you. I dream of us watching Daniel graduate from college, say his vows at his wedding, and raise his own family. I dream of being at Kelly's wedding, and holding her first baby. I dream of you being there for my girls and grandgirls. I dream of years of family dinners and holidays with you sitting next to me.

"I dream of taking baths with you, taking vacations with you, taking my last breath lying next to you. I dream of standing in front of God and taking you as my wife, but death can't do us part. You will be my wife in the afterlife, the next life, for the rest of eternity. I want to hear you call me husband forever. KD, can you make my dreams come?"

KD says, "I will, baby!"

John gets down on one knee. He looks directly in her eyes as he pulls a ring box from his pocket. KD's eyes get wide with disbelief. He opens the box to reveal a platinum ring with the biggest diamond KD has ever seen. KD gasps as a tear roll down her cheek. Her friends get excited at the sight of the ring.

John says, "KD, with you, I have my best friend, the love of my life, my girl, my joy, and my happiness in one person. I am committed to you, your peace, your joy, and your happiness. You with me is all I want, and I'll do any and everything it takes to keep you in my life. I talked to Daniel. He gave me his blessing to ask you to spend the rest of your life as my wife." John slides the ring on her finger; he asks, "Will you marry me?"

KD embraces John as she says, "Yes!" Everyone claps as the happy couple hugs. Mrs. Daniels does a church-lady shout just as Daniel predicted. KD's friends excitedly cheer. Lourdes and Langley happily clap even though they don't fully understand what's happening. Everyone congratulates the couple. The girls post the video on their social media pages, and text the video to John and KD. John also posts the videos on his pages.

Everyone sings happy birthday. John tells her to make a wish and blow out the candles. She closes her eyes. She wishes John will love her forever and that he never leaves her. After she blows out the candles, John kisses her forehead.

That night, they lay in KD's bed, talking. John asks, "Did you enjoy your birthday dinner?"

KD says, "I did!"

John asks, "Do you like your gifts?"

KD says, "I love them! Everything was lovely. Thank you for putting so much thought into my special day."

John catches KD staring at her ring. John asks, "Do you like the ring?

KD says, "I love it, baby! It's the most beautiful thing I've ever seen!"

John says, "When I saw it, I knew it was the one. I'm glad you like it."

KD says, "You really surprised me today. I did not see any of today coming."

John says, "You don't think we are ready or you don't think I'm ready?"

KD says, "I've been so happy just being in a relationship with you that marriage never crossed my mind."

John says, "Do you want to marry me?"

KD says, "I do!"

John says, "I want to marry you, and don't doubt that or my commitment to you. This is what I want. I wouldn't have asked if I didn't. Trust me, KD! Trust this!" KD kisses him.

She says, "I love you so much." She rests her head on his chest.

John plays with her braids. He asks, "When do you want to get married?"

KD answers, "I don't want to distract you. I know you have a lot going with the expansion. We can get married when you come home from your trip."

John replies, "I can do both."

KD says, "No, baby, planning a wedding and making a big business move is a lot. You need to focus. We can have a beautiful fall wedding."

John asks, "Now or later is cool with me. I just want you forever. I'm so proud to be marrying you."

KD answers, "Baby, I'm proud to be the one you want to marry, but you have a lot going on, and it's important to you and our kids. It would be selfish of me to distract you."

John says, "Don't change your mind!"

KD says, "You don't change yours!"

John says, "My mind is made up! This is what I want!"

KD says, "Baby, don't you want me to sign something? I will sign whatever you want me to."

John says, "All the documents are in the safe. When you are ready, sit down and take your time to thoroughly read them. You will see, I was fair. My new will is with the documents. I need you to read that too. I'm leaving the business to Kimma, but you, Little Man, and Kelly will be well cared for. Okay?"

KD says, "You should leave the business to Kimma. That's your family's legacy. I don't want any parts of that. It's not your money. I want you!"

John says, "Take your time and thoroughly read the agreement and will. Let's talk about it."

KD says, "I'm sure you were more than fair."

John says, "I promise your needs and wants will be fulfilled to the best of my ability."

KD replies, "I promise to do the same."

John says, "I want our marriage to be drama-free. I want us to go into this marriage with no secrets. I'm not trying to hide anything. I want you to feel comfortable talking to me about everything, even money. Money is a part of marriage and you need to know what you're getting into. You need to know what to do if I die first. All my wishes are in my will, and it is up to carry out those wishes."

KD says, "Baby, I will honor your wishes."

John says, "You should think about what you want, write it down, and put in the safe. I will honor your wishes. We should also make sure Kelly and Kimma know what we want."

KD says, "You're right!"

He says, "We'll have them over for dinner to talk about the documents and future."

KD says, "Sounds like a plan."

John says, "I'm not trying to step outside my lane, but have you checked in with DJ lately?"

KD asks, "What do you mean?"

John says, "He needs to know you're good."

KD asks, "Like you and I are good?"

John says, "That too, but do you ever talk about the things he saw between you and the ex? He said he saw somethings. He remembers the rape, and he said it wasn't the first time. He feels guilty about not being able to help you. He knows and accepts you must work because you pay for everything, but Ladybug, he's not getting enough of you. He quietly sacrifices because he respects how hard you work. You need to check in with him."

KD says, "I don't know what to say to him."

John says, "Ladybug, you know you can tell me anything. I want to be here for you. If Bradley hurt you, you can tell me, no judgement ever."

KD says, "I don't want you to know how weak and broken I was in that marriage."

John says, "Bradley is the weak one."

KD says, "I hoped he wouldn't remember the horrible things that happened. My daughter and I tried to shield him as much as we could. John, what do I say to him?"

John says, "The same thing you said to me. He's becoming a man. He can handle the truth. He's ready for your truth. Trust me, he checked me today, tough. He let me know he wasn't having any bullshit. He made sure I knew that he wouldn't accept any disrespect.

"Ladybug, you need to let him sit you down and talk to you as a man, not your little boy. He needs to be able to express himself, and you need to listen. Don't try to fix it! Just listen to his perspective on things. Let him get everything off his chest. Accept his truth and be honest and open with yours."

KD says, "I will sit down with him."

John says, "Now, that we are going to be a family, we should establish a space to make him comfortable to express himself. When I was a child, I never felt safe to express myself. I went along with what my parents wanted. I had to deal with my emotions alone. A boy needs to learn how to talk things out, make compromises, and have dialogue with his family.

"People say men don't do this well, men don't do that well. It's because no one teaches us as young men. He's a smart boy and understands a lot more than an eleven-year-old boy should understand. We have the tough, adult conversations now, and it'll save us later. You understand what I'm trying to say."

KD says, "Yes! We've been in a tight space all his life, so I can only imagine how much he has built up inside."

John says, "I'm going to stay in my lane because he is Kelly's father, but I want to knock Bradley out. I bet he sent those flowers to fuck with us."

KD says, "How can a man you never see or talk to still manage to fuck up your day?"

John asks, "When did he start hitting you?"

KD says, "I was pregnant with Daniel the first time he hit me. Things weren't good before he hit me, but that was the end of my trying to make the marriage work. That morning, we were arguing about having the baby. He didn't want me to have the baby. I didn't want to have an abortion. My daughter walked in the room just as he hit me. She froze. I was more focused on how she felt than how I felt."

John says, "How did you forgive him?"

KD says, "I never did! We just resided together, so my daughter could have both parents. I slept on the couch until, eventually, he stop coming home."

John says, "You never have to worry about any of that with me. When we disagree, we will talk it out. We talk about everything. We listen to each other, keep no secrets, use kind words, be patient, and always give each other the benefit of the doubt. You never have to worry about me cheating. I'm not worried about you cheating. It's you and me until the Lord calls us home, deal?" John reaches out his pinky finger.

KD says, "Deal," as she locks her pinky finger with his.

John falls asleep with a sleeping KD on his chest and is immediately awakened by his ringing phone. He doesn't recognize the number. John answers the phone. "My baby boy, I'm so proud of you," a familiar voice says.

John says, "Momma!"

His mother's voice says, "Son, it's so good to talk to you!"

John says, "Momma, it's good to talk to you!"

She says, "John Michael King, you're a good man. You've made me so proud."

John says, "Thank you, Momma!"

She says, "Son, I have to go, but know I love you!"

John says, "Momma, I love you!"

She says, "Son, I love her. She's good for you. I can tell you love her, and she loves you, too! Son, be strong! Keep your faith! I love you!"

John says, "I love you, Momma!"

When his mother hangs up, John jumps out of his sleep, waking KD.

KD asks, "John, are you okay?" John is visibly shaken.

John says, "I was dreaming, Ladybug, I didn't mean to scare you."

KD says, "Baby, you're upset," she rubs his back. She asks, "Do you want to talk about it?"

John kisses her forehead; he says, "I'm good," he put his head in his hands.

KD rubs his back and says, "Awe, baby, we can talk about it!"

KD knows he's crying. She hugs him and rubs his back. John says, "I dreamt of my mother. It seemed so real. I miss her so much."

KD hugs him to console him. She kisses his shoulder as she rubs his back. She empathizes with him.

John says, "I'm good. Come on, let's go back to sleep." KD lays on his chest. John looks at the ceiling until he falls asleep. At four in the morning, John is awakened by a text from an unknown number that reads: Sorry, John. John looks at the phone, and the cryptic message is of no importance to him, so he disregards it. John lays the phone down and tries to go back to sleep.

When John and KD leave KD's apartment to go to work, they find their cars vandalized in the parking structure. KD's tires are slashed. John's windows are shattered, tires are slit, the body of the car is keyed and spray painted, and sugar and water fill his gas tank. Screwdrivers are plunged into the radio and steering column.

John and KD stand next to their cars looking at the damage. John says, "It was probably Raina. I got a text from an unknown number early this morning. She's the only person I know who is up that early. She must be extremely mad because she is normally too concerned with her image and career to take risks."

KD says, "John, I can understand a woman not wanting to let go of you, and that could make her do things outside of her character."

John smiles. He says, "I hope you never want to let me go."

KD says, "Your wish is fulfilled."

John says, "You never want to let me go?"

KD shakes her head no. John says, "I never want to let you go. You're my Ladybug, always and forever!"

John and KD hug as the driver of the mysterious black Benz watches them. John says, "Ladybug, I'm sorry about your tires. You know I'm going to replace them."

KD says, "Thank you!"

Daniel comes to the parking structure. He curiously enquires about the damaged cars, but John and KD are evasive.

John looking for the tow truck, looks out and onto the street. He notices an idle, running car. The car gives John an uneasy vibe. He stares at the car and he can feel eyes behind the tinted window staring back at him. The car is the same year and make as Raina's, but it's a more expensive model.

The tow truck finally arrives to tow their vehicles away. Henson arrives to pick them up. Henson drives Daniel to school before taking KD to work. While driving to his office, John receives a series of taunting text messages from the same unknown number that refer to the damage done to his car. The last message states: Congratulations, you cold-hearted son of a bitch. I hope you liked your engagement gift because I really enjoyed giving it to you.

John, very irritated by the last text message, responds: Hopefully, you find a man that loves you as much as I love KD so you can leave me the fuck alone. Fuck you and those cars. When you have real love, material shit means nothing. If you think your shenanigans cause tension in our relationship, you're wrong. They bring us closer because we are happy. Why would such a smart woman act so stupidly? There was no reply. John words were too honest and mature for Raina to respond.

Raina sits at the anchor desk. She takes a deep breath. The cameras cut to her. She gets the cue. Raina welcomes the viewers back to the Monday morning broadcast after a commercial break.

Raina says, "Detroit's most sought bachelor, John King, is officially off the market. Last night, Mr. King and his fiancée attended the Annual Lexsor-Satchel Black-Tie Gala. The couple looked stunning as they posed for pictures on the red carpet."

A clip of John and KD posing for pictures plays over Raina's shoulder. As Raina continues to talk, a clip plays of a female reporter on the red-carpet asking John, "Did the king finally find his queen?" John grabs KD's hand and flashes her ring. The reporter asks, "Did you pick out the ring yourself?" John gives the thumbs-up. The reporter says to KD, "He chose well!" KD looks at John and touches his face. John kisses KD's hand before they walk into the event.

When the camera cuts back to Raina, her co-anchor looks at her with empathy. He knows Raina is still in love with John. Raina contains her personal emotions and says, "We wish the happy couple a long, blissful marriage." On the inside, Raina is boiling with disappointment because she wants to be the one engaged to John.

KD and John are cooking in John's kitchen as Daniel sits at the table, doing his homework. The dogs are under the table as usual they are never far from Daniel. John opens the refrigerator door as he and KD laugh. Suddenly, KD is frozen with shock. KD can't speak or move. John turns to see panic on her face. He asks, "Ladybug, what's wrong?"

She points to the front room. She says, "Someone is in there."

The intruder turns to see she is pointing at him. He finally gets the door open, and takes off running out of the front door. John rushes to put KD and Daniel in the pantry. He hands her the phone to call the police. John gets a gun out of the lock box in the kitchen, and whistles for the dogs to follow him. He and the dogs take off after the intruder who is running to a waiting black Chrysler at the end of John's driveway. The intruder had too much of a head start, so they aren't able to catch him. The dogs chase the Chrysler until John whistles for them to come back.

He stands in the middle of the street watching the car drive down the street. He gets a good look at the car and license plate. John and the dogs run back to the house to check on KD and Daniel who are shaken up, but safe in the pantry.

The police arrive quickly. John opens the door to let them into the house. KD and Daniel are sitting on the couch. The cops immediately begin to question KD. She hugs Daniel as she explains what she saw. KD says, "We were in the kitchen. I felt like someone was looking me, so I looked up. There was a pair of eyes in the darkness. As he turned, I could see an outline of his body. It seemed like a tall man from the shape of the shoulders, but I really couldn't distinguish much else. When he saw me point at him, he took off running."

John says, "I chased him down the driveway. There was a black Chrysler waiting for him. I wrote down the license plate number." John hands the officer a sheet of paper.

The officer asks if there's anything missing. John says, "We are in the process of moving. Everything is in boxes, so it's hard to tell. I couldn't imagine what he or they were after because the only thing of real value in here are the two people sitting on the couch."

The other officer asks if John knew how the intruder got in. John explains that he found the sliding door leading to the pool open. The officers check around John's house and the backyard, but find no sign of forced entry or any evidence of an intruder.

The officers tell John that the case will be assigned to a detective and to inform the detective if he discovers anything is missing later, so the detective can amend the report. When the police leave, John and KD decide to go to KD's apartment for the night. KD's apartment is also in disarray. KD's and Daniel's things are packed in boxes and prepared for the movers who are scheduled to come in the morning.

Before the movers arrive, they eat breakfast. After breakfast, KD takes Daniel to school before going to work. John and the puppies are home alone when the movers knock on the door. John lets the movers in and puts water and food in the doggie dishes before he takes the dogs for a walk.

While John is out with the dogs, a tall man dressed in all black running clothes sneaks into the back of the building. His face is hidden by his hoodie, sunglasses, and a black mask covering his nose and mouth. With all the movement of the movers and the clever disguise, no one pays any attention to him. The man watches the movers waiting on the perfect moment to make his move. As soon as the movers carry the next load out of the apartment, he sneaks into the apartment carrying a water bottle.

Once in the apartment, he hurriedly looks around. He finds what he's looking for in the kitchen. He opens the water bottle. He pours green fluid into the dogs' water bowls and quickly exits KD's apartment. He heads to the back stairs just as John and the dogs get on the elevator to go back upstairs. The intruder leaves the building undetected.

John and the dogs walk into the apartment never knowing the stranger was in there. John takes the leashes off the dogs, so they can move freely throughout the apartment. The dogs follow John around as he showers and gets dressed. Before he leaves out of the door, he says bye to the puppies. As soon as John leaves the apartment, the puppies run to the kitchen to eat. By noon, the movers have all KD's, Daniel's, and John's things in their new home.

That evening, John's phone rings. He sees KD's name. It makes him smile. He answers, "Hey, Ladybug!"

A crying KD says, "John!"

John's mood instantly turns serious; he says, "Ladybug, what's wrong? Where are you?"

KD says, "I'm at the vet! Something is wrong with the puppies!"

John says, "I'm on my way!"

When John arrives, the vet is telling KD, "The dogs consumed antifreeze. Unfortunately, they didn't survive." John hugs KD and Daniel who are both crying.

John says, "When I took them for a walk this morning, they were fine." John is confused because he knows they didn't go anywhere near antifreeze when they were with him.

They go to KD's empty apartment to look around. John goes into the kitchen. When he sees the antifreeze in the doggie dishes, he calls the police. John is infuriated as he talks to the police. Daniel is so heartbroken that he continues to cry. John and KD console Daniel with hugs, and apologies puppies. Daniel tells them that he doesn't blame them.

The police get the footage from the surveillance cameras. They tell John the intruder hid his face from the camera, he wore gloves and took the water bottle with him. The detective adds, "From the intruder's behavior, it seems as if he knew the locations of the cameras, which apartment was KD's, and the fact that the movers would be on scene."

They give John a report number, and tells him, "Unfortunately, we have no evidence or witnesses." John knows that means that's the end of the investigation. When the police leave, they go to their new house. Despite the sadness of losing their puppies, they try to enjoy settling into their new home.

KD and Daniel are driving to meet John for dinner. KD notices a set of headlights in her rearview mirror. There is nothing alarming about the car, but for some reason KD's attention is attracted to the car. She keeps an eye on the rearview mirror as she drives. The car suddenly speeds up. KD gets over to the left lane, but the car follows. KD crosses back to the center lane. The car quickly follows.

KD senses harm. She drives a little faster, but the vehicle quickly catches up. The loud sound of metal clashing scares Daniel as the car smashes into the back of KD's car. Daniel screams. KD tries to assure Daniel that they will be okay. KD drives faster, but the car rams into KD's car three more times. KD holds the wheel steady as she tries to escape further contact with the menacing vehicle.

The vehicle pulls alongside KD's car. The car gets close; she and Daniel can see two masked men looking at them. Daniel calls the police on his cell. KD tries to remain calm. KD slows down to let the car pass, but it sideswipes her car hard enough to push her car onto the embankment and into the wall. The car quickly takes off into the darkness of the narrow interstate.

KD calls John, who has just pulled up at the restaurant. When John hears she's upset, he gets upset. She says, "John, would you come get us?"

He says, "KD, what's wrong? Where are you?"

KD says, "We are on the expressway just before the exit to come up for the restaurant. Someone purposely crashed into us."

John rushes to the scene of the accident. He is so relieved when he sees Daniel and KD are okay. He is angry when he sees her car. The officers let him into the area of the accident to get to Daniel while the police questions KD. Daniel hugs John as he tells John what happened. Daniel says, "Someone tried to kill us! They kept crashing into us until they ran us off the road. It was two men with ski masks covering their faces."

John says, "Little Man, I'm so glad you are okay, and I'm so sorry someone did that to you. You did not deserve that."

John and Daniel go over to KD as she talks to officers. John hugs her and kisses her forehead. John asks if she is okay. KD nods yes. The tow truck arrives to haul her car away. The officer gives John a chance to get KD's things out of the car. John tells the driver where to take the car.

After the car is loaded on the tow truck, officers tell John he can take KD and Daniel home. As John walks his family to his car, he says, "KD, starting tomorrow, you and Daniel will have personal protection. You and Daniel are not to go anywhere without the protection team." John gives KD a look that says: this is not optional and the topic is not up for discussion. John gets Daniel and KD to agree to comply with the security plan.

They pick up takeout and head home. When they walk into the house, they find their belongings scattered all over the first floor, but nothing is missing. They are puzzled how someone got into the house because there are no broken or ajar windows or unlocked doors. John thinks the person had to have a key.

KD goes into the master bedroom. She sees pictures pasted all over the walls. She gets closer to see the images on the pictures. Each picture is of John with a woman in an intimate situation. She calls for him to come to their bedroom. John walks into the room, and his mouth drops immediately. John says, "What the fuck is this!" John gets closer to look at the pictures. His heart races. He thinks KD is upset.

John says, "Ladybug, I haven't been with anyone else. I don't know where the hell these pictures came from." John calls the police as he looks at the pictures. John says, "KD, I haven't seen any of these women in years, I swear!"

KD says, "I'm good! We're good!" John reports the break-in and the dispatcher says detectives will be the scene soon.

As KD and John talk in their bedroom, Daniel checks the basement and the second floor to see all is well. John says, "What you are looking at is safe, meaningless sex. KD, someone is trying to break us up, Ladybug, don't let them. Especially over this old shit that doesn't matter."

KD says, "No one is going to break us up. Only we can break us up."

John says, "As long as you know that I've kept my promises."

KD looks closely at one of the pictures and says, "John, this looks like your old bedroom. "John looks closely at the picture.

He says, "I didn't take any of these pictures. I've never seen these pictures." John looks closely at the woman in the picture, he says, "That was like five years ago. Who would sit around with pictures of me for five years?" John looks at another picture; he says, "This is Raina from last year, but she wouldn't risk her career taking sexually explicit pictures of herself."

KD looks closely at another picture; she says, "John, all the pictures were taken in your old bedroom."

John looks at more pictures; he says, "This is crazy!" He snatches a picture off the wall; he says, "Look at this picture. This was a long time ago. Damn, Ladybug, I have a secret to tell you about her. I know we don't keep secrets. I was going to tell you the day I found out, but you were upset, and I didn't think it was the appropriate time for that conversation. Do you know her? Does she look familiar at all?"

KD says, "No, should I recognize her?" John sits KD down on the bed.

John is disgusted at the conversation he is about to have. John says, "First, I didn't know Bradley Jacobs was your ex until he knocked on the door that morning. I swear I did not know before that. When I saw you jogging the morning we met, that was the first time I ever heard of you. I heard Bradley was married, but never a name or face, so don't think you and I have anything to do with him. We were never cool, but we were cordial when we first met. He and I hate each other. Well, he hates me! I just reacted to his energy.

"The female in this picture is Heather. I only fucked with her that night to make Bradley mad. Years ago, we were all down in Miami for a work thing. I was in my room, minding my business, and she came messing with me. I didn't know she and Bradley were messing around.

"He smacked the shit out of her in the hotel lobby the next morning. I didn't even mess with her that night. After that situation, there was tension between us. For years, he was talking shit about me. I ran into Heather at a club one night. I figured what would be better revenge than to get his girl. That's the night in the picture. It was a one-time, revenge thing.

"When I spoke to your daughter the day your ex showed up at the apartment, she told me Bradley has a son with Heather, Bradley Jr. He is three years older than Daniel. But that's not it. Shit! I hate to tell you this. Don't trip, Ladybug, this shit happened years ago. I'm only telling you this because it may be linked to all this craziness. Please don't tell Kelly I told you this."

KD says, "Tell me. I'm not concerned with anything regarding Bradley. I'm not mad about something you did years before we met."

John says, "We're good? You're sure?"

KD says, "Baby, we're good!"

John says, "I heard through mutual associates that Bradley was messing with Camille. Camille had been trying to get at me for a while. We ran into each other at a club one night, she did something to me at the table in front of those mutual associates. I only let her do that because I knew word would make it back to Bradley.

"Bradley and I haven't seen or interacted with each other in years, but when we saw each other at your door, it was clear, old feelings had not died. There's something else you should know about Camille. When I talked to Kelly, I found out Jacobs and Camille had two children during your marriage. Camille is the woman he lives with now.

"Bradley came to the apartment and found out I was with you, and he flipped out. Imagine how he felt when I opened the door. The hate and anger he felt because I have the most prized possession in both our worlds. I got you. Daniel and Kelly love me. I got his family, and he is mad."

KD says, "He wouldn't care about me!"

John says, "I need you to think like a man for like five minutes. You were married to him for twenty years. You're his first love, the only woman to be his wife, the mother of his daughter, he will always care what you do. Especially when you're doing it with his biggest enemy. KD, I swear you and I have nothing to do with this stupid rivalry.

"I swear I didn't know who you were until the morning he knocked on your door. I could not believe out of all the women in the world, I was in love with Jacob's ex-wife. Here we are deep in some shit. Bradley, Raina, and the doctor are mad that we are together. Between the three of them, one of them is fucking with us. They are mad that you are with me. I can't see how any of them could have these pictures."

KD says, "There's no way that man cares what I'm doing."

John says, "You think that's how that works? No, Ladybug, he loved you. Don't ever doubt that. What happens is your ego and penis overrule your mind. His cheating wasn't about you. He got caught up being weak with the wrong women. He took his frustration out on you, but he is mad at himself."

KD says, "Three babies explain why he gave me so much hell about having Daniel. He told me, 'Don't name that bastard baby after me.' The mere thought of the possibility of him being the one doing this to us angers me so much. I hate Bradley."

John asks, "Are you good about what I told you?"

KD says, "I'm fine. Do you think he's still mad over Camille and Heather?"

John says, "Ladybug, Camille and Heather don't mean shit to him or me. Think about it. Someone broke into KD's house and threw her stuff on the floor. Someone crashed into and vandalized KD's car. Someone poisoned KD's puppies. Someone is leaving notes about KD on my windshield. Someone tried to break into my house when KD's son spent the night. KD and her son are having dinner with John, and someone is standing in the dark looking at KD. KD, this is about you."

"Someone is trying to get you away from me. Raina may be mad, but she doesn't have the heart to go this far. I doubt that doctor ever knew where I lived. Bradley is mad and he is acting like a little bitch. I can't prove it, but it's him. Who else would want to get KD away from me?"

KD asks, "You really think it's Bradley?"

John says, "I know Bradley has some hand in this. He is working with someone. It's someone who knows my moves. I can't figure out how someone hid a camera in my old bedroom all that time and I did not notice. Someone is on some slick shit. A very smart and technical person, KD, Raina is smart, but she did not know me seven years ago. The depth of her technical knowledge is a smartphone and Fire Stick. She doesn't know high tech shit. This is Bradley. I hate him, but I cannot deny that he is a genius with the computer. Think about it. Two men try to break in the old house, I shot them, and Bradley doesn't show up to get Daniel for a few weeks."

KD asks, "What the fuck is wrong with him?"

John says, "Bradley living with Camille is convenience. He doesn't love her. Having the same address means he's not paying child support. As far as Heather, she is fun and wild. She probably had him going for a minute, but I doubt it was deep. She has been with every man with a little bit of money in the city. After me, she was with two of my friends.

"Bradley is stuck and unhappy as fuck. He is bitter because he fucked up his own life trying to be in the streets chasing hoes who were chasing a bag. I can't believe Jacobs was dumb enough to get either of them pregnant. I know Heather is hitting him for child support. She was looking for a meal ticket, and he was dumb enough to fall into her trap."

KD asks, "If it is Bradley, what are we going to do to get him to leave us alone?"

John says, "He will slip up, and I will catch him slipping."

When Daniel comes to their bedroom door, they stop talking and rush to block his view of the pictures. They tell Daniel to go his bedroom while they wait on the police. As they walk into the living room, two detectives, Detective Vernon and Detective Stratman, knock on the front door.

John and KD recount the occurrences of stalking to the detectives. John gives the detectives a copy of the police reports from the break-in, the poisoning of the dogs, and tell them about the crash that happened just before they came home. John even gives the detectives the notes he kept in his center console.

The detectives ask about their prior romantic involvements. KD explains that she is divorced, and there were no relationships outside John and her ex-husband, Bradley Jacobs. They ask if her ex-husband has a history of violent behavior toward her. She answers yes.

John explains that he had a sexual relationship with the news anchor Raina Rhimes prior to meeting KD. He describes how things went sour after her birthday. John says, "I asked what she wanted for her birthday. She showed me a picture of this jewelry set. I got it for her. She started flaunting the ring on air as if it were something more than a birthday gift. Since the friendship ended, she vandalized my car twice. The last time I saw her she cursed me out and threatened to get back at me." That was the first time KD heard why John ended his friendship with Raina.

Detective Vernon asks, "Is there anyone else that could have a grudge against either of you?"

KD explains the history with Dr. Segal. She starts with the sexual harassment at the hospital and how that led to his departure. She tells them about the meeting at the restaurant, his approaching her in the grocery store's parking lot, and outside the club.

When John and KD show the detectives the master bedroom, the detectives ask John to identify each woman and give as many details as he can recall from the encounters. KD rubs his back as he recounts and recalls as much as he can remember about each photograph.

After discussing the photos, the detectives tell him to take his family somewhere safe for the night. They pack overnight bags, and head to a hotel. Once they are at the hotel, John makes the arrangements for a protection team to escort and secure Daniel and KD twenty-four hours per day.

John explains to Daniel and KD there will be three sets of four armed guards working in eight-hour shifts starting in the morning. John explains to Daniel why security is important and how much Daniel's safety means to him. John makes Daniel and KD promise to never go anywhere without security.

In the morning, KD rides in the black SUV with the protection team led by another black SUV with two armed guards in each vehicle to take Daniel to school. KD tries to console Daniel and apologizes that things have been crazy. Daniel isn't affected by the break-ins, but he is still sad about the death of the puppies.

Daniel asks, "Momma, can you ask John to get us new puppies? I miss the puppies so much."

KD says, "Son, I'm sure he will get you a new puppy."

Daniel says, "Momma, don't forget, okay?"

KD smiles and says, "I will ask him as soon as I see him." Daniel makes her pinky promise.

Daniel says, "Don't you miss the puppies?"

KD says, "I do!"

Daniel says, "If you say you want a new puppy, he will get one. He'll do anything for you."

KD says, "He'll do anything for you. John loves you."

Daniel says, "Tell him we want two." KD promises she will tell him.

The guard in the front seat, Miller, overhears the conversation and texts John to tell him Daniel is very sad and wants two new puppies. John thanks him for the heads-up.

After dropping Daniel off at school, KD stops by her mother's house to tell her mother about the break-in and the crash. Mrs. Daniels says, "Sounds like someone had a key. Someone who doesn't want you two together."

KD says, "John thinks it's Bradley. I don't know."

Mrs. Daniels says, "You think it's Raina Rhimes from the news?"

KD says, "You know about that?"

Mrs. Daniels says, "She talked about him on the news every day for a year. One day she's showing off a ring, the next thing I know, he's at church saying he's your boyfriend."

KD says, "Whatever happened between them happened before I met him. He says they were never engaged and the relationship was casual, but she was pissed when she found out about me. She slashed my tires. She came to his house Memorial Day night. He doesn't know I heard them arguing. She was drunk. She loudly cursed him out, but his story remained the same as if he were talking to me. Maybe what he says about their relationship is true."

Mrs. Daniels says, "Well, John is your business, and you don't have to worry what anyone else thinks of your relationship."

KD's phone rings. It's John. KD says to Mrs. Daniels, "His ears must've been burning!"

KD answers the phone, and says: "Hey, baby!"

John: "Hey, do you want to take a ride with me?"

KD: "Of course!"

John: "I'm pulling up!"

KD says to Mrs. Daniels, "Momma, I'll see you later."

Mrs. Daniels says, "KD, when you're not wearing scrubs, you're half-naked. Does your new fiancé mind that a smidgen of your ass is always out?"

KD says, "My fiancé loves my ass.."

Mrs. Daniels laughs and says, "Bye, Little Girl!"

KD smiles and says, "Bye, Momma!"

Mrs. Daniels says, "Be careful, Little Girl!"

KD replies, "I will, Momma! I love you!"

Mrs. Daniels says, "I love you, Little Girl!"

When KD walks out the door, she sees John sitting on the hood of a red 1967 Mustang. KD covers her open mouth with her hands. John says, "Come, hug my neck!"

KD says, "Baby, that's the car!" She runs over to John and jumps in his arms.

John says, "This was supposed to be one of your birthday gifts, but the mechanic couldn't get it ready in time." He hands her the keys. He says, "See how she rides." KD kisses him and thanks him.

The protection team follows KD as John explains how he got the car months ago from a car collector. John says, "It needs a few more repairs, but after last night, I thought you needed something to make you smile. The mechanic is going to come get it in a few days to finish the repairs. It'll take a week or so, but after that she will officially be yours."

KD says, "John, you're so good to me. I can't believe you got my dream car."

John says, "You're my dream girl. I'm supposed to be good to you!"

KD says, "Awe, baby, you are the man of my dreams. How could I ever thank you?"

John says, "Spend your life loving me."

KD says, "I can happily do that."

John smiles. He says, "I love you so much, Ladybug."

KD says, "I love you, baby."

John gives KD directions to get to the lot where he and his friends race. When they drive into the lot, KD asks, "Baby, do you want to drive?" The protection team parks on the street outside the entrance of the lot.

John says, "I'm good over here. You enjoy your car. Ladybug, push it!"

KD pushes the gas pedal to the floor. She takes several laps around the lot. KD hits a donut before stopping; she says, "Baby, that was so exhilarating!" KD puts the car in park.

John says, "Who taught you how to drive?"

KD says, "My daddy!"

John says, "You handled all that horsepower like a boss."

KD says, "Don't I always handle horsepower like a boss?"

John says, "Yes, you do! So, you like the car, Ladybug?"

KD takes off her seatbelt and gets in his lap; she says, "Baby, I love it! Thank you!"

John says, "I talked to the mechanic; your car is totaled. The insurance company says the repairs are too expensive. They rather write you a check."

KD says, "Thank God I have my dream car."

John says, "KD, I feel terrible about last night. I'll do anything to make it up to you."

KD says, "Baby, we'll get through this and everything else that comes our way."

John asks, "Do you believe that with all your heart?"

KD says, "I do!"

John says, "I do, too, and if two people touch and agree it shall be. KD, I don't want anyone else. I don't see anyone else. You've got to believe that!" John and KD lock hands.

KD says, "I believe that!"

John says, "Tell me you trust me!"

KD says, "John, I trust you!"

John says, "KD, I'm so relieved you believe in me. I believe in you, too!"

KD says, "Thank you, baby, for trusting me and know I will never hurt you."

John says, "With all this shit going on, are you still prepared to become KD King?"

KD says, "Absolutely!"

John says, "You want a big wedding or a small ceremony?"

KD says, "I want what you want!"

John says, "We can fly to Vegas, get married here in a church, or get married on the beach in the Caribbean."

KD says, "I just want to be your wife!"

John says, "Kiss me like you mean that!"

KD caresses John's head as her face moves closer to his. John closes his eyes, anticipating the warmth of KD's soft lips. KD softly presses her lips to John's. As their lips and tongue softly tangle, John's hands slowly move up KD's thighs under her skirt. His hands grip her butt. John leans his seat all the way back; he says, "Mm! Your kisses are so sweet. Give me another one." They kiss again. John says, "Look what you do to me."

KD says, "I feel you bulging out of your underwear."

John says, "I can't help it when you kiss me like that."

KD says, "I don't want you too. I love that you desire me."

John says, "Not just your body, but your presence, support, and your friendship. Your friendship is the most important thing I have. We have so much fun when we're together."

KD says, "I love that about us. I value your friendship, John."

John says, "I have the best friend I've ever had, the best woman I've ever had, and the greatest love all in one person. Nothing or no one will come between us. KD, someone is trying to break us up, Ladybug, don't let them. Don't ever leave me, Ladybug!"

KD says, "I'm not going anywhere without you!"

John says, "Promise me!"

KD says, "I promise I'm not leaving you ever."

John says, "Ladybug, I don't know who it is. It could be Raina, Jacobs, the Creepy Doctor, or someone else from the past. Someone is pissed that we are together. I hope this isn't too much pressure for you."

KD says, "Diamonds are made under pressure. We will make it through this stronger."

John says, "I love that there's no games with you."

She whispers in his ear, "I love you too much to play with you!"

John says, "You're really being naughty right now!"

KD says, "What! What am I doing?"

John says, "I'm pouring out my heart to you, and you are touching me like that!"

KD says, "I'm listening, baby, I swear."

John says, "I'm trying to behave."

KD says, "I doubt that. The way your hands are squeezing my ass!"

John says, "They are? I didn't even notice!"

KD says, "You didn't notice you pulled my panties to the side when you were kissing me either, huh?"

John says, "Did I? That was a force of habit! Since they're already in position." John winks and smiles at her.

KD says, "Kiss me!" He kisses her.

John says, "Come here! Let me kiss them!" He pulls her shirt, putting her breasts to his lips. They look at each other as KD pushes him inside her.

KD caresses his face; she says, "Ah! Baby, you feel so good," as the back of her neck tingles.

John says, "Ladybug, you do!" John tightly holds her close to him. Pulling and pushing her, making her body grind on his.

KD asks, "Baby, you like that?"

John says, as he kisses on her neck, "Can't get enough of it!" John lightly bites her neck. John says, "Ladybug, I love you so much, baby."

KD whispers, "John, I love you so much."

John's eyes roll in the back of his head; he says, "Shit! KD, baby!" She hugs and kisses him as pleasure runs through his body. John hugs her; he says, "Ladybug, I can't live without you!"

KD says, "You never have to!" They kiss. KD gets back in the driver's seat. KD buttons her shirt; she asks, "Do you want me to take you to the office?"

John says, "No, take me home. I need to clean our house, so we can go home."

KD says, "I'll help you!"

John says, "We need to let whoever know that they will not run us away from our home or our relationship."

KD says, "You're right!" As she drives home, KD says, "The boy wants me to ask you for two new puppies."

John says, "I can take Little Man today or tomorrow to pick them out."

KD says, "Go today!"

John says, "So you wanted new puppies, too, huh?"

KD says, "I loved having those puppies."

John says, "I'll text her right now to let her know we'll be there after Little Man gets out of school."

KD says, "You know what he said?"

John asks, "What did Little Man say?"

KD says, "If I say I want a new puppy, you will get it because you'll do anything for me. I told him that you would do anything for him because you love him."

John says, "You both were right. I'll do anything for you, him, or Kelly."

KD says, "You have no idea how much we appreciate you, and I'll do anything for you!"

John says, "The feeling is mutual."

They go home to clean up their house. The protection team checks the house for bugs and cameras. Painters come to repaint the master bedroom. Locksmiths come to change all the locks. The protection team installs camera all over the exterior of the house, the basement, and garage. KD and John have the house clean and restored by the time Daniel is out of practice.

John tells KD he wants to go to pick up Daniel alone, so they can talk. I want to check-in with him to make sure he's okay with everything going on. She says, "I will go shopping to get the things I need to cook." Henson drives John to pick up Daniel. One security car watches the house. The other car follows KD.

Daniel is happy to see John standing next to the black Range Rover. Daniel and John greet each other with their special handshake before getting in the car. John asks, "How were school and practice?"

Daniel says, "They were okay. Where's Momma?"

John says, "She went to the store to get food. I wanted to talk to you."

Daniel asks, "What do you want to talk about?"

John says, "I wanted to make sure you were okay about last night and to see if you want to come home with us?"

Daniel says, "Yes! I want to be with you and Momma."

John says, "If you ever feel otherwise, you'll let me know, right?"

Daniel says, "You're my family! Where else would I want to go?"

John says, "I hope nowhere. I want you to feel safe and protected with us. I'm going to do everything I can to protect you and your mother, you know that, right?"

Daniel says, "Yes!"

John says, "I want the best for you, and I want you at home with us."

Daniel says, "I wish I never had to leave." Daniel took the conversation where John wanted: Bradley Jacobs.

John says, "You don't like spending time with your dad?"

Daniel says, "No!"

John says, "What do you do over there?"

Daniel says, "I read a lot of books, play on the computer, play video games, practice my jump shot, and do my homework."

John asks, "So, that's why you have a huge vocabulary! You read a lot of books."

Daniel says, "Books are a great escape from reality."

John smirks. He says, "You're an impressive young man." Daniel thanks him. John asks, "Does Bradley hang out with you or take you to do fun stuff?"

Daniel says, "Not like you. We write codes on the computer together every now and then, we talk here and there, but it's not authentic or adequate bonding time." John smiles because he is impressed by Daniel's word choice.

John asks, "What about your brothers and sister?"

Daniel asks, "How do you know about them?"

John says, "It's a long story."

Daniel says, "Bradley comes over every now and then. Brady is always there. We are cool, but not close. We're more like friends then brothers. We play video games, basketball, and ride our bikes sometimes. My little sister is sweet; she doesn't bother me."

John asks, "Is Camille nice to you?"

Daniel says, "You know Camille?" John reiterates it's a long story.

Daniel says, "We don't interact much. She's polite when we do."

John asks, "Does your father ever have access to your bag or your keys?"

Daniel says, "I've never seen him go in my bag, but he could get to it. He knows where it is. My keys stay in my bag. I leave it in my room in the closet." John and Henson make eye contact in the rearview mirror.

John asks, "Does he ever ask about your mother, like where she's going or what's she doing?"

Daniel answers, "Sometimes when we're in the car, he makes small talk like how she is doing, but nothing deep. He knows I'm not giving him any information about my mother. If you are wondering how he found out that my mom was dating you, it wasn't me. I know better. Some guy called and told him while we were in his car. He seemed extremely jealous. He just kept saying [mocking his father's voice], 'John King! I can't believe KD is messing with King. Out of all the men in the world, why, King? I can't believe KD and King are together."

John asks, "Does he ever hurt you or make you uncomfortable?"

Daniels says, "It's awkward and uncomfortable being around him. I can't forget or forgive how he treated to my mother."

John says, "You will tell me if he ever makes you uncomfortable or hurts you? You know you can tell me anything. I'm always here for you."

Daniel says, "I know and I appreciate that about you."

John says, "I appreciate you. Let's go pick up our new puppies, so we can go home."

Daniel excitedly asks, "We're getting new puppies, today?"

John says, "Anything for you, Little Man!"

Before going to the store in her new car, KD stops at Tri's house. As soon as Tri opens the door, she says, "Get in here! How are things going with that fiancé of yours?" Tri admires the engagement ring and bracelet that John gave KD for her birthday.

KD says, "Tri, things have been crazy."

Tri says, "Come into the kitchen. I'm cooking!"

KD asks, "You're cooking?"

Tri says, "Well, if you come into the kitchen, you could be cooking." KD washes her hands and goes straight to the stove to see what's cooking. Tri sits at the counter and asks, "What's up?" KD adjusts the fire under the frying meat. She stirs the pasta boiling in the pot.

KD says, "Someone is stalking us. They broke into our house last night. [KD adds seasoning to the meat and stirs the sauce.] Nothing was taken, but they specifically threw my and John's stuff all over the place. They did not touch anything that belonged to Daniel or the grandkids.

"After the proposal, someone vandalized our cars. They poisoned our dogs, and crashed into my car while I was driving on the expressway with Daniel. Daniel and I were staying at John's house one night, and John shot two people trying to break in. Someone has been leaving letters on John's windshield saying I'm a whore and I'm cheating on him. But here's the topper, John thinks it's Bradley."

Tri says, "Bradley? Why Bradley?"

KD says, "John thinks Bradley is mad were together. Bradley had an affair with a woman who made a pass at John. Bradley found out the female was trying to get at John, and Bradley has held a grudge all these years. But get this, Bradley had a child with her and two children with another female while we were still married. John had sexual encounters with both women. John says the encounters were revenge to get at Bradley for talking shit about him.

"When I met John, neither of us knew the other knew Bradley. In all the months we've been together, I was so happy with John that I never said Bradley's name. Bradley popped up at my apartment one day, and John just happened to be there alone, and that's how John found out about Bradley.

"In October, we were at a Halloween party, someone dressed in the same costume as John came up behind me and kissed my neck, touched my breasts. I noticed the kisses and touch were not John's. When I looked up, I saw a familiar smile. I could've sworn it was Bradley Jacobs, but why would Bradley want to touch and kiss me, yuck?"

Tri asks, "Do you think Bradley is stalking you?"

KD says, "At first, I thought no, but the more I think about it, the more it seems plausible. Bradley loves to hurt me. He has gone out of his way to torture me in the past. He sees I'm happy. Why wouldn't he want to ruin what I have with John?"

Tri says, "John posts a lot about DJ. I know that stings a little bit that John is at every game. They hang out and do all this father and son stuff. K, it's adorable."

KD says, "I know! I love their relationship. John has been great with Daniel and Kelly. He gave Kelly a job. She's making more money than me. I couldn't ask for more with John."

Tri says, "John is giving Bradley a lot to be jealous about. Bradley could be acting out."

KD says, "He does seem suspicious. He showed up at my apartment when he knew John was alone. He had to be watching, right. He had to be watching us to know which costume John would be wearing."

Tri says, "It sounds like he has been watching you for a while now."

KD says, "Something changed Bradley. He is not the man I married, or I married a man I really didn't know."

Tri says, "What happens in the dark will come to light. If Bradley has a hand in this, you can file a petition to relinquish his parental rights. Prayers going up."

KD says, "What does he hope to gain? I'm happy where I am. I'll never look back!"

Tri says, "K, I'm so happy for you. Look at God, giving you beauty for your ashes. Focus on the blessing. The burden is lifted."

KD says, "Thank you! Before we met, he was dating someone else."

Tri says, "The girl on the news. One day she's flashing a ring. Next thing I know, John is picking you up from Mena's. What happened?"

KD says, "John swears they were never engaged and the relationship was casual. They had a falling out about her implying they were engaged on the air. She must've heard that he proposed because she slashed my tires the next day."

Tri asks, "Do you think she's behind the other stuff?"

KD says, "Anyone is capable of anything when they aren't getting what they want."

Tri says, "That is true!"

KD says, "Guess who keeps popping up out of nowhere."

Tri asks, "Who?"

KD answers, "Remember, the creepy doctor? John has checked him three times for pulling up on me like I don't have a man."

Tri says, "Where in the hell did, he come from?"

KD says, "John and I were having dinner at my favorite spot. John left the table for a minute, and boom he popped up out of nowhere. He showed up two more times. John checked him. That didn't work, so he pistol-whipped him."

Tri says, "Dang! K! John is playing no games!"

KD says, "The only reason he hasn't gone to see Bradley is the kids, but he wants too badly!"

Tri says, "K, don't let Bradley, Freak Nasty MD, or the News Girl bother you two!"

KD says, "As much as they are on our nervous, the relationship is secure!"

Tri says, "Let me help you. How can I help you?"

KD says, "The thought of someone watching or following us has me creeped out. John hired security for Daniel and me, but I still feel uneasy."

Tri says, "Let me see your phone," Tri goes into her settings. Tri shares KD location to her own cell phone. She says, "I will always know where you are. If you need us, Mena and I will come to get you no matter what, hell or high water. We are not going to worry about exes, the surgeon, the reporter, or anyone else. They will get fucked up. Enjoy your man, your engagement, and let's plan this wedding."

KD smiles and says, "Thank you!" KD cuts off the sauce and stirs it.

Tri says, "Thank God you have a man that will do what needs to be done."

KD says, "We have cameras all over the house. What else can I do to be safe?"

Tri says, "Create safe words the family can use to alert each other when something is wrong. When you are out, make sure you get a good look at every person and car coming near you. If something doesn't feel right, it is not. Trust your instincts, and get the hell out of there. Try not to be alone, especially at night. Carry pepper spray, a taser, a knife, or anything you can use to defend yourself. Don't leave your purse unattended or consider not carrying a purse. Try something small and compact that you can put on your waist, ankle, or arm. Don't leave anywhere without a fully charged phone.

"Also, there's an app you can download that will record your calls, if Bradley or Raina calls either of you, record it just in case you need to report it. Write down everything suspicious that happens, include the time, date, and all the details you can remember. Check DJ's bag and all his things when he comes home from his weekend visits. Make sure he never takes a key to Bradley's house ever again. There's software that you can install on your devices to detect if someone is tracking you. Most importantly, you and John should know each other's every move. Be vigilant and watchful. K, be careful."

KD says, "I will!"

Tri says, "We are going to figure this out! It's going to be okay!"

KD says, "I hope you're right about that! I have to get to the store, so I can go home and cook for my boys." KD stirs the meat before she cuts off the eye. She drains the pasta and runs it under hot water. KD adds, "I think you can take it from here."

Tri says, "You call me to let me know you're okay, or if you just need to talk."

KD says, "I will!" They hug, and Tri walks KD to her car. Tri admires her new car.

Tri says, "Be safe, K!"

KD says, "I will! I love you, Tri!"

Tri says, "I love you, K!"

KD secretly goes to the range where John takes her. She buys two knives and pepper spray. The owner of the store shows her how to strap the smaller knife to her ankle and the bigger knife to her waist. The owner also shows her how to use the pepper spray to avoid spraying herself. She also buys a small wallet that she can strap to her wrist or ankle.

After leaving the store, KD visits John's daughters and Kelly at work. She knocks on Kimma's office door. Kimma is on the phone, but waves to invite KD in. Kimma gets off the phone and gets up to hug KD. She says, "Hi, Stepmom! What are you doing here?"

KD says, "I came to check on my girls and bring lunch. I haven't seen or talk to you, the twins, or my own daughter in a few days. I get jealous because John gets to see you all every day. I missed you." KD hands Kimma one of the lunch bags.

Kimma, taking the lunch bag, says, "Aww, this is so sweet. I missed you too! I promise to check in more." Kimma opens her bag. She is delighted. She says, "This looks good!" Kimma calls Kenna, Kera and Kelly. She tells each one of them to come to her office ASAP. Kimma and takes the first bite, and she rejoices, she says, "Stepmom, this is so good!"

KD smiles and says thank you; she asks, "How have you been and how are our Lovebugs?"

Kimma says, "I have been busy but good, and the girls have been bugging me to bring them over to see you. They ask me every day, a hundred times a day!"

KD says, "They are always welcome!"

Kimma asks, "I'll bring them by soon. How are you? How's work?"

KD says, "I've been good. I've been enjoying my son, my new house, and my fiancé. I have taken some time off. It feels good to be home when everyone walks through the door."

Kimma says, "You deserve some time to enjoy yourself."

KD says, "I really don't want to go back."

Kimma says, "Don't! What did Daddy say?"

KD says, "I haven't told him."

Kimma says, "Tell him! He will support you." Kenna walks into Kimma's office.

Kenna says, "Hey, Stepmom, what are you doing here?" KD gets up to hug Kenna.

KD says, "I haven't heard from you, so I came to check on you and bring lunch." KD hands Kenna one of the lunch bags. Kenna happily takes the lunch and sits to open the bag.

Kera comes through the door. She says, "It smells like Stepmom cooked for us."

KD says, "I did," KD hands Kera a lunch. KD and Kera hug.

KD adds, "How are you two?"

Simultaneously they answer, "Good!" Kenna starts to eat.

Kenna adds, "Now that we have this food, we are great!" Kera starts eating just as Kelly comes to the door.

Kelly says, "Hey, Momma! What are you doing here?"

KD hands Kelly her lunch. KD says, "I wanted to see my girls."

Kenna says, "How have you been, Stepmom?"

KD says, "I can't complain. Kenna, how are the boys?"

Kenna says, "They are well!"

KD says, "You have to bring them over soon to play with Daniel."

Kenna says, "I will!"

Kimma says, "How has Daddy been treating you?"

KD says, "We're happy!"

Kimma says, "That's good! I am happy that you both are happy."

KD says, "Thank you!"

Kimma asks, "Where is your fiancé?"

KD says, "He is meeting someone somewhere for something. He'll be here way later."

Kelly says, "Momma, this is so good. I was so hungry. Thank you!"

KD says, "You're welcome! You haven't called me, Daughter, what have you been doing?"

Kenna says, "She's been hanging with her secret boyfriend."

Kelly says, "Kenna, wow, you're snitching!"

Kenna says, "Sorry, Little Sister, but that's what big sisters do."

KD says, "Why is he a secret?"

Kenna says, shaking her head, "Precious, sweet, Kelly keeping secrets!" Kimma laughs.

Kelly says, "If I tell you, you will tell Stepdad, and Stepdad will have a fit. Don't mention this conversation to him at all, please."

Kenna says, "I can't wait to see Daddy's reaction when he finds out his favorite daughter disobeyed him. Stepmom, record his facial expression when you tell him."

Kimma says, "Kelly, honestly, Dad is going to be livid when he finds out, so you need to let your mother do all the talking."

KD asks, "Why would John be angry?"

Kelly says, "Stepdad warned him to stay away from me."

KD asks, "Do you like this guy?"

Kelly says, "We're just talking. It's not serious."

KD says, "Invite him to dinner tomorrow."

Kelly says, "Stepdad will not appreciate me bringing him to his house."

KD says, "He'll understand! Tomorrow at eight, okay?"

Kelly says, "Momma! No!"

KD says, "I want to meet him. I will talk to John. It'll be okay. What's his name? Where did you meet him? How does John know him?"

Kelly says, "He works here. His name is Todd. Momma, he is thirty-nine. Stepdad caught him flirting with me and threatened him. He told me he is too old for me and not to shit where I eat. I think his exact words to Todd were, 'If you touch my daughter, I will kill your old, nasty, slut ass.' He turned to me in front of Todd, and said, 'Kelly, you should choose better men to share your space and time with. He is no good for you. Trust me, Baby Girl!'"

Kenna says, "Daddy thinks Kelly wouldn't be able to handle a relationship with Todd."

Kimma says, "Kelly, Todd is very experienced with women. Be careful and think thoroughly through your decisions regarding him."

Kenna says, "You worded that so perfectly, Sis." Kimma winks at Kenna.

Kelly says, "I respect that, Kimma; I will!"

Kenna says, "Stepmom, Todd has worked here for years. Todd and Dad are friends. Like, hang out, double-date, party together, fly out of town with a couple of female friends."

KD says, "I see the problem. Kelly, I will talk to John. I promise, he'll be cool."

Kimma says, "Stepmom! Dad is going to be livid with Todd. This will end their friendship."

KD says, "You can't keep this a secret very long. It's best to tell him now."

Kenna says, "Kelly, let your mother handle it."

Kimma says, "Stepmom, your hands are full with this one!"

KD notices Kera is quietly picking over her food. She asks, "Kera, are you okay, Honey?"

Kera says, "I'm a little tired."

Kenna asks, "How are you enjoying your engagement?"

KD says, "I'm on cloud nine."

Kimma asks, "Have you started planning the wedding?"

KD says, "No! The only thing we agreed on is we are getting married in September at my mother's church."

Kimma says, "I will help you?"

KD says, "You are already so busy. I couldn't ask you to do that."

Kimma says, "I insist! I have a good friend who is a wedding producer. I will call her and we will sit down and talk to her."

Kelly says, "Momma, I'll help, too!"

Kenna says, "We will all help."

KD says, "You all are so sweet. I appreciate that."

Kelly says, "Momma, do you think Stepdad would mind if I moved in for a little while. My lease is about to expire, and the commute in and out the city is a monster."

KD says, "I'm sure he won't mind."

Kenna says, "Stepmom, you're supposed to move the kids out, so you can pop that thing."

KD says, "John will always make a way to do that."

Kimma says, "If I weren't married with kids, I would move in to save my money!"

Kenna says, "Think about that, Sis. There was a reason we didn't go back after college."

Kimma says, "You're right, John would be all in my business."

Kera says, "KD will be there to keep him calm."

Kenna says, "He's not going to treat Kelly like he treats us. If we went back home, John would be all over us like we were teenagers." Kimma laughs just as John walks pass her office door. The women stare at him as he passes the open door. He briefly looks into Kimma's office as he passes, but keeps walking. He thinks about what he saw. There was an extra, familiar female in there. John backs up to look again.

Kimma says, "Stepmom, can he smell you or something?" Everyone turns to look at the door.

John says, "Future Wife, what are you doing here?"

KD says, "I came to have bonding time with my girls."

John asks, "You cooked for them. Did you bring me something to eat, too?"

KD says, "You weren't supposed to be here."

John says, "Well, I guess, I'll let you bond with the girls." John looks sad.

Kimma says, "Good afternoon, Mr. King."

John waves at the girls before turning away with a disappointed demeanor. Kenna says, "Daddy, you can't share KD with your own children?" John doesn't answer. He walks away with his head down. Kenna says, "Stepmom, you hurt his feelings."

KD gets up and walks to the door. She calls his name. John turns around. KD says, "Come here, Future Husband." John walks back to her. She hugs his neck and kisses him. She asks, "How was your meeting?"

John says, "It's over. You really didn't bring me lunch?"

KD answers, "You said you were coming home after your meeting and going to the office later."

John says, "I can't believe you didn't bring lunch for me."

KD says, "We had a miscommunication. Don't be like that!"

John begrudgingly asks, "How is your day going?"

KD says, "It's going well! Will you be home for dinner?"

John says, "Yes!"

KD asks, "What do you want for dinner?"

John resentfully says, "Whatever you want."

KD kisses him again; she says, "I'll see you at home." John smacks her butt as she turns to walk away.

John says, "Ladybug, be good!" She looks back and winks at him. He walks to his office.

Kimma says, "What did you do to him? He's like a little lovesick puppy."

Kenna says, "I can't believe what I just saw. Stepmom, he is for real hurt."

KD says, "I'll go talk to him before I leave."

Kelly says, "Momma, the food was great, but I must go. Stepdad hates if we don't stick to the schedule."

Kenna says, "Stepmom, thanks for lunch. I need to go, too."

KD says, "Okay, my girls! Have a good rest of your day. I will check on you all soon, and Kelly, I'll see you and your friend tomorrow eight o'clock. No is not an option."

Kelly says, "Okay, Momma!" Kelly kisses KD's cheek before she leaves. KD and Kenna hug before Kenna leaves. KD says bye to Kimma and Kera before exiting the door.

Kera rushes out the door behind KD. Kera grabs KD's arm. KD turns around. KD asks, "Kera, baby, are you okay?"

Kera asks, "Stepmom, can I talk to you in private?"

KD says, "Of course, Kera!" Kera leads KD to her office. KD asks, "Kera, what's wrong?"

Kera says, "Stepmom, I messed up!"

KD says, "Baby, you looked terrified. What's wrong?" KD hugs her.

Kera says, "My dad is going to be mad at me."

KD says, "Your dad is going to support you. Whatever is going on, we will be there for you."

Kera says, "I'm pregnant, and I don't want to be with the father. Daddy will be disappointed because I'll be the only one to have a baby out of wedlock. I don't know if I can do this alone."

KD says, "You may be single, but you are not alone. You have us. Whatever you need, I'll be there. Your father will be there. Your sisters will be there. Sit your father down and talk to him."

Kera says, "I can't. I'm the baby. It'll hurt his feelings."

KD says, "He's going to notice sooner or later. You might as well have the conversation now."

Kera says, "Do you think I should have it?"

KD says, "Babies are hard work, but they are blessings. I know it's scary now, but once you hold that baby in your arms you are going to be in love unlike ever before. Creating a life is a miracle. An innocent piece of yourself in this tiny bundle of joy that needs you and loves you is so special. You'll love being a mommy. However, I will support you either way."

Kera says, "Do you think my father will want me to have the baby?" KD says, "Yes, he going to love his baby's baby."

Kera says, "Can you talk to him, please?"

KD says, "Are you sure you don't want to be the one to tell him?"

Kera says, "I'm so positive!"

KD kisses Kera's forehead. KD pats her back; she says, "Baby, it's a lot right now, but it will be worth it once you hold that baby in your arms."

Kera says, "I think the thought of my life changing scares me."

KD says, "Your life will drastically change, but, Kera, honey, I promise, this baby will bring you so much joy!"

Kera and KD hug. Kera says, "Thank you, Stepmom"

KD says, "You're welcome, baby!" KD hugs Kera and promises that everything will be okay.

After leaving Kera's office, KD peeks into John's office. He is lost in thought. She quietly comes in and locks the door. John looks at her. She asks, "Baby, are you okay, you seem distracted? I'm worried about you."

John says, "Don't worry." She walks over to his desk. She sits on his desk.

KD says, "I locked the door."

John asks, "What are you trying to do?"

KD says, "Make you feel better."

John stands up. He says, "You want to make me feel better?"

She says, "John, for real, what's wrong? Something is bothering you."

John says, "You focus on making me feel better. I'll worry about everything else."

She asks, "Are you sure you don't want to talk about it?"

John says, "What I want to talk about is you didn't bring me anything to eat."

KD says, "I brought me." John smiles.

John says, "You know that's my favorite, but you didn't bring me any food and they had a whole meal."

KD replies, "Baby, you said you weren't going to be here. I hadn't talk to the girls in a while. I wanted to check on them and let them know I was thinking about them."

John says, "You left me out. How could you leave me out?"

KD asks, "I didn't mean to make you feel left out."

John says, "KD, I would never feed them and not feed you. You hurt my feelings. You're supposed to always think of me."

KD says, "I'm sorry! I would never purposely leave you out. I always think about you. I put your food in the microwave with a note that says, 'Baby, I went to check on our girls. I will see later.' I really thought you were coming home after your meeting. If I would've known you were going to be here, I would've brought it. Baby, it brings me joy to take care of you."

John looks at her. He says, "Ladybug, I was so hurt when I thought you didn't think of me."

They hug. KD says, "Baby, I will always think of you. Don't ever think your well-being is not valuable to me. Do you feel better?"

John goes to kiss her, but he is distracted by a text. As he reads the text, he says, "I have to make a run. See you at home."

KD kisses his cheek; she says, "Baby, what's up? Something is bothering you." John looks at her. She says, "You're tensed. You're distant. Something is wrong. I can see it on your face."

John says, "It's…it's…" he can't find the words to explain his thoughts.

She asks, "Is it work? [John doesn't respond.] Is it the kids? [John doesn't respond.] Is it a woman?"

John pauses for a moment before he says, "Yes, and her name is KD. Ladybug, I want to be a good man to you. I want to build a life with you. I can't tell you what I fully don't understand, but I promise, when I figure things out, we will talk about everything. I promise, I've been faithful to you. I'm preparing to spend my life with you. I'm not intentionally being distant, and I don't want you to worry. I'm going to make this run. I'm going to clear my head and check my attitude. When I get home, I will be the normal John you're used to and we will not talk about this." He wraps his arms around her.

KD says, "OK! Baby, be careful. See you at home." They kiss.

John says, "Ladybug, be safe!" She winks at him before leaving his office.

That evening, John makes it home for dinner. KD plays cool, but she is curious and worried about what has him distracted. John asks, "How did your bonding time go with the girls?"

KD says, "The girls are really warming up to me. Hopefully, they feel my love."

John says, "I think so."

KD says, "I want us to be very close. I think we're getting there."

John says, "I think so, too!"

KD says, "I love that they call me Stepmom like Kelly calls you Stepdad!"

John smiles and says, "It's cute!"

KD asks, "John, we can always talk about everything, no secrets, right?"

John says, "Always! What's up?"

KD says, "Our daughters, there are some things we need to talk about."

John says, "Who did what?"

KD says, "Kelly wants to move with us. She wants to know how you feel about that."

John says, "Kelly is more than welcome here, always, anytime."

She says, "I'm glad you said that because I invited her and the guy she's dating to dinner tomorrow, so we can meet him. Can you be home around eight?"

John says, "Yes, I can be here."

KD says, "Baby, before you freak out, I want you to think. Kelly is young and she's learning. She has to learn to make good decisions. She has watched me make some bad decisions. I have talked to her. I have tried to prepare her, but it is on her to make those tough decisions."

John says, "Right!"

KD says, "John, look at me. See, I'm calm. I need you to stay calm."

John puts his fork down; he says, "Hell no! I told him to stay away from my Baby Girl. Hell no! He is not welcome in my home with my daughter. I told Kelly we don't shit where we eat."

KD says, "She heard you and she is scared you are going to be mad at her. If she interested in him, she needs to see who he is for herself."

John says, "KD, Todd is horrible. I saw them eyeing each other. I explained why it's inappropriate for them to date. I tried to stop it before it started."

KD says, "When you tell a girl no, you might as well tell her to do it. If we play it cool, she may be a little less interested. Can you be supportive of Kelly for me, baby?"

John says, "I will always be supportive of Kelly, but Todd, hell no. If he touches her, I will fuck him up. Ladybug, how can my friend who is forty date my twenty-two-year-old daughter?"

KD says, "I'm not thrilled about the potential relationship either, but Kelly has to be responsible for Kelly."

John says, "Kelly needs protection from men like Todd because she is young, vulnerable, impressionable, and naïve. Todd is a dirty piece of shit who would fuck over Kelly."

KD says, "Future Husband, stay calm for me, please, baby! It's only dinner. You can make it through a few hours."

John says, "For you, I will!"

KD says, "Baby, I have something else I need to tell you." She rubs his arm.

John says, "What's up?"

KD says, "It's about Kera, baby." John gets quiet. KD adds, "She's very scared to talk to you and you need to listen to her."

John asks, "She's pregnant?"

KD says, "She doesn't want to be with the father. She thinks you are going to be mad because she is going to have a baby out of wedlock. Are you mad?"

John says, "No, I am not mad. She has to live life her own way."

KD says, "Baby, she is terrified. You need to find her first thing in the morning and let her know we have her back."

John says, "I will!"

KD says, "You promise?"

John says, "Ladybug, I promise!"

KD says, "Can I ask you a personal question?"

John says, "Of course!"

KD says, "When we talked about our marriage and life together, you said you would support me in my decisions. Remember that?"

John says, "Yes, I will! What's up?"

KD says, "I've been thinking. I want to be home when you come home from the office and Daniel comes home from school. I want the grandkids to spend more time here. I want our girls to spend more time here. Kera is going to need support, and I want to be available for her. I don't want to go back to work. Is that too much to ask?"

John says, "No! If you don't want to work, you don't have to. I would never ask you to support this household. Besides, the things you want, I want, too!"

KD says, "Are you sure?"

John says, "Ladybug, I want you home more than you want to be home."

KD says, "I'm so blessed to have you as my soon-to-be-husband."

John says, "I'm the blessed one!"

KD rubs his arm; she asks, "Are you going to tell me what's bothering you?"

John says, "Ladybug, I'm good."

KD says, "Look at your leg." John is unconsciously shaking his leg. KD adds, "You're talking to me, but you're not looking at me. Something has you distracted. Is it work, the kids, or….?" KD pauses.

John says, "I thought we weren't going to talk about that?"

KD says, "We aren't. You're right! I'm sorry!"

John grabs her hand. He says, "I do have a lot of my mind. I promise you, everything on my mind is about us. I'm not trying to shut you out. I need a minute to process everything. Once I can put words to emotions, we will talk about everything. I am not having doubts or fears. It is not like that. I'm planning and preparing. I want our life together to be perfect.

"As the man, it is on me to plan and lead this family. I'm just trying to position things the best I can. I want to lead our family and make things easy for you without taking away your independence or making you feel constrained. I want to be a good husband. If I'm being honest, that's something I have never been. I have about ten months to figure it out. That's all it is, I swear! Ladybug, I need you to trust me, and let me figure out if I'm making the right moves."

KD says, "I can respect that!"

John says, "I want to make you happy. I hope I make you happy."

KD says, "I am the happiest I've ever been."

John says, "I want it to stay that way. I apologize if I seem distracted. Ladybug, I promise you, I'm not thinking about another woman. I got everything I need at home with you. Ladybug, this relationship will not work if you can't get over my past. I promise that the past is the past. I'm in this with you one hundred per cent."

KD says, "John, I'm so sorry. You're right. Every point you made is valid. I trust you and I didn't mean for my concern to come across as distrust. I would like a do-over. John, there's been a lot going on, I'm checking in with you to see how you are emotionally."

John asks, "Can I be honest?"

KD answers, "Yes!"

John says, "I'm stressed, Ladybug. Your safety is of great concern to me. To know someone is out there trying to hurt you and my hands are tied has me stressed. I don't know what to do. The police aren't protecting us. I'm literally stuck between a rock and a hard place. Ladybug, I want to fuck Bradley up, but I know that would hurt Kelly.

"I can't hurt her. I love her. I couldn't look her in the face if I hurt her father. That bastard is not giving us the same consideration. He's hurting her mother and not giving a fuck. She hasn't said anything, but she may feel stuck between choosing his side or my side. Ladybug, you're my woman. You're my responsibility. If he hurts you, I'm going to hurt him."

KD says, "Baby, I am so sorry that you are carrying this burden. I empathize with you. Hearing you say that enlightens me to the depth of thought you have giving to this dilemma. I wish I knew what to say or what to do to make it go away. I know Kelly, and I know she would never blame you for Bradley's actions. She knows how he acts toward me.

"I'm sure this whole situation is more about his hate for me than you. Baby, maybe we should pray and honestly talk to Kelly about the situation. As a parent, that's all we can do. If you have to handle Bradley, he brought it on himself. He came fucking with us."

John says, "Can I ask you something?"

KD says, "Yes!"

John says, "Hypothetically, Bradley does something to you or Daniel. I react. Kelly doesn't like how I react. She gets mad at you for being with me. Are you going to break up with me because you feel like I'm coming between you and your daughter?"

KD says, "Baby, you have given this a lot of thought. You are in a tight spot. But, John, I'm not leaving you over Bradley. Know that you have done everything right. John, we love our kids. As parents, we do everything we can to love and support them. But, this is one thing Kelly is going to have to deal with. Bradley came fucking with us for no reason.

We are getting married; Kelly, Bradley, and everyone else is going to have to deal with it."

John says, "You have my back on this!"

KD says, "I have your back!" She reaches out her hand. John takes her hand. She asks, "Now, that we've honestly talked about the situation, do you feel a little better?"

John asks, "How do we get through things?"

KD answers, "Together! We communicate and talk about everything."

John says, "You're right! And, I promise when I figure things out, we will talk about everything. I just need a little emotional leeway and space to figure out my next move. You've got to trust this is not about sex or some chick that doesn't mean shit to me. Okay, Ladybug?"

KD answers, "Okay, baby!"

Lying next to a sleeping KD, John pulls out his phone to text Kera. John writes: Baby Girl! I will never be mad at you for living your life your way. I will love you always and I love the baby already. KD and I will support you and the baby in every way. Please have breakfast with me at our favorite spot before work so we can talk. You can tell me everything you need to get off your chest. Goodnight, Kera! Love you!

Kera replies: Thank you, Daddy! I would love to have breakfast with you. Goodnight, Daddy!

John writes: See you in the morning, my sweetheart! I love you!

Kera replies: I love you more!

Darkness and quietness shroud John's old neighborhood shielding a tall person dressed in all black inching into John's old backyard. The veiled prowler pours gasoline along the perimeter of the house and John's boat. Another hidden man breaks into the house to douse every room with gasoline. The masked men light matches. One throws a match onto the boat. The other arsonist sets the house on fire. They hop in a car to quickly flee, unseen by anyone.

John rubs KD's back as she sleeps on his chest. John's phone rings. It's the security company calling to let him know that the received a fire alert from his old home. John texts the protection team to ask them to check on the house. The head of the team video calls him to show him his house and boat are completely engulfed in flames.

John looks at the phone. He covers his mouth as he sits up. He can't believe what he is seeing. His movement wakes up KD. She looks at his face; she asks, "What's wrong, baby?"

John says, "Someone set my old house on fire. My boat, the house, they are destroyed."

John shows KD the phone. She looks at the phone; she says, "Baby, I am so sorry."

Fire trucks are on the scene trying to put the fire out. KD covers her mouth as she watches the fire blaze. She gives John the phone. John thanks Taylor, the head of the security team, and hangs up the phone.

KD says, "John, maybe, we should take a break."

John says, "KD, those are things I can replace or live without. I can't replace you or live without you. You just said you're not leaving me over something Bradley did."

KD says, "John, I'm worried about you getting hurt. I'm not saying we should break up. Daniel and I can move out to make him think we are not together."

John says, "We are not running from Bradley. I will be fine. We will be fine if we are together. I can't take you leaving me. If you try to go away, I will find you and bring you home."

KD says, "Baby, I couldn't handle something happening to you, especially if it happens because you're with me!"

He says, "KD, I appreciate your thoughtfulness, but I'm not trying to hear what you're saying, respectfully. Ladybug, go back to sleep!" KD puts her head back on John's chest.

KD says, "Baby, I'm scared."

John says, "KD, I'm not going to let anyone hurt you or Daniel. I promise you."

KD says, "Who's going to protect you? I can't survive life without you, John. How can I look your kids in their faces if something happens to you? They will hate me if you get hurt. John, can you try to understand the position I'm in."

John says, "Can we talk about this another day with level heads? Ladybug, no one should make big decisions when they're emotional. Baby, your emotions are talking right now. You're not thinking clearly. I'll be alive and alone, no you, no Daniel. Ladybug, that's not the life I want. If you leave, you're letting him win. We are not doing that! You promised me you were with me and you would fight for this. Are you keeping your promise?"

KD says, "Yes, baby, I am, but...." John cuts her off.

John says, "Stop this crazy talk. You are not leaving me, and you're not taking Daniel from me. Do you hear me?"

KD says, "Yes!"

John says, "Whatever happens, we will make it through stronger. Remember you told me that?"

KD says, "Yes, and I meant it!"

John says, "Can we go to sleep and wake up like this didn't happen? The house and boat were insured. It's nothing. I don't ever want to hear you talking about leaving me. Please, Ladybug, go back to sleep." KD starts to respond. John says, "Don't say anything other than goodnight, John. Baby, I love you."

KD smiles and says, "Goodnight, John, baby, I love you."

John says, "I love you, KD, goodnight."

John, KD, and Daniel are walking into their dark house. Daniel runs off and John calls out to him. Daniel doesn't respond. John panics. He calls Daniel's name again and again. Still no response. John and KD look for Daniel in the dark, empty house. John and KD are worried as they walk into a dark room searching for Daniel. He asks KD, "Baby, do you see him?" When John turns to look at her, KD is gone.

John panics. He runs through the house shouting KD's name louder and louder. His heart is pounding so hard that he can feel and hear the echo of each beat throughout his entire body. He is sweating. The house gets darker and darker. John hears a door slams, and he runs in the direction of the noise as he shouts KD's and Daniel's names. John comes to a locked door. He beats on the door shouting KD's name. He kicks the door in to see a massive, dark figure holding KD and moving a knife toward her throat.

Before the knife touches her, John wakes up. John opens his eyes in a hazy panic. He notices KD sound asleep snuggled next to him. He immediately calms down. He lays looking up at the ceiling, thinking about the stalking ordeal. He knows it's Bradley, but his love for Kelly cautions him to not react.

The next morning, John meets Kera for breakfast. She explains what happened in the relationship with the father of the baby. When she told him she was pregnant, he asked her to marry him. When she said no, the father of the baby cut all communication. Kera explains the father was nice, intelligent, and a good man, but she wasn't ready to settle down and she never intended to get pregnant.

She says, "I thought we were always careful. Daddy, it is possible that he did this on purpose because he kept asking for more.

John is more than supportive and understanding. John tells Kera he understands why a man would want to settle down with her. He also tells her that she has every right to make the best decision for herself. He explains how settling down before he was ready led to two divorces. He assures her that he is not disappointed in any way by her pregnancy; he promises that he will love and support her whichever decision she makes.

Kera is moved by his encouragement. When Kera asks if she should have the baby, John affirms that he wants this baby, and he vows to be there for her and the baby. Kera tells him she appreciates his support, and she loves him so much. He tells her he loves her more.

After breakfast, John and Kera survey the ruins left by the fire. The remains of the boat are hauled away. A wrecking crew comes to remove the debris of what remains of the house. John talks to Kera about selling the land because he doesn't want to rebuild the house. Kera is empathetic about his loss. When she asks what happened, John pretends to be clueless.

Kera says, "I smell gasoline. Did someone set this fire?"

John plays it off; he says, "Why would someone do that?"

Kera says, "Good question! Is something going on you're not telling me?"

John says, "Daughter, my life is an open book to you."

Kera says, "Yeah right, Daddy, I don't believe that!"

John says, "We talk about any and every thing. You know everything important."

Kera says, "Daddy, if something is going on, you need to tell me."

John says, "Everything is good. You focus on growing my healthy granddaughter."

Kera says, "You want a girl?"

John says, "I need another beautiful grand girl."

Kera smiles. Kera says, "Daddy, I don't think I'm ready to do this, especially alone."

John says, "You'll be a wonderful mother, and you are not alone."

Kera says, "KD said the same thing."

John says, "She and I are here for you. She's quitting her job. She is serious about supporting you through this, and you know I am there for everything."

Kera says, "Thank you, Daddy! I love you and KD."

John says, "We love you, too!"

That evening, Todd and Kelly come over for dinner. John is so calm during dinner that Kelly and Todd are frightened by his politeness. KD appreciates John for being hospitable. As the evening is coming to an end, John takes Todd into his man cave for a private talk. Todd compliments John's new home. John asks Todd how things are going with Kelly. Todd explains they are only friends.

John asks, "Have you touched my daughter?"

Todd says, "Absolutely not, King."

John stares at him. John says, "Are you sure about that?"

Todd says, "King, I swear."

John opens a hidden display case exposing his gun collection. Todd begins to look at the weapons. He's fascinated by the exquisite gun collection. Todd asks [pointing to a weird looking weapon], "What is that?"

John says, "A grenade launcher, and I will fuck your face with it if you don't end this shit with Kelly. I told your rabbit ass not to pursue my daughter. You did it anyway like I'm some bitch, like fuck what I said. You have twenty-four hours to come up with a reason that you can no longer have any contact with her.

"I don't give a fuck about your feelings or intentions. I care about my daughter's well-being and we both know you're no good for her. You're too damn old for her. She is still a damn child and you're fucking forty.

"The fact you didn't listen to me the first time, I'm going to let it slide because my girl told me to be calm and civil. Monday morning, you have an interview with a good company for a great position making a hell of a lot of money. You're going to end this shit with Kelly, never tell Kelly about this conversation, take that job, and never have contact with my family again. Do we have an understanding?"

Todd says, "We have a clear understanding."

John says, "Take my daughter straight home. You will not get out of the car, walk her to the door, or kiss her. Don't even touch her hand. And, I will have someone follow you, so I will know what happens."

John says, "For the record, I would have never gone behind your back to pursue someone in your family, especially after we talked and you expressed you didn't want that. I thought we were better than that. I considered you a friend. I could've fucked your mother and sister. They both were throwing it at me, calling me after I met them at the picnic. They were begging for it. Unlike you, I did the honorable thing. But that's what makes me, me and you, you.

"You don't fuck with your friend's daughter. You're lucky I'm with KD and I don't fuck around anymore. It's only because of KD that I'm not balls deep in your mother's and sister's mouth just to fuck with you. Get the fuck out my house with your disrespectful ass, and let's never see each other again."

Immediately, Todd sees things from John's point of view. Todd feels guilty because he sees he truly hurt John. Todd and John go back to the dining room where KD and Kelly are waiting. John smiles like all is well. Todd plays along, as he and Kelly say goodbye.

On Monday, Todd takes the new job, and cuts all communication with Kelly. Kelly calls KD to tell her Todd ended their friendship.

KD asks, "How do you feel?"

Kelly says, "Stepdad was right. I should've never talked to him."

KD says, "I'm sorry things didn't work out the way you hoped."

Kelly says, "We were only friends. He was honest about seeing other women, so I thought talking to him would be harmless."

KD asks, "How deep was this friendship?"

Kelly says, "We didn't, you know. One part of my mind said run because he was with other women. The other part of my mind was intrigued by his reputation and demeanor."

KD says, "Men like Todd are seductive and dangerous."

Kelly says, "Do you think Stepdad said something to him?"

KD says, "I'm 100 per cent sure he did. I told him not to get involved and to let you navigate this yourself. Are you mad at him?"

Kelly says, "No, he was only trying to protect me."

KD says, "I don't like that you are disappointed. I want to protect you from every letdown. Wisdom comes from learning lessons. I hope that you learned from my mistakes and I hope you protect yourself in the future. Although John shouldn't have meddled in your friendship, I am happy with the results. Todd is not the kind of man I want you to you know, especially the first time."

Kelly says, "Momma, that was two years ago."

KD says, "Kelly! What? Why didn't you talk to me?"

Kelly says, "Mommy, I protected myself and everything was fine. I was smart about things."

KD says, "Kelly! Baby! You were supposed to talk to me before and after."

Kelly says, "Momma, you prepared me very well for life physically, emotionally, and spiritually. I knew you couldn't handle the conversation. Just know I was safe and everything was fine before and after."

KD says, "Kelly, baby, be wise with your choices concerning men. Decisions like that can't be undone and the consequences can be life-long."

Kelly says, "Momma, I am wise because you raised me. I wasn't trying to make Todd my husband. I saw who he was. I wanted to get got. He had a little appeal to him that made me consider making him number two on my list."

KD says, "You be sure to keep the number on your list reasonable."

Kelly asks, "What number is Stepdad on your list, Momma?"

KD says, "Kelly!"

Kelly says, "Come on, Momma! I learn about life from you. What number is Stepdad?"

KD says, "Four, Kelly!"

Kelly says, "Momma, for real? That's it! So, what number is your first husband?"

KD says, "One!"

Kelly says, "So were with two people after the divorce?"

KD says, "No, those other two incidents happened in college before we were married."

Kelly says, "Does Dad know you cheated on him in college?"

KD says, "No, but he cheated on me, so I cheated with number three."

Kelly asks, "What about number two?"

KD says, "I guess I wanted to get got."

Kelly says, "Momma! Who's the best?"

KD says, "He's walking through the door, now!"

Kelly asks, "Is it exceptional?"

KD says, "Incredibly!" KD and John look at each other as he walks through the door. KD smiles at John. He smiles back.

Kelly says, "Oh wee! I'm happy for you and Stepdad. Tell him, I have the best stepdad ever. I appreciate him, and I love him."

KD says, "Okay, baby, I will! I love you!"

Kelly says, "Momma, you deserve all the love Stepdad gives you. I am proud of you for taking a chance on love. Don't worry about me. I'm okay about the Todd thing, so don't be upset with Stepdad. Momma, I love you, too!"

KD says, "Awe, that warms my heart. Call me tomorrow to let me know how you're feeling."

Kelly says, "Okay, Mommy, bye!"

KD says, "Bye, baby!"

John walks up and hugs KD; he asks, "Was that Kelly?"

KD answers, "Yes! We know you said something to Todd."

John replies, "Why would I say something to that man after you told me not to interfere?"

KD says, "Because you are John King and you get what you want."

John says, "You're damn right, I said something to his snake ass. I considered him a friend, and he approached my daughter after I asked him to stay away from her. The things I've seen his slut ass do. She's too inexperienced to handle him. Are you mad at me?"

KD says, "The same thing could've been said about me dating you. Is it fair that you judged him based on his past?"

John says, "You and I are different."

KD asks, "How?"

John answers, "You were trying to get into my pants first."

KD replies, "What?"

John says, "The night on the boat, you were trying to get it. Your exact words were, 'Please, don't stop.' I had to tell you no. The first time you spent the night I wanted to cuddle, but you wanted more. I could feel the desire in you, your kiss, your heartbeat. One morning, we were kissing on your couch. It was innocent at least on my end. You tried to unzip my pants. I had to stop you."

KD is appalled. John and KD stare at each other. KD can't say anything because she knows he is telling the truth.

John says, "Look me in my eyes, and tell me you did not want it on the boat, the couch, or the first time you spent the night. If anyone needed protecting when we first met, it was me."

KD says, "You knew what you were doing. Seducing me. Giving me what I hadn't had. You were making your way in my head, lowering my inhibitions. You weren't that innocent."

John says, "I was taking my time to build a bond, a relationship with you. I genuinely liked you from the moment I saw. I knew Todd didn't have those feelings for Kelly. I saw the way he looked at her. She's a very beautiful, attractive, sweet, young girl. Todd didn't see her heart or mind. All he saw was her body. Her prince will come and he will like her for her, all of her."

KD hugs his neck; she says, "I am so glad you did things your way!"

John says, "So, we're good?"

KD says, "We're always good! You know what my daughter told me?"

John asks, "What did Kelly say?"

KD says, "Basically, she told me she was trying to get it."

John says, "Wow!" He adds, "She gets that from her mother." KD hits his arm.

KD says, "I can't believe you." John laughs.

John says, "I'm joking!"

KD adds, "She told me to tell you she has the best Stepdad ever. She appreciates you, and she loves you."

John says, "I love her, too!"

KD says, "Things turned out perfectly even though you didn't listen to me."

John says, "I did what I thought was best."

KD says, "I think the lesson in this situation is I need to trust my man because he always looks out for me and does right by me."

John says, "I like that thinking, Ladybug. Anything else I can do for you?"

KD hands him the pan and says, "You can cook."

John says, "How about you put on a pretty dress and we go out to eat? Pretend like our life is normal for a night. Daniel can order takeout. Security can stay here to watch the house while we are gone."

KD says, "You're going to take me out on a date?"

John says, "Yes!" They kiss. John says, "Go get pretty. I'll talk to Daniel."

John tells Daniel that he is taking KD out for a few hours to have some adult time. He explains that it is important for couples to have some alone bonding time. Daniel understands. John gives him a credit card and permission to order all the food he wants and to stay up late to play as many video games as he wants. John hands Daniel some cash to tip each delivery. John tells the protection team to stay with Daniel, and the only visitors expected are food deliveries. John exclaims that no one else is to go near the house for any reason.

John and KD dress in a manner to let whoever is watching know they are unbothered. John makes sure to keep KD close to him. His charming smiles keeps a smile on her face as they walk into the restaurant and are immediately lead to their table.

John pulls out KD's chair. He helps her sit down before taking his seat. KD looks at the menu. She says, "What are you in the mood for?"

John says, "The pasta looks good. The filet mignon looks good. I think I'll go with those. What about you?"

KD says, "I think I want seafood."

John says, "Looking as good as you do in that dress, you deserve all the seafood you want."

They laugh. KD asks, "You like my dress?"

John says, "I love you. The dress is a bonus, and taking it off will be my blessing," he winks at her. She smiles at him.

After dinner, John and KD exit the restaurant in high spirits. John pays the valet. The valet pulls his car around. John opens the passenger's side door. He helps KD get into the car. The mysterious black Benz slowly pulls up next to John's car. The passenger's side window slowly rolls down. Flames accompanied by the thunderous sounds of a barrage of bullets send everyone outside the restaurant scrambling to find cover. John pulls KD to the ground and cover her with his body as he reaches under the passenger seat for his gun. John tells KD, "Stay down!"

John creeps around the front of the car. He aims and quickly fires back hitting the car five times, shattering the passenger's side windows. The rapid fire he returns is so powerful that the Benz abruptly flees. John is so angry he chases the car, firing into the back window. The sounds of shattering glass and a speeding car scare the restaurant's patrons cowering under the tables. John rushes back to KD. He asks, "Are you okay? Are you hurt?"

KD says, "No! Are you?" John says no, helps her get into the car, then hops in the driver seat. The tires screech as John hurriedly pulls off.

John and KD make it home safely. They check on Daniel who is asleep with a game controller in his hand, a pizza box on his chest, and fast-food bags all over his bed. KD looks in the empty bags; she says, "The boy ate all this; I can't believe he's not sick."

John says boys are like garbage disposals. KD opens the pizza box; she says, "He ate the whole pizza." John replies that's why he's knocked out. John puts the box and bags in the trash while KD cuts off the game and TV. They tuck him in and cut off his light.

They go into the master bathroom, so KD can clean the cut on John's hand. As KD cleans the cut on his hand, she notices a hole in his shirt and blood on his sleeve. She takes off his shirt. She sees John was grazed by a bullet. KD asks, "Does this hurt?" as she cleans the area with a cotton ball and peroxide.

John says, "It stings a bit, but I'm good!" John notices her knee is bleeding. He says, "Let me look at your knee." John sits her on the counter of the sink. He washes his hands. John says, "Ladybug, this is going to burn," as he puts peroxide on her knee and clean it with a cotton ball. KD bites her lip as John puts antibiotic ointment on the scrape.

He asks, "Are you okay?"

KD says, "I'm fine!" KD looks at her knee; she says, "My hero saves me again!"

John says, "I'm your hero!"

KD says, "The way you handled tonight was very sexy. You made me feel safe and secure."

John says, "I'll always make sure you're safe and secure." She kisses his lips. John smiles and asks, "You thought I was sexy," as he gets closer to her.

KD says, "Incredibly!"

John pulls her face to his, so he can kiss her as his hands rub her legs and thighs. John whispers in her ear, "I am sorry someone tried to ruin our date!"

KD says, "We're safe, we had a good time and that's all that matters!"

John says, "I'll never let anyone hurt you!"

KD says, "I appreciate that and I appreciate you!" She kisses him.

John says, "I love your kisses!"

KD says, "I love yours!"

John kisses KD's neck as he pulls her panties off. KD holds on to his back as John kisses from her neck to her breasts. The passionate kisses ignite scorching hot flames in her body.

KD unzips John's pants. KD sticks her hand in John's underwear to massage him. She pulls him out of his underwear. She rubs him against herself. John lifts her up, putting her thighs over his forearms. He slides into KD as they kiss.

He wraps his hands around her neck, placing his thumbs gently on her throat as they continue to kiss. The way John has her folded in his arms leaves her vulnerable. KD's hands hold on to his wrists as John takes powerful and swift strokes into her.

KD is somewhere between amazement and hurting like hell. Her eyes roll in the back of her head as she uncontrollably moans and calls his name. The sounds she's making encourage John to give her more pleasure.

Every time she expresses her pleasure, John lowly and empathetically responds, "Hmm! Mm-hm," to acknowledges her pain as he strives to give her more pleasure. She can feel John all through her midsection. As the energy and pressure flood every corner of KD's mind, her folded body relaxes in his arms. KD caresses the back of his head and neck to comfort him.

John says, "Ladybug, I love you!"

KD says, "I love you, too!"

John says, "Ladybug, that was so sexy. The way you were calling my name, that look on your face, and the way you were moaning made me want you more and more. I tried to fuck your mind."

KD says, "You did!" John smiles. He kisses her.

John says, "I can do it again?"

KD says, "I can't even think about another round."

John asks, "Ladybug, it's like that? You have never tapped out."

KD says, "Baby, I can't even move. I just want to stay wrapped in your arms?"

John, still holding her trembling body, says, "I can definitely make that happen." She rests her head on his chest.

The next morning, John and KD wake up to images of John beating Dr. Segal with the gun on the news. A reporter interviews Dr. Segal who proclaims he didn't provoke the attack. Dr. Segal says, "I spoke to John's fiancée. Suddenly, Mr. King attacked me with a gun. He hit me over and over in my face and head with his gun." Dr. Segal tells the reporter his lawyer is planning to sue John King for pain and anguish.

KD looks at John as images of him beating the doctor tarnish his clean reputation. She says, "This is why rich businesspeople don't fight in the street like irresponsible teenagers. John, you have too much to lose to make poor decisions."

John says, "Ladybug, you're right. I can't believe he's playing the victim. He started the whole thing."

KD says, "When people have less to lose, they are the victim. Now, Creepy Creepo has you looking like the big bad wolf, ruining your clean image."

John says, "This is the worst possible time for this."

KD says, "Fix this!"

John says, "I will figure it out, Ladybug, I promise."

John and KD get calls from their daughters. They explain Dr. Segal, who has a history of harassing KD, pulled the gun on John and John took the gun.

Later that day, KD asks the protection team to guard the house to ensure Daniel is safe while she makes a quick run. She promises to return soon. The team leader tells her that is not a good idea. He reminds her that a half of the team's orders are to secure her twenty-four hours a day, but she insists she will be okay, and the entire team should stay with Daniel.

KD has dinner with Nanette, Laura and Karen at a restaurant near the hospital. As they eat, KD tells her friends that she is considering not coming back to work because she wants to spend more time with her son. She explains that she has missed so much over the last five years, and she doesn't want to miss one more thing. They are sad that she is quitting, but they understand.

Nanette says, "You can tell the truth. You want to be at home with that fine fiancé of yours. I understand. If I were in your shoes, I would be at home with him, too." Everyone laughs.

Karen asks, "How is it being engaged to The King?"

KD says, "He's a regular guy and we have fun doing the same things other couples do."

Laura says, "He is nowhere near a regular guy. KD, I saw a picture of him with his shirt off. My husband doesn't look like that at fifty-three."

KD says, "I'm very fortunate."

Nanette says, "I'm so happy for you. You took a chance and look what happened!"

Laura says, "I've watched your relationship grow on his social media pages. Your relationship looks like a dream."

KD says, "Dreams can be complicated."

Laura says, "Hang in there, KD! Things will settle down after the wedding."

Karen says, "Nothing worth your time is easy."

Nanette says, "John is worth a tussle with a lion."

KD says, "A tiger, a bear!"

Laura says, "Oh my!" They laugh.

Nanette says, "This morning, I saw John on the news beating up the pervert surgeon. What happened?"

KD says, "The video didn't show what triggered John. He keeps approaching me. John asked him to leave me alone. The creep pulled out a gun. John took the gun from him."

Laura says, "Dr. Segal was always strange. He was obsessed with KD from day one."

Karen says, "Remember the day Bradley came to the hospital and the surgeon got jealous?"

Nanette says, "He acted as if you were his girlfriend and as if he wasn't married."

Karen says, "He does strike me as the stalker type."

Nanette says, "It's weird that he is still obsessed with you after all these years. KD, be careful! He's not right in the head."

KD nods. She says, "That part. He makes me feel threatened."

Laura says, "He is very intelligent, but socially inept."

Nanette says, "I am so glad John whipped his creepy ass."

KD says, "I hate everyone thinks John is the bad guy. No one knows how he has harassed me over the years. John was only trying to protect me."

Karen says, "The truth will come out. John will be vindicated. What man wouldn't protect his woman from a predator! After what he did to you, he needed someone to teach him a lesson."

After eating, they walk back to the hospital. They hug and promise to keep in touch before saying goodbye. Laura, Karen, and Nanette go into the hospital. KD walks into the parking structure. As KD walks up the stairs, she hears footsteps. The footsteps give her an uneasy feeling. KD stops and listens, trying to distinguish if the footsteps are getting closer. She thinks someone is coming down the stairs. She turns to go back down the stairs.

The lights in the stairwell go out. KD is scared, but remains level-headed. She tiptoes down the stairs trying not to make a sound. She secures the pepper spray in her hand, preparing to defend herself. When she turns the corner, she sees a masked man coming up the stairs. She quickly turns to run. Filled with fear, she heads for the door. Before she can get through the door, she is grabbed from behind.

A gloved hand covers her mouth to muffle her scream. She's lifted into the air. KD is terrified, but she fights back. She bites his hand. She sprays the man in his face. The man drops her to cover his face. KD lands on her feet and scrambles to get away. The potential abductor misses a step and tumbles down the flight of stairs. KD makes it up a few stairs. Suddenly, another masked man appears out of nowhere.

She sprays him with the pepper spray, but he manages to grabs her. He carries her down a few stairs before she pushes her feet against the wall, making them fall back. She and the second man wrestle on the stairs. She sprays him again. The pepper spray made the man loosen his grip, so she manages to get away from him.

She quickly runs down the stairs, but the first man catches her. She tries to spray him, but he knocks the spray out of her hand. He grabs her by the throat and squeezes. KD discreetly pulls the knife from her waistband to slice the man's wrist before sticking him in the chest. He lets her go. KD kicks the bleeding man as hard as she can in his groin, making him fall to his knees. She kicks him as hard as she can in the face. He falls. She steps on the knife, pushing it further into his chest before she runs down the stairs.

The second man chases her and catches her just as she makes it to the door. They fight over control of the door. KD can't over power the man, but she doesn't give up. KD puts up such a fight that the man gets frustrated and slams her on the stairs. As he lifts his hand to smack her, she reaches for the knife strapped to her ankle. She jabs the knife into the man's side. She pushes the knife into him as far as she can.

While the man is distracted by the pain, KD rushes through the door. She runs between parked cars when she notices a third veiled man running toward her. KD darts across the parking structure to the opposite stairwell. The man chases her to the main floor. He reaches out his hand to grab her. Boom, the would-be attacker body flies into the air and falls on a speeding car. KD keeps running until she is almost hit by a patrolling security car.

Trevor panics as he recognizes KD. He sees the blood on her clothes, so he quickly exits the car to check on her. KD explains three men tried to abduct her. Trevor quickly secures her in the car and takes her to the security office as he calls the police.

Someone tells Nanette to check on KD in the security office. Nanette rushes to the office, but the guards won't let her enter. Nanette can see a crying KD covered in blood. Nanette texts Laura and Karen before she calls Daniel.

Nanette: "Hey, Daniel, it's Nanette, I work with your mother. Remember me?"

Daniel: "Yes! Hello, Ms. Nanette!"

Nanette: "I need to tell John something very important. Do you have his number?"

Daniel: "Well, he is right here, you can talk to him."

Daniel hands John the phone; he says, "It's my mother's friend from her job. She says she has something very important to tell you." John looks concerned as he takes the phone.

John: "Hello!"

Nanette: "John, I'm Nanette, KD's friend! The police have KD at the hospital in the security office. They won't let me talk to her. She has blood on her clothes, she is shaking and crying. She looks terrified. We just left her less than ten minutes ago, so whatever happened just happened!"

John: "I'm on my way."

John tells Daniel his mother needs help with her car before he hurries out the door. By the time John is dropped off at the hospital by one of the protection team's SUVs, the parking lot is full of police cars. John goes to the security office. He talks to Trevor and Fordham who are empathetic to John because they know how much he loves KD.

Trevor says, "I was making the rounds. KD ran out of nowhere. She was panicked and had blood on her clothes. She said three men were trying to abduct her. I put her in my car. I asked was the blood on her clothes hers. She told me she fought with two men and stabbed them."

John is furious but maintain his composure. He asks, "Where is she? Is she hurt?"

Fordham says, "She is in the hospital with the Detroit Police. She was scared, but she didn't seem hurt. Come on, I'll show you where they have her."

John follows Fordham to hall that leads to the room where KD is being examined. Fordham points and says, "She is in the room where the police are guarding the door."

John sees Nanette, Laura, and Karen yelling at the officer guarding the door. John thanks Fordham and rushes down the hall. Nanette yells at the officer, "She is afraid and alone. She needs her friends. We need to see her now."

Karen says, "She is scared. She needs us."

Laura says, "At least tell us what is going on!" The officer doesn't even acknowledge their presence. John walks over to the angry women. John touches Nanette's arm.

Nanette says, "John, you're here! She was fine at dinner. We walked back to the hospital. We said goodbye. Ten minutes later, someone told me she's in the security office, crying and covered in blood. They won't let us see her. We don't know what is going." John thanks Nanette for calling him. He tells them he will find out what's going on and let them know.

John's stoic demeanor calms the angry women immediately. John leads them to the chairs against the wall. Nanette says, "Tell her we are right here and we are not leaving until we know she's okay!" John promises to give KD the message before he walks toward the room. The women sit down, nervously waiting to hear how KD is doing. John talks to the officer and the officer lets John enter the room.

John walks through the door to see a female detective, doctor, and nurse examining KD's body for evidence. They take pictures of the bruises on her arms, thighs, back, and neck as KD recounts the event. His heart breaks at the sight of KD's blood-soaked clothes and shoes bagged in evidence bags. The usually boisterous John is silent.

KD has on a gown and her back is to the door, so she doesn't see John standing there. When the detective and doctor are done with the exam, the nurse gives KD scrubs, socks, and some slippers to wear home. Before the detective, doctor, and nurse leave the room, the detective asks KD if she needs anything. KD asks for her phone to call her fiancé. The detective says he's already here. KD turns to see John standing there. The doctor, nurse, and detective leave the room.

She cries as she runs into his arms. She says, "Baby, you're here!" as she wraps her arms around his neck. John holds her. She tightly squeezes him as she exhales the angst of the ordeal she survived. In John's arm, she feels safe.

John says, "Ladybug,"

KD says, "Baby, I,"

John cuts her off. John asks, "Did they?"

KD quickly answers, "No!"

John asks, "Are you hurt?"

KD says, "A little sore!"

John asks, "Could you see who it was?"

KD says, "It happened so fast. It was so dark."

John says, "KD, I am so sorry that happened to you."

John asks, "Did they take anything?" KD says no. John asks, "Was it Bradley?"

KD replies, "It was dark, but I could tell there was three Black males who were taller and bigger than me. I couldn't see faces or features."

John says, "What did it seem like they wanted?

KD answers, "Me! It was clear they were here to take me."

John says, "Ladybug, I am going to figure out who did this, and I will kill them all. This isn't sliding whether it was Bradley or not. I'm not letting anyone get anyway with hurting you."

KD says, "I was so scared, baby!"

John says, "You fought back and survived. Thank God you're smart and strong."

KD says, "Baby, don't tell Kelly and Daniel about tonight. I don't want them to worry, but make sure they understand they need to be safe." John looks at her arms and neck.

John says, "I will talk to them, but, KD, how are you going to explain these bruises? [John looks at her back.] They are going to think I did something to you. Little Man will freak out if he sees these bruises on your neck.

"I know Bradley is the father of your children, but if he did this [John is still looking at the bruises], I am going to kill him. Look at these bruises. I can't believe this happened. He has gone too far."

KD says, "I'll wear makeup for a while. Baby, go get some ice, maybe I can stop the bruises from getting worse."

John says, "Your friends are out there. They are worried about you. They said they aren't leaving until they know you are okay. What do you want me to tell them?"

KD says, "Tell them I'll let them in after I get dressed."

John says, "Don't leave this room without me!"

KD says, "I won't!" She goes into the restroom. She cries as she scrubs her skin with disinfectant soap. She is disgusted at the thought of the attackers touching her. She tries to scrub the memory away, but flashes of the attack fill her mind. John tells her friends that she'll let them in as soon as she gets dressed.

John goes to the nurses' station to ask for ice packs. While walking back to the room, John runs into Detective Vernon and Detective Stratman. John asks about the investigation. They explain that the surveillance video is dark. Detective Stratman says, "We can make out three male attackers dressed in all black. They were masked and wearing gloves. We can see everything happening just as KD explained."

Detective Vernon shows him the pepper spray and knives KD used to defend herself. He says, "We have samples of their blood. If they are in the system, we will find them. They are probably the same men who tried to break into your house. We will compare the samples from both scenes."

Detective Vernon explains he hopes the suspects' DNA is in system otherwise they'll have very little to go forward with the case. Detective Stratman tells John that the car the three suspects fled in was stolen. He says, "We found the car on fire not far from the hospital, but don't be discouraged. We found a lot of blood in the stairwell. The way KD stabbed them, they are going to need medical attention ASAP or they will die."

John asks, "Can I watch the video?" Because he is John King, hometown hero, they let him watch the security footage. He studies everything about the suspects. His body shivers as he watches KD fight for her life. He says, "She fought hard."

The detectives agree. Detective Vernon says, "She is alive because she fought so hard. She was smart and quick."

John asks if he can get a copy. They tell him no, but they hint that if he happens to record the video on his phone, they wouldn't say anything.

John records the video before going back to KD who is ready to go home. John pops the ice packs and shakes them. He places one on each side of her neck. He asks, "Did you talk to your friends?"

KD answers, "Yes, they just left."

John says, "How are you feeling?"

KD says, "I'm sore, but I'm thankful I'm alive and glad you're here."

John hugs her; he says, "I'm so happy you are alive and well."

KD says, "Let's go home." John grabs her wallet, phone, and keys.

As they walk toward the door, John asks, "Where did you get knives and pepper spray?"

KD says, "Tri told me to start carrying pepper spray and a knife."

John says, "Thank God your friends are smart and give good advice. Thank her for me."

KD and John talk about what happened as he drives her car home. John asks, "KD, didn't I say you and Little Man are to go nowhere without the protection team?"

KD says, "You did, more than once. I thought I would be okay."

John says, "I'm not victim blaming. I'm saying I need you to be safe. You can't take risks even if they are small."

KD says, "You're right!"

John says, "You are not to leave the house without me or the protection team. You are not to drive yourself anywhere. KD, you can't take any more chances. Do you hear me?"

KD says, "I hear you, baby! I promise to follow the plan this moment forward!"

John says, "We have got to hear each other. I need to do better with complying with your wishes, and you can do better with complying with my wishes. I hired security to keep you safe when I am not around. KD, security can't secure you if you don't follow the plan." KD can't give a rebuttal because she knows he's right.

John parks the car in the garage. He kisses KD. He says, "You had a rough day, so I will leave that alone. I want to check in with you before we go in the house. Do you need to talk? Do you need me to do anything? I can stay home for a few days with you."

KD says, "I'd like that!"

John asks, "Are you going to tell your mother? We can have her come over for a few days."

KD says, "For now, let's keep this between us, but talk to everyone about being cautious."

John says, "I can handle that. Anything else?"

KD says, "You go distract Daniel while I go to our room. Tell him I had to use the bathroom, and I'll come say goodnight before he goes to bed."

John says, "I can do that." They kiss. John says, "I thank God for keeping you safe. Baby, I can't lose you."

KD says, "Thank God, he spared me! Lord knows I don't want to leave you! I love you!"

John says, "I love you more!" John goes in the house. He goes upstairs to Daniel's room. Daniel is totally into his video game. John sits next to him and pretends to watch. KD sneaks into their bedroom on the first floor. She showers and washes her hair. She covers the bruises on her neck with foundation. She puts on a smile and hides her fears as if she had a perfect day before she goes to say goodnight to Daniel.

While sleeping, KD has a nightmare about the attack. She jumps up panicked, waking John. He hugs her. He asks if she's okay. She cries; she says, "John, I hurt two people. What if they die?"

John says, "What if you didn't? What could have happened to you? They had bad intentions toward you and you have a God-given right to defend yourself. Daniel needs his mother. Kelly needs her mother. Your mother needs her daughter. I need my wife. My kids and grandkids need KD. Were we supposed to lose to save some scums' life? You did the right thing, KD!" His kisses her forehead. He lays down and pulls her to his chest.

KD says, "You're right! I didn't want to die, be kidnapped, or raped. I felt like they were going to take me and hurt me."

John says, "Feel secure that you did the right thing."

KD says, "Baby, why won't whoever leave us alone?"

John says, "Ladybug, I don't know. We need to be watchful because if they catch us slipping, it won't be good for us."

KD says, "What are we going to do?"

John says, "Keep you and Daniel safe. I talked to him while I was in his room. I'm going to call Kelly and Kathy tomorrow, okay, Ladybug."

KD says, "Okay!"

John says, "Do you want to watch TV or listen to some music to calm your nerves?"

KD says, "I'll watch TV!"

KD lays on John's chest watching TV. She and John don't sleep much. They are both too shaken up by the possibilities of what could have happened.

John spends the next few days comforting KD who is afraid of the dark and afraid to be alone.

Someone anonymously emails Raina cell phone video of the shooting outside the restaurant, so Raina has the exclusive on the situation. She is more than delighted to report tarnishing news to fuel the fire burning John's reputation. Raina's deceitful smirk irritates John's soul as he watch Raina report the shooting. KD says, "I want to smack that smile off her face."

John says, "I should call and cuss her out. I hope people see that her dumb ass is enjoying throwing dirt on my name because she can't have me."

KD says, "Don't give her the satisfaction of knowing you're bothered."

John says, "You're right! She's taking pleasure in spreading lies. You see what I meant when I said she has some ways about her."

KD says, "I see. She's manipulative and evil."

John says, "Ladybug, I don't care what anyone says. I will protect you at all costs."

KD says, "I know she is doing everything she can to make you look bad, but you keep your head up. You were not wrong. You have the right to protect yourself just like everyone else."

John says, "Thank you, Ladybug!"

That night, KD is sleepless. She looks at John sleeping peacefully. She crawls over to his side of the bed. She kisses his cheek and rubs his arm. She whispers his name in his ear. John opens his eyes. She kisses his lips and her hand tenderly rubs down his chest. John grabs her hand just before she reached his underwear. John says, "I can't!"

KD asks, "What's the matter, baby?"

John says, "Ladybug, I walked in that hospital room and saw you hurt and crying. [John pauses. His eyes fill with tears.] You were so vulnerable and fragile. My mind went somewhere that I don't even want to think about. I can't get those images out of my head. I thought they…. [Tears roll down the side of his face. KD hugs him.] I can't even say it."

KD hates to see him cry. She says, "John, I'm sorry," she wipes his tears. She feels empathy for his emotions. She rubs his arm to comfort him. She says, "I'm so sorry that I worried you." His tears invoke hers.

John says, "Never in my life have I not been able to perform. Don't be mad, Ladybug, I need a little time to get my head together."

KD says, "I understand, baby, I'm not mad." They hug. She says, "It's okay!"

John kisses her forehead; he asks, "You can't sleep?"

KD says, "No! My dreams terrify me."

John asks, "Do you want to talk about them? Maybe it will help if you get it out."

KD says, "No!" She says, "Tell me a story."

John says, "Once upon a time there was a very lonely man named Ron who lived on a farm. One day, Ron was riding his tractor, plowing his field when he saw Kacey moving into the house next door. When she smiled at him, she stole his heart. Ron was crazy about Kacey before he talked to her. When he found out Kacey was a widow, Ron was set on stealing her heart and never giving it back.

"Ron made every excuse he could to be near Kacey. He started doing nice things for her and helping her around her house. One day, he sent her flowers, so she cooked a nice meal to thank him. When he tasted the food, he knew he had to marry her. Ron did everything he could to get Kacey to fall in love with him, and out of the blue, he saw love in her eyes. Ron sold his farm and Kacey sold her house. They got married and moved to an island. They had two kids and lived madly in love for the rest of their lives."

KD says, "That's a cute story. I really enjoyed it."

John says, "I'm glad you enjoyed my story."

KD asks, "Did John ever see that look in KD's eyes that Ron saw in Kacey's eyes?"

John says, "All the time!"

KD says, "KD loves John more than Kacey loves Ron."

John says, "John loves KD more than Ron loves Kacey."

KD kisses John. She says, "Thank you, baby, your story calmed my nerves."

John says, "I'll stay up with you. We can keep talking."

KD asks, "Are you sure? I know you are tired of staying up with me."

John says, "I'm sure! I'm here for you."

They talk for a minute before John gets a bright idea. He says, "Hey, let's go to my parents' cabin for a weekend getaway. It's quiet. It's cold outside, so no one will be anywhere around. Just us. No television, no news, no social media, no cell phones, no bullshit. We can have time to ourselves to reconnect. I can get my head right."

KD says, "That sounds nice! I'd love to go."

John says, "In the morning, I'll rent a car. I'll go to the grocery store to get your favorite foods and snacks. Make sure Daniel knows to call Kelly if there's an emergency. Let Kathy know we won't have cell service. Ask if she can keep an ear out for Kelly and Daniel."

KD says, "I'll call momma when she gets up, and I'll talk to DJ before he goes to school."

John says, "We'll have a good time!"

KD says, "I always have a good time with you!"

John says, "I always have a good time with you!" John reaches out his hand. He says, "Let's cuddle!" KD settles his arms. John says, "If you have another bad dream, I'm right here. Wake me up if you need to."

KD says, "OK!"

John says, "I wish you sweet dreams!"

KD says, "Thank you, baby!" John kisses her forehead. KD says, "I love you so much."

John says, "Don't ever stop!"

John instructs the protection team to guard the home while they are away before he and KD load the SUV John rented for the trip. John grabs four guns and several boxes of bullets. KD watches him put the guns in his bag. He tells her, "We should be fine, but if anything pops off, we need to protect ourselves."

John pulls out of the driveway with keen awareness. He vigilantly watches for any suspicious vehicle. As he drives north, they talk about the pending nuptials and the grandbaby on the way. They are excited for both events. John asks, "Would you mind if the baby calls you Nanna?"

KD smiles as she asks, "You think Kera would let her baby call me Nanna?"

John says, "I am Poppa and you are Nanna! This is the first grandbaby we're going to raise together."

KD says, "If Kera is comfortable with her baby calling me Nanna, I would be delighted!"

John says, "It's going to be so cute to see you holding and caring for our new grandgirl!"

KD says, "I love babies, and I'm definitely going to love a baby that looks like you."

John says, "You think the baby will look like me?"

KD says, "All your kids and grand babies look like you. This baby is going to fit right in."

John says, "I'm praying for a girl!"

KD says, "I will pray with you."

John says, "Thanks, Ladybug!"

When they get to the cabin, KD cooks. John cleans up the cabin, puts fresh linen on the bed, and lights the fireplaces. After they eat, they sit by the fire, cuddling under the blanket. KD's kisses and touches excite John. They stare in each other's eyes as KD takes one of her legs out of her pants. She unzips John's pants. They continue to kiss as she slides down John. John's facial expression shows how much he missed her. John lets KD enjoy herself until he can no longer contain himself. He picks her up and carries her to the bedroom.

He undresses her. She undresses him. He puts her in the bed. He gets in the bed. They are face to face on their knees. They kiss as John slides back and forth, stimulating her feminine treasures. The pleasure they put on each other's face shows they needed this time to reconnect.

John turns her around. She bends over. John slides into her. John can't get close enough, so he lifts her legs from the bed. He holds her bent legs in his hands. John feels so good to KD that she can't handle it. KD falls in the bed, shaking. John watches her shake from the extreme pleasure racing through her body. She looks at him and pulls him on top of her. They kiss. She wraps her legs around him. He wraps his arms around her. They kiss and make love until they fall asleep.

In the morning, KD makes breakfast before John takes her outside to practice shooting. John is so proud of her. She is much more confident with the gun. He tells her, "Ladybug, you're ready. If something pops off, you will handle it."

After shooting practice, John takes KD to the lake to go fishing. They relax on the boat and enjoy the cold fall air with their baited hooks in the water. They catch several fish, but she makes him throw all the fish back into the lake after they takes pictures with them.

John lights the bonfire and the grill to make dinner. They eat before they cuddle under a blanket by the bonfire. With KD lying on his chest, darkness in the sky, and the fire warming them, John relaxes so much that he falls asleep. KD eases out of the chair and goes into the cabin to use the restroom. On her way back outside, she stops in the kitchen to get something to drink.

As KD sips a bottle of water, she sees something moving beyond the backyard in the trees. She cuts off the light to get a better look. She makes out a man moving through the trees. She sees another shadow slowly approaching the house. She hurriedly gets down on the floor. She tells herself to not panic. She gets down and crawls to the walkway. She whispers John's name, but he doesn't wake up. She sees an ink pen on the counter. She throws it and hits the open door, but he doesn't wake up.

She whispers, "Shit" as she rushes to grab the three of the guns from the table. She puts two in her waistband and gets the third gun ready to shoot. She gets up and walks toward the door. She aims the gun carefully to ensure John is not in her line of sight as she cautiously approaches the door. She sees a man dressed in all black with a black ski mask holding as axe approaching John. She shoots as she continues toward the door. The first two shots hit the man holding the axe, making him fall back into the fire.

John wakes up from the noise. He sees one man rolling in the bonfire and another man walking toward him holding something in the strike position. KD shoots the second man in the shoulder, making him drop whatever he was holding. KD keeps shooting to keep the men away from John. When she runs out of bullets, she sits the empty gun on the floor as she reaches for a gun in her waistband and continues to shoot.

John manages to crawl into the house under the bullets whizzing toward the stalkers. The first man crawls out of the fire. He and the second man run off, dodging the powerful rapid gunfire. KD keeps shooting until the men are no longer visible. John makes it to KD. She hands him the last gun from her waistband.

John says, "Ladybug, I told you, you would handle the situation. Girl, you saved my ass!"

KD says, "I'm not letting anyone hurt you!"

John says, "That's why I love you!"

They survey the premises. KD says, "I think they are gone."

John says, "How the fuck did they find us way up here!" John loads all the guns.

KD says, "Do you think we should go home?"

John says, "Yes, let's hit the freeway." They put out the bonfire, load the SUV, lock up the cabin, and pull off as fast as lightning. John says, "We may be able to catch up with them."

KD says, "Are we calling the police?"

John says, "So, they can tell us there's nothing they can do? Nah. We are going to have to handle this ourselves."

KD says, "John, I…."

John cuts her off; he says, "Just like you popped their asses tonight, you can do it again. KD, you are much stronger than you realize. Look at what you have survived. You are tough, smart, you have incredible drive, you are a fighter. Ladybug, they are coming at us unprovoked, we have a right to defend ourselves. The police are not doing anything to protect us.

"I know Bradley is the father of your kids, but I can't keep letting him come at us. I want to fuck him up, but I think about Kelly. I don't want to hurt Kelly. I chill for Kelly's sake, but Bradley 'The Fucking Loser' Jacobs is testing my patience."

KD says, "I'm sorry that he is doing this. I really don't know why he is bothering us. Everything I told you about him and I is true. We have not communicated since that night, nor have I given him the impression that I want to communicate with him."

John says, "I know you haven't. I don't think that at all. Bradley knows he has me between a rock and a hard place, and he's taking advantage. He knows I don't want to hurt Kelly."

KD says, "Thank you for thinking of my daughter. I know this isn't easy for you."

John says, "We're family. That's what families do. There's always a way to hurt someone in a non-violent manner."

KD says, "Bradley should be at home with his son. What the fuck is he doing way up here fucking with us?"

John answers, "Getting his ass popped and burned. The way he fell in that fire was like a movie. Ladybug, that was so sexy! I got excited watching you handle that gun."

KD laughs. She says, "You're so silly!"

John says, "Seriously, how are you feeling emotionally?"

KD says, "I can't believe what just happened. I couldn't let someone hurt you. I will kill to keep you safe." John takes her hand and kisses it.

John says, "They aren't dead or dying. They're a little hurt, but they will live. Sometimes, you fall in the ditch you dig for someone else. We were minding our business. They have no business all the way up here bothering us. You did the right thing. Okay, Ladybug?"

KD says, "Okay!" They make it home to find all is well.

On the last day of school before Christmas break, John picks up Daniel from school. Daniel is confused to see John. Daniel says, "What are you doing here? It's Thursday, isn't Bradley picking me up?"

John says, "No, you are not going to Bradley's house ever again."

Daniel says, "My mother didn't tell me anything."

John says, "Do you want to go with Bradley or come home with me?"

Daniel says, "Go home with you."

John says, "Get in the car and don't worry about Bradley. When your mother asks why you are home, tell her Bradley didn't come, so you called me."

Daniel says, "I probably should wait for Bradley. I don't want to get my mother in trouble."

John says, "Your mother will not get in trouble. Do you see Bradley?" Daniel says no. John says, "Little Man, he is not coming. He's never coming again. You never have to deal with him again. Your mother never has to deal with him again."

Daniel asks, "Are you sure?"

John answers, "I promise! That man is out of your life for good!"

Daniel happily hops in the car and says, "So long to that sucker."

John says, "Let's swing by the video game store."

Daniel says, "You are a man after my own heart."

John laughs. He says, "Son, let's go home and enjoy our first Christmas together." When Daniel hears John say son, Daniel's heart smiles.

On the way home, John and Daniel plan activities to do over Christmas break. John offers Daniel two options. He says, "We can stay home, enjoy two weeks here in Detroit as a family. We can invite the g-sons over, and you all can play video games until your brains explode. We can eat whatever you want. Or, we can go on a family vacation."

Daniel says, "Man, that's a hard choice, but I want to stay home. I can't believe there's no more Bradley. I get you in my life, and get him out of my life. This is the best Christmas ever. [John smiles listening to Daniel's glee.] What did my mom say when you told her about Bradley?"

John stops smiling instantly; he says, "I didn't tell her and we're not going to tell her. Sometimes, a man protects his woman by handling the situation before the woman is aware of the situation. She doesn't need to worry about Bradley. She's been so stressed out lately. I don't want to put any more pressure on her. You and I have it handled. We're just going to tell her he didn't show, so I picked you up."

Daniel says, "I get it! Bradley did something bad and you're keeping it a secret. Bradley can be an asshole, but he must've done something extremely bad if I'm never seeing him again."

John says, "Little Man, you are so smart. It's something for adults to worry about. I got it handled, so you don't have to worry. I promise it is handled."

Daniel says, "I trust you, John! I'll keep the secret!"

John says, "My man!"

Chapter Four

It's a cold, snowy holiday season, but KD enjoys time with her kids and fiancé at their home. The house stays busy and full with the grandkids running around with Daniel. There are no incidents over the Christmas season, but KD and John remain cautious.

After the new year, John and KD are relaxing in bed when KD's friend calls, asking for a favor. Her friend's son is sick, and she needs to take him to the doctor. KD agrees to cover her friend's shift since everyone in the house has plans. Kelly and Daniel are spending the day with Kenna and her sons. John is going to play basketball with friends.

John and KD decide to ride with the security team. Before KD gets out of the car, John tells her to be careful and he loves her. They kiss, she tells him she loves him too. After KD is safe in the hospital, the security team drops John off at the gym to meet his friends.

After a competitive basketball game, Castle suggests that they settle the "Who's the Best Athlete" debate by racing their go-carts. The wintry conditions make for an interesting race. Only a good driver can navigate the frozen ground of their make shift track. They get their go-karts and line up to race in the coldness blowing from the Detroit River.

After the first two races, John and Rocco drive up to the starting line. When the flag goes down, John and Rocco take off as fast as they can. When John tries to make the turn, he realizes his steering wheel is jammed. John tries to slow down, but his brakes are not engaging. He struggles to steady the car. Before he can make another move, an axle breaks, causing him to veer into to Rocco's Lane. Rocco quickly maneuvers to dodge and pass John.

John rolls into the fence at full speed. The velocity propels him into the air. He flips over and over until he crashes into the opposite wall. John is thrown from the car just before it burst into flames. His friends run to check on him as they call 9-1-1 for help.

The Detroit Fire Department is on scene within a minute because the station is only a few blocks from the lot. They quickly extinguish the fire and render aid to John. An ambulance arrives to take John to the hospital where KD is working.

As John is pushed through the emergency room door, he and Nanette recognize each other. He is conscious, but having trouble speaking and can barely move. Nanette rushes over to him. She says, "Oh my God, John," as she tries to see how she can help. John points to Nanette's pen. She hands him the pen and holds her pad while he writes.

She runs alongside the bed as he writes a message. He passes out and drops the pen before he can finish the sentence. Nanette picks up the pen and reads the message: KD I love y. Nanette runs to find KD, who has no idea what is going on.

Nanette finds a smiling KD coming out of a patient's room. Nanette is hysterical and out of breath. Nanette's hysteria concerns KD. Nanette, out of breath, says, "KD, you need to get downstairs to the emergency room, now. John is hurt. It looks bad! He sent you a message."

She hands KD the note and says, "Go check on John, I'll finish the shift for you." KD reads the note in a panic. She takes off running. She pulls out her phone. Focused on getting to John, she runs non-stop down the stairs as she calls Kimma. Kimma panics when KD tells her John is hurt. Kimma contacts her siblings, and they rush to the hospital.

By the time KD makes it to the waiting area, the accident is breaking news. The images of the mangled, torched go-cart make KD sick to her stomach. John's friends run into the emergency. They offer KD comfort with promises that John will be okay.

Tri and Mena call to offer support. As soon as she hangs up with her friends, Mrs. Daniels calls to say she is on her way to the hospital. KD calls Kelly, who is with Kenna and Kera. They are on the way to the hospital. Isaac arrives with Isaiah just as Kimma is pulling into the hospital's parking lot. The news vans arrive at the hospital just in time to catch Kimma, Isaac, and Isaiah rushing into the hospital. Alex is on his way home from a business trip.

John's friends explain to KD what happened during the accident as Kera, Kenna, and Kelly run straight into a crying KD's arms. Kenna's sons and Daniel are panicked and scared. Kera, Kelly, Kenna, and KD hug the boys as Ms. Daniels rushes into the waiting room in tears. Although KD appreciates John's friend's support, the presence of Wesley makes her uncomfortable. She looks at Wesley with untrusting eyes. He can feel her hate. Wesley leaves, and something in his body language didn't sit right with KD.

As Mrs. Daniels and Kelly comfort KD as she hugs Daniel, Detective Vernon and Detective Stratman walk into the waiting room. Detective Vernon says, "We are sorry to bother you at this time, Ms. Daniels, but we believe someone tampered with Mr. King's go-cart, causing it to malfunction. Has there been any suspicious activity since the attempted kidnapping?" The word kidnapping shocks everyone.

Everyone says in unison, "Kidnapping," in an aggressive tone. They all stare at KD who says, "I'll explain!" Isaiah and Isaac ask KD about the kidnapping, but the detective tells them to let KD answer. KD says, "Well," she hesitates to answer, but continues, "We went to his parents' cabin a few weeks ago. On our second night there, two men were trying to break into the cabin, so we came home early." KD didn't want to worry her family with the truth.

Kenna says, "Stepmom, what the hell is going on?"

Before KD could answer, Kelly says, "John mentioned a black car, an expensive black car with tinted windows. It's a BMW, no, he said a Benz, yeah, a brand-new Benz has been following him. He said the car stuck out because it didn't have a license plate. At first, he thought it was Raina, but the car was a more expensive model." The detectives take notes.

KD says, "He hasn't mentioned anything about a black car to me."

Detective Stratman asks, "Ms. Daniels, have you noticed a black car following you?"

KD says, "I haven't left the house much since the incident."

The detectives ask John's friends if they know anything, but they are clueless and just as shocked as his children. They thought the accident was purely an accident. The detectives tell KD, the family, and John's friend to contact their precinct if anyone hears or thinks of anything.

When the detectives leave, Kimma says, "Kidnapping, a black car following Daddy, men trying to break into the cabin, KD, what is going on?"

KD says, "I told your father to tell you all what was going on a long time ago, and he promised me that he would."

Kenna says to Kelly, "Little Sister, you didn't think to mention anything to us?"

Kelly replies, "He swore me to secrecy. You know how he is. He didn't want to worry you all. He swore he had things under control, and he could handle the situation."

Kimma asks Kelly to tell them everything she knows about what's going on. Kelly says, "He told me someone is trying to break up the relationship he has with my mother. Weird things have been happening and he was being followed. He told me not to worry because he will protect my mother and brother. That's all I know."

Kimma says, "KD, what is going on?"

KD says, "Things have been crazy lately."

Daniel says, "Someone crashed into momma's car as we were riding on the freeway."

KD says, "Daniel and I were meeting John for dinner, and someone crashed into us and totaled my car. Before we moved, someone broke into my apartment to poison our puppies. Someone broke into the new house to vandalize it. One night we were at John's old house, and an intruder was in the front room looking at me. Speaking of John's old house, someone burned it down along with his boat."

Kera says, "That's why Dad was acting so suspicious after the fire."

Kenna asks, "When did this all start?"

KD says, "The minute the proposal video was posted on social media."

Kera says, "What about this kidnapping the detectives mentioned?"

KD says, "I was in the hospital's parking garage. Three men tried to take me."

Everyone gasps in disbelief. Kelly asks, "Momma, why didn't you tell us?"

KD says, "I didn't want you to worry."

Kelly asks, "How did you get away?"

KD answers, "I did what I had to do."

Mrs. Daniels says, "KD! I can't believe you didn't tell me."

KD says, "Momma, I'm fine! I didn't want to worry you!"

Isaac asks, "Has anyone checked to see if Raina is behind this?"

KD says, "The police talked to Raina. She admitted she vandalized his car and she sent some text messages after seeing the video, but denied being involved in any of the other incidents."

Alex asks, "Did they talk to the guy involved in the altercation at the club?"

KD says, "The police questioned him, but they said he had an alibi."

Isaiah says, "KD, there is a succession of women who do not want to see Dad with you."

KD says, "The police have questioned several women from John's past. They don't think any of them were involved."

Kimma says, "Who would go this far?"

KD says, "We have been asking the same thing."

Isaac asks, "KD, could there be someone in your past behind all this?"

KD says, "The only thing in my past is an ex-husband. The police talked to him." John's friend leaves one by one as minutes turn to hours of waiting.

After three hours, John is finally out of surgery. Dr. Aleem Parvesh comes to speak to the family, "He will fully recover, but it will be a long, hard healing process. He is going to be immobile for several weeks, so he will need round-the-clock care.

"He has several broken ribs, a broken arm, a broken leg, and he has a concussion. We successfully stopped the bleeding in left lung. He is going to be in a lot of pain for a month or so. You all can go see him. Brace yourself; it looks as bad as it is. He is sedated, so he'll be asleep for a while."

Daniel gets up, but KD stops him; she says, "Let his kids see their father."

Kera says, "Stepmom, are you sure?"

KD says, "You all should have a private moment with your father."

After John's kids go into the room to see him, Daniel says, "Momma, I want to see John."

KD says, "You don't want to see him like that. He's not going to look like himself."

Daniel says, "But how will he know I'm worried about him and love him?"

KD says, "He knows in his heart that you love him, and he can feel your love even in his sleep. Son, you've got to be strong for him and me. With everything that's going on, Son, I don't know if I can hold it together if you break down." Mrs. Daniels hugs KD and wipes her tears.

Daniel says, "Momma, I promise I will be strong," as they lock pinky fingers.

Kimma comes to get KD and her family; she says, "We think you all should be in here with us. We are family, and Dad would want you in here." KD did not want to see John hurt. She reluctantly walks into the room comforted by her mother and daughter.

The sight of John is too much for KD. She loses all control of her emotions as she leans over to kiss him. Kelly, Kimma, Kenna, and Kera all surround her and rub her back. KD gently lays on him, balling her eyes out. KD cries so hard that everyone in the room is silent and sullen with their own emotions compounded by her emotions.

Just before sunrise, John opens his eyes. He feels KD's hand in his. He squeezes her hand, waking her. KD calls out to everyone, "He is awake!" They all rush to his bedside. John looks in KD's eyes and he knows he must be strong and fight through the pain and for her. She looks at him, and thanks God he is alive.

Four weeks at home, John is feeling better. The doctor wants him to avoid strenuous physical activity for two more weeks. John's heart skipped a beat when the doctor told him and KD no intimacy for two more weeks. KD had to encourage him to hold it together.

Daniel comes in the house from school and runs straight to see John with the puppies. Daniel brings him water and a protein bar; John thanks him. They talk about sports and school.

Daniel says, "I miss hanging out with you."

John says, "As soon as the doctors clear me, we will spend a lot of time together. We can do whatever you want."

Daniel asks, "Can we go shopping?"

John says, "You want to go shopping?"

Daniel says, "I need some clothes that girls will like. I'll never get the older girls to see me if my momma keeps dressing me like a little kid. I need some clothes to make me look more mature, especially on free dress days. You have great style. I want to dress like you."

John says, "We will get you a new wardrobe. We can even do some things to make your uniform pop. You're going to have girls all over you. How is school going otherwise?"

Daniel says, "School is fine. I just miss you."

John says, "I miss you, too, Little Man."

Daniel asks, "When you marry my mother, will you call me son, and can I call you, dad?"

John says, "You are my son. We don't need a marriage or a piece of paper to prove that."

Daniel says, "It's cool that you call me your little man, but I would like to be your son."

John says, "Did you talk to your mother about that?"

Daniel says, "Yes! She told me to talk to you. She said we should settle things in our relationship between us like men and quit using her as our middle man because she's a woman."

John says, "She's right. Son, we should feel comfortable enough to talk to each other about whatever we need to talk about. If you feel comfortable calling me dad, I'm comfortable with it. I love you, and I will be here for you for the rest of my life no matter what is going on."

Daniel says, "I will be here for you for the rest of my life. I love you, Dad," they hug.

John says, "I love you, Son!"

KD comes into the room. She tells Daniel to go to the kitchen to eat. KD sits John's plate on the table before she sits on the bed. John begins to eat. John says, "This is really good, but I want to eat something else." KD smiles but ignores that comment.

KD asks, "Did Daniel talk to you?"

John says, "He did!"

KD asks, "What happened?"

John says, "We talked like men."

KD says, "John, you are incredible with my son. Thank you for accepting him and loving him. You are an awesome man." She kisses his forehead; she says, "Thank you, baby!"

John says, "You're welcome! You're an amazing woman, and Daniel is an awesome young man. I love you both."

After John is done eating, KD gets up to take his plate to the kitchen. John grabs her arm and pulls her back to the bed. KD asks, "What are you trying to do?"

John says, "I'm trying to knock into the back of your c-section scar."

KD says, "No!"

John says, "Ladybug, I need you. We have never gone this long without loving each other. Come on, Ladybug, I need it."

KD says, "No, the doctor said we have to wait two more weeks."

John whispers, "Two more weeks might take me out. It's a medical emergency. You are my caretaker, so you need to attend my needs."

KD says, "The doctor said no strenuous or prolonged activity."

John says, "You can ride it. I won't move."

KD says, "I can't go against your doctor."

John says, "Come on, Ladybug! Just a little bit. Please!"

KD says, "John, no!"

John whispers, "Lock the door!"

KD says, "I cannot believe you have me doing this." KD sits the plate on the table and locks the door. She lifts her skirt, pulls off her panties, and crawls into bed.

John says, "Ladybug, I need to feel you."

KD says, "You better not get hurt."

John says, "I'll be fine. I promise! Come here," he reaches out his hand. She takes his hand. John says, "Kiss me, Ladybug!" KD bends over and slowly kisses him. She holds him in her hand as her tongue traces all around him. John rests his head on the pillow and relaxes. He appreciates her willingness to please him. When her lips surround him, he lifts his head and stares into her eyes. He says, "When you look at me with those pretty eyes while you do that, oh my God, it's magical, baby!" She rubs all over him as she pleases him.

He says, "Ride me, baby!" She slowly lowers herself on him. She braces her weight on her toes and holds on to the headboard. John says, "Oh, Ladybug, I missed you!" She tries to be gentle. He says, "No, baby, give it to me!" He grabs her hips pulling her all the way down.

KD says, "Baby, we need to take it easy."

John says, "I need you to take all this dick."

KD laughs. She says, "You talk so much shit. You know what I meant."

John says, "Okay, I'll be careful."

After John is satisfied, KD gives him a sponge bath. KD says, "You're handling this well."

John says, "Only on the outside!"

KD says, "You know I don't mind taking care of you. I will always be here for you. Whatever! Whenever!"

John says, "I got a real one. I don't doubt that, but I hate being totally dependent on you for everything. I'm sitting here thinking who could be this mad at me. I can't think of anyone. Raina can't even be this mad. After the marriages, I told myself not to lie to women. Every woman I was with knew what was up. I never led a woman to think things were more than what they were. I knew a few wanted more, but they said they understood."

KD says, "Sometimes a woman will say she accepts something when she really doesn't. John, they said they understood, but hoped you would change your mind."

John says, "Ladybug, what did I do to deserve this?" KD holds his hand next to her heart.

KD says, "I wish I knew the answer to that, but I have to believe our trials aren't always retaliation or karma. Baby, the things we go through is undeserved sometimes."

John says, "KD, I hope you know when I say I love you, I need you, and I want only you, I mean it. I haven't used those words loosely ever in my life." KD kisses his hand. He says, "I've never loved anyone or been loved like this. Someone knows that, and they want to take my happiness. You and Daniel make me happy."

KD says, "You make us happy."

John says, "How would a stranger know which car was mine?"

KD says, "Good question. They wouldn't."

John asks, "Do you think Raina did this to me? She knew which car was mine."

KD says, "You spent a year with her. What do you think?"

John says, "Messing up the cars, no doubt that was her, but this is not her style."

KD says, "Then it's probably not her, but it's someone familiar with you and your habits. Think about everyone who has been around when you all raced. Who would betray you or benefit from betraying you?"

John says, "Ladybug, this is some shit."

KD says, "It is! Have you talked to the kids?"

John says, "Yeah! The girls are mad at me except Kelly."

KD asks, "What did you do?"

John says, "Why do you think I did something?"

KD looks at him with a face that says I know it was you; she asks, "What did you do?"

John says, "They called me a chauvinist and misogynist. They think I don't trust them because they're women. I was only making sure we're on the same page. Ladybug, I'm not a misogynist or a chauvinist, am I?"

KD says, "Awe, baby, of course, you are."

John says, "What? Ladybug!"

KD says, "It's okay, John, it works for us, but your daughters are not like me. You like getting your way and being in control. I like giving you your way, and I don't mind that you love to have control. I'm naturally a submissive person, which works well with your dominant personality. Kimma, Kenna, and Kera are you. They are strong, smart, and driven. Baby, who raised them?"

John answers, "I did!"

KD says, "Who taught them everything they know about the business?"

John says, "I did!"

KD says, "Baby, you can trust our girls. They will do right by you and the company because that's what they were raised to do. They're bosses, baby, just like their daddy. When you check with them to see how things are going, you need to check your tone and talk to them like they are executives, not your daughters.

"You should trust them as much as you trust yourself because those girls are you. They love you and look up to you. They want to make you happy, despite the fact you treat Kelly differently. They tell me all the time that you are easier on Kelly than the rest of the girls.

"You confide in Kelly as a friend in your personal time, and you treat her like an employee at work. The other girls were very upset that you told Kelly things that you hadn't shared with them even after I asked you to tell them what was going on. You said that you would talk to them. I trusted that you kept your word. Your children were looking at me as if I were hiding something. I don't have to think how they felt because their faces said it all. Now, I would tell you about yourself for not doing what I asked you to do, but I'll save it for another time.

"I get you're building a relationship with Kelly, but the mutual respect you have with her can come across as favoritism, and our other girls resent that. All our daughters deserve mutual respect at work and a loving, concerned dad off the clock. You understand what I'm saying?"

John says, "Yeah, I hear what you are saying."

KD asks, "Can you do better for me?"

John says, "I'll do better!"

KD says, "Will you call to apologize for me?"

John says, "Would you grab my phone for me?"

KD says, "Of course," as she hands him the phone, "I'm going to go wash dishes. I'll check on you in a little while." John tells her okay.

John calls Kimma. When Kimma answers, he asks, "Are Kenna and Kera with you?"

Kimma says, "Yes!"

John says, "Would you put me on speaker?"

Kimma says, "Okay!"

John says, "You three are my light and pride. The bond a man has with his daughters is so important to him as a father, and I never want to break that bond with either of you. I love each of you more than you ever will know. I realize it's not easy being my daughter and working with me. I recognize that I can be controlling and demanding.

"As your father, I want to say, Daddy apologizes for making you feel less than. That was never my intention. I know you all are smart and capable. Never doubt that I am proud of each of you or that I trust you. I am well aware that you all are beyond capable and highly intelligent.

"It is an honor to be the father of three beautiful, intelligent women. You three are amazing women. You all were born with good souls. Everything you do, you do with pure intentions. Only by the grace of God was I blessed with great kids despite my flaws.

"As your employer, Mr. King would like to thank you for all your hard work. I have the utmost confidence in your skills and ability. I appreciate your loyalty to our mission. Most importantly, I trust you. I did not mean to upset you earlier. I unfairly disrupted your workday. As your father, I apologize for my tone and approach. That will never happen again. Mr. King is going to let you do your jobs. Call if you need to; otherwise, I'm at home trying to heal. Okay, my daughters?"

They say unison with a sweet tone that only a daughter could use, "Okay, Daddy!"

Kimma says, "Thank you, Mr. King."

Kenna says, "Hey, Daddy!"

John says, "Yes, daughter!"

Kenna says, "Tell KD, thank you!"

Kera says, "We know she told you what to say, but it was sweet and we appreciate it."

John says, "For the record, I spoke from my heart. She did not tell me what to say, but she did help me see that I was wrong."

Kimma says, "Dad, we love KD, don't mess up."

John says, "I hear you, baby! My daughters, I should have been open and honest with you about what was going on before the incident like KD told me to, but I didn't want to worry you. I realize now I should have trusted you were mature enough to handle the truth. I can see how you were blindsided at the hospital.

"I hope you understand, I was protecting you and not shutting you out. It was easier to talk to Kelly because she already knew some things, and I asked her to keep my situation a secret while I figured things out. I apologize because I mishandled things. Forgive me?"

In unison, they say, "We forgive you!"

John says, "No more secrets, I promise. I love my girls, and I love that you all care enough to be concerned." They tell him they love him before they hang up.

KD is cleaning up the kitchen when an unknown vehicle parks in front of their house. The protection team rushes to the car. The driver identifies himself as a courier. He says he has a package for Ms. KD Daniels. Security escorts the courier to the door. He rings the doorbell. He stands surrounded by the armed protection team when KD cautiously opens the door. He asks if Ms. KD Daniels is home. When she says I'm KD, he tells her she's been served as he hands her an envelope from family court. KD's heart pounds faster than ever before. She closes the door and anxiously opens the envelope, thinking Bradley filed for full custody of Daniel.

She is relieved when she reads Bradley Jacobs relinquished his parental rights of Daniel James Jacobs. KD didn't see that coming at all. She rushes to show John. She is so happy when she hands him the paper. John calmly says, "I'm happy that you are happy."

KD joyously says, "Baby, isn't this great? Maybe, he is going to leave us alone."

John comforts her by rubbing her leg and says, "I hope so!"

KD says, "As happy as I am that Bradley gave up his rights, I am sad that my son doesn't have a father. It's going to hurt him when I tell him his father gave up on him."

John says, "Daniel has a father. I may not be his biological father, but I am his father. I am here for him, and I am not going anywhere."

KD says, "You're right, John. You've been an excellent father to him!"

John says, "Let me talk to Daniel. I'll make sure he is okay."

KD says, "Do you want me to get him?"

John says, "Can we talk alone?" KD goes to get Daniel. When he comes into the room, John says, "Son, sit down. I need to talk to you." Daniel says okay and sits down. John says, "You are a great person, no matter what anyone else says or does. Sometimes people really want to do right, but they don't have the strength, courage, or know-how.

"Look, I don't know Bradley Jacobs personally, so I can't say why he does what he does. Don't you ever let anything that man does or says affect who you are and what you do. You are a remarkable young man. Since the day I met you, I've loved and admired you, your heart, your spirit, your courage, your integrity, your intelligence, and your goodness. You have a bright future, and I'll be there for every moment, God willing.

"I have to tell you something. Today, your mother received a letter from the court. Jacobs is no longer legally your father. That means, he will no longer be responsible for you financially. He will no longer have any contact with you. He will no longer have a say in the decisions regarding you. That decision is about him, and has nothing to do with you."

Before John could say anything else, Daniel excitedly asks, "Does this mean you're going to be my father? Will you adopt me?"

John asks, "Is that what you want?"

Daniel says, "I want that more than anything!" Before John could respond, Daniel runs to tell KD who is nervously sitting on the couch. KD's mouth drops.

Daniel asks, "Momma, why do you seem mad? I thought you would be happy for me. I am finally getting the father I always wanted. He loves me, he plays with me, and he comes to all my games and competitions. Momma, why aren't you happy for me?"

KD says, "Daniel, it's not that. I'm shocked. I wasn't expecting you to say that."

Daniel says, "I know I am only a kid, but can we just this one time do what I want?"

KD walks to the master bedroom. Daniel follows her pleading his case. Daniel artfully articulates how having John as a father and role model will be beneficial for him. KD hears him, but is too overwhelmed to respond. She asks, "John, what is he talking about?"

Daniel tells KD, "You told us to work our relationship out between us, so we decided John is going to adopt me." She looks at John. She goes to speak, but John and Daniel affirm that things are decided. Daniel says,

"You can't say we need to work things out amongst ourselves and when we do, you get mad."

John says, "He said what he said and he meant what he said."

KD doesn't say anything. Daniel says, "I should be able to have some say in my life. I had to spend the last five years with Bradley Jacobs because no one cared how I felt. I am free now and I want John to be my father."

John says, "He is an intelligent young man. He should have some input in his life. It will help him learn about making tough decisions and being responsible."

Daniel says, "You feel me, Dad?"

John says, "I'm with you, Son!"

Daniel says, "Girls always flip-flop. What is that about?"

John says, "You're the smart one, you tell me because I can't figure it out."

Daniel asks, "Why can't they just say what they mean? It's so confusing."

John says, "Who are you telling!" KD listens in disbelief of the entire conversation.

Daniel says, "Dad, would you like some ice cream and root beer to celebrate?"

John says, "Son, I would love to celebrate with you and enjoy some ice cream."

Daniel says, "Dad, I'll be right back with *your* dessert. Would *you* like it in a mug or bowl?"

John says, "Mug!"

Daniel asks, "One or two scoops?"

John says, "We're celebrating, give me two!"

Daniel says, "You have a point. Dad, I will be right back." Daniel looks at KD; he says, "You don't get any ice cream," before he leaves the room.

KD sits on the bed. She asks, "What if we break up? He can't take another man leaving him."

John says, "He needs a father. Why are you so against me being the man in your life? I wouldn't leave him for any reason. Besides, we aren't breaking up."

KD says, "I love that you are the man in my life. It's not that. It's a lot to ask of you."

John says, "But, you didn't ask, and I can handle it. I am here because I want to be here. I want to marry you. I want to be a part of Daniel's life. I want to be there for the hard times, the big moments, and I want to share all those moments with you."

She kisses him; she says, "I want to share those moments with you, but this is a big commitment. I know that I love you and I want to be with you, but I also know that relationships aren't always happy. When you aren't happy with me, your relationship with him will be affected."

John says, "Daniel is a part of you, and I love that, but that's not the sum of our relationship. Daniel and I have our own bond, and that bond isn't taxing or a burden to me. And, I need you to have faith in us. We're going to make it.

"We'll raise our son. He's going to be healthy and happy. He'll go to college and we will be empty nesters. The grandkids will come over on the weekends. We'll cook and let them run around. Then, one day our son will get married and have kids, and they will come over and run around. We are going to grow old together. We will have matching rocking chairs. There will be times we get on each other's nerves. We may argue and yell at each other, but I will never make Daniel feel the brute of my anger."

KD says, "John, I admire the man you are. Being so willing to take on a great responsibility. God has truly blessed me."

John says, "Destiny! This is our destiny. God has blessed us both to live out our destiny."

KD asks, "John, baby, aren't you going to discuss this with your kids before you make this decision?"

John says, "My kids already accept Daniel, but I will talk to them."

KD says, "You're going to talk to all six kids and seven grandkids?"

John says, "For real, this time, I will talk to each one of them individually. Do we have a plan? No backing out or having doubts. You can't be in this and be afraid. Have faith in us!"

KD says, "If you look me in my eyes and say this is what you want, I will wholeheartedly agree to the adoption. I'll sign the papers, go to court, whatever you and he want me to do."

John says, "This is what I want," looking in her eyes with a straight, serious face.

KD says, "Then, that is what I want." She kisses him. She says, "I love you so much!"

John says, "I love you so much! Now, you need to go talk to him because he is mad at you!"

KD replies, "I'll go to talk to him."

John says, "Let him make my float first!" John laughs. He adds, "Mad you're not getting one?" KD rolls her eyes at John. He winks at her and sticks out his tongue.

Chapter Five

KD, Tri, and Mena are enjoying each other's company at a restaurant. They laugh and talk, unaware they are being watched by Raina. KD explains that tomorrow will mark one year of her meeting John. Suddenly, KD hears someone say her name. She looks up and straight into Raina's smiling face. All movement at the table stops. The energy at table immediately lets Raina know her presence is not appreciated. Tri is highly pissed and her face doesn't hide her feelings. KD leans back in her chair and says, "How may I help you?"

Tri says, "K, who is this?" Tri asks to make Raina feel trivial. Mena, on the other hand, has no idea John had a relationship with Raina before meeting KD.

When KD doesn't answer Tri, Mena asks, "K, who is she?"

Raina sticks out her hand and says, "I'm Raina, I'm a friend of John's." KD doesn't extend her hand, so Raina puts her hand down. KD looks at her with a sharp face. Raina corrects herself, "I was his friend a year ago; we don't communicate anymore."

Mena says, "If you were friends with John in the past, your business was with John, in the past. You have no need or reason to speak to KD, in the present."

Tri says, "This better not be some bullshit."

Raina says, "This is not like that. I have no ill-intent."

KD says, "Is that why you slashed my tires and called me bitches on Memorial Day?"

Raina says, "Yes, I tore up John's car, but I didn't touch your car, I swear. And, I'm sorry about that night. I was drunk and, in my feelings, I said some very hurtful things. I was very much out of character. I unfairly took my anger at him out on you. Please accept my apology."

Tri asks, "Get closer to your point! What do you want?"

Raina says, "I'm coming with information from one woman to another."

KD is not interested in what Raina has to say, but gives her a chance to speak. KD points to the empty chair next to Tri. Raina sits and says, "When I was with John…" KD gives her that look again, so Raina rephrases the statement. She says, "I heard about what's been going on, and I wanted to let you know that I had nothing to do with anything other than vandalizing John's car after I saw the proposal video.

"I think you should know when I was friends with John, a black car followed me to and from John's house. I could never see the driver, but the car would closely tail me, especially at night. I would randomly find weird notes on my windshield. John always ignored my warnings. I think it's the same person. Whoever it is has been sending me emails. From the content of the emails, I can tell the person has been following you."

KD says, "Thanks for letting me know." KD thinks Raina is done. When Raina starts talking again, KD rolls her eyes.

Raina says, "Look, one day, I was the happiest woman in the world in love with the man of my dreams. The next day, the same man wouldn't answer my call, wouldn't call me, wouldn't talk to me. I went to see him, and he was so cold. He had never been that way with me.

"Finally, I got him to answer the phone. He was cordial enough for me to get the closure I wanted. I said what I needed to say, and he said what he had to say. At that moment, I realized there was nothing I could do because I'm not the one, and I accept that.

"I have not and will not contact him again. You have my word. I've moved on. I've found a good man, and as you know, there's nothing like the love of a good man. Cas reached out to me and comforted me, and he made me feel better. Cas said John plays with women for a year, then pushes them away. He told me John will be done with you before the wedding."

Tri and Mena stand up. Tri says, "Bitch, you need to get the fuck away from here." Cas, standing at the door, calls Raina. He waves at her to come to him.

Raina gets up and says, "Ms. KD, I'm trying to save you from the heartache I experienced."

Mena says, "Bitch, your ass is going to ache if you don't get the fuck away from this table."

Tri points her finger in Raina's face; she says, "You, dingy, dumb bitch! Just like Rudolph, no one lets you play reindeer games because no one likes you."

KD, frozen and speechless, stares at Raina as her heart crumbles and her mind explodes with fear and insecurity. As Raina puts her hands up and walks away, Tri says, "Get you and your good man fucked up, talking that dumb shit."

Mena says, "The audacity of that bitch," as she sits down.

Tri says, "I should've knocked that bitch in her shit when she first walked up. I knew she was on some bullshit."

Mena says, "K, don't let her bother you. She's bitter." KD is unable to move or speak. She stares at Raina and Cas as they joyfully leave the restaurant. KD is so focused on Raina that she can't hear Mena or Tri talking.

Tri says, "K! K!"

Raina doesn't know KD but knew her biggest fear; she says, "I have to go! I'll call you!" KD puts two hundred-dollar bills on the table, grabs her jacket and keys, and rushes out of the restaurant. Tri and Mena try to talk to KD, but KD rushes out of the restaurant. As soon as she gets in her car, the tears flood her face as she drives home.

KD is so embarrassed that she locks herself in her room. She calls Kelly. Kelly tells KD she'll come straight home as soon as she can get away from work. KD texts the protection team to ask them to pick up Daniel from school. Tri and Mena call her phone, but she doesn't answer. She responds with a text that says: I'll call you later.

John repeatedly calls, but she sends him to voicemail each time, which has never happened before. John texts, but KD ignores them. John knows something is wrong, so he calls Kelly. Kelly tells him that her mother ran into Raina, they had a conversation, and now KD's hysterically crying.

John rushes home from his office. As he pulls up, Daniel is getting out of the protection team's SUV. John says, "How was school, Son?"

Daniel says, "It was cool, Dad. Where's my mom? She promised to pick me up today," as they walk into the door.

John says, "She's in the house, but I'm going to be honest with you. She's not happy with me, right now."

Daniel asks, "What did you do?"

John says, "Remember, I told you I can be an asshole. I was an asshole to someone else, and to get back at me, she said something to upset your mother."

They go straight to the master bedroom. Daniel knocks on the door. Daniel says, "Hey, Momma! Are you in there? You promised to pick me up. Are you okay?"

KD tries to conceal her emotions. She says, "I'm good, Son, how was school?" John motions his hand to tell Daniel to get KD to open the door.

Daniel says, "It was cool. Momma, are you coming out? I'm hungry."

KD asks, "Is John home?" John signals Daniel to say no.

Daniel can't lie to his mother; he hesitantly says, "He's here!"

KD says, "Tell your father to cook you something to eat."

Daniel says, "Momma, are you mad at me? Why won't you open the door?"

KD says, "Baby, I could never be mad at you. I'm just had a bad day."

Daniel asks, "Momma, what's wrong? What happened?"

KD says, "Ask your father."

Daniel asks, "What did he do, Momma?"

KD answers, "John, talk to your son."

John says, "Ladybug, talk to me. You're not answering my calls or replying to my texts. What's wrong?" She doesn't answer. John says, "KD, open the door and talk to me." John knocks on the door. He says, "Baby! Please! Don't shut me out! Tell me what's wrong. Give me a chance to address your concerns." KD doesn't respond. John says, "Whatever, you're mad at it's only fair you allow me a chance to address and fix it."

KD, not wanting to hear John say anything else, says, "John, get away from the damn door, and go to the fucking kitchen to feed your son."

Daniel rushes away from the door because he knows to get out of the way when adults are mad. Daniel says, "Oh boy! She cursed! She is beyond mad at you. Whatever you did, it must've been extremely bad." John follows Daniel to the kitchen.

John says, "The past came back to bite me in the ass."

Daniel says, "My Granddaddy told me the past is never the past. It's always there waiting to be the present."

John says, "Well, that is true."

John and Daniel sit at the kitchen table. John, looking through takeout menus, asks Daniel what he wants to eat. Daniel says, "Italian," John orders everyone's favorite entree. While they are waiting on the delivery, Kelly runs through the door. Kelly speaks to John and Daniel as she takes off her shoes and jacket.

Kelly asks, "How is she?"

Daniel says, "She won't open the door. She's super mad at John. She cursed at him, twice!"

Kelly says, "Oh, she's big mad. I'll talk to her."

Daniel asks, "What happened?"

John stops Kelly. He says, "Kelly, Daniel, I have not cheated on your mother. I love KD! I wouldn't do anything to hurt her."

Kelly says, "Stepdad, we know! Mom knows, too. She's having a moment."

John says, "As long as you know I have been faithful to KD since the day we met."

Kelly says, "We know, Stepdad! We trust you!"

Kelly goes to the master bedroom and knocks on the door. She says, "Momma, it's Kelly. I'm alone." KD opens the door. Kelly hugs her mother; she asks, "Momma, you know John loves you. He is not thinking about that woman. Why are you letting her bother you?"

KD says, "She knew exactly how to hurt me. I froze. I couldn't say shit. She left the restaurant with this huge smirk on her face."

Kelly says, "Momma, you know she was trying to get back at him by hurting you because she can't have him."

KD says, "What if it's true? What if he gets bored with me? John is super impulsive."

Kelly says, "Momma, he's in the kitchen looking like his whole life is in disarray. Momma, you need to talk to John."

KD says, "Raina is beautiful and twenty years younger. If she couldn't keep his attention, I know I can't!"

Kelly says, "Momma, stop it! You are one of the most beautiful women in the world."

John knocks on the door. He says, "Kelly, will you come out here for a minute?"

Kelly says, "Momma, let me see what John wants."

Kelly leaves the room to talk to John. John whispers, "Please get your mother to let me in."

Kelly says, "You probably should give her a minute."

John whispers, "I need to get in there, now. I'll give you everything in my pocket, right now, if you get me in there." He pulls out his car key and a wallet full of hundreds."

Kelly says, "I can have your car?" He gives her the money and car key. Kelly says, "Wait, right here!" Kelly goes into the room. She comes right back out. Kelly says, "You can go in there."

John and Kelly look at each other as he walks in and she walks out. Kelly shakes her car key and runs to put on her shoes. She grabs her jacket and leaves out the door. Kelly hurries to the car. She takes off to go get her friends. John walks in the room to see KD lying at the foot of the bed, looking up at the ceiling. She won't look at him. Her dangling feet shake as she sniffles and wipes the tears.

John walks over to the bed and sits beside her; he says, "KD, talk to me." KD doesn't say anything. She wipes her tears. John says, "How did we promise to always get through things?"

KD says, "Together!"

John says, "Ladybug, you're shutting me out, and I can't take it. We keep our promises, KD. Get up, stop crying, and talk to me. Tell me why you are upset with me." KD sits up. John wipes her tears; he says, "Ladybug, I don't like seeing you cry. Come here!" KD scoots closer to him. John wraps his arms around her, and she hugs him back.

She asks, "John, are you going to leave me?"

John says, "Never!"

KD asks, "Are you really going to marry me?"

John says, "I will marry you right now."

KD says, "John, why did you adopt my son if you aren't going to marry me?"

John asks, "Why would I adopt your son to play games with you? Why do you doubt me? Where is your faith in us? You know the only reason we aren't married is you said to wait, right?"

KD, gets in his lap, and says, "I know!" John caresses her hair. He kisses her forehead.

John says, "KD, I have never lied to you. I will never lie to you. I love you, and I'm in love with you. We are together for the rest of our lives. If the Lord calls me home first, I'll be on the other side waiting on you. You better not get with another man. You save it for me."

KD laughs and says, "You better do the same."

John says, "I will!"

KD says, "Raina and Cas are a couple. I saw them together today."

John asks, "What did they say that upset you?"

KD says, "I told you, baby, I don't like him. He's not your friend. He has a grudge against us. There's something about his eyes and spirit that's not right."

John says, "Ladybug, you're right. I see it now. Did he say anything to you?"

KD says, "No, he sent the killer mockingbird. She came over to our table like everything was cool. She starts talking about a black car used to follow her, getting emails from our stalker, talking to you to get closure…"

John interrupts. He says, "Ladybug, that's a half-truth. She called from a number I didn't recognize on a line I never gave her the number or permission to call. She asks why her and not me. I told her the truth hoping that would get her to leave me alone. We hung up, I got busy, and forgot all about the call. I wasn't keeping a secret. I never intended to talk to that girl. I won't do that again. I will make sure you know of any contact with any female that's not family. Okay?"

KD says, "Okay, I will do the same!"

John says, "When I come to you to tell you I had contact with a female, you need to trust and believe in me. Just like I need to trust you." KD reaches out her pinky finger. John locks his pinky finger with hers. John kisses KD. He says, "Finish your story!"

KD says, "She said you were the man of her dreams. One day you just stop talking to her, and she was hurt. She found a good man who loves and comforts her. She said [KD mocks Raina's voice.], 'Cas told me John plays with women for a year, and he'll be done with you before the wedding.' Tri and Mena hopped up and checked her; I sat there too embarrassed to speak. What if Cas is right, you get bored, and move on with someone else?"

John says, "That's what you think of me, of us? That hurts my feelings, KD. I've been true to you. I'm committed to you. I have never been faithful or committed to any woman. I haven't even thought about another woman since the day we met. Hearing you say that hurts."

KD says, "John, baby, I don't mean to hurt your feelings, but I have this nagging insecurity that you will leave me. I try to tell myself that I'm just insecure, and I'm letting the baggage of my first marriage haunt our relationship. John, don't ever think I don't believe in you or trust you because I do. I love you so much. My fears are about me. You have done nothing to bring about those fears. Don't be mad, baby!"

John says, "I'm not mad, Ladybug, but I am hurt! I got something for Cas and Raina."

KD says, "Baby, promise you will stay away from them. Don't call them or go play basketball with him. I don't trust Cas."

John says, "I don't either. He was out of line. I don't care about him being with Raina. I knew he liked her, but to send a message to my girl was out of line. While Raina is worried about us, she needs to focus on her relationship with a married man. Cas isn't leaving his wife."

KD says, "Until we find out who's in the black car and what's what, let it slide, Baby, please." KD grabs John's cheeks. He kisses her hands and promises to stay away from Cas.

KD looks down with tears flowing down her face. John says, "Look at me!" KD looks at him, "Don't doubt me or my love for you. Those two bitter people want to hurt you because hurting you hurts me. You're the only way they can get to me. They know that because they know I love you. You're crying and I'm hurt while they are somewhere laughing. This is why I need you to have faith in us, so when people come talking shit, it won't bother you."

KD says, "Honestly, I never felt good enough for you, so when she started talking, all my insecurities came up. Baby, why would you love and choose me out of all the women you've been with? I hate to say it, but I do have fears. I don't mean to, but I do. Raina is young and beautiful. She...."

John cuts KD off, "She is young and beautiful, and I wasn't faithful to Raina. I saw other women while we messed around. She knew that. Honestly, Raina was never a factor. That was sex with a beautiful woman. I want you! I'm committed to you and have been since day one. My desire for you is not affected by your age or some superficial quality some other woman possesses.

"I know you know in your heart, mind, and soul how I feel and that I've been faithful. Ladybug, aging isn't easy for any of us. I look at myself and I can't believe I'm my father's age. I can't change my past, but I promise you that is the past. I'm fully in this relationship with you."

KD says, "Baby, I never want to hurt you. I never want to hear you say I hurt your feelings. I do know you love me and you are faithful. You are always available. You are always honest about your whereabouts. If you're not at work, you're with me or one of our kids. I should feel special that I am the one, and I am disappointed in myself that I feel insecure.

"What bothers me is you're somebody. Everyone knows you everywhere we go. When we walk into a room, every woman in the room looks at you with desire. I can only imagine what they say and do when I'm not around. You have so much access to everything. Baby, I'm no one with nothing."

John says, "You with me makes me feel like the whole world is mine. No money or woman can replace you. You're everything to me."

KD says, "You're everything to me, and no man could ever take your place."

John asks, "You know what women say when you are not around?"

KD says, "No!"

John says, "Me either! I don't give them the opportunity. KD, you are not interpreting the situation correctly. Everywhere we go, men desire you. You don't pay attention, but I see it. Men are constantly letting me know if I fuck up, they will gladly take my position. You don't notice it because you're happy in your relationship. Just like I don't notice females looking at me because I'm happy in my situation. I satisfied. I have everything I want here with you."

KD says, "Aww! Honey, that's so sweet. I have everything I want with you, and I want to be the only woman you want and need. I want that more than anything."

John says, "Ladybug, you are, and that's real." KD looks at and plays with her ring. John says, "Don't ever take that ring off!"

KD says, "I won't! Ever!"

John says, "KD, listen to me. (He stares directly in her eyes.) Every piece of me, every part of my life is yours. All of me is yours. Ladybug, you have nothing to worry about. You can be secure in this. I'm yours. I want to hear you say it."

KD says, "John Michael King is my man."

John says, "That's right, and I'm keeping my promises. Are you keeping yours?"

KD says, "I am!"

John says, "Tell me all of our promises."

KD says, "We promise to work through things together; talk our problems out; listen to each other; care for each other; protect and provide for each other; be faithful to each other; trust each other; be patient with each other, be kind to each other, and be honest with each other."

John says, "Cooperation, communication, consideration, compassion, protection, provision, fidelity, commitment, reliability, patience, kindness, and honesty. I'm adding assurance. You are always safe with me emotionally, physically, and spiritually. I trust you with my secrets. I tell you how I really feel because I know you never judge me. You make me feel secure in our relationship. Ladybug, I need that back."

KD says, "Baby, you do have that. I promise you will feel that from this moment forth. If I have to say it every day, I will."

John says, "See, how we can work through anything."

KD says, "Yes!"

John says, "To answer your question: why would I choose you. I already chose, and I choose you every day because you are the most amazing, caring, intelligent, beautiful, intriguing, attractive, sexy woman I have ever met. You complete me, support me, encourage me, you calm me, you care for me, and you bring me joy. KD, believe it or not, being with me is a part of your destiny. You are stuck with me." She kisses him.

She says, "I don't mind and I will never mind being stuck with you."

John says, "Yes, Raina is beautiful and successful. We were cool, but things were never serious. Let me ask you something."

KD says, "Okay!"

John says, "If I were the same person I am, but I worked in the factory instead of owning it, would you date me?"

KD says, "Yes! I like and love you. Your wealth has never been a factor for me."

John says, "I know you would, and I guarantee Raina wouldn't give a factory worker the time of day. Why would I want to be with a woman who is with me because I have money? You make me laugh, we have the most engaging conversations, you have a caring heart, you cook for me, you take care of me and my lovebugs. I love those things about you.

"Raina would never get on the floor and play with my grandgirls. My daughters would never call her to ask her to babysit. My kids trust you with their children. KD, that means something to me. Baby, I love that you are beautiful and down-to-earth. The superficial women I messed with before you were chasing a bag, and I was chasing sex. You and I have a relationship. You have every quality I want. I'm not leaving you. I'm not playing with you. I want to marry you."

KD asks, "What if I said I don't want to wait another day?"

John says, "We can do whatever you want."

KD says, "I want to marry you now."

John says, "You want to move the wedding up?"

KD says, "No, I want to elope tomorrow. We can still have our wedding in September. Everyone is so excited. We can't cancel."

John says, "Done!"

KD says, "Are you serious?"

John says, "Tomorrow, we will go to Vegas, get married, and come back home before our son gets home from practice tomorrow." KD kisses him.

Daniel knocks on the door. KD says, "Come in!"

Daniel opens the door; he asks, "Momma, are you okay?"

KD says, "I'm fine! Did you eat?"

Daniel says, "Yes, Dad had Italian delivered. I made you both a plate. They are on the table."

KD says, "Thank you, baby! We're coming to eat now. Where's Kelly?"

Daniel says, "She left in Dad's car."

KD asks, "You let her drive your car?"

John says, "It's her car now!"

Daniel says, "You gave her your car?"

John says, "She got me in the door. Son, you failed."

Daniel says, "You mean I lost out on a Lambo?"

John says, "And two thousand dollars."

KD says, "You're going to get your car back, right?"

John says, "I have you! I don't need a car."

KD says, "She's too young to drive that car around Detroit."

John says, "I'll tell her to be safe, but I can't take the car back. That car represents the old John. I need something less flashy and more fitting of a soccer dad."

KD says, "Let's go eat. What am I going to do with you?"

John says, "You're going to love me."

The next day after Daniel leaves for school, John and KD fly to Vegas, get married, and fly back home by the time Daniel comes home from practice. When he asks about their day, they smile and say it was good. He tells them about his day and how Breonna is his new girlfriend. KD asks who is Breonna.

Daniel says, "She's the most beautiful girl in the whole school. She's a good student and a cheerleader. If I could be frank, her body is so curvy and her hair is so shiny and silky. She has these long legs that look so soft in her tiny skirt. She smells like berries. She is so quiet and shy, but she's confident. I just want to hold her hand and play in her hair." KD didn't know her son had such mature feelings.

KD asks what happened to Naomi. John says, "Naomi is old news. You've got to keep up."

Daniel says, "Naomi is my friend. Breonna is my heart."

KD asks, "Son, you were kind to Naomi when the relationship ended?"

Daniel answers, "I'm not a jackass like the other boys. I was honest about my feelings and Naomi suggested we should be friends. She said we were better as friends, anyway. She supports my relationship with Bre, and I support her relationship with the other Daniel. He isn't as smart as me, but he's cool."

KD says, "I'm glad you were honest. Son, for me, always be honest with women."

John says, "Son, I'm happy for you. I am proud of the way you handled the situation."

Daniel asks, "Thanks, Dad! Can I take Breonna on a date? Kelly can drive us in her new car and bring us back home."

KD says, "You have to ask Kelly first. If she says yes, you and your father must go meet her parents. It's the gentlemanly thing to do."

Daniel begs John to help him go on a date with Breonna. John says, "We will work it out, Son, I promise." Daniel excitedly goes to do his homework.

KD says, "My baby is going on a date."

John says, "Don't worry, you'll always be the number one lady in his life. Did you hear the way he described Breonna? He could've been talking about you. He'll make good choices in women because he has an awesome model of what a woman should be and do."

KD is touched by John words; she smiles and asks, "How did you handle your girls dating?"

John says, "Like a maniac! I was all over them until they sat me down and told me I acting like a crazy person. I thought karma was going to kick me in the ass. Honestly, I've been blessed. Langston is a good dude. He's been a good husband and father. He was the first and only guy Kimma brought home, and they stuck it out through high school and college.

"Kenna and Kera dated, but nothing serious. Kenna met Yasir and they got married pretty quickly. He's been cool. She always seems happy, so I can't complain. Kera, unfortunately, inherited my player gene. She breaks hearts. I've had to console a few heartbroken young men over the years. I don't know what to say to her, so I mind my business. How was it when Kelly started dating?"

KD says, "We talked a lot about being safe and responsible. She didn't give me any problems. She always made curfew. She was always open and honest. I didn't even know she had sex two years ago until she told me when we talked about the thing with Todd."

John says, "We are blessed to have some pretty good girls. Don't worry about Daniel, he is a good boy. He will behave. Well, at least, he'll behave until he gets that first taste."

KD says, "You will talk to him about being appropriate and a gentleman?"

John says, "I will talk to him."

KD says, "Thank you for today, baby."

John says, "Thank you for the last year and the years to come."

KD says, "I love you, husband!"

John says, "I love you, wife!" John flashes his wedding ring. KD smiles. She asks if he likes the ring. John answers, "I love it. I was so thankful when you surprised me with it."

KD explains she bought the ring with the prize money she won at the costume party after he proposed. She says, "When I saw it, I knew it would be perfect. I looked through your jewelry box to see what size ring you wear."

John says, "You know me so well!"

KD says, "We have a deep connection. It's like I've known you all my life."

John replies, "I feel the same way! Now, you can't leave me."

KD says, "I am not going anywhere without you."

John kisses KD. He says, "I love being married to you already."

KD says, "I feel the same way."

KD and John are asleep when their phones receive a series of text messages early the next morning. John wakes up and grabs the phones to stop them from vibrating. John opens the video in the most recent text on his phone. He sits up and covers his mouth. He goes to the next video; he is speechless. He can't believe what he is seeing. He scrolls through all the videos seeing himself with different women, and he is appalled.

John opens KD's phone to see videos of him and KD. His heart breaks because he didn't want her involved. As he scrolls through the videos, KD's phone receives one more text message: John, I know you don't want your girl exposed. You have twenty-four hours to decide if it's worth a million dollars to you. Check KD's phone at this time tomorrow.

John shakes KD. He says, "Ladybug, wake up!"

KD wakes up startled; she asks, "What's the matter, baby?"

John says, "Brace yourself! The shit show has started again."

KD says, "What up?"

John asks, "We can talk about anything, right, and you won't shut me out?"

KD says, "Yes!"

John says, "I'm so sorry! I hate that I got you involved in this."

KD says, "You're making me nervous. Tell me!"

John hands KD her phone, "Look at the messages."

KD looks at her phone; she says, "Oh my god! John, I figured it was coming. Notice when the pictures were glued to the wall, I wasn't there."

John takes KD's phone and gives her his phone, he says, "There's more!"

John calls Kimma from KD's phone while KD looks through his phone. Kimma answers, "Good morning, Stepmom, what's going on this morning?"

John says, "It's Dad!"

Kimma says, "What's up, Daddy?"

John says, "I need to take care of home. Someone is playing on our phones."

Kimma says, "Daddy, be careful."

John says, "Kimma, Daughter, my firstborn, I love you."

Kimma says, "I love you, Daddy! Tell my stepmother and little brother that I love them and to be careful."

John says, "I will! Talk to you later, Daughter!"

While John calls his lawyer and accountant on KD's phone, KD continues to watch the videos on John's phone. KD says, "Damn! She had to study gymnastics." She goes to the next video; she says, "I'm going to have to try that." After she watches the next video, she says, "You have never done that with me." John finishes the call with his lawyer.

John says, "Give me that," he snatches the phone from her hand. He says, "I didn't give you the phone for you to do that. There are things I do to you that I didn't do with any of them."

KD says, "Looks like you've had an adventurous sex life."

John says, "KD, this is not the time for that. Stay focused, Ladybug."

KD says, "John, looking at those videos, I need to step my game up."

John says, "You're the best! You satisfy me in ways they could never understand. It's about the feeling, not the action. Not one of them feel like you. Stay focused, Ladybug. Any minute now, the house will be full of people. You need to get dressed, and decide if we're sending Daniel to school."

KD says, "He doesn't need to be here for the commotion."

They quickly get out of bed. John says, "Get Daniel's phone. I'll get us new phones and new numbers." She wakes Daniel to tell him it's an emergency.

Daniel says, "What's going on?"

KD says, "Get ready for school, meet your dad downstairs, he will answer all your questions. And, baby, I need your phone, permanently."

Daniel says, "Momma, why, what did I do?"

KD says, "Dad's going to get you a new one."

Daniel happily jumps out of bed; he says, "Smartphone upgrade! Yes!"

Daniel meets KD and John in the living room. John says, "Son, I know this isn't cool, but someone is playing on our phones this morning, and we want you to be safe. I am going to ask Kelly to get new phones with new numbers by the time you get home from school. [John hands him an old phone.] This is an old phone. Only use it if you have an emergency. If you need anything, call Kelly. She will know how to contact us."

Daniel says, "Okay, Dad!"

John says, "Eat breakfast, have a good day at school, and don't worry about us. Focus on school. Mom and I won't leave the house. We will be right here waiting for you to get home. Do not leave that school without security and come straight home after practice. Son, hug your mother before you leave. Here's some lunch money." Daniel eats his breakfast. He hugs his parents before he leaves.

KD hugs John. He asks, "Do you think it's Raina?"

KD says, "I believed her when she said she only vandalized your car. Maybe she was trying to tell me that she loves you too much to really hurt you." KD asks, "Do you think it's Bradley?"

John says, "I don't see how he would have cameras in my room, but I think it's him."

KD says, "Maybe, Bradley had a woman put the cameras in your bedroom."

John says, "Possibly! Prepare yourself! The police will see the videos."

KD says, "Maybe I'll feel better if I know exactly what they will see."

KD watches the videos of her and John as John talks to his lawyer and accountant. In the last video, KD and John are asleep in the bed. KD thinks it is odd to send that video but she keeps watching. At the end of the video, she sees something strange. She gasps. She pauses the video and says, "John, look at this."

John grabs the phone. She points to the screen. She says, "That night, I thought I saw a reflection of someone, but when I turned to look, I didn't see anything. I felt like someone was in the room with us." John looks at the phone in disbelief. John sees the reflection of the female intruder dressed in all black with a black ski mask covering her face in the mirrored ceiling. KD says, "That's a female. Look at the long blonde hair. Is there anything about her that's familiar?"

John is mortified that someone was in his room; he says, "Not at all!"

KD says, "She sent that last video to let us know she can get close to us."

John asks, "Who the fuck is she? Did you watch all the videos?"

KD says, "Yes, beginning to end, but I didn't see anyone in the other videos."

John asks, "How'd she gets in my house? That's creepy as hell."

John's lawyer says, "Maybe this could help the police figure out who sent the videos."

The accountant asks, "John, are you going to pay the million dollars?"

John says, "I don't want my eleven-year-old son seeing videos of his parents, so yes."

KD says, "No, he is not paying anyone any amount of money. What if you pay, and they still post the videos? How can you trust she will keep her word? Terrorizing and embarrassing us is worth more than money to this person."

John says, "KD, think about Daniel."

KD says, "Well, you better start thinking about what you are going to say to him."

John says, "Are you ready for everyone you know to see those videos?"

KD says, "John, I didn't do anything wrong, so I am not ashamed of my behavior."

John says, "I think you're right, but I don't know if I'm willing to take that chance."

KD says, "We really don't have a choice but to take that chance."

John tells his accountant, "She says no, so the answer is no."

John's lawyer says, "I suggest you deactivate all your social media accounts, now."

John gets his laptop to deactivate his social media pages. Just as he finishes, Detective Vernon and Detective Stratman knock on the door. John lets them in. They discuss the text messages and videos. They take the phones to see if they can trace the origins of texts.

John meets with the head of the protection team to discuss the pending threat. The protection team sweeps the house for bugs and hidden cameras, they check the security of their network, and they scan all the computers and tablets for tracking software. No threats were found. The head of the team assures John that the house is secure.

John turns to KD and says, "Prepare yourself; there's no telling what's next."

KD says, "Together, right, we'll get through anything together."

John kisses her; he says, "There's no other way."

That afternoon, a courier pulls into the driveway. The protection team gets the envelope from the courier. The head of the team opens the envelope. It's a note attached to banking information. The letter says: Send a million dollars by the beginning of the next business day, or your girl will be exposed by the end of the business day. The protection team contacts the detectives to give them the note.

John and KD debate paying the ransom, but again KD insists that paying is not an option. KD says, "No, John, you're not risking that kind of money to protect me. I will be fine. Daniel will survive this. This person will not extort you. You've worked hard for every dollar you have. This person doesn't deserve to prosper from your labor. No, John, you're not paying." John concedes, but fears that the videos will negatively impact Daniel.

John and KD talk about the consequences of not paying the ransom with Daniel before he leaves for school the next day. John says, "Son, I hate to put you in this predicament, but someone has intimate videos of your mother and me. We don't know who, why, or how. They plan to release them publicly. Son, I am so sorry all of this is happening."

KD says, "Son, you have to be strong because we have no control over this person."

Daniel is sad, but he says, "Okay," as if it's no big deal as he gets up to leave.

John says, "Son, that's all you have to say?"

Daniel says, "What can I say?"

John says, "Are you mad?"

Daniel says, "A nameless, faceless someone is exploiting my parents, my mother, yes, that is disturbing. It's infuriating, but let them post the videos. I know a boy at school that can hack anything. If those videos get posted, Viper can trace them, hack into their network, and steal all their data, then we can expose them."

John asks, "Son, can you discretely contact Viper? Let him know we may need him, and we'll pay whatever, but it must be top secret."

Daniel says, "Dad, I got this handled, nothing will come back to you and mom. If the videos get posted all I have to do is send the link to Viper. He doesn't talk business at school. Everything is done electronically and anonymously."

KD says, "Son, do not get in trouble."

Daniel says, "Momma, sometimes, I can take care of you. Viper is not a snitch. He's very professional."

John says, "Son, thank you!"

Daniel says, "We're family! We have each other's back." John and KD hug Daniel and tell him they love him before he leaves for school.

John turns to KD and says, "It's a waiting game, now!"

KD says, "It's a little empowering to think we may have a counterattack."

John says, "Thank God we have a smart son!" John gets a call from the detectives. When John answers, Detective Stratman explains they he found out that the banking information is fake. Detective Vernon chimes in to tell John the text messages came from a burner phone with no GPS that was immediately deactivated after the messages were sent.

Two days go by without a word from the stalker, so John goes back to work. He works so late that he is alone in the building with security and the environmental services crew. KD is home with Kelly and Daniel watching movies. The night protection team takes over and surrounds the house. John calls to check in with KD.

KD asks, "How is your night going?"

John says, "Busy preparing for a few important upcoming meetings. I missed being home with you."

KD says, "I missed you, too!"

John asks, "How was your day?"

KD says, "Besides missing you, it was cool. I'm watching a movie with my beautiful children."

John says, "I have a little more to do then I coming home to you."

KD says, "I'll run you a bath and message your back when you get home."

John replies, "You're so romantic! I can't wait."

KD whispers, "Husband, I love you!"

John says, "I like the way you say that. Can you say it again?"

KD says, "Husband, I love you. When you get home, I'll show you just how much."

John says, "Wife, I look forward to that."

KD says, "I love you, baby!"

John says, "I love you more!"

KD says, "Be careful, be watchful, be safe!"

John says, "I will!"

KD says, "See you soon!"

John says, "See you, Ladybug!"

When John hangs up the phone, he goes back to typing. It's dark and quiet around the building. Security surveys the premises with high-tech cameras when they notice movement on the perimeter. Two dark figures are approaching the security fence in the back of the building.

Security calls John's office phone to let him know what is going on and where. John tells the officer to have armed guards quietly approach with the lights off. John grabs his gun and cell phone. John calls the protection team to ask them to discreetly check on his family. The protection team checks the perimeter of the property to find no movement. The protection team thoroughly check the house, but there's no sign of danger.

John quickly but quietly makes his way to the location of the intruders. The security guards, Daryl and Taylor, pull up in the dark vehicle with the lights off next to John. John tells the guard to go around to the left and he'll go to the right. John reiterates be quiet, no lights, and guns up.

John quietly approaches with his gun up as two masked men squeeze through the hole they cut in the fence. John says, "On your knees!" Daryl, Taylor, and John have the two men surrounded. The two men slowly get on their knees. John says, "Masks off!" They slowly pull their masks off. Taylor shines a light on their faces.

John says, "Cas, you dirty motherfucker!" John walks up to Castle. John points the gun to his forehead. John asks, "Did you put your hands on my woman?" Daryl points his gun directly at the other intruder to prevent him from interfering with John's interrogation of Castle.

Castle says, "I never touched her."

John hits him with the gun; he says, "You're supposed to be my boy. We grew up together. You crossed me like this! You endangered my family. What the fuck is wrong with you, Cas?"

Castle says, "For once in your life, you weren't on top, and I enjoyed knocking you off the throne." John punches him in the faces. When Castle falls to the ground laughing, John repeatedly kicks him in the face until the laughter turns to groans of pain.

John tells Castle to get up. Castle spits blood on the ground. John says, "Take your shirt off! You too!" The intruders comply. John doesn't see any wounds on either of the intruders. John says, "Lift up your arms!" John looks for newly healed injuries, but doesn't see any scars. John asks Castle, "Did you have anything to do with what happened to KD at the hospital?"

Castle says, "I don't know anything about that."

John says, "I can't believe you turned on me. You're dating my ex. How does your wife feel about that? That's violates the brotherhood, but hey I am happy for you. You and I both know Raina would rather be with me. You're the rebound guy because she can't have who she really wants, but hey, you have to get what you can get however you can get it. Next time, you kiss your new girl, think about how my dick used to be all down her throat."

John beats and kicks Castle until he is covered with blood, leaving him unconscious. John says, "And, I enjoyed knocking your ass out." John turns his attention to the second intruder. He says, "I paid your ass a lot of money to leave us alone. What the fuck do you want?"

The second intruder says, "I want my wife back!"

John says, "KD is my wife. She doesn't want you. Nobody wants you, Bradley Dumbass Jacobs. You know what's funny. Heather wanted me. Camille wanted me. Truth, is you hate me because every woman in your life wanted me. KD will never leave me especially for you, but you already knew that. Why the fuck are you here, Bradley, you fucking loser, Jacobs?"

Bradley says, "I came to kill you. I came to kill the King, so I can get my wife and son back!"

John asks, "You mean my son. That's my son. He has my last name."

Bradley says, "He has my blood!"

John says, "That young man has nothing of you. You're a piece of shit. Did you have anything to do with what happen to KD at the hospital?"

Bradley says, "That wasn't us. The fire, the dogs, KD's crash, and your accident was us."

John says, "Was it you I shot in October?"

Bradley says, "That wasn't me!"

John says, "Why didn't you show up to get Daniel the last two weekends in October?"

Bradley says, "Camille had a baby. There were complications."

John says, "Congratulations! Wait, it's yours, right? You know how Camille gets it in. Has she gotten any better with her head game? She wasn't that great back in the day."

Bradley says, "Yes, it's mine! Another boy!"

John says, "Bradley, I don't really give a shit about you, for real. Back to my questions. Was that you standing in my living room?"

Bradley says, "That wasn't me."

John asks, "So you have never been in my home?"

Bradley says, "Only to set the fire."

John asks, "Did you send those videos?"

Bradley says, "What videos?"

John says, "You know, the videos of me and Heather, me and Tori, me and Nia, me and Roxa, me and Tanil." Bradley looks at John with eyes as sharp as a samurai sword when he hears Tanil. John says, "That's right, I fucked Tanil. We all know how much you wanted Tanil. I remember how you used to chase Tanil and how she shot you down every time.

"After the Heather and Camille thing, you were busy running your mouth about me, but I was too busy running through Tanil and two hundred fifty other women to care. Tanil, oh my god, sweet girl! Nasty as fuck, though. Quiet, good girls are so freaky when you get them alone.

"I see why you had a thing for Tanil. She resembles KD in a lot of ways. Sweet, kind, and that body! Tanil was unbelievable. Are you sure you never seen the videos?"

Bradley says with an attitude, "I have never seen the videos."

John asks, "Did you shot at us at the restaurant?"

Bradley says, "No!"

John asks, "Was that you dressed like me at the costume party?"

Bradley says, "Yes! I touched and kissed all over your girl, John King. It was just like old times when I used to fuck her brains out. I used to fuck her face and that fat ass. I could tell she missed me, too! You should've seen the smile on her face when I touched it." John kicks him in the throat. John keeps kicking him as he lectures him.

John says, "Keep your motherfucking hands off my wife. If you ever touch her again, I will kill you. I don't give a fuck. Don't ever disrespect my wife again! You keep testing me, you fucking rapist, woman beater. The sex doesn't count if you have to take it, punk motherfucker.

"The only reason I haven't pull this trigger is because I love my stepdaughter. Killing you would hurt Kelly, but if you fuck with my wife, I mean if you look at her the wrong way, I will air your bitch ass out. You punk bitch, rapist, woman beater piece of shit."

John stomps Bradley in the head until he passes out. Taylor asks, "You know these people?"

John says, "This snake ass piece of shit was my homeboy since middle school. And, this dumb, goofy motherfucker is my wife's ex. Thank God the kids look like her." John kicks Castle and Bradley as he answers Taylor.

Daryl says, "It's always your homeboy out to get you."

Taylor says, "It's always the ex!"

Daryl says, "That is true!"

Daryl and Taylor handcuff Bradley and Castle as John calls the police. When the police arrive, they find a bomb in the bag on Castle's back. Bradley Jacobs and Wesley Castle are immediately arrested. John, Daryl, and Taylor go to the precinct to give statements.

By the time John makes it home, everyone is asleep. John has never been this late. It's been hours since he last talked to KD. He has several missed calls and unread text messages from KD. John anticipates KD's anger. John carefully makes his way into the bedroom. He connects his cell phone to the charger before undressing.

As he showers and brushes his teeth, he thinks about the conversation with Bradley. He hears the remarks Bradley made about KD over and over in his head. He contemplates if Bradley is trustworthy. If Bradley was being honest, someone else is out to get him. John is frustrated trying to figure out who drives the mysterious black Benz.

John gently lays on the bed. John's movement wakes KD. KD doesn't open her eyes or lift her head from the pillow. She says, "Husband, you're so late? I called you more than ten times. I was so worried about you." KD reaches back for his hand. John doesn't want to tell her what happened, so he quickly deflects from the truth.

John takes her hand and scoot closer to her as he explains, "You're right, Ladybug, I was inconsiderate. I should have called you every hour. I apologize, that will never happen again." John wraps his arm around her.

KD says, "It's okay. I'm happy you're here and healthy."

John touches her hair and kisses her. He thinks about the conversation with Bradley. John looks at her. John asks, "Do you love me?"

KD opens her eyes. She answers, "Of course, I do! Don't ever question or doubt that. Is everything okay?"

John says, "Ladybug, I need your affection and attention. I need to feel your love."

KD turns to look at him; she says, "John King, my husband, the love of my life. I love you with everything in me."

John says, "Kiss me and hug me like you mean that." KD hugs and kisses him. They stare at each other.

She asks, "Baby, are you sure everything's okay?"

John answers, "With you in my arms, everything is perfect." Her lips make their way to his. They kiss! John says, "I missed you all day, Ladybug!"

KD says, "I missed you, too!"

John says, "I love you so much, KD!"

KD says, "I love you so much!"

John asks, "Can another man take you from me?"

KD says, "Never!"

John asks, "Do you ever think about another man?

KD answers, "No! Baby, what's up? What's wrong?"

John replies with a question, "Do you think any other man could love you better than me?"

KD answers, "No! Baby, I want John Michael King only!"

John asks, "Are you completely satisfied with me?"

KD asks, "Okay! Something is bothering you. Baby, what's wrong?"

John answers, "Please tell me you love me, you'll never leave me, or let another man love you. Ladybug, please just say it and mean it. I need to hear you say it."

KD sincerely says, "I love you. I will never leave you. I will never let another man touch me."

John says, "Show me right now how much you love me and I will do the same. I need you, Ladybug!" KD starts undressing. John kisses her abdomen as he watches her undress.

KD says, "You know I'll always do whatever you want me to do."

John says, "Kiss me, Ladybug!"

KD kisses on his neck. She whispers in his ear, "I'll do anything for you! Anything you want I'll do; all you have to do is just say what you want." She kisses down to his chest and past his abs. She looks at him as she goes lower to kiss him.

John says, "I had a long, stressful day, Ladybug, I need you. I need to feel you, all of you. I need to feel your love." KD can tell something is bothering him, but she understands things have been stressful. KD wants to comfort him so she complies with his requests.

Why John let Bradley get to him is something he can't understand. He knows his home is secure, but Bradley hit a nerve. John knows KD would never go back to Bradley, but he wants KD to convince him he is right. John reaches for her and pulls her up to his face. John says, "I want you so badly, Ladybug!" They kiss. John lays her down to kiss and touch all over her body.

John whispers, "I need you to put your all into loving me. I will do the same." KD submits to his will. John has KD profess her love and commitment to him all through the night. John affirms his love to her over and over again. The passion created by John's jealousy and KD's submission manifests the most intense lovemaking either of them have ever experienced.

While John is at work the next day, KD gets a call from Terrence, a lifelong friend, asking her to have lunch with him. KD is excited to hear from him because they hadn't talk in a long time. KD texts John to tell him she's having lunch with a friend. John replies: Okay, Ladybug, have fun! Be careful! John assumes she's hanging with Tri or Mena.

After a few hours, John calls the protection team to check on her. They tell him she's eating at a restaurant with a guy. John gets confused and concerned. John borrows Jayme's car to rush over to the restaurant. He pulls up to see, KD and Terrence walking arm in arm into the parking lot. They stop and stand next to Terrance's car. Terrance says, "I can walk you to your car."

KD says, "That's okay; my car isn't far!" Terrence hugs and kisses KD on her cheek.

When John sees the kiss, John hops out of the car and rushes toward them. Terrance says, "It was so good to see you!"

KD says, "Don't let this much time pass again."

Terrance asserts, "Let me walk you to your car."

KD says, "I'll be fine. I promise." She knows security is watching her.

Terrence says, "You have to introduce me to your man before I leave," as he gets into his car.

KD waves and says, "Okay!"

Terrence says, "I hear he is fine!"

KD says, "He is so fine!"

Terrence says, "God blessed you girl!"

KD smiles and says, "I'm so blessed."

Terrence says, "I'll call you!"

KD says, "OK, Terry, drive safely!" KD walks to her car. Out of nowhere, a force snatches her from behind and scares her. She says, "John, you scared me!" She recognizes his cologne.

John holds her close to him; he says, "I can smell him all over you." The scent of another man makes John angry, so he squeezes tighter. KD tries to pull away from him. John being forceful makes her uncomfortable. John whispers, "Are you keeping your promises?"

KD asks, "Are you?" John immediately feels guilty, calms down, and lets her go.

John says, "Look at me, KD, I saw him kiss you, and I got jealous. I apologize. Let's just go home!" He tries to touch KD, but she jumps away.

She says, "You promised you would never touch me in anger."

John tries to hug her; he says, "Ladybug, I'm sorry!" KD pushes John away from her.

She says, "You think I would do something that foul knowing I'm being watched? John, would I do something that dumb and risk losing you? Terrence is my mother's best friend's son. He's visiting from out of town. We've been friends since we were newborns. He's like my brother. He has kissed me since we were one, and he's been gay since we were three. I wouldn't do that to you, John. I would never betray you. You are my husband. That wasn't an intimate kiss. That was family affection. We had lunch and talked about you the entire time."

John is apologetic and remorseful; he says, "KD, I lost my head! I trust you! I know you wouldn't play me. I was stupid, KD. Let's go home to our son." John tries to hug her.

KD pushes him away; she says, "You go home to your son!" KD gets in her car and pulls off. The protection team pulls up next to John.

John says, "Nothing happens to her. Follow her. Let me know where she goes." The protection SUV pulls off quickly to catch up to her. The second protection team vehicle is securing the house where Kelly is home with Daniel.

KD goes to her mother's house. KD texts Kelly to tell her she is staying at Grandma's house. Kelly asks if she's okay. KD replies she and John had an argument and she just needs a minute away from him. KD cries in the bathroom. Mrs. Daniels hears her crying, but she knows KD won't talk about it. KD gets in the bed with her mother.

Mrs. Daniels asks, "Do you want to talk about it?" KD nods no. KD falls asleep curled in ball. She dreams about John all night.

At five o'clock in the morning, she dreams about being in the parking lot with John, but instead of arguing, they are kissing. Instead of feeling anger, they feel love. John kisses her with so much heat and passion that she jumps out of her sleep, waking her mother.

Mrs. Daniels asks, "What is it, baby?" KD cries. Mrs. Daniels asks, "Did he hit you?" KD shakes her head no. Mrs. Daniels asks, "Did he cheat on you?" KD shakes her head no. Mrs. Daniels asks, "Do you love him, baby, with all your heart?" KD nods, yes. Mrs. Daniels asks, "Do you want to be with him?" KD nods yes as she continues to cry. Mrs. Daniels says, "Baby, go home to your man. You tossed and turned all night. I couldn't sleep a wink."

KD hops up, put on her clothes, and brushes her teeth as she listens to the voicemail John left her as he stood in the parking lot watching her drive away. KD rushes to her car, calling John, but he doesn't answer. KD, followed by the protection SUV, rushes home to be with John, but Daniel and Kelly are home alone. KD asks Daniel, "Your Dad didn't come home last night?"

Daniel says, "No! I haven't seen him. I thought he was with you."

KD asks, "Did he call?"

Daniel says, "No!" Kelly says she hasn't seen or talked to him either.

As KD gives Daniel money, she notices his shoes, his slacks, and the scarf hanging around his neck. She smiles at him.

Daniel looks at her, he asks "What?"

KD says, "You look so much like John!"

Daniel asks, "Do you like my new clothes? Dad picked them out!"

KD says, "You're very handsome!"

Daniel asks, "Kelly is taking Bre and me to eat after school. Do you think she will like my clothes?"

KD hugs Daniel. She says, "She won't be able to take her eyes off you! Have a good day at school and enjoy your date!"

Daniel says, "Thanks, Momma!"

KD tells one protection team vehicle to get Daniel to school and the other car to search for John. KD tells the protection team she'll wait at home while they look for him. KD showers and hurriedly puts on clothes. KD calls all of John's kids. No one has talked to him, so KD calls Jayme. Jayme tells her John left in her car and the app on her phone says the car is still parked by the restaurant. KD is too panicked to wait on the protection, so she dashes out of the house to go check the restaurant's parking lot.

She walks around the parking lot, calling his phone. She hears his phone vibrating in the bushes along the fence. She puts her phone in the hidden pocket in the waistband of her yoga pants and bends down to pick up his phone. As she continues to search the lot, she finds his keys and wallet. She puts them in her jacket pocket. She runs toward her car as she dials 9-1-1.

Before she gets to her car, a gun is pointed in her face. A car pulls up next to her. A masked man takes the phone out of her hands as the operator answers the phone. The masked man points to the open trunk. KD gets in the trunk. The man says, "If you make a sound, if you move, if you breathe too hard, I will kill you. Don't be slick or cute! There'll be a gun pointed at you." The man points at the center of the back seat. The rear center console is down. She can see there's a gun pointed at her. The man closes the trunk.

As the car pulls out of the parking lot, she quietly gets her phone. She tries not to move too much as she shields the phone from the person sitting in the back seat. She puts the phone on silent and turns off vibration. She texts Tri: Are we still meeting for seafood this afternoon? She prays Tri understands the text as she checks to make sure her location is still being shared with Tri. Once she sees her location is being shared with Tri, she quietly puts the phone back into the secret pocket of her pants. The car stops. The trunk opens. A man pulls her out of the trunk.

They take her through the doors of an abandoned warehouse. The men lead her to a locked room. When they open the door, she sees John who has a small bump on his head and a little bruise on his cheek. John looks up and is so relieved to see KD. He thanks God she's okay, but at the same time he feels he failed to protect her. They rush to each other and embrace. KD says, "John, baby, look at your face!"

John says, "It's okay, Ladybug! Did they hurt you?"

KD says, "No! John, I'm so sorry about last night! I should've gone home with you."

John says, "No! Ladybug, it's on me! I know your heart. I shouldn't have jumped to conclusions. I shouldn't have scared you. I handled the situation terribly. Ladybug, I would never hurt you."

KD says, "It's okay! I should have told you I was meeting Terrence. He has been in my life all my life. I consider him family. Baby, I forgot we hadn't had that conversation."

John says, "I was supposed to give you the benefit of the doubt. I saw him touching you, and I lost my fucking mind. I'm going to work on controlling my temper."

KD says, "I thought about how you must have felt. If I saw you with a woman, I would've been hurt. I have to give the respect I want. I don't blame you for getting angry. I will never do that to you. You never have to worry about or question if I desire another man. I don't want any other man. You have to know that."

John says, "Ladybug, you see what happens when we don't work through things together. Ladybug, we were vulnerable because we were not together. I swear to you, we will never work against each other again. We keep our promises, Ladybug."

KD says, "You're right! I can't keep letting things come between us. It took this to happen, but, baby, I get it now. John, I swear to you, I will keep my promises to you." John kisses her and holds her. KD says, "Baby, your face!" She kisses his bruised cheek.

John says, "I'm good!" KD rubs his wounds with her thumb. John asks, "Did you see any of their faces, where we are, anything?"

KD says, "A silver car, a big black gun, three Black men but their faces were covered, some hallways, we are in an abandoned plant or warehouse, but nothing looked familiar."

John says, "I was on the phone, leaving you a voicemail as I walked out the parking lot. Someone tased me, then hit me with something hard. I woke up in this room."

KD hugs him and whispers, "Thank God, we are together. When I couldn't find you this morning, my whole world was in complete chaos."

John says, "Did you talk to my baby boy?"

KD says, "I sent him to school."

John says, "What the fuck are we about to do?"

KD says, "Pray!" KD secretly prays Tri will understand the message.

John says, "If this is it for me, KD, know that I love you, and you and my baby boy will be taken care of well."

KD says, "Don't talk like that. How do we get through things?"

John says, "Together!"

KD says, "I need you, not stuff or currency!"

John says, "I need you, too!"

KD sits between John's legs leaning against his chest and wrapped in his arm. Suddenly, the door opens, they grab each other tighter. Two men walk into the room. One man puts food next to them, and the other man grabs KD's leg. KD screams, "John!"

John holds her with all his might. John shouts, "Let her go."

KD holds on to John as she kicks the attacker and screams, "John, don't let me go!" The man laughs as he pulls KD's leg. John tells her he has her. In the tussle, KD sees a healed cut with impressions of stitches on the masked man's wrist. KD panics and looks into his eyes. She recognizes his eyes. She screams, "John, baby, please, don't let me go!" She kicks and hit the man with all her might.

John says, "This is my wife, man, come on, let her go."

The man asks, "What are you going to do if I don't?"

John says, "I will kill you!"

The man says, "But I'm the one with the gun."

The other man says, "Man, let's go and stay focused!" The man lets KD go. He laughs and touches KD on her butt as she crawls closer to John.

The other man says, "Stop messing with her. We have things to do." John hops up. KD rushes behind John. John punches the man in the face, so hard that he stumbles back.

The other man grabs John to give the man a chance to catch his footing. John starts punching the man holding him. KD punches and kicks the man who grabbed her as she tries to stop the fight. She yells, "That's enough," as she works her way between the men and John. She pushes them away from John. The men leave and lock the door. KD checks to see if John is hurt.

John says, "I'm okay! Are you good?" John wraps his arms around KD and kisses her forehead.

KD says, "He was one of the men who grabbed me at the hospital. I saw the cut on his wrist."

John doesn't get a chance to respond. A woman walks into the room before he could speak. KD and John stare at her. KD recognizes the hair from the video. The lady says, "Aren't the displays of affection cute! You two are adorable."

KD says, "We must be, the way you're stalking us."

The woman says, "Bitch, don't be too cute."

John says, "Who are you, and what do you want?"

The woman answers, "You don't remember me, John?"

She takes off her mask; she says, "John, you really don't remember me?"

John says, "No, I do not remember you."

KD says, "You did all this for a man that doesn't even remember you? That's insanity!"

She says, "I did all this to make John see me, so he can apologize for how he hurt me."

John says, "Whatever I did to you, I am sorry."

The woman asks, "Is that an apology, Playboy King? Sounds like a weak ass apology. You could at least say it like you mean it." She pulls out a gun and walks over to KD and John. KD moves in front of John.

John says, "What's your name?"

The lady says, "Carmen! John, do you remember me, now?"

John asks, "Carmen, when and where did we meet?"

Carmen says, "John, we were neighbors for years. All the nights, I watched you bring female after female home wondering what I did or didn't do. You forgot all about me, huh, John?"

KD says, "You've been this mad for this long over a man that doesn't even remember you?" Carmen smacks KD. KD says, "I'm going to let you have that one because you have the gun, but bitch, don't put your hands in my face ever again."

John moves KD behind him, completely shielding her from Carmen. John says, "Woah! You're mad at me, so focus on me."

Carmen says, "John, teach your bitch not to talk when no one is speaking to her."

KD disrespectfully points her finger in Carmen's face and says, "You teach me, bitch!"

Carmen says, "Oh, bitch! You like to talk shit."

KD says, "Put that gun down, and we can more than talk. I'm sick of you, bitch!" KD reach over John to hit Carmen, but John uses his elbow to stop the punch and backs away from Carmen who is increasingly getting upset. Carmen has the gun pointed at John's chest.

Carmen says, "John, get your bitch before she gets fucked up!"

KD says, "You get me, bitch!" John tries to keep both ladies calm fearing Carmen might pull the trigger.

Carmen says, "John, you need to train your chick." Carmen tries to hit KD by swinging over John, but John moves KD out of the way. KD swings again, but John blocks the punch.

KD says, "You hate me because I have what you want. You vested a whole year of your life into two people who don't give a fuck about you. Only a desperate, lonely bitch would be that damn psycho. You're a sad bitch!"

John says, "Ladybug, please relax!"

Carmen says, "Yes, Ladybug, you need to listen to your man and relax."

KD says, "Carmen, you need to get a man to listen to, and leave mine the fuck alone. You crazy bitch." Carmen tries to get around John. John moves KD out of Carmen's reach. He knows that last comment had to hurt. Carmen is visibly pissed.

Carmen steps back and cocks the gun; she says, "John, if you love your bitch, you better shut her up. Before I pop both of you motherfuckers."

John says, "Ladybug, please calm down!"

Carmen says, "John, you have until midnight to remember me and apologize for exactly what you did, or you won't like what I do to your bitch!"

When Carmen leaves, John turns to KD. John says, "I know this shit is crazy and you have to be stressed the fuck out, but, Ladybug, you have to survive."

KD says, "I'm tired of that bitch and Raina coming at me about my man. Crazy bitch has us locked in here like some damn movie. Black people don't even do shit like this."

John hugs her; he says, "I'm tired of the shit, too, but I need you to stay calm." John looks around the room. John sees a vent. John puts his finger over his lips. KD looks at him. He points to the vent. KD nods.

They walk over to the vent. John points to KD, then to the vent. KD grabs John's shoulders. He lifts KD. She lifts the vent cover. She crawls into the vent. John climbs up the wall and into the vent. KD crawls through the vent and John follows her to an empty room.

John quietly listens for footsteps. When he is sure no one is in the room, he opens the vent and jumps down. KD jumps into his arms. They quietly tiptoe toward the door. John peeks out the door. When he sees no one is in the hall, John pulls KD's hand and they take off running. They make it down the hall. Just as they turn the corner, Carmen sticks a gun in John's face.

Carmen says, "Nice try, John!" John throws his hands up and backs away, keeping KD blocked from Carmen. Carmen leads them back to the room. John sits in the corner on the blanket. KD leans against the wall visibly frustrated. Carmen says, "It's a camera watching you, so don't be smart." Carmen looks at KD. Carmen points the gun at KD; she says, "Sit your ass in the corner with your little boyfriend."

KD says, "Fuck you!" KD sits between John's legs. She leans her head on his chest.

Carmen says, "Good girl!" Carmen closes and locks the door. She yells, "John, get to thinking and maybe I'll let you and your little girlfriend go."

KD yells, "Wife!"

Carmen yells as she walks away, "Shut the fuck up!"

Tri checks her cell phone and sees KD's text and location. Tri calls Mena. When Mena answers, Tri says, "Hey, Mena! Something is up with KD. Give me ten minutes to leave, and meet me at the fifth precinct."

Tri and Mena explain to Detective Vernon and Detective Stratman that they know KD is in trouble because Tri is allergic to seafood. Tri says, "She came to me concerned about her safety. We talked about code words. She's trying to tell us that she is in danger." Tri shows the detectives KD's location. Tri says, "I googled the address. That's the old, abandoned warehouse that's about to be renovated. It was just on the news. Something's not right."

Mena says, "Why would KD be in an abandoned warehouse for several hours?" Detective Stratman says, "She's an adult. It's not illegal for her to be there."

Mena says, "But she has no reason to be there. It makes no sense."

Detective Vernon says, "We will look into it." Tri and Mena leave the precinct unconvinced that the police will help.

Mena says, "We've got to go check it out ourselves."

Tri says, "I told KD, if anything went down, we'd come to get her."

Mena says, "Then, that's what we'll do!"

Tri says, "I need to get some intel on the building."

Mena says, "We need to get equipped, so we can go in blazing."

Tri says, "I'll meet you at your house in a half-hour."

Mena says, "Okay."

As Tri and Mena drive to the warehouse with a printout of the layout of the building, KD convinces one of the men to let her use his phone to call her mother to pick up her son from school. KD asks her mother to pick up Daniel Jacobs from schools. Her mother knows something isn't right because Daniel's last name is now King, and the protection team takes Daniel to and from school. Mrs. Daniels asks, "Are you okay?"

KD says, "No, Momma, I'm still at work." That was confirmation to Mrs. Daniels that something is wrong because KD officially quit working when John had the accident. KD says, "Momma, John and I love you and DJ so much."

Mrs. Daniel says, "We love you and John, too!" Tears roll down KD's face. Mrs. Daniels knows KD is sending her a distress message.

KD says, "Bye, Momma!"

KD told Mrs. Daniels to call Detective Vernon or Detective Stratman if anything strange ever happened. When Mrs. Daniels calls Detective Vernon's cell to say something is wrong with John and KD, and give him the strange number KD called her from, the detectives decide they better check out the warehouse.

Mena parks the car near the warehouse, so they can plan their entrance. Mena says, "Tri, are you ready for what we may have to do?"

Tri says, "Let's go get our girl!"

Mena says, "It's best that we go through that door. The angle of the building will hide us." Mena and Tri check their weapons before they get out of the car. They quietly sneak into the building. Tri follows Mena as they carefully move through the halls checking every room.

Mena hears someone coming their way. She motions for Tri to follow her into an unoccupied, dark room. Tri slides to the left of the door. Mena goes to the right of the door. They prepare themselves for the possibility of what could happen if anyone walks through the door. Tri sees a metal pipe lying on the floor. She slowly bends down and quietly picks it up. Tri prepares herself to swing the pipe as hard as she can.

Mena and Tri hear footsteps and feel dangerous energy quickly approaching. Tri's heart is beating fast as adrenaline floods her body. Mena, the well-trained soldier, is calmly preparing her mind and body to attack. The voices of two men resound throughout the hallway. Mena and Tri know the men are coming into the room.

Tri braces herself for the moment someone comes through the door. She is nervous, but intent on doing whatever she has to do to rescue her friend. Mena's military mind is ready to attack whoever steps through the door. Tri adjusts her grip on the pipe.

A male voice says, "Yes, they are in here."

The second voice says, "Grab a box." One of the men takes a step into the room. Tri swings the pipe so hard and so fast that the man doesn't see it coming straight at his face. He falls to the ground knocked out cold.

The thud of his body falling alarms the second man. Tri takes the gun from his waistband. The second man pulls out his gun and cautiously enters the room. Mena kicks the gun out of his hand as he enters the door. Tri rushes to pick up the gun. Mena kicks the man again. The man grabs Mena. They tussle in the doorway. Tri points the gun at the man, but she doesn't think she can get a clear shot without also hitting Mena.

Mena punches the man. He slams her against the door. Tri puts the gun in her waistband to secure the pipe in both hands. She swings, hitting him behind his knees, making him fall to his knees. Tri quickly hits him in the back of his head, pushing it forward just before Mena kicks him in the face. As his head bounces back, Tri hits him with the pipe again.

Tri beats both men in their heads until blood spatters covers the floor. Both men are knocked out cold. Mena says, "They're out! Let's go!" The victory gives Tri energy. The excitement of facing danger was exhilarating, so now she is hyped for another fight.

Tri and Mena continue guardedly walking down the hall. A man comes from behind and grabs Mena. She immediately kicks him in the groin as hard as she can, making him slowly fall to his knees. Mena turns and kicks him repeatedly in the face, breaking his nose. He passes out. Mena jumps up and comes down with her knee on his head.

Tri says, "Damn, soldier, the army trained you well."

Mena says, "It's Sergeant Major," as she bends down to take his gun. Tri bashes him in the head with the pipe a couple times just for batting practice. Mena hears KD and John talking. Mena tries to open it, but the door is locked. Tri goes back to the last man they left unconscious. She searches his pockets for a key.

When she finds the key, she rushes back to the door. Mena stands guard, while Tri unlocks the door. When Tri opens the door, she and KD instantly meet eyes. KD is so relieved.

Tri says, "I told you we would come to get you!"

KD says, "Thank God you understood my message! Tri! Mena! Thank you so much!" John also thanks Tri and Mena as he and KD run out of the door. KD hugs Tri and Mena.

Tri says, "Let's get out of here!"

Mena says, "Let's go back the way we came." John asks if they have another gun. Tri gives him the guns she took from the men they left unconscious in the room. John puts one gun in the back of his waistband and cocks the other gun as he walks behind KD; Mena and Tri lead the way. When they turn the corner, bullets fly from three guns. Mena and John shoot back. Tri immediately grabs KD and pulls her in the opposite direction.

John tells Mena, "Get KD out of here! I'll take care of them." KD doesn't want to leave John. She reluctantly runs with Tri. John yells, "Go with your friends, Ladybug! I'll be right behind you." KD calls his name. John says, "Go!"

Mena hands him the gun she took from the man they left unconscious in the hallway; she says, "Kill them all!"

John takes the gun and secures it in his waistband; he says, "That's the plan!"

Mena runs behind Tri and KD. Tri pulls KD as fast as she can down a flight of stairs then down a dark empty hallway. Tri, KD, and Mena run until Tri sees a familiar door. Now that she knows where she is going, she runs even faster.

John readies himself to face the three shooters. Shielding himself behind the wall, John aims at the first man, shooting him between the eyes.

John aims at the next man, then shoots him in the head. The third man is the one who touched KD. John says, "See, how God balances things. I have a gun, now, and I'm probably a better shot than you."

The man says, "Come on, old man, let's see." The man sticks his face out just enough for John to get a shot.

John says, "You should've learned to respect your elders." The man is dead before his body hits the floor. John walks down the hall. He shoots the three men Tri and Mena left knocked out in their heads several times. John makes sure the six men are dead before he cautiously continues down the hallway searching for foes.

Tri, Mena, and KD are just a few feet away from the door they came in when Carmen comes out of the shadows holding a gun; she says, "KD, you wouldn't want to leave before the party is over." Carmen has her gun pointed at KD. Mena and Tri point their guns at Carmen.

KD says, "Bitch, I'm so sick of you!"

Carmen, with a condescending tone, says, "Why? We were having so much fun."

KD says, "There's nothing fun about being here with your obsessed ass."

Carmen says, "KD, you seem ungrateful of the party I planned for you."

KD says, "You planned this shit for you."

Carmen says, "I think you're right!"

Tri says, "Be a real bitch! Put the gun down and fight!"

Carmen says, "I see you brought your friends to the party. I hadn't expected more guests."

Tri says, "If her girls aren't invited, it's not really a party."

Mena says, "Look, I don't know what the fuck is going on and I don't give a shit. We are walking out that door. Whether we have to shoot our way out or walk out peacefully. Bitch, you choose."

Tri lowers her gun. She says, "Put your gun down, and fight KD one-on-one."

Carmen says, "Let's get it popping."

Carmen puts her free hand up as she slowly lowers to put the gun on the floor. As she slowly rises, Tri quickly hits her with the pipe as hard as she can. Tri says, "Dumb bitch!" KD stomps her several times in the face and head. They run out the door and straight into Detective Vernon and Detective Stratman with guns pointed at them. The three ladies put their hands up.

Mena says, "You're a day late and a dollar short."

KD excitedly says, "John is still in there." As soon as she finishes her sentence, shots ring out in the building. Detective Stratman requests back.

As soon as John cautiously turns the last corner, bullets fly in his direction. He dives into a doorway. There are two shooters standing at the end of the hallway. There's one on each side of the hall. John stays shielded in the doorway while he thinks of his next move. He surveys his surroundings to find a way to get the advantage.

KD turns to run back in the building. Mena and Tri stop her. KD screams at the detectives, "Go get John!" Mena and Tri take KD to Mena's car to wait for the detectives to rescue John.

John peeks in the room behind him. He sees a vent facing the hallway on the opposite side of the room. He quietly makes his way into the room and over to the vent. He quietly climbs up to the vent. John sees the two shooters slowly walking down the hall with their guns positioned to shoot. John aims his gun. As they walk pass, John shoots one in the head.

John quickly turns the gun to the second shooter and pulls the trigger. The sound of the first shot warns the second shooter who jumps and alters the pathway of the bullet. Instead of the head, the bullet hits the second shooter in the shoulder. The second shooter starts blindly shooting in John's direction. John quickly jumps from the vent, knocking the shooter off his feet. John drops his gun as he lands on the second shooter.

John is so full of adrenaline and anger that doesn't realize he is shot in the abdomen.

John grabs the last living male kidnapper by his collar and snatches off his mask. John says, "You, motherfucker!" John immediately begins beating the man in his face and head; he says, "You had something to do with what happened to KD at the hospital."

Dr. Segal can't answer because he is too focused on John's powerful punches. John tightly holds Dr. Segal by the collar; he says, "I told your ass to stay the fuck away from my wife. What the fuck is wrong with you?"

Dr. Segal cries as he answers, "KD is my soulmate. I love her. I can never stay away from her." Dr. Segal points his gun at John. John grabs the gun. They wrestle for control of the gun. The weight of John's hand makes Dr. Segal squeeze the trigger as he and John battle to point the gun at the other. A bullet goes into the ceiling. John kicks Dr. Segal, making him unbalanced and giving John the advantage.

John pushes Dr. Segal's hand, making the doctor aim the gun at his own forehead. John squeezes Dr. Segal's hand, forcing him to pull the trigger. Dr. Segal shoots off half of his own forehead off. Tiny specks of skin, bone, blood, and brain matter splatter over John, the wall, the floor, and the ceiling. John lets Dr. Segal's body fall to the floor. With the threat gone, John begins to feel lightheaded from losing blood. He stumbles over to the gun he dropped. The pain is radiating throughout his abdomen. He picks up the gun, and continues down the hallway.

The detectives survey the building with their guns up. They come across Carmen who is still out cold. Detective Stratman handcuffs her. While they look around the building, checking the corpses John left behind, they find the makings of a big bomb. Detective Vernon says, "They were building a bomb. Who are these people?"

Detective Stratman says, "KD and John are lucky her friends came when they did."

KD's anxiety is on ten, looking for any sign of John. The detectives come outside with a cuffed Carmen. KD gets out of the car; she shouts, "Where is John?"

Detective Vernon says, "We saw about eight dead men, but not one was John."

Carmen laughs before she says, "Well, whatever happened to him, he deserved it." That comment pushes KD pass her threshold of tolerance. KD punches Carmen so hard that Carmen passes out again.

KD says, "This stupid bitch had us locked in there all day. John has got to be in there."

Detective Stratman says, "We didn't see John, but we saw a big ass bomb in there."

Tri, Mena and KD in unison say, "Bomb!"

Detective Stratman says, "KD, thank God, your friends came when they did."

Just as he ends the statement, John emerges from the door. He falls to his knees. KD runs over to him, screaming his name. John, bleeding from a gunshot in the abdomen, says, "It's okay, Ladybug, I killed them all. They will never bother us again."

KD applies pressure on the wound; she says, "John, I love you, baby, you're going to be okay!" John loses consciousness. KD screams his name trying to wake him up.

The ambulance comes to take John to hospital, a squad car takes Carmen to booking and processing, Detective Stratman and Detective Vernon take KD, Tri, and Mena to the precinct to give their accounts of what happened, and the coroner comes to get the corpses after the bomb squad removes the explosive material.

At the precinct, each woman accounts her story separately. When it's KD's turns, she starts her story with the disagreement she and John had on the night before. She tells the detectives what John said happened to him and how she went looking for him.

When KD is done with her story, Detective Vernon says, "When your friends came to report you were missing, we didn't take it seriously. It wasn't until your mother called that we figured we better go check. We thought the situation was settled when we arrested your ex-husband and Wesley Castle. We didn't know there was another stalker."

KD is confused; she says, "Arrested Bradley and Castle! What do you mean?"

Detective Vernon asks, "John didn't tell you?"

KD says, "Tell me what?"

Detective Stratman says, "Bradley Jacobs poisoned the dogs. Wesley was in the car with Bradley when Bradley crashed into you on the freeway, they, also, set John's house on fire, and Bradley paid Wesley to tamper with John's go-kart causing the accident."

KD says, "What?"

Detective Vernon says, "Bradley wanted to scare you away from John."

KD is livid. She asks, "How did you find out? What happened?"

Detective Stratman says, "Bradley Jacobs and Wesley Castle planned to kill John. We arrested them the night before last in the parking lot of John's office. They were released on bond this morning. John didn't tell you anything about what happened the other night."

KD is astounded. Shakes her head no. She says, "John hasn't mentioned anything."

Detective Vernon says, "Bradley and Wesley planned to put a bomb in John's car. Bradley and Wesley confessed to their involvement in those four incidents, but they swore they didn't have anything to do with any of the other events. We thought they were lying."

KD says, "You're telling me Bradley Jacobs caused John's accident."

Detective Vernon says, "Mr. Jacobs was jealous of your relationship with John. He figured if he killed John, he would have a chance to get you back. When Bradley said he wanted you back, we had to pull John's hands from around his throat. It took five or six officers to keep John from attacking Bradley in the precinct. John had to be cuffed to a chair to keep him from going after Bradley. John should've been arrested, but the captain felt bad for him and dropped him off at home. John didn't mention any of this to you?"

KD says, "No, he did not, but it explains a lot." She pauses for a second. She asks, "Can I go now? I need to see my husband."

The detectives take KD, Tri, and Mena back to Mena's car. When they get in Mena's car, KD says, "Tri, give me that pipe. Mena, let's swing by Bradley's house before you drop me off at the hospital."

When they pull up in front of Bradley's house, Bradley is getting out of his car with Braely, Camille, and the new baby boy. KD quietly gets out the car and sneaks up behind Bradley. She swings the pipe as hard as she can, hitting Bradley in the back of his head so hard that he falls, hitting his face on the concrete.

The thud makes Braely and Camille stop and turn around. Camille sees KD standing over Bradley, beating him with the pipe. Camille gets a glimpse of Mena and Tri leaning against the car watching with a protective stance. KD hits him in the back his head again, leaving him disoriented; she says, "Turn your ass over, so you can look me in my face." Braely screams. KD tells Braely, "It's okay."

Camille says, "It won't be okay with you hitting her daddy with a pipe!"

KD says, "Take your kids in the house." Mena and Tri can't believe what they are seeing.

Camille says, "You need to leave or I'm going to call the police?"

KD says, "Oh, really, I didn't call the police when you stole and fucked my husband." KD's anger at Camille makes her hit Bradley harder.

Bradley grabs his head and turns to face KD; she says, "Motherfucker, have you lost your mind? What the fuck is wrong with you, Bradley, Dumbass Jackass, Jacobs?" KD repeatedly hits Bradley as hard as she can. Braely screams, "Daddy."

KD tells Braely, "I know you love your daddy. My daughter loves him, too. Do you know Kelly? [Braely nods yes.] Kelly is my daughter."

KD tells Camille, "Bitch, take the kids in the house. She doesn't need to see this," as she repeatedly hits Bradley across his chest.

Camille sends Braely in the house. Camille, holding the car seat, says, "The police will be here to arrest you!"

KD says, "I'm not worried. My new husband can afford the bail." KD continues beating Bradley with the pipe. She says, "Do you have any idea what this dirty motherfucker did to me?"

KD hits Bradley's knees as she says, "Did this rat bastard tell you about the time he was living with you, but came to my home and raped me?"

As she continues to hit him with all her might, she says to Camille, "You need to take that baby in the house and let us talk." Camille goes to stand on the porch, so she can listen. Braely watches from the window.

KD says, "What did I ever do to you to make you hate me so much? All I ever did was love your black ass. You, heartless son of a bitch," as she beats his ribs. She says, "Bradley, I don't fuck with you. I let so much shit slide, but you have gone too far. Did you ever think how this shit affected Daniel? No, because you don't give a fuck about anything or anyone outside yourself. You, selfish bastard," she repeatedly hits Bradley as she talks.

She puts the pipe on his chin; "Tell your mistress that you raped me six years ago." KD turns to Camille; she says, "How old is your daughter about six or seven? That means he was with you when he raped me." KD says, "Bradley Jacobs tell her the truth."

Bradley says in a voice cracking with pain, "It's true! It's true!"

Camille looks at KD. KD asks, "We're good?" Camille turns to walk through the front door, but she doesn't close it, so she can hear what they talk about.

KD asks, "Why won't you leave me alone, Bradley?"

Bradley says, "Because I still love you."

KD says, "You were out making babies with two bitches. You made my life hell. You never loved our son. You used him as a pawn to fuck with me. That doesn't sound like love."

Bradley says, "I fucked up, KD, but if you give me another chance, I can make it right. I can do right by you and Daniel."

KD says, "Bradley, you have completely lost your good sense. There is no way in hell I would leave my husband to go back to the hell that is you. I can't believe you paid Cas to do that to John."

Bradley says, "He has my family. You and Daniel love him more than you ever loved me."

KD says, "I did everything to try to make our marriage work. Nothing I did was good enough. You wanted out, so I let you go." KD beats Bradley about his head and face as she talks to him. Bradley cries out in pain. He begs KD to stop. Mena and Tri enjoy watching KD beat Bradley; it's a small portion of payback for all the bullshit he put her through.

Bradley says, "It wasn't you. KD, I'm sorry. I have changed. I can be the husband you want." Bradley's response hurts Camille's feelings. She goes into the house and shuts the door. She gets Braely out the window and cut off the lights.

KD says, "That's some bullshit, Bradley! You wanted out, so stay the fuck out! Stay the fuck away from my son and my husband. Don't fuck with me Bradley or you'll meet the bitch you should've met ten years ago." KD jabs him in each knee, his chest, his face, and his groin with the pipe. She continues to hit him with all her might. Bradley screams out in pain, but doesn't fight back. He begs her to stop.

She says, "I want you to hurt like John hurt. You could've killed him and for what! The man is doing what you didn't want to do, you should've thanked him. You are a selfish bastard! I want you to lay in bed for weeks in so much pain you can't move, and Ms. Camille has to wash your slut ass!

"While you were hounding me to abort Daniel, you had two babies with two bitches. I was your wife. I was faithful to you for twenty-two years. You treated me like shit. This is for every time you hit me, every time you raped me, and every time you hurt me.

"Don't fuck with me, Bradley! Leave us alone. Don't think about us. Don't ask Kelly how we are doing. Daniel and John are no longer your concern. What kind of man gives up his son to let another man adopt him? And, the only reason my man hasn't been over here to check you is it'll hurt our daughter. We all know you prefer to fight females, anyway. You, punk bitch!" KD repeatedly hits Bradley in the face with the pipe with all her might. The last blow was so hard it knocks Bradley's two front teeth out.

Full of frustration with Bradley Jacobs, she walks toward his car. She steps on Bradley teeth as she approaches the car. When Bradley hears the crunch of his teeth underneath her foot, he cries out, "KD, my teeth."

KD says, "Crying like a little bitch! [She mocks him.] KD, my teeth. Fuck you! I should knock out some more." KD gets the pipe ready to swing. One by one, she breaks every window, every light, and both side view mirrors. She furiously beats every part of his car before she walks back to Mena's car. Mena and Tri hurry to get back in the car as KD approaches.

She gets in the backseat and says, "Take me to see my man!" Tri and Mena look at her with unbelieving faces. KD sits back, exhales, and lays the bloody pipe in her lap. She excitedly says, "Let's go!"

Mena says, "Yes, ma'am!" Mena pulls off to take KD to the hospital.

Tri takes the bloody pipe from her lap. Tri says, "We better get rid of this."

Mena says, "Definitely!"

The weight of the past with Bradley, the physical and mental pain are lifted. He no longer invokes fear. She has looked the monster in the eye and survived. Bradley is no longer a foot taller or a hundred pounds heavier. She has confronted the beast, conquered the beast, and made the beast a mere mortal. She can hear John's voice in her head telling her she is strong and she is a fighter. She can hear him saying, I'm so proud of you, Ladybug.

When they arrive at the hospital, Tri and Mena walk KD to the door. They hug, and she thanks them for saving her and John.

Tri says, "That's what friends are for!"

KD says, "I love you both so much! Thank you so much!"

Mena says, "We love you, too. Go see about your man!"

Tri says, "I know he's going to be fine!" KD thanks them again before she runs through the emergency doors. The receptionist tells her where to go. She rushes to waiting room.

She sees John's kids in the waiting room. She runs over to them. Kimma says, "He's in surgery."

As KD sits to talks to John's children, Tri and Mena drive to the river. Tri throws the pipe in the river. Mena drives homes. Before Tri gets in her car to go home, they check in with each other about the violence they committed. They hug and agree what was done had to be done.

Kenna asks KD, "What happened?" KD starts the story with the argument the night before in the parking lot, and she ends with the conversation she had with the detectives about her ex-husband. KD is covered in blood, but everyone assumes the blood is John's as they console her. She doesn't mention going to Bradley's house. She apologizes to John's children for her ex-husband's behavior, but she assures them that he is going to jail.

While everyone tries to figure out who is Carmen, the surgeon comes out to say the surgery was successful. Dr. Curran says, "John will have a scar to show off to his friends and grandkids, but no internal damage was done. The bullet went straight through. It didn't hit any organs." The doctor tells them he is awake and they can go see John. Everyone thanks God as they walk toward the recovery room.

Before KD can walk through the door, Detective Stratman and Detective Vernon approach her. Detective Vernon says, "Ms. Daniels, may we speak to you in private?"

KD says, "Of course." They ask her to have a seat. KD sits down.

Detective Stratman asks, "Where did you go after you left the precinct?"

KD asks, "Where was I supposed to go?"

Detective Vernon says, "Straight here, one would think."

KD chuckles and says, "That's the logical answer."

Detective Stratman says, "Someone said you were at Bradley Jacobs' house breaking his ribs, fracturing his jaw, breaking his nose, bursting open both knees, splitting his scalp, destroying his car, knocking out a few teeth, and cursing out his girlfriend."

KD asks, "Why would I do that?"

Detective Stratman says, "We're asking the same question. Why would you do that?"

KD asks, "Did Bradley tell you I did that to him?"

Detective Vernon says, "Bradley refused to talk, but you were identified as the assailant."

KD says, "Someone is mistaken. I haven't been anywhere near Bradley since he raped me six years ago while my son begged him to stop. He heard and saw everything. My son still remembers every detail of that night. We have an agreement: I wouldn't report the rape if he stayed away from me. I upheld my end of the deal."

Kimma comes out of John's room; she says, "Stepmom, Dad is asking for you."

KD says, "I really need to see him. May I go?"

Detective Vernon says, "Mrs. King, stay out of trouble. We like you, but we never want to see you again. Do you get what I am saying?"

KD says, "I get it. I feel the same," as she gets up.

Detective Stratman says, "You should probably wash the blood off your face and hands before you go in there."

Detective Vernon says, "I don't remember that much blood on you when you at the precinct."

The detectives say goodbye to KD and walk away.

KD runs to wash the blood off her face, arms, and hands. She borrows a pair of scrubs from her friend. She puts her clothes in the hazardous waste bin. She scrubs her hands, arms, and face again with antibacterial soap. She rushes to see John. When she walks into the room, John's face lights up; he says, "Ladybug!"

She rushes to gently hug and kiss him; she says, "I'm so happy you're okay."

Kimma says, "KD, with this over, you and dad can move on."

KD hugs Kimma; KD says, "I pray so."

John's kids go home, so John and KD can be alone. John asks, "Are you okay?"

KD says, "I'm fine!"

John says, "I know you are. Lay with me," he asks, "Where are your friends?"

KD lays in the bed with him as she answers, "They went home."

John asks, "Did you thank them for me?"

KD says, "I did!"

John says, "They saved us, Ladybug!"

KD says, "Thank God Tri understood my message! I had my phone in my pants sharing my location with Tri the whole time. I prayed she and Mena would find us."

John says, "You have true friends, Ladybug, and that's a blessing. Did you call to check on Kelly and Daniel?"

KD says, "Kelly is home with Daniel, and they are fine. He enjoyed his first date. Breonna kissed his cheek."

John says, "That's my boy."

KD says, "I looked at him today. I noticed how much he looks and acts like you. He really looks up to you."

John says, "I pray that never changes. I never want to disappoint him."

KD says, "You won't!"

John says, "I remember Carmen now. She lives in my old subdivision. We met at one of our neighbor's houses at a backyard barbeque years ago. We spoke here and there, but that was it. Her name is Carmen Jones like the movie. I never touched her. I never paid her any attention. I never even held an intimate conversation with her, so how did I lead her on or hurt her."

KD says, "Baby, ignoring her was as hurtful as giving it to her and taking it away."

John says, "I thought I was doing the right thing. You know I don't mess around at work or in my neighborhood."

KD says, "You did the right thing, and sometimes people misread your intentions. Just find peace in the fact that you did what was best for you."

John says, "That's why I love you! You always know what to say."

KD says, "Our relationship has been the most beautiful and the most disturbing time of my life. The fact that so many people we weren't even thinking about would go through so much to break us apart is disturbing. The fact that nothing they did could break our bond is beautiful."

John says, "Ladybug, nothing could keep me away from you. Everything they did brought me closer to you. That's crazy, huh!"

KD touches his bandages; she says, "Baby, your once beautiful, perfect body is scarred. I'm so sorry!"

John says, "I'm just happy that we are both alive." She kisses his bandages.

KD asks, "Who shot you?"

John says, "Your old friend, the creepy doctor."

KD asks, "What would he be doing with Carmen?"

John says, "Losing his mind. Literally!"

KD asks, "Why didn't you tell me about Bradley and Wesley?"

John pauses. He looks at KD. He says, "What good would it do to hurt you and Daniel? He's out of our lives, and that's all that matters."

 KD says, "Baby, we said no secrets."

John says, "You're right. I should've told you. I thought I was protecting you and our son."

KD says, "Speaking of Daniel, how are we going to explain all this when we get home tonight?"

John says, "We are going to tell him the truth. The truth about tonight, that night. It's a lot to handle, but it's best he hears the whole truth from us tonight before it hits the news."

KD says, "I knew something was up with you that night. You were so late, and the crazy questions you were asking. What happened?"

John says, "Remember the day you were at the office with the girls?"

KD says, "Yes."

John continues, "My lawyer and I met with a family attorney that morning. The family attorney said the best way to handle the situation is to get him completely out of the picture. That afternoon, my lawyers offered Bradley a bag of money to leave us alone and relinquish his rights to Daniel. It only took him a minute to gladly take the money and sign the paperwork, so that should've been the end of it.

"Right after we hung up that night, I got a call from security saying intruders were breaching the security fence in the back. I went to see what was going on. It was Bradley and Cas talking about, they came to kill me. We were all talking shit. Emotions got hot when we exchanged low blows. Ladybug, I tried to stomp a hole in their heads."

KD says, "What did Bradley say about me that made you feel some kind of way?" They look at each other. John smirks, he doesn't want to tell her. KD says, "It's okay, you can say it."

John says, "He said it was him dressed like me at the Halloween party and when he touched you down there, he could tell you missed the way he used to fuck your brains out. He said some other very vulgar stuff that I didn't appreciate."

KD laughs. She says, "Baby, he did not touch me there, and that other comment is irrelevant. What did you say to get back at him?" John doesn't want to say. KD says, "John, you love to talk shit, so I know you said something."

John smiles and says, "I didn't say anything about you or us."

KD asks, "What's her name?" John doesn't want to answer, but KD gives him a look.

John reluctantly says, "Bradley had a big crush on this young, beautiful girl he worked with named Tanil. She was fresh out of college, but she was mature, smart, and focused. Bradley chased after Tanil like a sick puppy, and she turned him down every time. We were cordial. I never looked at her in that way while we were working together. She was too young for me. Years later, I ran into her and well you saw the video. Ladybug, all that was years ago. It's the past, don't think about that stuff."

KD says, "Honestly, why did Bradley's comment bother you so much?"

John says, "It's hard to hear another man talk about being intimate with my wife. I know you were married to him, and of course you performed wifely duties. Those parts of your body belong to me. You have over twenty years of history with him, and although I know you wouldn't, I got jealous at the thought."

KD says, "As long as you know, I would never see Bradley in that way again. If I could erase that man out of my life and keep my children, I would. When I did those things with Bradley as his wife, Bradley was a different man. I don't know and I don't want to know the person he is today. For him to brag about doing those things to me is so degrading to me as a woman. It's such a violation of the bond we once had. He is a miserable son of a bitch."

John says, "Ladybug, after tonight, we never have to mention his name."

KD says, "Well, we may have to. I went to his house tonight."

John says, "You went to his house? What did he say?"

KD says, "I didn't go to talk."

John says, "What did you do?"

KD says, "I made him feel a little of what you felt when you had the accident."

John says, "Do I need to call my lawyer?"

KD says, "That's probably a good idea." John looks at her, trying to gauge the truth. KD says, "I hit him a couple times."

John says, "KD, you hit him?"

KD says, "When the detectives told me he and Cas were responsible for your accident, I was hell bent on making him hurt the way you hurt after the accident. Every part of your body that was hurt, I hurt him in the same area and some extra parts. We'll see how much Camille loves him with a few teeth missing."

John says, "Ladybug, are you serious right now?"

KD says, "Yes! I beat his ass with that pipe Tri had."

John looks at her like he can't comprehend what she is saying. He says, "My little, sweet, KD, went over to big, mean Bradley's house and beat him with a pipe."

KD says, "I let all the shit he did to me slide, but hurting you, hell no, that wasn't sliding. He's here in the hospital somewhere. Camille snitched on me. The detectives just left asking why. I told them I haven't seen him since he raped me. If he presses charges, I will let Daniel tell what he heard and saw that night he raped me. I don't think Bradley wants to press the issue."

John says, "My Ladybug took her power back. Bradley will never make you feel fear again."

KD says, "I'm not having anyone hurt my man."

John says, "You love me, huh?"

KD says, "I love you so much!" They kiss. She adds, "I'm so sorry for everything Bradley and Dr. Segal did to you. I feel badly that you experienced so much pain because of me."

John says, "You do not have to apologize. What they did has nothing to do with you."

KD says, "I will spend my life making it up to you!"

John says, "I will gladly take you up on that offer!"

KD says, "Are you still happy you married me after all this?"

John says, "Absolutely!"

KD says, "Baby, I can't believe the storm we made it through."

John says, "How do we get through things?"

KD says, "Together!"

John says, "Don't ever forget that. We made it through this year, so we can make it through anything, together!"

KD says, "I love you so much!"

John says, "I love you so much!" KD kisses him. John interlocks his fingers with hers. John asks, "Are you upset that I paid Bradley to give up custody of Daniel?"

KD says, "Honestly, Baby, I feel like you saved us from him. I'm thankful. I prayed for a long time that Bradley would leave us alone. You have been more of a father to Daniel in a year than Bradley has in eleven years. I'm grateful. Thank you for loving us the way you do."

He says, "KD, you are my destiny. No one or nothing can change that." KD kisses him again. When the doctors release John, John and KD go home to talk to Daniel and Kelly. They tell them everything. They answered all their questions. They did not sugarcoat or water down any of the details. Daniel and Kelly accepted and appreciated the truth. Neither Kelly nor Daniel was upset with John. They both thanked him for protecting and loving their mother.

By the morning, details of the traumatic ordeal are breaking news on Raina's broadcast. Carmen's mugshot projects over Raina's shoulder as she explains how Carmen Jones, a wealthy real estate developer, and Dr. Rothman Segal, a prominent surgeon, conspired to kidnap John King and his fiancée, KD Daniels. Raina's exclusive brings her so much attention that she obsesses over the story.

Raina reports every detail she finds out about Carmen Jones and Dr. Segal. She gives an in-depth report on their education, career achievements, family background, and personal lives.

Castle's wife, Beverly, begrudgingly agrees to a brief interview. Beverly Castle is bewildered by Wesley's behavior. She says, "This is so out of character. The last eighteen or so months have completely taken me by surprise. If you would have asked me two years ago if I saw this coming, I would've said no. John has always been cordial and respectful toward me. John and Wesley have been good friends since I met them as teenagers. I can't explain Wesley's actions. Beverly explains that she was hurt and embarrassed by Wesley's actions, but he is no longer her concern because she has filed for divorce.

Over the next few weeks, Raina gets her hands on the police reports on the attempted break-in that led to John shooting two people, the vandalism of their home, the poisoning of their dog, and the attempted kidnapping in the hospital's parking structure.

Raina has an expert enhance the quality of the surveillance video of the attempted kidnapping at the hospital. Raina reveals the men's identities and criminal histories. She reports the attackers are deceased, and their lives were taken by John during his escape from the warehouse.

What still isn't clear to Raina is the connection between the deceased men in the warehouse, Dr. Segal, and Carmen Jones or why they put such an elaborate plan together to kidnap KD and John. Raina also doesn't understand how Bradley Jacobs and Wesley Castle fit into the plan.

Raina wants the whole story. She is determined to put all the pieces together. She goes to every court hearing, which is detailed in weekly investigative reports on the Friday evening broadcast. Raina is the first to report that Bradley Jacobs and Wesley Castle take plea deals instead of going to trial.

As a part of their plea deals, Bradley and Wesley Castle must account their involvement in open court. Raina reports word for word of their confessions given in court. Their confessions give Raina the who did what and how, but doesn't really explain why, so she petitions the court for interviews.

Carmen Jones' lawyer argues her mental health issues make her incompetent to stand trial. KD and John's lawyer met with Carmen Jones' lawyer and the prosecutor. John and KD want to move on and focus on their family, so the parties come to an agreement that Carmen would serve her time in a mental institution and she won't be released until she is deemed fit for society.

In her determination to get the whole story, Raina connects with Todd to see what he knows while she waits on the court to respond to her petition. Their conversations about John quickly turn into a conversation about their interest in each other. They start dating and quickly become a hot topic on her morning broadcast. Raina is succeeding in her professional and personal life and it gives her confidence to take chances. Raina asks the judge and the institution for permission to interview Carmen Jones.

Carmen's lawyer, popular Detroit defense attorney Cavell Hawkins, preps Carmen to ensure the public sees her as misguided and harmless. Before Carmen is allowed to speak, her lawyer explains her history of dissociative personality disorder and paranoia. He emphasizes she is on a new combination medicine and attends daily group therapy and weekly individual therapy.

He says, "The medication has given her clarity, and she sees the harm her behavior caused. She is apologetic and understands it is crucial to take her medication with fidelity. We are hoping to have her back to her successful life as a realtor/broker soon."

After completing his speech, he consents to the interview. Raina and Carmen start the interview with a smile, a pleasant greeting, and an unspoken acknowledgement of the shared experienced of being hurt by John.

Raina asks, "Who is Carmen Jones?"

Carmen says, "A simple girl who got lost in a fantasy."

Raina asks, "How did all this start?"

Carmen answers, "I met John in passing maybe ten years ago. I instantly fell for him, hard, but never had the courage to approach him. I watched him from afar for years, but I don't think he ever saw me, which was disappointing."

Raina asks, "How did you have so much access to John over the years?"

Carmen admits, "I lived a few houses from him in the cul-de-sac of our subdivision, so I knew his schedule. I developed that subdivision. My agency sold John the house. After we sold him the house, I secretly made a copy of his key. John never had the locks change."

Raina says, "So you were the one who put the photos of John in John and KD's home?"

Carmen replies, "Through my connections, I was able to get a key to gain access to their home. I thought KD should see what she was getting into."

Raina asks, "How did you get the intimate videos and photos of John?"

Carmen says, "The burdens and joys of technology. I had someone hack his laptop's camera. He kept his laptop in his bedroom. I watched John a lot over the years, which is how I found out that you were in a relationship with John."

Raina says, "That made you unhappy with me?"

Carmen says, "It wasn't personal."

Raina says, "The notes on my windshield, the black car following me, that was you?"

Carmen answers, "I wanted you out of the picture."

Raina says, "You quietly watched John for years. You saw him with me and numerous women, and no one was harmed. What made you go as far as you did this time?"

Carmen answers, "When John started dating KD, I immediately knew this relationship was different. John's energy was different with her. They went on dates and spent a lot of time together, but the killer was John didn't see any other women. His fidelity was a threat to me getting what I want. He was in love and I couldn't stand it." Raina could relate because she felt the same way.

Carmen explains, "I followed John and KD for months. I watched the progression of their relationship, and the men stalking KD. KD had three men madly in love with her, and she didn't even know it. I saw how her ex-husband and Dr. Segal lusted after her. As I sat watching John and KD in the darkness, I saw her admirers watching from the opposite direction, which is how I was able to record the incident between John and Dr. Segal."

Raina asks, "So you were the anonymous source who sent me the video?" Carmen admits to being the source, and editing the video to make John look like the aggressor. Carmen says, "When I saw Dr. Segal sit on John's car, I knew things would get violent. I recorded the whole incident. I cut out the beginning which shows Dr. Segal instigated the whole situation."

Raina asks, "What about the other videos and pictures I received? Were they from you?" Carmen confesses she sent the images to ruin John's clean reputation.

Raina asks, "How did you meet Dr. Rothman Segal?"

Carmen answers, "After the fight outside the club, I followed and approached Dr. Segal outside his home. It was easy to convince Dr. Segal to help me break up KD and John." Carmen explains the intention was never to hurt John or KD. Carmen says, "Dr. Segal and I wanted to split up the relationship. Our plan was to use fear to drive the couple apart."

Raina asks, "How did the deceased men in the warehouse fit into your plan?"

Carmen says, "They were unemployed felons I hired to terrorize the couple. They needed fast money, and I paid more money than a legitimate job." When Raina asks about the attempted abduction, Carmen says, "That was all Dr. Segal's idea. He had followed KD for weeks. He was seething with anger that John had a hold on KD. He hated that John would intercede whenever he tried to talked to KD. Dr. Segal wanted an opportunity to talk to KD alone.

"He told the crew no guns because he didn't want her to get hurt. He hadn't planned for KD fighting like a trained ninja, stabbing everyone, and getting away. Dr. Segal had to stitch up the wounds to keep his plan a secret. I had no part in that plan."

Raina asks about the kidnapping. Carmen explains, "The plan was to make John and KD think the other died in the explosion. No one was going to be harmed."

The hour-long interview with Carmen Jones is the highest-rated news broadcast in Detroit's history. Even John and KD snuggle in each other's arms and watch the entire broadcast. Carmen comes across as honest and apologetic, but John and KD aren't convinced that Carmen is sorry for her actions. With the success of Carmen's interview, Raina is granted permission to interview Bradley Jacobs and Wesley Castle.

Raina starts the interview with Wesley by discussing the long friendship between him and John. Raina asks Castle when his feelings toward John change. Castle admits he was jealous of John's good fortune. John always attracted attention and good things always went his way.

He says, "I never thought about hurting John, but when Bradley approached me, I agreed to help him with his plan. I enjoyed hurting John more than I wanted the money from Bradley. I was blinded by hate and jealousy. I should've been focused on what I had going on. When Bradley approached me with his plan, I should've told him no and tried to convince him not to go forward with his plan. John had been my friend since sixth grade. I know his kids. He knows my kids. I disappointed everyone, including myself. I regret getting involved in the situation."

Castle ends the interview by saying, "KD and her son didn't deserve the terror we caused. I was so focused on hurting John that I terrorized an innocent woman and child. Only a monster would do that. I have never in my life hurt a woman or child. When I look back at my actions, I am so ashamed of myself. I will never forgive myself. I've hurt and embarrassed my entire family. My kids won't speak to me. I lost my job, freedom, and love. I have nothing left."

When Raina interviews Bradley, he explains how the rivalry between him and John began several years ago when the women he was having an affair with began secretly communicating with John. He goes on to say the rivalry coupled with the desire to get his ex-wife back drove him out of his mind.

He admits he was obsessed with getting his wife back and that killing John sounded like a good idea. He says, "I couldn't accept that the love of my life was in love with my biggest enemy. When I heard about the relationship, I was livid. I was so set on putting an end to the relationship that I didn't consider the impact of my actions on my children."

Raina asks Bradley about his marriage to KD. Bradley admits getting married at twenty-two and not having a chance to explore started to get to him about year ten of the marriage. He says, "I'd only been with one other woman before we got married. I started to wonder what it was like out in the world. I got caught up and things got out of control. I ruined my marriage. KD was the perfect wife and mother. She did everything a woman should do as a wife and mother. She raised our daughter well. She cared for me like a king, and for some reason all she did wasn't enough.

"She spoiled me, and I took her for granted. I had this idea that more was out there and I was going to find it. When we first divorced, I appreciated my freedom, but I quickly saw the grass wasn't greener. No woman did a fourth of what KD did. I was stuck because I had been so cruel that going back wasn't an option.

"When I found out how much she was in love with King, I wanted blood. He was posting pictures and they looked so happy. I saw KD loved him more than she ever loved me. My son was never happy with me. I acted out of character and disappointed my daughter, my family, myself. I have lost everything: my job, my girlfriend, and my dignity. My children won't even answer my call. KD knocked three of my teeth out. All I can do is serve my time and apologize. I'll be a better man when I get out."

Raina's interviews gain national attention and break local ratings records. By the beginning of summer, Raina is the premier news anchor in Detroit. She becomes the highest paid and most recognizable anchor in the city. When KD and John are old news, Raina begins producing weekly thirty-minute investigative segments highlighting local crime.

Raina is also prospering in her personal life. Todd leaves the player life behind. She often discusses their relationship on the morning news, so it only makes sense that Todd proposes on the show. Raina has the final piece to her power couple puzzle.

John and KD gather their family at Kimma's house the night before John leaves for his business trip. The whole night KD is quiet and melancholy, but she hides her feelings behind a smile. When they get home, John sits KD down to talk.

John says, "Ladybug, we're not breaking up. Why are you so sad?"

KD says, "I miss you already."

John says, "Ladybug, I'm right here, right now. I know it's a long time, but this trip is going to be good financially for our family. I know money is not your concern, but it's mine. I am the provider. I'm going overseas to build my business. I'm not going near a woman. You are my wife. I don't ever want to hurt you. Believe that and believe in me."

KD says, "Baby, I do believe in you. If the vibe I am giving contradicts that, I apologize."

John says, "Can you genuinely smile for me? I don't want to waste our last night together being sad. Ladybug, every night for the next three months all I am going to have is the thoughts and memories of your face tonight. Smile and love me."

KD smiles at him, she says, "I do love you. Husband, I love you so much."

John smiles at KD, he says, "Show me!" KD kisses him. John says, "That's my Ladybug. That beautiful face giving me a beautiful smile teaches me what life is all about." KD kisses him again. John says, "Keep going, I'm trying to learn some more."

KD says, "You're so silly." John and KD laugh and hug. She adds, "I'm going to miss you, baby."

John says, "I'll miss you, too!"

Chapter Six

Dr. Emberly Wakes examines KD. Dr. Wakes says, KD: "KD, you're pregnant!"

KD is in disbelief. She asks, "I'm what?"

Dr. Wakes says, "I'm pretty sure there's a baby in you, but let's take a test to confirm."

KD is confused. She looks at the doctor and says, "I'm fifty. How is that possible? You know my troubled history with fertility."

Dr. Wakes says, "When was your last period?"

KD thinks about it. She remembers having a period a week before the night Bradley and Wesley were arrested. John was so sweet. He went to the store to buy her tampons and Midol. She remembers the cramps being so bad that John laid in bed with her holding a heating pad against her abdomen after he made her soup and tea. KD explains to the doctor her last period was in March. Dr. Wakes does count the weeks, she says, "That sounds about right."

Dr. Wakes says, "It's possible for a woman to ovulate and conceive at your age. It's rare, but it happens. About fifteen weeks ago, it happened to you." After the doctor runs a few tests, Dr. Wakes says, "Congratulations Mrs. King, you are going to be a mommy again!"

KD asks Dr. Wakes, "What is the likelihood this baby will survive? I don't want to tell my husband only to disappoint him."

Dr. Wakes answers, "You are in good health. You live an active, healthy lifestyle. You are in a healthy, supportive relationship. Yes, your history concerns me, but history doesn't have to repeat itself. I was there for your first two healthy deliveries, and God willing I will be there for your third.

"For now, I want to see you every two weeks. I want you to continue to move, but not your usual vigorous exercises. Walk instead of run. Instead of weight training, do some yoga. Cautiously riding a bike is okay. Continue to eat healthy. Try to stay as stress-free as possible. Don't worry about your history. Try to enjoy the remaining six months of your pregnancy. I am going to give you a prescription for some pre-natal vitamins.

"KD, it's okay if you want to give yourself some time before you tell Mr. King. Forty weeks will be ideal, but you can still have a healthy and happy baby at thirty-two or thirty-five weeks. Just think, you're almost half way there."

On the drive home, KD decides to keep the baby a secret. She doesn't want everyone to be disappointed if history does repeat itself. That night, she dreams she and John are kissing when she whispers to him, I'm pregnant. He stops kissing her to smile at her. He says, "You'll be so cute with a big belly."

She smiles and asks, "Are you going to still be attracted to me?"

John says, "I will love and adore every inch of you!"

They begin to kiss again and just as things are about to heat up, KD jumps out of her sleep. She rubs her belly as she looks at John's side of the bed. KD whispers to her belly, "Be strong for your mommy!" KD gets on her knees to pray. Tears began to flow down her face. She pleads with God, "Please, don't take my baby!"

She lays prostrate, crying and praying like Hannah prayed in the temple. She promises the Lord that she will be the best mother she can be and raise the baby to recognize him as the one and only Lord and savior. She prays every night for the life growing inside her. She prays for the health and joy of the life growing inside her.

Over the next few weeks, Kelly notices KD is quiet, distracted, and nervous. Kelly tells Kimma, Kera, and Kenna that KD is having a hard time being separated from John for so long. Kelly explains what happened when KD met Raina, and how KD has been struggling to feel secure in the relationship.

Kimma says, "If dad breaks her heart, I will never forgive him."

Kelly says, "Stepdad won't leave Momma. He is just as much in love as she is. I just need to get her to relax."

Kenna says, "We need to get her mind off him. We should have a girls' night slumber party."

Kelly says, "That's a good idea. Daniel is away at basketball camp. I'll invite her best friends. A distraction would be good for her."

Kenna says, "I'll bring the alcohol. Who's got the menu?"

Kimma says, "I'll handle the food as always."

Kera says, "No one told you to be the good cook!"

Kimma says, "Kelly, you have to get her to stay home Friday night."

Kelly says, "I'll tell her I need some mother-daughter time. She'll make time for me."

Kera says, "Sounds like we have a plan."

Friday evening, the doorbell rings, Kelly is in the kitchen pretending to prepare to cook, so KD answers the door for her best friends, John's daughters, and his granddaughters all holding overnight bags and food. KD is pleasantly surprised; she says, "What are you all doing here?"

Kera, holding her sleeping newborn baby, says, "We're having a ladies' night. We are about to have some grown folks' fun." KD is so excited to see the new grandbaby. Kera says, "I'm going to lay her down, so we can commence to having fun."

Kimma says, "Sorry, I had to bring the girls. Langston is hanging out with his frat brothers."

KD says, "It's okay, they are always welcome here." KD bends down to hug Langley and Lourdes before they run into the house and straight into the master bedroom to watch their Papa's big television.

Kenna, also holding a box, says, "Stepmom, we are about to get you so drunk that your head will be spinning for days," as she walks through the door. KD laughs.

KD says, "How in the world did they get you two over here?"

Mena says, "Kelly called!" KD hugs Mena and Tri.

Tri says, "You know when you need us, we will be there!"

KD says, "I'm so happy you're here," as they walk in the house.

The women gather around the table to eat. Kenna pulls a variety of bottles of alcohol out of a box; she says, "Since we're spending the night, no one needs to worry about driving. Let's get drunk AF."

Tri says, "I'm ready."

Mena says, "Let me pop the first bottle." She picks a bottle of tequila.

Kenna says, "Nice choice." Kenna hands Kera a bottle of lemonade. She says, "Sorry, Lil Sis!" Kera smacks her teeth and rolls her eyes. Kenna says, "What! You are breastfeeding. You can't drink alcohol." Kera rolls her eyes again. Kenna adds, "That's what happens when you pop it and don't make him stop it."

By the time they are done eating, the alcohol is kicking in. Kelly pulls out an adult game, and the women get comfortable in the living room to play. The game quickly turns into a conversation about sex. KD quietly sits listening to the other women talk about sex.

Kenna asks, "Stepmom, why are you so quiet?"

Mena says, "She's shy."

Kelly says, "She's not that damn shy when she's with Stepdad."

Tri says, "Kelly, spill the tea because KD is never going to tell."

KD says, "Kelly, do not embarrass me!"

Tri says, "Kelly, you've already started, you might as well finish the story."

KD says, "Kelly! You wouldn't embarrass your mother."

Tri says, "Kelly, tell it all."

Mena says, "Come on, KD, it's girls' night!"

Kelly laughs and says, "Okay, last summer, [As soon as Kelly starts talking, KD puts her head down.] Stepdad was supposed to be out of town, so I went to surprise Momma with some mommy-daughter time. Shouldn't have done that because Stepdad was in her room putting it down. I mean, he was knocking it back." KD covers her face. The other women laugh.

KD says, "Kelly, baby, Daughter, don't do this to me!"

Mena says, "Kelly, you have to finish the story!"

Kelly continues the story, "I went to knock on her bedroom door, but before I could knock, I heard the bed rocking, Stepdad talking shit, and banging it out. He was like, [Kelly gives her best impression of John's voice.] 'Damn, Ladybug, baby, yes, fuck me just like that. KD, baby, throw all that ass back.'

"They were clearly having a good time, so I dared not disturb them. I made myself comfortable on the couch. It got quiet for a little minute, and only for a minute, so I fell asleep. Next thing I know, the bed is banging, I mean crashing. They went all night. I mean all night."

Tri asks, "Was that a special night or the norm?"

KD answers, "It was just another day."

Tri says, "So all night, all the time?" KD raises her eye brows and shyly smiles.

Mena says, "Well, shit, KD, you're the soldier, I was just in the army." Everyone laughs.

Tri repeats, "All night!"

KD says, "Every night!"

Mena says, "That's why you are always glowing and shit. Talking about I've been running and working out."

Tri says, "You're not sad. You're having withdrawals."

Mena says, "You should be sleepy, you haven't slept through the night in over a year." Everyone laughs at Mena and Tri.

Tri says, "If you can take it, you deserve it! You deserve a good man that gives you good love. Two awesome people found each other and fell in love. Nothing is more beautiful. I'm so happy for you, K."

Mena says, "Me, too! I bless this union, and I pray God does as well!"

Tri says, "I'm so proud of you, K." KD thanks Mena and Tri.

KD says, "Kelly, I cannot believe you did me like that."

Kelly says, "Sorry, Momma, it's girls' night. The tea gets spilled at girls' night."

Mena says, "Now, John's daughters know their daddy's fiancée is a big freak, which probably explains why their daddy is so in love."

KD says, "Mena, he loves me because I'm a good person!"

Tri says, "It's okay, K, that's how it's supposed to be. You're a lady in the world with everyone else, and a freak in the bed with your man. You're supposed to put it on his ass, so he knows what's up."

Kera says, "She's right, Stepmom! I'm happy to know you take care of him in every way."

Kimma asks, "How long did you make Daddy wait?"

KD shyly answers, "Almost two months."

Kimma says, "Were you in love?"

KD says, "Yes!"

Kenna asks, "Who said I love you first and when?"

KD says, "When everyone left on The Fourth of July. I told him it was time for him to verbalize his feelings for me."

Kera asked, "When did you fall in love?"

KD says, "I liked him immediately. I was attracted to him immediately. One night, we were on the phone, he was talking, and I was falling in love. We had been dating for almost a month."

Kelly asks, "What made you fall in love with Stepdad?"

KD says, "He was open, honest, vulnerable, intense, attentive, sweet, and sexy."

Kelly asks, "What was your relationship like back then?"

KD answers, "We were in the late nights and early mornings phase. It was fun and exciting getting to know each other. No pressure, no worries, just all this energy and attraction. The nagging desire to be together all day. He spoiled me, not with material things, but with the little things that I hadn't had from a man. He gave me attention and affection. He was always honest with me. He showed up for me. If I didn't feel well, he came home early to cook for me. He went to church with me. He did everything to let me know I was special to him."

Kelly asks, "How have things changed in a year? Not considering all the bullshit, just talking about Stepdad as a man, a boyfriend, a lover, a friend, and a partner."

KD says, "We know each other now. We love each other now. We are committed, so we're vested and that adds pressure. But, really, nothing has changed. He is still the man I'm excited to see and talk to. I still have incredible fun with him. There is still the same energy and attraction. He's still honest with me. He is forthcoming about his whereabouts. He always shares his feelings. We communicate about everything. His relationship with Daniel still amazes me."

Kelly says, "Stepdad is a great guy, isn't he, Momma?"

KD says, "He is an amazing man! When we met, he was upfront about his past. With me, he has been a good man every minute of every day since day one."

Kimma says, "I'm so happy he has you to love him and care for him."

Kera says, "KD, you have made him a better man."

Kenna says, "KD, him with you is a very different him, and it is for the better for us all." KD smiles and thanks John's daughters for their compliments.

Kelly asks, "When did you know Stepdad was in love with you?"

KD says, "His affection toward me always felt genuine, but his birthday last year was the telling moment. The whole week was magical."

Mena asks, "Has he ever changed? Has he ever done or said anything to make you question or doubt him?"

KD says, "No! Never!"

Tri asks, "Have you felt this way before?"

KD says, "No!"

Kelly says, "Stepdad called me a few days after we met. He told me he wanted me to get to know him because he was going to be with my mother. He sounded so sure. He was honest with me. He answered all my questions. He spoke with confidence, no hesitation, no doubt. He told me nothing or no one compares to KD, you were special to him, and the bond you and he have meant so much to him. I believed him.

"Before we hung up, he promised me that he would do right by my mother and I never have to worry about my mother being hurt in any way by him. He and I have been super tight ever since we had that conversation. Something told me he was not lying."

Kimma says, "He speaks so highly of you, KD, in a way we have never heard him speak of anyone other than our grandmother."

Kera says, "That is true!"

Kenna says, "After Memorial Day, I talked to him about you, just him and I. While in the conversation, I was thinking my father is really in love for the first time in his life. By the end of the conversation, I loved you because he talked about you in such a loving way."

Kimma says, "After we met for the first time, I went back to his office alone later that day. We had a long talk about you, and I knew this relationship was something different for him. When I got to know you, I was like Dad is right, she is special. We are so happy that he has you. Even our brothers love your relationship, and they've hated every woman Dad's hung out with over the years."

Kera says, "He and I also had a heart-to-heart talk. He told me he purged his phone on the day he met you because he knew you were the one. I was chewing gum, and the gum fell out my mouth when he said that. When I got to know you, I understood why he felt that way."

KD says, "Aww, Kenna, Kimma, and Kera, your words are so sweet. I love all of you and the babies. I'm so honored that you all have accepted me and my children into your family."

Kelly says, "Group hug!" They all surround KD in a group hug. After the hug, Kelly starts the game back up. Kelly and KD stare at each other and smile. KD figures out what Kelly was doing. As they continue the game, John video-calls.

KD answers the call with a smile. She excitedly says, "John, our girls are here," she turns the phone to face the girls, and they say hello. Kimma, Kenna, Kera, and Kelly tell him they love and miss him. He tells his daughters and Kelly he loves them. Mena and Tri say hello. John says hello to them.

KD says, "I'll be right back," she rushes to her bedroom to talk to John. KD sits on her bed. She shows Langley and Lourdes the screen. John says, "Lovebugs, I miss you! I love you!" They tell him they love and miss him too. KD shows him the sleeping baby. John says, "I cannot wait to meet Summer in person. She is adorable."

KD says, "She looks just like you. She's so beautiful."

John is struck by KD's radiant smile and glowing skin. He says, "Ladybug, your hair is growing so much. It's so pretty and healthy. It's so long!"

KD asks, "Do you like it?"

John says, "I love it! It's so sexy! I can't wait to get my fingers in it. Ladybug, you're glowing."

KD says, "Thank you, baby!"

John says, "How was your day?"

KD says, "Kelly and I had a mother-daughter day. I met Kelly's new boyfriend. I think you will like this one."

John says, "I better!"

KD asks, "Baby, how are you?"

John says, "I'm good now that I'm talking to you. I am missing you like crazy."

KD says, "I miss you so much. I'm counting the days until you come home."

John says, "Ladybug, this is the last time I'll ever leave you. I've been thinking. How can I be a better husband? What should I do differently in this marriage? When I come home, I'm going to give the girls, including Kelly, more responsibility. I'm going to slow down, so I can be present in our marriage. I want to be a good husband to you, Ladybug!"

KD says, "I would never ask that of you. I understand how important your work is to you."

John says, "When we first started dating, I asked that of you. Not directly, but I manipulated things to get what I wanted. I understood how important your work was to you, but I wanted more of you and more time with you. I pretended like I didn't know about Daniel's tuition being paid because I didn't want you to be mad at me."

KD says, "I knew it was you, but you played it off so well I couldn't question you."

John says, "I could've been an actor."

KD says, "You're so naturally charming that you get what you want from people."

John asks, "Have I charmed you?"

KD answers, "I'm enchanted!" They both smile. She asks, "How did you celebrate your birthday?"

John answers, "I had a steak and thought about you!"

KD says, "We'll do something special when you get home. I'll make you a cake and we'll have the kids and grandbabies over for dinner."

John says, "I look forward to that. Ladybug, go back to your guests. I'll call you tomorrow."

KD says, "I hate to hang up!"

John says, "I'll be home before you know it."

KD says, "I love you!"

John says, "I love you, too!"

KD goes back to the party. Everyone is having a great time when Mena asks KD why she isn't drinking. KD tries to play it off, but Mena insists she takes a shot of tequila to relax. KD pushes the shot glass away.

Tri asks, "Are you taking medication?"

KD says, "No, I'm just not in the mood for alcohol."

Kimma asks, "Stepmom, are you okay?"

KD says, "I'm fine! Nothing is wrong."

Tri says, "Either you are taking medication or and I know it's not the or, is it? It can't be!"

Kelly says, "Momma, you're worrying me. Are you sick?"

KD answers, "No, I'm fine, I promise."

Kelly slides a shot toward KD; Kelly says, "Then, take a sip and relax!"

KD pushed the alcohol away; she says, "Please don't mention this to anyone especially John because I haven't told him." When everyone agrees to keep her secret, KD says, "I'm pregnant, but don't get excited. You know my history of miscarriages, so I'm waiting until John comes home to talk about it." Each one of the women sit with her mouth opened.

KD says, "Trust me, I'm just as shocked as you."

Kelly says, "Momma, I noticed you've been distracted lately, but I thought you were just stressing over Stepdad."

Kera says, "Dad would want to know either way."

KD says, "Since I met him, he's been talking about this trip. I'm not distracting him. I'm doing everything the doctor told me to do. I need John to be focused on his goals. If I tell him, he will want to come home, and I couldn't live with that. I want him focused on his success. If all goes well, he will have time to enjoy the pregnancy. I would hate to get his hopes up and disappoint him."

Kimma asks, "How far along are you?"

KD says, "I'm eighteen weeks!"

Kelly says, "Momma, how do you feel about this? Stepdad is going to blow his top."

KD says, "If I can make it to eight months, I will allow myself to feel. I know the disappointment all too well. I can't look at John with that disappointment on his face."

Tri says, "KD, that baby is going to make it. If that baby survived this long, that baby is already strong and determined."

KD says, "Babies: one boy, one girl!" Everyone gasps.

Kimma says, "Twins! Dad is going to be so happy!"

KD says, "Don't get excited. My age, my history, the babies are underweight, especially the girl. I pray that both babies have John's intensity and will to survive. When I think about them, I think about them as John's babies. I see them as strong, and that gives me peace and comfort."

Kelly says, "Mom, you don't eat. Every time I see you with food, you're just picking in it."

Mena says, "KD, sweetheart, you've got to eat."

Tri says, "KD, why aren't you eating?"

KD says, "The smell of the food, the anxiety I feel, and the stress of my history takes my appetite away. I want this and I know John would want this if he knew. I'm scared!"

Mena says, "Fear isn't a bad thing, but it becomes bad when you let it rule you. KD, you are letting fear ruin the possibility of you getting what you want. That baby girl needs you to eat."

Kelly says, "Momma, you have to start eating properly."

Tri says, "Kelly, do her like she did you as a child. Make her sit at the table until she eats."

Kelly asks, "What did the doctor saying about the babies being underweight?"

KD says, "My daily calorie intake should be 2,200, but I'm only eating about 1,600."

Mena says, "KD, I know it's hard to force yourself to eat, but, sister, eating is the means to get what we all want. We all want these babies. We already love them because we love everything that's a part of you. For us, please start eating more."

Kelly says, "I'll be checking on you every day. If you don't eat enough, I will call Stepdad!"

Tri says, "What would John say if he knew you weren't eating enough?"

KD says, "Point made! I'm going to eat as I'm supposed to."

Tri says, "Let's pray for the babies' health." Everyone stands in a circle and hold hands. They bow their hands as Tri prays for the healthy delivery and long life of both babies.

After they pray, Kenna breaks the silence, she says, "Stepmom! I'm sorry, but I can't wait to get excited. Daddy is about to have another set of twins."

Mena says, "KD, you don't look pregnant."

KD says, "I had no idea. I had no signs or symptoms. When the doctor told me, I was in disbelief."

Tri says, "Eighteen weeks ago was stressful."

KD says, "I know exactly the night it happened. John came home very late. He was in his feelings with everything that was going on. All the stress he was under had him on ten."

Kenna says, "I can't wait to see Dad's reaction when he finds out. He is going to be so happy."

KD says, "After he kills me for not telling him."

Kimma says, "KD, no one can blame you for not telling him. You have a very valid argument and thorough plan. I understand why you are waiting and eventually he will see you were looking out for his best interest. He is going to appreciate that."

KD says, "I'm breaking my promise to never keep secrets."

Kera says, "But, you are protecting everyone. Daddy will understand."

Mena says, "You're about to be a mommy of a baby again!"

KD says, "I haven't even begun to process that yet!"

Tri asks, "I will pray every day for you and the babies. When you hit eight months, we will begin to process the situation and plan the baby shower." KD accepts Tri's proposal. After that night, the ladies orchestrate a coordinated effort to support KD.

Two weeks before John is scheduled to return, KD walks the dogs along the river. KD rubs her burgeoning belly bump as she stops to enjoy the cool breeze. She takes her eyes off the dogs for a second to watch the water hit the riverbank. Without warning, the dogs take off running and barking loudly. KD turns to go after the dogs, but she sees John. John bends down to hug the dogs. When John stands up, he stares at KD who is so happy to see him. KD waddles over to him and straight into his arms. They kiss.

John bends down to kiss her baby bump. He says to her belly, "Daddy's home and he's never going to leave you again." He stands up and says, "I couldn't wait another day?"

 KD asks, "How did you know?

John touches her nose. He says, "Your nose, hair, and skin changed. I understand why you didn't tell me. I didn't want to pressure you. I gave you space to work things out, but, Ladybug, I don't ever want to do that again. We should work through things especially important things together." He kisses her.

KD places his hand on her stomach. KD says, "Meet your son [she moves his hand over] and your daughter. I just don't want to disappoint you!"

He says, "Ladybug, you won't disappoint me. It's all in God's hand."

KD kisses him. She says, "Are you sure you want all this? Babies and marriage are a lot with all you have going on with your business."

He says, "God is blessing me with everything I want with you! I love you, Ladybug! I want this," he rubs her belly.

KD says, "I love you, John!" He picks her up and kisses her. He tells her he loves her and their babies.

As promised, John gives Kimma, Kenna, Kera, and Kelly promotions and more responsibilities. Kimma is named the CEO and Kenna, the CFO, is her right-hand woman. Kelly is named the CTO. John sells all his properties for three times what he paid for it. He sells his property management company, so Kenna can focus on the family business. Kera excels at her position as COO while being a new working mom.

KD gives birth to healthy twins via c-section as the clock strikes midnight. The twins make news as the first babies born in the new year in Detroit. One of Raina's co-anchors, Stacy Smith, interviews a smiling John and joy-filled Kathy holding the twins in the nursery while KD rests in her room.

John explains he named the twins to honor their grandparents. He says, "Our son, John Carlo King, is named after my parents: John and Carla King. Our daughter, KD Kathleen King, is named after my wife's parents." When Stacy asked who the twins look like, John says, "They look just like me, but have their mother's beautiful eyes." John's elation is evident as he holds his son throughout the interview.

After seeing how great KD's wedding dress turned out, John encourages her to make more dresses. Eventually, he surprises her with a remodeled boutique in Downtown Detroit to sell her original designs. John becomes Mr. Mom, spending his time with the twins, his grandchildren, and Daniel, while KD makes and sells her dresses.

The End